DIGGING
IN THE DIRT

WALTER CLEARFOSTER

To Denning and Liam.
Writers taken too soon.

Acknowledgments

I'd like to thank Aja Pollock for her copyediting, my beta readers for their time and attention to detail. Thank you to Debbie Dove and Polgarus Studio for proofreading and formatting my manuscript. Thank you to Jan Lewis for her bold cover design and her patience. Thank you to Ben Mandefield for his creative input. Thank you to my friends and family, for their encouragement. And finally, my thanks to 'Officer X' for his invaluable contribution to my book, and for keeping us safe.

ONE

I'VE BEEN WRITTEN off so many times, you'd think they'd have run out of ink by now. I've never understood quite why. I could put it down to arrogance or the complacency of others. It could be to do with the fact that I'm a woman in a man's world. But I hate playing the gender card and want to keep it firmly in its pack. Playing cards like that is a victim's mentality, and I don't want to be one of those. Especially not like my mother, who was a determined victim. I don't even feel guilty about the fact that I despised her. I despised her more than I despised my father, even though he was the violent one. I despised her for making excuses for his behaviour. I despised her lack of pride and weakness. I despised her for falling for his lies when I could see through him like I could see through a window.

Children know these things, but I just wasn't clever enough to keep my big mouth shut or hide my expressions of disdain. It took me years to understand that you should choose your battles and that it's simpler to let others think they're in control. But my damned ego wouldn't let me. I also think my mother hated me because I was, in her family, the unwanted anomaly: the first girl in fifty years. I think she wanted boys because she couldn't stand the competition. It's sick to think that parents envy their own children. That's probably why I don't have them myself, just in case I end up messing it up like her.

I see them everywhere—my parents, that is. They formed the blueprint for most of my relationships in life. When I see a bullshitter, narcissist, or psychopath, I think father. When I see a servile, weak, pathetic female, I think mother. This explains the many conflicts that I have had. Most of your relationships are determined by how your parents behave towards you and how they treat each other. Isn't that what they say? If that's so, then I was screwed from the beginning. That's the thing about childhood programming: you can spend the next forty years undoing the first five. Some spiritualists believe that you choose your parents. Why on earth would I do that? I must be into self-harm. Some say that I should be grateful, that family is family, that blood is thicker than water. But the problem with blood is that it clots.

But the past is what made me the person I am. Does that make me feel better? Not always. There must be a part of this where I can decide. How free are we? I like to think we can make our own choices, that we can lock out the influences that make us feel like we're strange because we don't fit. I've never liked the crowd and I'm not a follower. I'm a one-woman clique. But I know that it's cost me and caused great pain to others. It's taken me years to realise that some games you have to play. I guess it's just as bad for men as it is for women in that we're both victims of patriarchy.

I wasn't strategic enough and had no concept of the bigger picture. I'm starting to understand that you can't take on the world on your own and expect to win. There's a side you show others and there's a side that's just for you. It's called compromise: one of many words that are alien to me. I guess that's what growing up does for you. I really need to get over myself. I don't need to be right anymore. But you know what they say about old habits. They not only die hard; in some cases, they're indestructible. And they can resurface when you least expect them to.

But what concerns me right now is that I've been well and truly fucked over. I'm on the run. I should be on the way back to England after snatching Karl Yumeni, a suspected international terrorist and first-rate scumbag. Instead, all of my team is dead. I can't trust my agency. I'm injured and lucky to be alive. I'm in my homeland of Germany, which doesn't hold the best of memories, for some of the reasons I've already told you. And I've never felt so solitary, which for me is saying something, as I consider myself a lone wolf. I have one chance left, and that's to contact my mentor, Lothar Litze, a man I haven't seen in years. I hate asking him for help, but right now, pride is a luxury I can ill afford. Especially if I want to stay alive. And I really want to stay alive. Getting shot at is an occupational hazard, but this time it feels different. Not many people know about this mission as it is on a need to know basis. Which drives me to the conclusion that this assignment is compromised. But by who? It feels personal, like a betrayal. Funny because I always feel this way, so maybe this is a self-fulfilling prophesy. My rage is keeping me going. My old habits of anger and determination burn into me and I welcome them like old friends. That's good, because they distract me from the pain I'm currently in. I'm not enlightened enough to walk away just yet. Revenge has consumed me, and I feel no shame about it. I can't believe I've messed this up so badly, but I can't beat myself up too much. I guess nobody is perfect, and my foe has proved this. Not killing me was their second-biggest mistake. Going after me was their first.

TWO

MY MIND STARTS to drift. All sorts of thoughts come into my head. When you face the possibility of your mortality, the brain has a way of trying to make sense of everything. Flashbacks of my life come in like gate crashers at a bad party: family; sorrow; Ben & Jerry's ice cream; sex; the illicit affairs with married men that I have no guilt over; the men and women I dumped and who dumped me; the marriage proposal I turned down because I was too scared; the people I've killed and the fact that they're laughing, waiting for me in hell; chocolate; the films I'll never see; what the big deal is with Jimmy Choos; the sounds and smells of the Caribbean.

Music also enters my consciousness. Songs load in my mind as if it's an iPod on shuffle. One track that I hear is that song 'Once in a Lifetime' by Talking Heads. The line that resonates with me is 'How did I get here?' How the fuck did I get here? To answer that question, you have to trace it back to Osama and the boys. After 9/11, security agencies were springing up almost faster than McDonald's franchises. Everybody was calling themselves security consultants. With states throwing trillions at the war on terror, like money was the cure for everything, who could blame these companies? The powers that be spread their legs, put their collective arses in the air, and waited to be fucked by the unregulated and the unscrupulous. And I queued up, with my strap-on at the ready.

My background wasn't conventional. I wouldn't have lasted five seconds in the army, where many security consultants come from. People like me, who have problems with authority, shouldn't join the forces. The ones who recruited me weren't looking for those who came through the system. They were looking for something altogether different: the raw potential that they could develop and train to create elite operatives.

I was fourteen when I was recruited by the Facility. There is no direct German translation for this word, not that it is necessary as we understand English quite well. Their origins are unclear and still a mystery. They have an international covert scouting network that looks for particular character traits. They hide in the shadows. A secret group that works in a parallel universe. There was more talent available than was evident, and they needed very special recruiters to spot the people they were looking for. I was part of that group: the ones the others dismissed; the ones who got overlooked because they didn't fit in. I was perfect for them, but it takes a special person to spot ability that most people miss. Someone with an immense mind who appreciates talent. Someone who trusts it, respects and nurtures it. A visionary.

Someone like my mentor.

After my time with the Facility, I became a security consultant. It suited me as I preferred the freedom of being a freelancer. I could take the jobs I wanted, as and when I felt like it. And I could build up my reputation steadily. In the beginning, they gave me work that I couldn't mess up. Imagine how that felt, doing menial tasks because they didn't yet trust me. But I played along with them. Being underestimated has its advantages; it means that nobody expects anything. Once I proved myself, clients trusted me, and I got more substantial assignments. Over time, I began turning work down. That's the position I wanted to be in. It wasn't that hard to be good in this business, but it was hard to be great. Clients like it if you're professional, punctual, and consistent, and don't ask too many questions. After a while, they get the measure of you.

Then I got the opportunity to lead this team in Germany in March 2013, through a casual contact, someone that I was sleeping with at the time. Karl Yumeni was the contract and on every most-wanted list. He was as nasty as they come, but very elusive. You didn't get to be as successful as he was if you weren't ahead of the game. This was supposed to be a simple snatch operation. The agency I work for is called Coba Security. They didn't tell me who their client was, but they wanted Yumeni alive. I guess I was flattered that I got the job. At the time, I wondered why. There were people more experienced. But nevertheless, it was given to me. In retrospect, it had setup written all over it, and I never saw it coming. But they saw me coming.

The team was put together relatively quickly, and I realised it was too quick. Moving fast is not always the best idea in the world. You need time for people to gel no matter how highly trained you are. And it's always better to work for people you know and can trust. But in this game trust is a rare thing. I wish I'd turned it down. I'd refused work before without a thought, but the money was too good, which is always a sign of something. Also, it was a chance to go back home. I had unfinished business. I was probably too eager, and my employers sensed it. My willingness to oblige might as well have been tattooed on my forehead. Being told that you aren't good enough has its consequences. The need to prove myself has become a recurring preoccupation in my life. I have my father to thank for that.

My other team members, Avery, Gains, Madison, and Blake, were all ex–US Special Forces. They were all Caucasian, quite good-looking but not idiosyncratic enough for my tastes, with jarhead hairstyles and recent tans, which suggested they had spent time abroad. But my guess was that it wasn't for a holiday. It looked like they were enjoying the fruits of their lucrative security contracts, judging by the expensive designer suits they were wearing at our first meeting. They looked the part and had assured body language. You didn't have to be in the military to see that. Presence is a thing you can't define. It's a thing you feel.

And they seemed more than happy for me to lead the team. They had no ego about it, which surprised me. What surprised me more was that none of them came on to me. Maybe I was threatening to them. Perhaps I wasn't their type. But as I think that, the voice in my head berates me and says, *Really? Get over yourself, you're not eighteen anymore.* The voice in my head is a great leveller. I should listen to it more. I didn't get to know the others in the team much as there was no time for small talk. It was very professional and respectful, but cold. I like to crack jokes to break the tension, but somehow, I sensed these guys were not the joking kind. Given what I do for a living, I never know when it will be my last time to laugh, so I try to make the most of it.

We spent a few days together being debriefed in our training facility in Hertfordshire. It was very intensive and well-rehearsed, considering the short window available. But because of the intel, we had to move quickly. The target would be in one of his warehouse storage facilities in south-western Germany. Plan A was that we were going to breach the warehouse.

I feel comfortable with men. I had good training in my family, being the only girl among five siblings. It was a fight for survival, and I learned a lot from my brothers. They all had their different character traits, and we took turns to fall out and make up with each other, as families do. Some of my brothers were protective when they felt like it or competitive when it suited them. It gave me a good grounding in how to survive in a male-dominated world. To be honest, part of me liked the fact that I didn't have a sister. It meant that I stood out. I liked being the centre of attention. Regarding not wanting competition, maybe I'm much more like my mother than I care to admit.

Blake, our driver, drove us in a black BMW six-seater SUV from Frankfurt am Main Airport. The journey to the warehouse location outside of Mainz took about sixty minutes in total. The Wednesday midday traffic on the autobahn was surprisingly smooth. It was a beautiful day with a clear blue sky and sunny; just how I liked it. The weather made my mood about returning to my homeland a little better. It was weird coming back, and I didn't think I'd return so soon, as there were lots of bad memories. I guess I was running away from my past, but this assignment gave me a chance to perhaps face my demons. But I probably allowed the emotion of returning to my homeland to cloud my judgement.

We parked about five hundred metres from the target building, offloaded and checked our weapons, and attached our comms system, but there was no camera to send back surveillance feeds to the agency. Which is what they wanted. This was supposed to be a deniable op: a black bag within a black bag. As it turned out, this was a suicide mission.

The four of us made the rest of the journey on foot and took up our positions. We waited for almost two hours, and it felt like it. Some people aren't cut out for this kind of work. It can test your patience. Surveillance isn't glamorous and doesn't suit many people's psychology. They feel the need just to do something. But sometimes impatience can get you killed. Patience is not a natural trait of mine, as my mentor, Lothar Litze, kept telling me. I used to lose it when he trained me, and he used to taunt me about it. He said that impatience is a fear of what we can't see, that things are always working behind the scenes, and that the universe hates queue jumpers. I never knew what he meant, and to be honest, I still don't. Maybe when I've experienced enough, I'll be ready to understand it all. I suppose I'm too impatient to comprehend.

The target was in a dirty grey, rectangular, featureless building that, from a distance, looked like a collection of well-ordered large shoe boxes. The grimy windows matched the exterior. The warehouse was bordered by a steel fence with barbed-wire coils at the top, which looked like something out of a war movie. The expanse of concrete ground buried the discreet flecks of grass straining through its gaps.

Yumeni finally left the building through the front with his three black-suited, sunglass-wearing bodyguards in a wedge formation, with their client in the middle. He looked as smug in real life as he did in the photographs. I wanted to shoot him there and then, but I reluctantly obeyed my instructions. Things must be desperate if you want a lowlife like Yumeni to still be breathing. I'd seen the file on him, and it's not recommended bedtime reading. The ones who wanted him alive must have had a moral compass without a needle. But he was the reason people like me exist. A thought that almost makes me ashamed.

I sent Avery and Madison to the left of the warehouse perimeter as Gains and I took a right. Blake stayed with the SUV. We were all in radio contact, ready for my sign. I waited until I was sure. But before I gave the signal to move, I momentarily looked in the direction of my advance team. Something in the air didn't feel right. It was as if I had a premonition. Like I could see or smell impending death.

Then it happened.

The sniper's bullets obliterated Madison's head like a great firework display. I could hear the blood hissing in my earpiece, spraying its random patterns across the ground and in the air like an out-of-control hosepipe. His headless body dropped to the floor, unaware that his brain was gone, still twitching, determined to cling to life.

Avery was next.

The bullet smashed through his throat, but he was still alive.

Just.

He instinctively placed his right hand on the entry wound, which was as pointless as using a finger to try to plug a huge dam, as he gurgled, drowning in his own blood. There was no need for another bullet, but the sniper shot him again anyway, blowing half his face off this time. Not to show him any mercy, but to make sure.

Exactly what I would have done.

Yumeni's bodyguards had already hustled him into the vehicle, speeding off even before they had time to close the car doors properly.

Before I could take cover, I was hit on my right shoulder, spinning me to the ground. As I lay on my back, I saw Gains's head for the last time before it was perforated by the sniper's bullet. I could see daylight through his skull. Then he lurched forward, like a tree being felled. He landed, just missing me, on my right. Gains's left eye dropped out from what was left of his shattered eye socket onto the ground and stared back at me, but it couldn't relay images of my contorted expression as I stared back at him, wondering how this operation had gone belly-up. He also couldn't see my look of pity, which was pointless now. I got back to my feet in a crouch, kept quiet, and ran to some nearby undergrowth for cover. *Must get to the vehicle*, I thought, and ran, keeping low and zigzagging to avoid being hit, hoping the trees would provide natural cover.

The speed at which I was running meant that everything in my peripheral vision was a blur. It felt like I was moving faster than normal, even if it wasn't true. The twigs and undergrowth cracked under my weight as I raced to my exfil point. I was in sight of the vehicle, but my hope was extinguished as I saw a confused-looking Blake at the wheel.

But I wasn't fast enough to beat what came next.

The rocket-propelled grenade tore through the still air, hissing and spinning towards my only means of escape. Blake didn't stand a chance as the missile ruptured the fuel tank, exploding the vehicle in a mini Hiroshima with successive explosive bursts, ending in a massive fireball. I could hear Blake's screams as the shock wave sent me back on my arse. I rolled over onto my stomach, got up, and ran into the woods for cover.

I felt my senses heighten. I could have sworn that I could hear birds from many miles away hatching from their eggs, the insects in the ground clawing away at the mud, distant conversations with faint echoes, and the leaves making crashing noises as they fell to the ground, as I ran for my life through the undergrowth. I could hear my heart pound in my chest as if it were trying to escape my body. I had to check myself as I realised that it was the adrenaline kicking in and I was hallucinating. Fear can do that to a person. It can play tricks on the mind. I had to stay calm and remember to control my breathing. My mentor always told me I should focus on my breath when I'm anxious. I was bleeding and willing myself to get over the line. They always said that I had a strong survival instinct, and it's served me well so far. If they were going to take me, I would make sure they would have to work for it.

THREE

IT'S HARD TO tell how many are after me. I thought it was one shooter; it may be more. I manage to find cover in the dense trees. I know that whoever is out there won't have a clear line of sight now, but they're turning the tables by playing the waiting game. My injury isn't fatal, which is good news, but it is painful. As luck would have it, the bullet grazed the part of my right shoulder that wasn't protected by my vest. I sit down under an old pine tree. I just need to settle for a while. I look around and see the sunlight cut through the foliage, casting various shadows and creating colours, bouncing and reverberating off the trees and rocks, illuminating the scene before me.

I listen to the faint cacophony of wildlife, which sounds like a meditation CD on a loop track. I'm glad that I can still appreciate the beauty of it all. And in a way, it helps clear my head as I contemplate my next move. I tie a handkerchief above my wound, using my left hand, my teeth, and a pen to twist the knot tighter, forming a crude but effective tourniquet. It's fortunate that I have it with me since I don't normally carry hankies and don't know many people who still do. They seem quite old-fashioned now. I was given it by one of the stewardesses on the flight over, and I kept it because I like the simple design.

I'm hopeful that I've evaded the sniper, for the time being, but I can't stay here. Much as I like the woods, I don't want to be here at night. I have no shelter, no food, but there is always plenty you can eat in here if you're desperate. I'm not just yet. I saw a documentary on children in the South American rain forests who catch and cook tarantulas on a stick. They roast them over a fire like marshmallows, and they make a squeaking noise as they burn because of the air inside them. I could barely watch it and turned my face away from the screen. What is it with spiders? I'm like many people in that regard, despite my courage in other areas; I have a primeval fear of them. I can't even explain why. Those children put my courage into perspective.

I have to do something. I was taught by my mentor that doing something generally has the same outcome as doing nothing. I always choose to fight. That's my nature. When there is a choice between fight and flight, I always fight, regardless of the potential outcome.

Pride's a bitch. Another old habit of mine.

I default to my warrior gene, especially when I'm threatened.

I decide to chance it and walk further into the woods. I'm not quite sure where I am, but I must rely on all my senses for clues. Being here reminds me of my childhood. After school, my friends and I would play Cowboys and Indians. I always played on the Indian side because I related to the underdog. I knew enough back then to work out that the Westerns were bullshit and that Hollywood glossed over reality to suit its purposes.

Now I'm a gun for hire. How ironic.

I probably don't look like someone a hitchhiker would pick up, so I decide I'll steal a car and do whatever is necessary. That's what I was trained for, but my survival instinct is innate. I've learned various strategies that help overcome childhood and adulthood problems. It could be as simple as allowing someone to think they're in control. I became good at that. Manipulation is misunderstood; it has negative associations, but it's a necessary technique. We all do it to some degree, though we might call it something else.

I want to survive, even if it means turning to the last person in the world I want to go to for help. This is a measure of my desperation, and my mentor would know it only too well. No doubt he would throw this in my face. But better to be embarrassed than dead. Litze said to me that if I was ever in trouble, I should send him the unique text code. Like I said before, I hate asking him for help. That's partly due to my pride, but partly because we didn't exactly part on the best of terms. That's putting it mildly.

Litze's memory of our last time together would end with my shooting him.

FOUR

VERY FEW PEOPLE get the drop on Lothar Litze, as he's the toughest bastard I've ever known. They used to call him die Silberfuch (the Silver Fox) because of his prematurely greying hair. I could see why women were drawn to him. He was timelessly handsome. His eyes were Paul Newman blue, and he had a square jaw, hard facial features, and soft wrinkles that enhanced his looks. He was tall and lean rather than overly muscular but moved with a grace that came with an inner confidence and a spiritual authority that very few people have. Litze was ex-Stasi and one of the best of his generation. A highly skilled operative in weapons and hand-to-hand combat, he had led many covert missions during the Cold War.

There is much I don't know about Litze. But I know his past was troubled. I think he enjoyed training us at the Facility. It gave him a focus. I know he was married to a lady called Silke whom he'd met while he was on a mission in the late sixties. It was more lust than love at first sight. The love part grew over time. I wonder how hard it must have been to have a relationship in this line of work. That's why I prefer casual relationships. Killers don't make great companions, and besides, I've never met anyone yet who had the courage and the wisdom to leave me alone. I know Litze and his wife sometimes worked undercover as they both felt they could be more convincing if they were a couple.

While it's an unspoken thing in the service, agents regularly use sex to get information. I wonder how my mentor felt about his wife fucking other men. Equally, Silke had to cope with the attention Lothar was attracting from other women. I wonder if they shared stories with each other about their conquests, or had a silent agreement not to discuss it. I wonder if they got turned on by it and used it to spice up their sex life, but that's me being mischievous. I don't believe in God, but if there is one, maybe he invented sex to test the integrity of any relationship. The fact that for most of the time they could separate the sex from love gave them a greater resilience. From what I heard, they had a deep love and respect for each other, meaning that they could survive almost anything. They also planned to give up, retire from the service, and start a family. It was something that kept them going, but that dream was to be short-lived.

As I got to know Litze, he started to confide in me more. I took it as a compliment that he was beginning to trust me. Tears settled in Litze's eyes as he spoke to me about Silke. He probably wasn't used to people seeing him cry. But he had no shame in revealing this to me, whereas I have a problem with showing emotion.

He told me about Silke's assignment in Paris to meet a top US diplomat with information about an impending attack in Europe. Lothar didn't want her to go, but she insisted. Litze knew her too well to try to talk her out of anything, as it was her single-mindedness that had attracted him to her in the first place. She wanted to do this one last job before they retired. She arrived at the Ritz in Paris on September 12, 1988. Someone had left the diplomat with not only a bullet between his eyes but a bomb vest strapped to him, which was triggered when Silke opened the door. The explosion killed thirteen people: twelve adults, including Silke, and Silke's unborn child.

It must have felt to Litze like all the lights in the world went out when his wife died. And there were rumours that he was into drink and drugs. Which was understandable. But it was his human side that I preferred. Not the other part of him, which I didn't care for: the side that liked to prod and provoke, especially during our often-brutal training sessions. I also heard other rumours about Litze, that he was a traitor, that he was not all that he seemed, but I put that down to jealousy and trusted my instincts. Even I had my doubts and sometimes I hated his guts, but I believed that he was a good man.

He probably thought he was doing the best for me: that he was trying to prepare me for the tough world ahead. I consider myself physically very resilient. I was also one of the fittest in school, an all-round natural athlete, but I was no academic and hated classrooms. I wanted to be outside doing things. But Lothar was utterly ruthless and provocative. I was his project, and I believe he used me to help him cope with the grief of losing his wife and daughter. He pushed me to the very limits of my training, both physically and mentally. I think he enjoyed it too much for my liking at times.

The gun incident came after a gruelling twelve-hour training session. The program had intensified over that last six months, and I was near my breaking point. Many in the programme didn't stay the course. Some people were taken away and never seen again. I wondered what happened to them but couldn't afford to dwell on it too much. I fought everyone Litze put in front of me. There were some hard bastards that he lined up to fight me. He called them 'the Vienna Specialists'. They were some of his toughest men and women who enjoyed beating the crap out of people. I think Litze did this for his amusement. Some of my fellow trainees were not so lucky and were destroyed by these animals. But I was determined not to give Litze the pleasure, and I managed to get the upper hand.

There was one woman whom I particularly enjoyed fighting. They called her 'the Psycho Bitch'. She had one of those faces that you'd never tire of hitting and had an arrogance about her that let you know she looked down on you like you were nothing of consequence. She was aesthetically pleasing on the eye, if you like that sort thing, but she had a dead soul. I was looking forward to pulling the reins on her high horse.

She was a good fighter—I'll give her credit—but she was a poser. A vanity fighter. Vanity doesn't work too well on the street. I'm not an aesthetic fighter. I'm not an aesthetic anything. Some would call me an unconventional beauty. I was an ugly duckling at school who turned into less of an ugly duckling later. My body shape and my looks managed to form into something that aroused enough interest from men and women. And I don't get many complaints. My boobs are a reasonable size without inhibiting me physically, and my athletic physique means I'm a good all-round package.

I destroyed her techniques, which made her more frustrated. That's what I was taught by Lothar: the art of dismantling the opponent and their self-perception. I broke her arm and smashed her ribs, and I saved the best for last: her nose. I think Psycho Bitch was proud of that cute little nose of hers. Don't think she was after I made it look like a Picasso and flattened it sideways. It wasn't so much Cubism. I taught her an art movement called Realism.

Even when it was two on one, three on one, or more, I still saw them off. I must admit, Litze taught me well. I was just pleased I wasn't going toe to toe with him instead.

I'd jumped through every hoop he wanted me to. I was tired, hungry, emotional, and to be honest, seriously pissed off. But Litze kept on about my resilience. He questioned my mental toughness. He had an annoying habit of doing that. I felt he was picking on me. Like he was singling me out. He even made me do more exercises than my peers, and that hadn't gone unnoticed by the others. I think they were pleased and relieved that I received much of the attention, which deflected it from them. But I know what he was trying to do: he was trying to screw with me, trying to make me doubt myself, just like my father used to do. Just like all those dumb-ass teachers used to do. Just like all those people who never got me, which were most people. That's the history of humankind: if they don't get you or you don't fit the norm, they put you in a box. Well, boxes are for dead people, and tradition is for those who have no ideas of their own.

The reason I shot him seems silly, looking back on it, but Litze didn't think I had what it took. He would be particularly cruel and get personal about my family. Maybe I'd shared too much with him. That was my mistake, and he threw it back in my face. He used it as a weapon against me.

My hatred for him grew inside me like an uncontrollable weed. It was like he was trying to push me away, and he was succeeding. He knew what buttons to press as his goading intensified. I'd thought he was different from the rest. I'd thought he got me, thought he understood me. But he was like everybody else. Some people would call it assertive mentoring. I call it being a fucking sadistic bastard.

Litze found one trigger that he knew would rile me. It was the one thing that would set off my fight response, and he knew it. He said that I didn't have the guts to be a top agent and I'd end up like my mother, a compliant lowlife whore who couldn't stand up for herself. The woman who became my father's willing punching bag. The woman who was a disgrace to womankind. I knew all this and said it often enough. But I didn't want to hear it from someone else. It's as if families can criticise each other, but outsiders can't. I became unusually protective towards my family. It was like he was turning up the volume on my past. The noise in my head was intense. I just wanted it to go away. I wanted him to go away, so I took the easy way out. After I shot him, he merely smiled and said, 'Thank you for proving my point'.

FIVE

THE FACT THAT Litze was wearing a vest that saved him from the bullet I aimed at his chest was beside the point. My rage took over, and I pulled the trigger. I couldn't even remember whether he was wearing protection, which made it worse. It was like a blur. I lost control. I failed. He won. And I hated him even more. I tried to convince myself that I was angry at Litze, but I was deluding myself. I was angry at me. I'd let myself down. I'd let him down. I dropped the gun and fled. I ran before he could see me cry. I hated crying in front of people. Stupid, I know. But that was years of my defiance against my father. I didn't want to show him that he'd gotten to me. Privately, I cried like Niagara Falls, but I wasn't about to let him get the satisfaction. That's the last time I remember crying.

That was eight years ago, and I've never seen Litze since then. I've thought of contacting him many times, but I chickened out. I remember the times when we were tight. They were good times. He was the father, and, to be honest, the lover, I wish I'd had. I would think of my mentor often. When I used to get into close calls, I'd ask myself, 'What would Litze do?' That's how influential he was. But I ruined it.

This is my chance to make things good with him. Even though the circumstances are desperate. I'm asking him for help. And he'll know how hard it is for me. Just as well humble pie doesn't have a sell-by date, as I haven't eaten any for a while. It's about time for me to consume some. I eventually convince myself that I should face him now. I want to atone for things. The thought of our going to our graves unreconciled saddens me greatly. Elton John was right: sorry seems to be the hardest word. For me, it isn't the most difficult word. It simply isn't a word in my vocabulary. Again, it's like the tears that I refused to show; I mistook those actions as a sign of weakness.

If I can face my mentor, I can come through this. It's quiet in the forest now. The temperature dropped a little in the afternoon, but it's still mild. I decide to move further into the trees. I try to get orientated and remember not being too far away from the main road. But I still should take care because whoever is after me will be trying to second-guess me. As I hold my weapon in my right hand, the pain makes my gun feel heavier than usual, but I must get on with it. What would I do if I were after me? I wouldn't go into a forest alone. I'd probably bide my time. It depends of course on what they're being paid and the deadline for taking me out. The fact that I have cover gives me some protection. Would I risk it in here? The prey would be scared and have nothing to lose. Going after an average target isn't necessarily more straightforward than killing another assassin. Taking out someone in the same game can have a certain predictability about it. Better to live and fight another day and risk some loss of reputation or losing the second half of the fee, than die. I remember what Litze said: 'Impatience can get you killed.'

I should trust all my senses now. And I have to trust the most important sense of all: the sixth one. They say we females are more intuitive than men. Maybe. Maybe not. When I see how some of my kind behave at times, I wonder. Maybe I'm coloured by my experience of having a weak mother.

I go further into the woods. I don't want to stay here in the dark.

But I will if I have no choice. Maybe I'm overthinking this. Litze would often say that about me. I'm feeling tired and hungry. I've managed to stem the flow of blood from my shoulder, but my gun feels heavier than before. I hold my weapon in my left hand and clench my right in an attempt to reanimate it. Part of the training I did with Litze was to use my weaker side. We did this a lot in our combat drills. I wasn't bad at shooting with my left, but I always favoured my right.

My movements across the ground are becoming more tentative now. I don't want to take the chance of being heard. But my hunter has the same problem. There is no way they can come after me without making a sound unless they can walk on air. I think I hear something and stop suddenly. I'm trying to take my mentor's advice: don't think, feel. What am I feeling now? The forest smells good to me. I can still hear the faint sounds of birds bouncing off the trees. I'm trying to revert to a time when we used our intuition more, before 'civilization' crushed the life out of it with its so-called progress. The woods feel more imposing now. As if they're trying to reclaim me as part of the ecosystem. It's been a while since I felt in tune with nature, but I would have preferred better circumstances. I go inside myself and feel the air change. I lick my right index finger and hold it up to the air. Not exactly scientific, but good enough, as I feel a light breeze cool my saliva, confirming my earlier thoughts. My instincts told me there was a clearing to the right of me. There is enough light to see where I'm going, but I don't want to use my torch, for obvious reasons. I'm hoping I'll be able to keep my date with destiny and face my mentor after all.

***

I can't remember how long I've been in here. To me, it feels like an age. I guess it seems like that when you become the prey. Or it depends on your perception of time. My natural impatience means that time seems longer to me. I know only too well what Litze would be saying to me now. I see the clearing as confirmed by my finger test and am pleased. But I don't want to get ahead of myself. I've done that more times than I can recall and learned valuable lessons along the way about making assumptions.

The opening forms a sizeable oval shape in the brush ahead of me. As if it's man-made rather than natural. Although it feels like a portal into another world that I'm hopefully escaping through. Walking towards it, I can see a steep bank, down which runs a well-trodden path that descends for about one hundred metres, leading to what looks like a minor road. I know that if I walk into the open, especially with it being still light, I'll be exposed, but I have to risk it. Staying in the woods isn't an option for me. I decide to run to the bushes on the other side of the road. A moving target will be harder to hit. Like I said before, if they want me, they'll have to work for it.

I'm still fast and am hoping this will save me. My specialism was the one hundred metres at school, but I learned to train for longer distances as I got older. Aided by gravity, I make ground very quickly and am pleased that the sniper at least isn't here. But I still need a vehicle.

This road doesn't look like one that's used very regularly, so I decide to walk south. I hope that I'll hit some habitation soon.

I was offered an agency mobile, which I declined. I don't trust any communication device I haven't vetted myself, and I told Coba so. Technology has moved on so much that these days, you can track a mobile which has been switched off. You can even turn a mobile on remotely. Being naturally cautious, I always carry a separate mobile and use the ghost network, which is untraceable. This was introduced to me by Donny Walsh, one of the world's top hackers and yet another person I've fallen out with. For me, relationships feel like a minefield where I can't avoid setting off the explosions.

My main concern now is to get a car and drive to the location where I used to train with Litze, using my phone GPS to help me get there. I wonder about lots of things: I wonder how my mentor is. I wonder if he's managed to come to terms with his past and the death of his wife, Silke, and their unborn child. I wonder whether he's still training protégés in the Facility. I wonder what he'll look like. Though I can't imagine that he'll have changed that much. He went grey quite early in his life, so his hair at least won't have changed.

He'll probably think that I have a nerve contacting him after all these years. I wonder whether I was fair to him and myself. I've put off this moment, and to be honest, I know why: I was a coward, and I couldn't bear the thought of facing him. It will be humiliating for me. I thought I was somehow strong, but you can only kid yourself for so long. No matter how much you try to bury or avoid things, reality catches up with you in the end.

I now don't believe in coincidence. In a weird way, I believe I somehow conspired to make this happen so that I'd have to face the great Lothar Litze again. There is only one way to prove to him that I'm serious about needing his help. The fact that I'm asking for his help is bad enough. The real proof to him will be the code words I'll use to contact him. I daren't utter them. And he knows that. He wasn't supposed to know, but the ever-resourceful Litze found out and would tease me mercilessly about them. The thought of them makes me cringe. He's only one of a handful of people who know these words. For me, they aren't words. They're more like major embarrassments.

SIX

THE WALK SOUTH is pleasant, and the scenery momentarily helps me forget my circumstances. There's nothing better than connecting with nature. And if I'm going to die today, I can think of worse places. The German countryside is breathtaking. The trees have a calming effect on me, towering over me like giant sentries cloaked in their magnificent greenery. The smells seem uncorrupted by the current clumsy inhabitants. I'm not aware that anyone is hunting me now. But to be honest, part of me doesn't care anymore. This is perhaps reckless, but it's my way of confronting my fear. We all have to die sometime. Over the years, my martial arts teachers taught me to fight without fear, live without fear. When you fight without fear, you never actually lose. Like the samurai: learn to detach yourself from the outcome. Easier said than done, but I'm getting better at it. My mentor was pretty good at it, but sometimes, I thought he had a death wish. Given what had happened to his wife, I could understand it. When you lose the one thing you will take a bullet for, it's hard to find meaning.

I've walked for the best part of an hour without seeing one car. I'm tired, hungry, and thirsty. And I can't feel my injured shoulder. This isn't looking great. My hope is that I'll find a residence soon, steal a vehicle, and get to my destination. The place where Litze and I trained wasn't high-tech, but it was extremely useful. Litze didn't believe in high-tech for the sake of it. He'd become disillusioned with the direction the world was going in. He was an analogue man in a digital world, and he felt mankind had lost its way. Litze wasn't a fan of consumerism and had become cynical about how many manufacturers would make things designed to break down, so we would buy more things. They called it 'planned obsolescence'. He laughed when "the powers that be" used jargon to disguise their true meanings, as if they were somehow ashamed of them. He also laughed at the term 'extraordinary rendition.' For the uninitiated, this sounds like a night out at the opera listening to Pavarotti singing 'Nessun Dorma' instead of someone being made to sing by more nefarious means. Who are they fooling? The powers that be do like to airbrush shit.

It wasn't just things that didn't last. Litze thought relationships succumbed to the obsolescence curse. Society had changed so much that you could change your partners more often than you changed your underpants. People didn't seem to give things time and gave up too quickly because of the choices available. He thought some people saw partners as the latest fashion accessories rather than people. Litze felt out of time and place in this world and saw himself as one of the last relics of a golden age. But he loved the thought of that. Litze wore it like a badge of honour that he would thrust in the face of those who were against his views. But he had calmed down over the years and realised that you should choose your battles. Something I am now starting to understand late in the day.

My eyes are tired now. Perhaps I'm straining too much. The light is fading, which doesn't help. My vision isn't perfect, but I can see enough in the distance that gives me hope. It's a good situation for me. From what I can tell, there's a farmhouse enveloped by acres of wheat fields, which looks so peaceful. And now, I'm about to disturb its serenity.

SEVEN

IT TAKES ABOUT ten minutes to walk to the edge of the farm. The wooden fence, adorned modestly with barbed wire, is low enough for me to jump over. This is a good thing, since my shoulder is causing me discomfort. I take my jacket off and place it over the wires to protect myself as I jump. The farm doesn't look secure, and I can't see any trespass warning signs, which feels unusual to me. Maybe people who live in the country are more trusting than city dwellers. I wade through the wheat fields while keeping sight of the farmhouse, which grows with every few strides.

The building looks like just another homestead. The roof is made of dark red slate, and the white walls have beams, with lines which resemble liquorice, running through their exterior. To the left of the farm, I can see an oak-panelled outhouse just a few yards away. On the right, behind the main building, is a large barn with a bell-shaped grey roof and brick-red exterior. There are no vehicles visible, but I hope that there will be a vehicle inside.

I raise my pistol with my good arm and move slowly across the front of the farm. I'm not here to negotiate. I'm going to take what I want and will kill if I must. I'm a killer; I know that. I've known that since before I was formed in my pathetic mother's womb. It's not as if this life comes with some manual or assassin's code of conduct.

I head over to the barn and see the large wooden doors slightly ajar, revealing a dark interior. As the sun is still out, it indicates to me that at least the roof isn't in disrepair. I'm very thirsty now and I notice a standpipe on the right of the building. When I finally reach the pipe, it comes up to my waist. I replace my gun in the back of my jeans. The tap is quite stiff, and I decide I'll use my left hand to turn it, which isn't natural for me but will be less painful. The tap squeaks as I twist it. The pipe trembles as the water pours over my hands, cleaning the dried blood from my fallen colleagues and my shoulder wound. Then I cup the liquid with both hands and drink greedily. I lower myself directly under the tap, allowing its contents to bathe me. My clothes absorb the water. This rejuvenates me as I drink some more. I didn't appreciate how dehydrated I'd become.

The next thing now is to find a vehicle. I retrieve my gun and point it at the barn doors. I revert to holding my weapon in my right hand as I gently creak open the doors with my left. The wood is solid and made to last. Litze would appreciate that. Every push I make lets more of the sun in, revealing more of the barn's interior. The building is deceptively bigger than it looks as I scan the inside. The neatly stacked straw bales are now casting shadows as I further let in the sun. With some relief, I can see to my right an old pickup truck. It's an orange Unimog. I don't know or care much about vehicles— my two eldest brothers were the petrol heads—but even I know they're made by Mercedes. Growing up with boys has its advantages. This mode of transport isn't exactly inconspicuous, as I think Unimogs are ugly, but it will have to do. I just hope that it still works.

My stride towards the vehicle is suddenly interrupted by the sound of something metallic falling to the ground. I pull my gun and swiftly point left, in the direction of the noise. My body tightens. Someone is in the barn, and I'm about to find out whether I'm prepared to cross that line again.

EIGHT

I HAVE BOTH hands on my gun this time as I move towards the target. Before I can call out, a figure slowly emerges from the shadows. She shields her eyes from the sun with her hands until she's under my silhouette. Then she places her hand down at her side. Most people I've pointed a gun at react by screaming, putting their hands up, or saying 'Don't shoot'. This girl, who I guess would be about fourteen years old, just looks at me, as if she wants a staring competition. She's blonde, skinny, blue-eyed, and is wearing a grey school uniform. The jacket lapels have a purple trim; she wears a crisp white shirt and purple tie, which isn't done up at the top, with a pleated, knee-length skirt. I hate uniforms and am so glad I'm not still at school. The little girl is as cool as they come. She doesn't flinch. The sun is at my back, so there is a possibility that she can't see my face. But I can't deal with possibilities, only certainties. I have a decision to make as to whether to kill her or let her live. Then she says something that surprises me.

'Looks like there are two of us that shouldn't be here.'

I don't reply. I just hold my position, pointing my gun at her head, right between those seemingly innocent blue eyes. It would be straightforward and quick enough. She wouldn't feel a thing. It would be clean, efficient, and clinical. The trouble is, my gun doesn't have a silencer, but there is no one else around. The sound would carry, but I'm in the country. The sound of a gunshot wouldn't be that unusual. But I can't squeeze the trigger. Not yet. I'm intrigued. I wonder why she didn't speak to me in German. Then I remember that I don't exactly look like a local.

'So, what now?' says the girl.

I still don't reply.

'You're not much of a talker, are you? People say I talk too much and don't listen enough. That's what gets me into trouble.'

If the girl is nervous, she isn't showing it. She displays a maturity that belies her years. She's a beautiful girl, but there's something about her that seems sad. Something very familiar about her. We stare at each other, and time appears to stand still. It's as if I'm looking back to the past and she's looking into the future.

'If you're going to use that thing, get it over with. You'd be doing me a favour.'

So, she wants to die? I think. I decide to reply. 'How come?'

'Well, school sucks for a start.'

I can relate to what she's saying. 'So you should be at school now?'

'Unfortunately', says the girl, betraying no signs of nerves or fear. I'm trying to hide that I'm impressed. But the fact that I haven't killed her yet is a sign that at least she's gained my respect. She's no typical fourteen-year-old.

'I bet you didn't like school either. You don't seem like the indoor type to me.'

I say nothing.

'You look like you're running from something. You and me both.'

I still aim the gun at her, but to be honest, I don't know why. She's just a kid. But there is something quite unnerving about her.

'My name is Brigitte. What's your name?'

I can't believe this. I'm pointing a gun at her head, could kill her any minute, and she wants to make small talk.

'Are you alone?' I ask her.

'It depends on what you mean by alone', replies the girl. 'If you mean right now on this farm, then I'm the only one here. In my life? I've always felt alone.'

She pauses for a while, then she says, 'Until now, that is.'

Is she trying to fuck with me? What does she mean? Is she referring to me as if I'm some long-lost soulmate? She's nothing like the others whom I've pointed a gun at. Like the ones who talk nervously about everything and nothing; the ones who beg for mercy; the ones who beg for their lives, which would never work with someone like me; or the ones who piss themselves instead.

'Take the truck. That's what you came for, isn't it? There's plenty of fuel; the key is in the ignition, and there's a first aid kit in the back.'

I still point the gun at her head. But I don't quite know why I haven't killed her. Why am I hesitating? *Shoot her, Becker. You've done it before!* I've pulled the trigger many times in my career, with many different guns and mostly without a thought. But the trigger on my Glock feels heavy to me now. It's as if an invisible force is stopping me from pulling it. Oddly enough, my fingers feel sweaty. I'm overthinking this. She's evidence of my existence. Collateral. One more on the list of kills I've made, for which I'll have to bear the consequences at some time to come.

I believe Brigitte though: I would be doing her a favour if I killed her. She isn't happy. What happened to her that she wants to die? She's a kid. A brilliant one too; probably too bright for this world. She's a deductive reasoner who works things out for herself. So she'd probably be a threat to most people. Especially people with power. But she can see through them. That makes her dangerous. That also makes her very lonely. She's probably bored at school because they can't keep up with her. That makes her restless. They no doubt put her in a category. Maybe she's considered a so-called special needs child. She isn't mad; she's just too sane. She's probably been told that if she works hard, gets her exams, goes to university, gets a good job, marries a guy called Heinz or Fritz, has kids, settles down, and continues the family line, she'll live happily ever after. That's all right for most people. But she isn't most people. She doesn't believe in duty. For her, there is a depressing preordination about it. She's desperate to be herself, but she feels trapped, crushed. She's the square peg, and her corners have been cut off to fit the round hole. But that never actually works, because if you're tough enough, the corners eventually grow back. You can't change people. It always ends in tears. She knows this. She's always known. She wants to live her life, not somebody else's. She's figured it out: the fairy tale she was sold from very young is full of shit.

'Take me with you', she says, breaking my concentration.

'You're crazy', I say.

'You're the one holding the gun.'

The girl has a point. I finally lower my weapon and head towards the truck.

'Does it get any easier?' she asks.

'Does what get any easier?' I stop momentarily.

'Life.'

I think about lying to her, but you can't kid a kidder. And I don't want to be yet another adult who deceives her.

'No, it doesn't.'

'Thank you for your honesty.'

I look at her one last time, smile weakly, and get into the vehicle. The keys are in the ignition like she said. The tank is full, and I drive out of the grounds.

I didn't have to kill her in the end. Someone else already beat me to it.

NINE

I MAKE GOOD progress towards my destination. The speed is a steady sixty miles per hour. Although I will the vehicle to go faster, I know that's my impatience again. I keep checking the wing and rear-view mirrors just in case I'm being followed. This seems academic as I could not outrun anybody in this thing. If they're going to get to me, I'll have to fight rather than run. There's no radio either, which annoys me a bit, but I tell myself I should be grateful for a vehicle. It was handed to me on a plate by a disillusioned little girl. Brigitte's stare is etched into my mind like a lithograph, and I'm glad—no, relieved—that I didn't cross the line in her case.

The sun starts to set in the west, making the scene more exotic. There's an eerie calm on the roads. I do encounter some traffic; though it's nothing to cause me immediate concern, I'm still on my guard. I manage to stop momentarily to tend to my shoulder. The first aid kit is where Brigitte said it was, in the back. I clean the wound with some wipes from the kit and some mineral water that I found in the boot. I replace my tourniquet with a large flesh-coloured plaster and then wrap my shoulder with a bandage. It doesn't seem to hurt as much, but maybe that's because it's starting to numb. Or maybe my mind is too busy to register the pain. I'm trying to piece everything together. Calling the agency is not an option now because it's compromised. I have no choice but to go dark until I can unravel this mess. Lothar Litze, assuming he's still alive and still willing to talk to me, would be a great sounding board. He was always adept at seeing things that I couldn't see. Knowing where the pitfalls were and helping me come to my own conclusions. One thing is for sure: my haste probably led me down this road, and it's a hard lesson. They say people don't change unless they experience enough pain. How much pain do I need? I'm not always good at picking up clues, but it's about time that I do. There are repeat patterns I need to address, and he's the only man in the world who can help me. I think of the eight years of lost time and experience, but I try to console myself with the fact that everything has its time. I had to learn from my mistakes. Even Litze would appreciate that.

The thought of meeting him again fills me with a mixture of indescribable excitement and trepidation. There is hardly anybody that I know who can evoke those feelings in me. It's as if he's emitting a homing signal to my soul. And despite everything I've tried to avoid him, I'm being pulled in. I bow to the inevitable and now must face him.

Litze would love this if he could read my mind right now.

TEN

I'VE BEEN TRAVELLING for about two hours now and am ready to take a break. The journey is only a further forty-five minutes at the most. But I think I'm ready to stop. The evening sets in and the darkness cloaks the scenery. The trees look like black silhouettes against the navy-blue sky, and the stars come out, twinkling in various sizes and with various degrees of intensity. I pull over to the side and get out of the cab. I need a stretch. Being sat on my butt all this time isn't the world's greatest exercise plan. I love working out. Well actually, that's not strictly true. I hate the gym, but I love the results. I have to work out due to my profession, as I'm not getting any younger. And if you're wondering about my age, then I'm going to take out the gender card from the pack and plead the fifth. But I'm mostly comfortable in my skin. I've met some beautiful women in my time who hated their bodies. That's the problem with the objectification of women. We're taught the wrong things at school, and not accepting your body is one of them. I'm not saying I'm there, but I'm mostly at the place I want to be.

I'm tired, but sleep will have to wait. Not the best idea as I know that a break will refresh me enough to keep going. I've been warned by others about my tendency to work through things and that I don't understand the importance of taking breaks. I feed on stress. As I get older, I sure appreciate them even more. I was always impressed with the way my mentor managed to maintain himself over the years. During our fight training, he seemed to defeat others without breaking a sweat, whereas I expended more energy than I needed to. Litze would say it was because I wasn't relaxed. And because of that, I used unnecessary energy. He said I needed to slow down to speed up. My impatience meant that I wasn't always mindful. I got better over time, but I wondered whether I was a good student because I didn't always agree with him. I didn't always listen, and to be honest, I probably thought I knew it all. That all seems very silly now. The reality is that I didn't know diddly, and my current predicament proves that.

ELEVEN

APART FROM MY shoulder, I feel like I'm back in the land of the living. I never realised how dangerously close I came to falling asleep at the wheel. I now can't stop thinking about the place where it all started. The place I'm returning to, which made me who I am. This is the closest thing I've known to a real home and a semblance of family. Litze gave me strict instructions on what to do. If I do this, he'll finally take me seriously. I never really believed he did. I look at my phone hesitantly. He'll think that I have a nerve contacting him after everything we've been through, but it's something I need to do, and to be honest, I'm doing it for myself, not him. This has been eating away at me like woodworms in a rotting tree. Or sometimes it felt like a load on my back, like a giant rucksack. Try as I might, I can't bury the past. I must face up to it. It's hard to feel like Superman when you're drowning in Kryptonite.

I need to get a hobby. All this introspection is not good. I could take up knitting, but I'd only use the knitting needles to stab people. I could turn the car around and go someplace else and disappear. But I'm here now. And to be honest, that isn't my style. I want to settle this once and for all. Whoever went to this much trouble to get me will try again. I need to finish this.

***

I turn off the main autobahn heading south-west of the Rheinland-Pfalz region and into a minor road towards a small village called Troppen. I slow down and drive for a further ten minutes until I reach a farmland gate. If I remember correctly, this is where Lothar told me to contact him. Why here of all places? He never said, but my woman's intuition tells me that it has something to do with his late wife, Silke. It's the way he spoke about this place. There was no anxiety when he talked. His voice was soft, almost a sombre hush as he spoke, seemingly out of some reverence or respect. Something happened here. While I respect his privacy, I am nosy as well. Eight years on, I'm feeling more courageous. I decide that I will ask him when I see him. I believe that maybe it will help him to speak about it. I want to show him that I've changed, that I've become a better listener. I got the impression that he didn't have that in his life. Not really. People are polite, or they pretend to listen, but do they? Not in my experience. I want to be the one who listens to him; that's if he feels I'm worthy.

I take out my cell phone. There's just enough battery power left to send this code. I stare at it for what feels like an age. I walk around in circles for a while. I start to enter my message, then I delete it again. I do this I think five or six times. I'm still procrastinating. All the things that Litze told me not to do, I am still doing. It's as if I'm reverting to my childhood and I'm eight years old again. My stomach tenses, as if it's in one of those knots that you can't undo. My throat is dry. I can barely watch as I type in the words. I squirm as I look at my message one final time. Then I press send. You win this one, Litze. My humiliation is complete.

TWELVE

MY TEXT MESSAGE travels through the ether and cannot be unsent. Like an insult that cannot be taken back. Now all I have to do is to wait. I'm assuming he's on the same number. Knowing Litze, he will be. Surely, he'll take me seriously now as I've done the very thing I said I'd never do. It's cold and dark now. I'm hungry, but I'm even more tired. I should be OK here, but I don't want to be in the dark. There are some blankets in the vehicle now. They should keep me warm, but they smell of the farm they came from.

It's been five years since I gave up smoking. When I say, 'gave up', I don't mean I was a smoker; I used cigarettes to calm my nerves. Lothar wouldn't have approved. He taught me how to calm myself, but I momentarily lost my way. Anyway, I don't like the taste of them, but occasionally, it's nice to try one. I could do with a cigarette now. Then I try to talk myself out of it and focus on my breath. I've tried dope, but again, that just makes me hungry and horny, which isn't such a bad thing. I think of driving off, but that's me being scared again.

I can't seem to sleep. My mind is racing and I probably don't feel like it now. Now I must wait. I've sent my message, and I want to get it over with. I'm assuming Litze hasn't moved far since I left. He is a man of routine. I'm assuming a lot of things. I would've heard something had he died, I'm sure of that. I believe he's alive. We both are alive so we can square this circle. He can't be dead. We will forever be connected. I hope he's alive so that I can finally move on. Litze is the most important piece in the jigsaw. Then I can finally look at it one last time and put it in its place.

I climb back into the truck and cover myself with the blankets, lying across the back seat. I'm drowned in tiredness. I'm too tired to care, too tired now to be scared. I must sleep. Even in this desolate place, I think I'm safe. This is Lothar's secret place, but you can never be 100 percent certain. I must trust now that everything will be OK in the morning if I'm lucky enough to greet it.

***

I don't feel that rested. My body feels stiff from sleeping in the cab. I look through the window and see the dawn emerge. I think I'm awake and check myself. I wipe away the condensation from the window and believe that it feels too real to be a dream. This place looks different in the day. It's altogether friendlier. I get out of the vehicle just to confirm to myself that I'm awake. The first thing I hear is the sound of birdsong. Better than any alarm clock in the world. And I see fields of green and gold side by side, going to the edge of nowhere and beyond. It's breath-taking in its simplicity. I needn't have worried. It feels safe here, and I understand why this is Litze's's secret place. Many people have secret places, whether they're real or virtual. We all need these havens. It's our chance to reconnect with ourselves and recalibrate.

I wonder how many times Lothar came here in the past and whether he still does now. It's hard to believe that he wouldn't, but it might be too painful for him. I look around for clues as to why this place might have meaning for my mentor, but there is nothing that is obvious here. But that's typical of his style.

The air feels good, and I inhale as if for the first time in my life. But I'm trying to remember the things that I was taught about focusing on my breathing and living in the moment. It's the thing we human beings do without thinking, without paying much attention to it. When I'm anxious, I sometimes forget to do the very thing that I need to calm myself down. We all do. I was just at this moment testing the fact that this wasn't a dream, and I was indeed alive. And it felt good. My stomach reminds me that I'm not asleep and talks to me in its rumbling dialect, complaining I've neglected it. I notice that there are some apple trees in the distance, which means at least breakfast and perhaps lunch are taken care of. I grab about a dozen apples, some from the tree itself and some from the ground, and stuff them in my various pockets, hoping that I won't need them, that I'll get other food later. I give them a quick wipe. The green and red fusion of colour makes them look appetising. They also taste and feel good as they crunch impressively in my mouth.

Lothar hasn't replied to my text, which doesn't unduly worry me. It may be for security reasons. Litze has many enemies, so he has to be careful. He could be dead, but I have this feeling that he isn't, and I can't explain why. I wonder how long I'll wait before I give up and continue on my own. I don't have many friends here. I don't have many friends anywhere. As for my family, well, that's another story. I decide that if I come out of this alive, I'll make more of an effort with others. I've been accused of being arrogant or aloof. But that's a self-defence mechanism. I can't engage with people; it's hard to when you don't trust easily. I look back at the way I treated some people, and I cringe. And the missed opportunities to say sorry. I hope that finally facing my mentor will be an important first step to my rehabilitation into becoming a half-decent human being.

THIRTEEN

IT'S EASY TO lose track of time here. I think it's about three in the afternoon. It's so peaceful here that I don't even feel the need to check my watch or my phone. It's like at last, I'm in alignment for the first time in ages. And it's made me realise that I haven't taken any opportunities to pause for breath. Something I need to do more often. Something that was drummed into me, but I neglected to listen. Maybe that's why my mentor chose this location: to make himself and me appreciate just 'being'. I wonder what he thinks when he stays here. The years of his past will be catching up with him, but I am grateful that even if he doesn't have many friends now (many of his contemporaries would be dead), he still finds some peace in this sanctuary.

I eventually look at my spare mobile and still no response. But my screen shows it's 3.10pm, so my guess is not far off. Litze didn't say how long I should wait for him if I needed his help. But maybe that was the point: he was trying to test my patience or even my faith. I wonder whether he'll still come, especially after the circumstances of our last meeting. But I cling on to the hope that despite all we've been through, it would take more than a bullet to destroy that invisible connection between us. I hope he'll forgive me and he's a man of his word. But I know I was a cheeky bitch, and I had a real nerve.

Even my injured shoulder seems better as I rotate it, trying to restore some feeling. I look skyward and am excited about doing something I haven't done since childhood: I want to climb an oak tree that has caught my attention. It's probably at least a thousand years old and, like many, is succumbing to the effects of climate change. The trunk is so huge; I estimate it would take a chain of at least twenty-five adults to circle it. The base splinters off into branches and sub-branches like a mind map. I could happily study the intricate patterns all day. There's something comforting about staring at this tree. It represents everything that is currently lacking in my life regarding safety and security.

I wonder how many people before me have climbed this tree. I envy its all-seeing, being, and patient quality as I negotiate the climb towards its summit. Though, I decide I won't go all the way. I can see enough where I am. The view is great as my eyes scan the vast expanse of land. The rows of green-golden fields bathed in the warm afternoon sun seem to go on forever. I can make out specks of farm buildings in the distance. Litze used to tell me when I got stuck on a problem that I should look at things in a different way, change perspective, or even walk away from it completely and come back to it. I guess climbing this tree is my way of looking at my situation from another perspective. I'm trying to work out how I got into this mess and what I could have done to prevent it, like a detached observer. It doesn't take much working out. It was greed that got in the way of my better judgement—that and this stupid desire to prove myself. I have more money than I know what to do with, but it made me think that somehow, I was invulnerable. That's the mistake that some of these rich pricks make, and unfortunately, I've become one of them. I admire the ones who have vast wealth but don't have the need to show off or prove anything. That's one of the ironies of my profession: I was sent to take out some of these scumbags, but at the same time, I've become the very thing I hate.

So why don't I just walk away? Because at the end of the day, I'm a killer, and for the most part, I've accepted my nature. But even I am coming to the realisation that something must change. The world always needs rat-catchers. There's a belief amongst some that our kind is necessary. It's just that those people don't want to know how we work. Pest control is shitty work, but there's no paradox here: you have to understand the pest to hunt it in the first place.

I can only work out so much on my own, and being here is doing me a lot of good. But Litze had this incredible mind. He could see all the angles and made you think things through, and was unusual in that regard. I know his mentorship benefited many under his care. And I liked the fact that he sought no recognition. He wanted to develop people for their own sake. It gave him great satisfaction to see others grow, even though his methods at times were questionable.

As I sit in the tree, I wonder how long I can remain here. Part of me wants to stay for longer, but I know that isn't realistic as I want to fix this thing I'm in. I decide that I'll give it one more day here, then I'll have to do the one thing that I'm having trouble with at this moment: trust my judgement. And that very thought scares the life out of me.

FOURTEEN

IF I DECIDE to leave before Lothar arrives, I'll use my bank card to get money and risk buying food. Blake, along with everything that I need, has gone up in flames in that SUV. I won't risk using agency cards as they would be traceable. And I have enough money of my own in untraceable, encrypted accounts. That's due to the genius of my old friend and hacker Donny Walsh.

I first set eyes on this six-foot-five man-mountain on a tube train in London. The Piccadilly line was busy that morning, and there was hardly room to breathe, let alone stand. I really should've waited until the next train, but I didn't want to be late for my appointment with a contact I was due to meet in Knightsbridge. I stood in front of sliding doors of the train, and Walsh was revealed right in front of me, staring with laser intensity through his light brown eyes. His hair was reddish brown, cut short at the back and sides, and the top resembled pineapple leaves. He was unshaven and had a long face, probably accentuated by his carrot-top hairstyle, with a square jaw. He looked like a mature student in his tightly fitting brown tweed jacket with tan leather elbow pads. His muscular thighs in spray-on blue jeans meant that I wanted to fuck him there and then.

The carriage looked more like a human sardine tin as the commuters contorted themselves to fit into the limited space. Walsh looked at me and sensed that I wanted to get into the train, so he reached out his hand and squeezed me in. This meant that there would be no such thing as personal space as people rubbed against each other in the hot and steamy confines of our metal container. I could think of much more pleasurable ways to get up close and personal but needs must. Since we were practically fondling each other, Walsh and I decided we might as well talk to each other. He didn't have to reach out his hand and pull me in, but there was something about him, and I believe he saw something in me: like there was a connection. Sometimes you can tell in an instant. It was like he was offering the hand of friendship, which was a compliment since he didn't have many friends to speak of.

Donny Walsh called me 'Becks' for short. He was the only one who did that. When we were on speaking terms, Donny told me that he had a way of making you disappear or creating new identities through technology. I didn't understand how he did it, and I think his ego prided itself on the fact that this stuff was all above me. But frankly, I didn't care. I had no intention of competing with his genius. Not that I or anyone ever could.

Walsh was probably the most diversely talented person I'd ever known. He had this ability to turn his hand to almost anything. I was astonished by his range of skills, from design to intricate drawings, various prototypes, engineering, making costumes, and his extensive research. He seemed to have intimate knowledge of most things. Many of his projects remained unfinished, as he got bored and moved on to the next thing. Donny always appeared to be working on something, but we never discussed his work. Partly because it would have been way over my head, and partly because I respected his privacy. Also, I didn't tell him about everything I did. He knew I was in the security profession, and if he wanted to find out, he easily could have. He liked to take things apart to see how they worked and had supreme confidence that he could put them back together. He was like a modern-day Michelangelo. We had many things in common; one of them was our inability to maintain relationships. Walsh was much more of a lone wolf than me. I admired the fact that he stubbornly refused to play the game. His deep cynicism about human beings made me look like Pollyanna. Another thing I liked about him was that he never once tried to hit on me. I thought that perhaps he was gay, but that was my ego's way of protecting myself from rejection. Donny was just a genuine guy who cared for me. So the fact that we too are not on speaking terms is even sadder. I've realised that this lone-wolf stuff isn't always what it's cracked up to be and accept that at times, even I need a helping hand and shouldn't be too proud to ask for help. I know that when I see Litze again, Walsh will be the key to whether I succeed. That's if he still wants to talk to me after what happened four years ago. I didn't shoot him, if that's what you're thinking. I did something that in his eyes was much worse.

FIFTEEN

I CONVINCED MYSELF that I acted out of love after it happened. You probably find it hard to believe that I'm capable of such an emotion after what you've heard. But it's true. If you see a friend spiralling out of control and you have the power to do something, what will you do? Walsh's snooping was getting out of hand. There's a saying that curiosity killed the cat. Well, I feared that Donny was beginning to run out of lives. His interests not only extended to engineering and design projects, but he was also hacking into US military databases. This was reckless stuff. Although Donny was careful to cover his tracks, I knew if he continued down this path, he would eventually be caught. And I could see what lay ahead: the men in the shadows would parcel him up and deliver him to the US according to their 'Do as I say but not as I do' extradition treaty with the UK, and he'd face up to sixty years in prison. But Walsh was either too stubborn or too arrogant to fully comprehend the consequences of his actions. And as close as I thought we were, he wouldn't listen to me. Walsh was becoming more distant, dismissive, and irresponsible, like he was asking to get caught.

I also told him that he would be lucky to get out alive after what he was up to. I warned him that not everybody believed in due process, and there were those who could make people like him disappear. But Walsh still wouldn't listen. His hubris made him think that he was invincible, and I was becoming more worried. My feelings surprised me because sometimes, I've been called cold. Looking back, I don't think that's true. It's just sometimes emotion isn't a luxury I can afford, though my mentor would probably disagree.

I knew Donny had elderly parents, but he didn't talk about them much, so I assumed he wasn't close to them for some reason. I also wasn't aware Walsh had any close friends apart from me to speak of. The fact that there was no close family or friendship group meant that I was running out of options. He was also drinking more and I suspect taking drugs. It wasn't to excess, but it was enough to cause concern. I also believe his loner status meant he had few points of reference to curb his behaviour. And I should know about that.

I tried to get through to him, as I didn't want to give up just yet, not until I was satisfied that I'd tried everything. But he accused me of nagging him, which seemed to make him more determined to continue. I'm a lousy friend normally, but I persisted in trying to get him to see sense. I even backed off for a while, but that didn't appear to work either.

We never had sex, and I don't know why. During our time together, we were single and mostly available. But looking back, I'm almost glad we didn't. It was an unspoken thing between us which knew that friendship was the purest form of relationship and that sex would cloud things. I didn't need to sleep with someone to love them. Nor did I need to prove my love for someone by sleeping with them. Something I learned the hard way.

Walsh was on his way back home to his flat in Camden Town from Covent Garden one winter's evening. He set off at about 7.30pm and the journey on foot would take approximately forty-five minutes, which he'd made countless times without any thought for his well-being. Not because London was safe, because it wasn't. Crime in the city had worsened over the years, but Walsh was determined not to give in to fear. Also, being a big guy, he walked confidently, trying not to project a victim posture. While that was no guarantee, studies say that a positive demeanour can significantly improve your chances of safety. He loved walking, though not because he could enjoy the fresh air. If he wanted clean air, he was better off moving out of the city. Donny preferred to be outside rather than being stuck on a tube train, which he only used for convenience. There was no need to use a car in London. He'd passed his test some years before, but he was a reluctant driver and only used it when he was travelling out of the capital. If he was going to go anywhere, he favoured the bus. At least he could see the landmarks he was travelling to rather than be stuck underground.

The snatch squad of three had been following Walsh for about ten minutes on foot, without being noticed. That was no achievement as they could easily blend in with the crowds at that time of the evening; the city was still teeming with people. Along with New York and many other cities around the world, London is yet another city that never sleeps. The team followed him to a newspaper vendor on the corner of Montague Street, adjacent to the British Museum, where he took his free copy of the *Evening Standard*. So far, the surveillance was going to plan. Walsh turned right into a small side road, then took a few more turns and eventually walked onto City Road, which carried traffic like a pulsating main artery carrying blood cells. To the left, Madame Tussauds was about fifteen minutes away, and to the right, this major road headed out towards Whitechapel to the east. Walsh would often take random walks when the mood took him, because although he'd lived there for many years, there were so many parts of the city he still didn't know and there was so much to explore. He also felt that

London was schizophrenic, as it had so many personalities that comprised different social and economic demographics, as well as a diverse society.

The snatch team was hoping that he was a creature of routine, as the success of their plan would depend on it. They pursued Walsh onto a minor road that led them onto Eversholt Street. This wasn't necessarily the quickest way to Walsh's home, but he liked to vary routes just to make the journey more enjoyable. Walsh turned around briefly. One of the team looked away, but not too suddenly, hoping he'd not been made. The team had earpiece communication and were careful not to put their hands up to their ears. Though they wouldn't have looked too unusual given that many people used Bluetooth accessories for their mobile phones, they didn't want to take chances. They hoped there were too many people around for Walsh to notice them. The team made a point of splitting up for that very reason. The target resumed his journey onward towards Eversholt Street, which would eventually change to Camden High Street. Walsh entered a Costa Coffee shop a few yards ahead and bought a hot chocolate. The team slowed their pace and held back. They knew Walsh was bright, and even though they'd covered their tracks, Walsh wasn't normal by most people's standards. He saw things that most didn't see, and they didn't want to give him any advantage.

Walsh left the café, deciding to drink and walk. This slowed his pace, which was good news for the surveillance team. He dumped his cup into a street litter bin and picked up his stride. It was much brisker this time, but nothing to arouse suspicion that he knew he'd been followed. The team thought there was no way that Walsh could distinguish them amongst the many that night. That would have been impressive, even for him. Walsh stopped to browse in the various shop fronts on the way. He wasn't a big shopper and anything that caught his eye he would mentally log for later. If he wanted to splash the cash, there were better parts of London where he could window-shop.

The team didn't sense anything unusual in that. Walsh was sticking to his normal routine. So far so good. His best chance of evasion was if he changed his routine significantly that evening, but he didn't. He would soon fall into their trap. But the team knew they would have to close in. What they had planned for him meant they could afford to. Walsh turned off onto another side road, not part of his usual pattern but nothing to worry about either.

Walsh walked past Camden tube and spotted a homeless person selling copies of the *Big Issue*. Walsh would regularly give money to the homeless through online charitable donations or, as in this case, on the street. The homeless person wasn't the usual guy. Nothing strange about that, though typically, the sellers had their preferred patches. Sometimes the *Big Issue* sellers worked in teams, which made sense, and they often shared their profits. The vendors had to adhere to a strict code of conduct, which included not fighting over other pitches.

That made it easy for the team, because this wasn't the usual guy. This wasn't a homeless person.

Walsh handed over his spare cash to the man. It was £5, twice the cover price of the magazine. The man shook Walsh's hand with both hands with what appeared to be extreme gratitude and some force. But the man just wanted to make sure.

Walsh felt a prickly sensation on his right palm. He probably thought it was grit on the vendor's hand. Nothing to initially arouse suspicion.

The target walked away. He made it about a few yards, then tiredness and nausea overcame him. Walsh tried to shake himself out of his stupor, but nothing he tried worked. Then he saw the nightlife of London slowly melt in front of him. He was willing his hands to hold on to the street railings, but they wouldn't obey, like there'd been a short circuit from his brain to his limbs. His legs finally buckled beneath him. The street seller stopped Walsh from hitting the ground. He was a big guy and in no fit state to prevent serious injury on the pavement. The vendor was joined by the other three team members, who ran to help. They bundled him into a blue van parked a few yards away. He was out cold. The combination of weight and gravity didn't make it easy for them to carry him. Also, the four-person squad had to do it without arousing attention. Not easy with a man of Walsh's size. I'd warned Walsh this would happen: the people in the shadows don't always believe in due process. They would take the law into their own hands. They would make him disappear. But the plan worked. They had counted on Walsh's sticking to his routine. His altruism was the thing that trapped him.

***

When he eventually woke up two hours later, Walsh found himself in a room with plain grey walls and no windows. Just a damp, mouldy smell, the kind you get in garages that haven't been used in years.

Knowing Walsh, his analytical mind would have been starting to put it all together. The *Big Issue* seller had drugged him with that handshake. The vendor was wearing a specially adapted ring, worn on the wedding finger of his right hand, with a powerful tranquillizer. The needle, housed in a micro-spring which was barely visible to the naked eye, was worn on the palm side of the hand and was only activated when the right pressure was applied, as in this case, with a handshake. The effect of the tranquillizer meant that he had a mild headache, and he felt hung-over.

He was blindfolded and tied to a chair. One of the assailants came closer and unbound his eyes. Walsh looked out and seemed nonthreatening. But that was the wrong assumption to make. Walsh was not just some geek they'd snatched off the street. He was a geek with attitude. Walsh lunged forward from his chair, head-butting the person who'd taken his blindfold off, breaking his nose, and sending him backwards into the table behind him. As the others pounced, Walsh got up and, in a slick hip movement, whipped the wooden chair against the left-hand wall, shattering it. If he was going to die, he wasn't going to go down without a fight.

Walsh was still unyielding, which surprised his kidnappers, as the tranquillizer should have slowed him down. It was as if he was trying to redeem himself for getting caught in the first place. But there was nothing Walsh could've done. These people were highly trained; the fact he had to be drugged for them to subdue him was of little consolation. The problem now was that Walsh's hands were still tied, but not his feet. That was an error by the hit team. The tranquillizer didn't subdue him. Fighting was in Walsh's nature. He'd been fighting something or someone all his life. Something we also had in common. The team leader fired a tranquillizer gun at Walsh's thigh, a stronger dosage this time, which felled him like a tree.

The kidnappers took no chances and secured Walsh properly this time. Despite the punching, kicking, and waterboarding, Walsh gave them nothing, apart from wisecrack remarks, which seemed to antagonise them even more. They continued for about two days without Walsh's sleeping. He was one of the toughest and bravest people I ever knew, but everybody has a weakness. They made it clear anybody he knew was fair game and threatened the people he cared about, leverage that normally works in these situations. Love can be found in the most remote corners of some of the coldest hearts. Everybody loves something or somebody. Walsh wondered whether he loved his parents. He used to say to me that he didn't like his parents, but he never elaborated as to why. I sensed that he didn't live up to their expectations. He had no contact with them. This situation would soon reveal whether he felt anything for them at all.

The intention wasn't to kill him, just to scare him, but they went one punch too far. Walsh stopped breathing. The hit team panicked and tried to revive him, but he lay there, his eyes closed, his skin ghostly pale, with lips turning blue. They slapped his face, but still no response. The team leader administered CPR in a frantic effort to reanimate him. They didn't want to go through the hassle of getting a cleaner or removing a body. They could do it easily enough, but it was more work than they wanted, and this wasn't the objective. Walsh's heart stopped for about two minutes, which seemed like ten to them. Eventually, after frantic efforts and nearly giving up, they managed to revive Walsh, but it was close. They finally dumped Walsh outside his Camden apartment block.

The abduction worked, as Walsh immediately stopped hacking military databases. He also destroyed all hard drives linking him to the various government websites he'd snooped on. The very thing I warned him about had happened. But at least Walsh wasn't playing with fire anymore. The people in the shadows don't play by the rules. Walsh realised he had had a close escape and his behaviour nearly cost him. But something about the kidnapping didn't feel right. Why didn't they just kill him and make him disappear or dump his body? Why didn't they fake his death? That would have been easy enough to do. That would have been simpler than just scaring him. Why did they keep him alive? Walsh saw the lengths they'd gone to just to keep him alive, even though they'd nearly killed him. There have been thousands of people who have disappeared around the world without a trace. He had been kept alive for a reason, but why? He did consider that the thugs wanted to blackmail him, which would have been the nightmare scenario. Many possibilities came to Walsh's mind over the following days. Eventually, the clues fell into place in his head. My warning him about the men in the shadows went off like alarm bells. An enemy would want you dead, but a friend or an interested party would want you alive. He didn't believe in coincidences. In Walsh's world, there were not many people to choose from. He had been kept alive by a concerned party. Also, when I saw him next, I couldn't look him in the eye, and that was my mistake.

SIXTEEN

IF WALSH DIDN'T listen to me much before, he didn't listen to me at all after he worked out that I'd set up the abduction to scare him. When I tried to call him many times, he hung up or the call was diverted to voicemail. Though we never had that conversation, I knew that he knew, and there would be no point in denying it. This may seem an extreme way of protecting a friend, but at least he's safe, even if it meant destroying our relationship. Part of me wishes I had seduced him after all. I really should have fucked his brains out. Given his intellect, that would've taken ages. I'm not saying that would have necessarily worked, but at least it would have been some distraction for him. I've used seduction many times for professional or personal gain, and if I don't mind saying so, I'm pretty good at it. Either that or men and women are easily swayed.

Sometimes I'd turn up in suspenders, stockings, and high heels, or just in my long coat, stark naked underneath. It's interesting to see the reaction of various men and women over time, and I learned plenty as my coat dropped to the floor, revealing my shamelessness. But Walsh wasn't like the others. He would have seen through it, or worse still, laughed at me. Maybe I underestimated my attraction to him. Or maybe the truth was, I couldn't face the rejection. Maybe I loved him too much. When you look back on any failed relationship, you realise that it was the things you didn't say that ultimately cost you. If I'm lucky enough to get the chance to speak to him, I'm determined that things will be different.

I knew about those in the shadows. I knew what they were capable of, as I was one of them. I didn't want them to kill him, just to scare him. I nearly lost him for good. In the end, I lost him anyway. Looking back, I probably should have trusted him to make the decision for himself. My inability to trust is an occupational hazard that Walsh had fallen victim to. I didn't trust him to make this decision, for better or for worse. He felt betrayed. They say it's easier to forgive an enemy. What I did in his eyes was worse than being betrayed. I'd killed his belief that in a hostile world, there should be at least one person you can rely on. I'm hoping that the passage of time means that he too has forgiven me. Not only was Walsh a world-class talent, but he was also world-class at bearing grudges, so I'm asking a lot.

I've used other people in the past with Walsh's expertise. Well, that's not, strictly speaking, true. There isn't anyone with his talent for what he does. I've used pale imitations. Bad photocopies. Poundshop versions of him. I'm sure there are those at least as good as or possibly better than him, but I'd have to get into a space rocket and travel further afield to find them. I need to know who set me up, as I feel like I'm working blind, fighting an enemy I can't see, smell, hear, taste, or touch. This is a real test of my patience, or lack thereof. It's just as well that I'm here in this place. It's so peaceful here. Like a work of a higher power. An energy field of love. It allows things to be, without judgement or expectation. My impatience is out of step in a place like this. In fact, it seems rude, so I stop complaining in my head and remind myself I should be grateful that I'm alive to complain about anything at all.

***

The evening draws in now, and I decide that this will be my last night here. I resist the temptation to text Lothar Litze again as I don't want to appear desperate. He's either not coming or, more likely, dead, but I refuse to believe it. I don't have a Plan B, but I can't afford to worry about that now as I return to my truck and finish my remaining apples. I'm tired now. I think it's the fresh air. It makes a nice change from some of the crap I've inhaled in some of the cities I've visited during my previous assignments. I'm not used to relaxing so much, but it's done me a world of good. I take one last look outside. I consider that whatever happens, I'm glad that I came here. If Lothar Litze is dead, then this is like he's trying to send me a message from the grave. When he first trained me, I found that I was a rather intense and restless soul with the weight of the world on my shoulders. In fact, I wanted to fight the world, only to learn the hard way that eventually the world always wins.

If he is dead, then the visit to this place is his last bequest to me. Telling me that I should take time out to be; that I shouldn't beat myself up so much and not to overthink things like I have an annoying habit of doing. I know I've come a long way from that time, but I know there is still much to do.

***

I check my phone; it's 3.30am. Earlier than I wanted to wake up, but I blame this on going to sleep too early and eating apples, which have settled on my stomach. And when this happens, I never normally get back to sleep, so I decide not to try. Especially when I look at the time. It's fatal for me when I want to return to sleep. It's like the secret is out and my mind can't erase it. My sleep pattern is all over the place, and I'm not an early riser. I'm shocked that I manage to get out of bed at all at times, as my body clock is set to get up at ten or eleven. Being a killer means that you can't have a restrictive routine. So I've learned to adapt and get up at hours that I'd rather not. And that makes me grumpy. I tell myself that this is not the best frame of mind in which to conduct an assignment. Litze taught me that I must remain impassive, calm, cold, detached. Even if it goes against my nature. I think he must have despaired at the times he had to mentor me. I'm enough to test anybody's patience.

I still haven't managed to sleep well. The light outside gives me clues that it's early as the shards of light from the sun greets me. I have a long day ahead, and I need all the energy I can muster. The first thing I want to do when I get out of here is to get some decent food. Then all my cognition will be restored, and I'll be able to piece together this mess. If I can at least get Walsh on my side that will be a great help. Just a couple of hours of uninterrupted sleep should do it. Then I'll be on my way.

I settle down, and I finally drift out of this world and into dreamland. I descend as if I'm walking down a spiral staircase, but the steps feel soft and featherlike. That's one of the great mysteries about sleep: some claim we leave our bodies and go to other worlds, or that we dream every night, or even that dreams are where we are at our most creative. I step deeper into the safety of my subconscious. Everything is slowing down to a nice calm. And I'm grateful for this respite, which is short-lived as a hard thump shatters me out of my unconsciousness. I reach for my Glock in a well-rehearsed move; like I'm on autopilot as the adrenaline surges through my body, reanimating it like the air in one of those party balloons with funny shapes, inflated at ultra-high speed, and dismisses any tiredness I may have had with utter contempt. I open the car door with the gun pointed. He's used to the sight of pointing a weapon at him. He looks at me, then the mobile message that I sent him. Then he looks at me again and laughs. It's more than a laugh. It's more like a roar. Lothar Litze does Schadenfreude really well.

SEVENTEEN

'WE MEET AGAIN', says Litze. His German accent is still quite strong, compared to mine. I've been away so long; my voice has picked up transatlantic inflexions. Partly due to my travels, and partly due to the influence of my fucking American father. 'Hello, Sam Becker, it's been a while. I saw your text message. You finally convinced me that you were serious. You used your middle names.'

Litze laughs again. He's enjoying this too much for my liking.

'It took a lot for you to do that. I know how much you hated them.'

He said hated. That's past tense. I still hate them. That's an understatement. Who in their right mind would call their children these names? One of many potential ways a parent can screw up a child is by the way they name them; that's if you believe in nominative determinism. If the names are terrible, like in my case, it's guaranteed to get you bullied if the other kids find out. It can change the way people perceive you. Luckily, I've managed to keep them a secret from most people. But why these names? It's as if my parents were trying to win a competition for how many syllables you can fit into middle names. And there's no way I'm going to reveal them to you here.

'You did say you'd have to be desperate to use those names again.

Things must be bad. Especially after the last time we saw each other, when you ran away. Not your finest hour, Becker! I've even kept that bulletproof vest as a souvenir.'

I want to speak, but the words don't want to come out of my mouth. I'm in shock. The great Lothar Litze showed up, and I feel like I'm fourteen again, like I've regressed back to my childhood. I swing between gratitude and awe. He still looks in good shape and the years have been kind to him. I don't know his age, and I've never asked him. Litze is probably about in his late fifties, pushing sixty. He has the same shock of short spiky hair, handsome features, and ridiculously blue eyes. He's wearing a brown suede jacket, open-necked shirt, and blue corduroy jeans, and what look like good-quality brown brogues.

'I see you've dyed your black hair, Sam, and you've changed the style. It's shorter and suits you.' A compliment from Litze is a rarity, unless, of course, I am still in my dream state. 'You can put the gun away now unless you do want to shoot me again. I'm not wearing a vest this time. But if you shoot me, at least it will be in my favourite place.'

I still can't speak. In fact, I don't know what to do. I'm not sure whether to hug him, shake his hand, cry, or scream. Uncertainty and confusion have gripped me. This is the man who made me the person I am today, and despite everything, he responded to my message. He said he would keep his word.

'Thought you might be hungry so I bought some breakfast.'

Litze pulls out a paper bag from his coat pocket and hands it to me. I finally put my gun on the seat beside me and take the package. They're freshly made—two cheese-and-tomato sandwiches. I only realise seconds after that I snatched them without saying thank you, but Litze doesn't take offence. He's used to my lack of social graces.

'Where did you get this?' asks Litze as he taps the door of the vehicle.

'It's a long story', I finally reply. I rehearsed a million times in my head the things I would say to him if we ever saw each other again. And this is all I can manage. Pathetic!

I devour the first sandwich quickly, not realising how hungry I've been. The second sandwich soon follows the first. I should eat more slowly, but my hunger consumes me.

'I think we should take my car. We can leave yours here', he says, walking away. I take a drink of water from the cab, and then I gather my things.

'Why here?' I ask him.

'Come, Sam, I'll show you', says Litze as he gestures me forward.

I close the vehicle door and follow him into the fields. The sun isn't quite out yet, but there's enough light. The dawn makes the surroundings feel sombre, beautiful, and at the same time serene. The birdsong is in full flow as Litze and I trudge through the fields, crunching the earth. I'm feeling more confused. What is he going to show me? There are no obvious clues here. We head in the direction of some more trees. An isolated clump in the distance. I don't know what kind. I estimate it will take about five more minutes to reach them at this pace. We make our human plough through the field, and Lothar doesn't look back at me once to check that I'm catching up.

All sorts of permutations race through my head. Maybe this is the place where he and his ex made love. It would be ideal here as there would be privacy. There's something very liberating about having sex outdoors. Or maybe he's buried something in the ground: Secrets of his past. His days in the service. Maybe some things that could bring down governments. Maybe it's documents to blackmail top officials with. Litze was a wily operative. Just when you thought that he was backed into a corner, he would always come up with something that covered his ass. That's probably why he survived for so long: he made himself useful—invaluable. He was probably worth more alive than dead. He knew way too much, but he had insurance. Litze was a master chess player. He was always two or three moves ahead.

We reach a cluster of trees. Then Litze slows his pace and finally stops. He looks back at me.

'You asked me why here, Sam?'

I nod to Litze.

He walks a few steps and then pauses in deep reflection.

'Look here', he says as he first points to the largest tree in the group. 'This tree is very significant.' I walk closer.

'Take a look at this', as Litze points to the ground. At first, I'm not sure what I'm supposed to be looking at. Then I see: There's a large branch on the ground. It's rotting. It looks like it's been snapped off. I stare back at him, confused, as if I'm somehow supposed to work out the meaning. During our training, Litze would often challenge me to think things through for myself. He was like that: always trying to test me, playing games. But this is too cryptic for me.

'This branch comes from the tree that I chose', says Litze.

'So you wanted to climb a tree? So what?' I say impatiently.

'Not exactly, Sam. This branch snapped from the weight of my body when I tried to hang myself.'

EIGHTEEN

I THINK HE said, 'hang myself', but I must have misheard him. Litze reads the puzzlement on my face.

'That's right, Becker. You heard it right the first time. I tried to kill myself here after Silke died. When you lose the one person you will take a bullet for, then you think: What's the point of living? I lost everything. Depression gripped me like a stranglehold. I think they call it the black dog? I couldn't snap out of it. I blamed myself for a long time for not protecting her. When she died, I thought I had nothing left to live for. You could say that I took the easy option.'

I listen, but I still can't take in that my mentor would try to kill himself. I think most people understand the journey of suicide but don't reach the destination. And I've had some bad times. Some close calls. Yeah, it's crossed my mind. But given my profession, I suppose you would think of suicide often. I know of people in my game who have killed themselves. Sometimes it's the individuals who are the least likely that do it. They call it smiling depression: people with a sunny disposition on the outside, but with a great inner turmoil inside. There's still a stigma to admitting to having mental health problems, like it's a weakness. But I didn't realise that things had gotten so bad that Litze had reached his last stop, his journey's end. Maybe that was my naivety: I didn't see beyond the surface. To me, he was a superman. He was like that to everyone. But we all have our fronts. And we never know what goes on in another's head when even they don't.

We still don't understand the intricacies of the human mind and how it works. We're ticking time bombs. Often, it's just a cry for help. But sometimes, the world is so fast—overloading us with information, noisy, dismissive, and uncaring—there's no time to be. You just want to switch life off like you would a television. I feared and idolised Litze at the same time. And part of me still does. That's the problem with putting people on a pedestal: the reality can never match the perfect image in your head.

'I decided I was going to do it, Sam. I'd thought of other methods, but for some reason, I chose to hang. And I wanted to be here. I love this place. So peaceful, isn't it?' he says as he looks around. 'It made sense for me to do it here. I hooked up the rope and brought a stool so I could kick it from under me. In my mind, I was going to die. This was somewhere secluded, so I wouldn't be found for days, maybe months. Some people commit suicide to try and grab attention in the hope someone will find them. But this was a serious attempt. I looked at different trees and even picked what I thought was the strongest one. I even kicked the trunk to test it. Crazy, no? The rope I bought was good quality, you won't be surprised to hear. I made sure that every detail was taken care of. I'd written my will and even left a note. I secured the rope to this branch', says Litze, pointing to the ground. 'I kicked away the stool, and I hung there for a few seconds. And to my shock, the branch snapped.'

'So what did you do then?' I ask softly.

'I laughed.'

'You laughed?'

'I laughed, and I cried', continues Litze. 'I thought to myself that I had failed at everything else. I couldn't even get this right. Anybody watching me with a rope around my head sitting on the floor laughing and crying like a madman would think I was crazy. They would probably be right. It must have been about ten minutes when I stopped laughing and my tears dried up. I looked at the branch on the floor; then this strange wave of relief came over me. I felt so peaceful at that moment. I took it as a sign that it wasn't meant to be: that even a wretch like me deserves another chance. I was ready to go, Becker, but something or someone else had other plans for me. I was trying to end my life instead of trying to find meaning or a reason to continue. So when I'm feeling depressed, I come back to this place to remind myself that I've been given a second chance. We all have opportunities every single day, and we don't grab them. You have been guilty of that as much as anyone.'

I look at the floor where the branch is, and I don't reply because I know he is right.

'I'm glad you contacted me. I knew you would eventually. Or at least I hoped. We're connected, you and me. I've always felt this. These things are rare. Our last time together proved that you weren't ready. You left the training too early. But I wasn't easy on you for a reason. I knew this would catch up with you. Like me, you've been given another chance. I'm glad you're still around to learn from your mistakes. I thought about you often during the years. I wondered whether you were dead or alive, whether you were happy; I even thought you'd got out of this life and disappeared. I sometimes believe that we've been talking to each other via our dreams. The fact that you contacted me is a good sign. It shows me finally that all I've taught you hasn't been lost. That maybe I've gotten through and at last, you're ready to watch and learn.'

It's Litze's long-winded way of telling me 'I told you so.' But for once I don't mind. I haven't seen this side of him before. I'm beginning to like him again.

'And one more thing', he continues. 'When you've rested and recovered fully, we're going to fight like in the old days. I've always maintained my practice like I said you should. I want to see how rusty you've become.' Litze smiles as he clenches his fists.

Only one word comes to my mind: Shit!

NINETEEN

THE DRIVE BACK to Litze's place takes about one and a half hours. We travel in the same battered old Fiat Punto he had back then. It would be quicker if it weren't for the stop at a petrol station along the way. I want some coffee just to keep me awake. I cut down to one sweetener, which is good for me as I have a sweet tooth. I wonder how Bad Kreuzberg has changed in the years I've been away. I used to like the fact that they'd resisted the temptation of Sunday openings. I believe a society needs to take a break. Advice which I ought to follow.

We arrive at Klosh Strasse 14, Litze's address. The same place he's lived for the last ten years. He switches on the light and curses when the landing bulb blows. He replaces it and resets the fuse box. Then he rants about how they don't make light bulbs to last like they did in the old days. He saw this documentary about Osram and other companies and their planned obsolescence policy, and he's not impressed. I'm used to hearing this from the old days, and I smile at the fact that he's still his old cantankerous self.

It's not his property. He rents, as many Germans do. I could afford to buy if I wanted, but I like the flexibility of renting under different pseudonyms, paying in cash mostly. I've stayed in a range of places, from hotels to bed and breakfasts to rented villas. I'm not ashamed to say that I'm not keen on slumming it. I like my comforts. I get paid well enough, so why shouldn't I? I believe that I need to be in the right frame of mind to do my job and don't subscribe to the view that luxury makes one sloppy. My sloppiness is down to complacency: something that my mentor has spotted a mile off and will soon expose.

I'm not looking forward to sparring with Litze again. I never beat him in our many bouts and I'm not convinced that this is going to change any time soon. He's over twice my age, but he seems to have far more time than me. As a highly skilled killer, you develop a repertoire of fighting styles. But I couldn't read him. Litze knew all my moves better than anyone. And that frustrated me. He would expose the fact that I'd been sloppy with my technique and I hadn't kept up with the basics. I hated basic training and could never understand why we did these drills. Then he would remind me that these were the fundamentals of life: if these weren't in place, then everything else would fail. Litze would be the first person to start training and the last person to leave. He trained like a demon, but I think he did this to occupy himself after the death of his wife. Litze had trained in many different martial arts and had no style loyalty. His main fight system was Shotokan, but his philosophy was 'Whateveryoucan'.

Unlike me, Litze isn't a person who is seduced by the trappings of materialism. When I enter his apartment, it's very much like when I last saw it. The furniture looks like it's from the fifties: He has a sturdy wooden table and chairs with matching cabinets and memories from his past inside. I notice pictures and ornaments, old-style china cups and saucers and crystal glasses, which look expensive and have probably been passed down to him from his family. They're to the left of me in the eating area. The living room is wood panelled and smells like it's been polished recently, which would be typical of

Litze's fastidious routine. There's a small coffee table without any traces of caffeine circles on the surface. There is a vintage radio with three knobs that's minimal in design on the sideboard to the right of the living room, and a small, old-style TV straight ahead, which I can tell has been overused due to the luminescent screen, which emits a ghostly residue. On the left of the television is a small bookshelf. I notice that there may be new additions, which I'm too tired to investigate now.

But the first thing I want to do is take a shower, as I smell, and eventually get a change of clothes. I go to the bathroom, strip, and throw myself gratefully under the warm water. The large waterproof dressing on my shoulder Litze gave me protects my wound. The steam quickly forms and rises like an apparition. The strong spray pummels my body, and I make sure that everything is washed away. Blood from my shoulder wound streams down me and eventually finds its way to the shower floor, swirling around my feet into the plug hole in the white enamel like an animated Rorschach ink test. I stay in here for what seems like an age. It's as if I want to wash the dirt not only from my skin but also from my soul. That would be a massive water bill in that case.

I dry myself and look in Litze's full-length mirror. I think I'm not in bad shape for my age. Apart from some scar tissue that I've collected along the way, like a suitcase that's collected stickers from its various travels—reminders of key events—my athletic frame has stood the test of time. But that fourth dimension will beat us all in the end. I look closer at the reflection, and the image that stares back at me is tired. I pull at my face. I don't have many wrinkles yet, but there's something different about my expression. I look haunted, and that's not attractive. I want to reclaim that joy I once had, but I'm struggling to find it now. It's the face of a woman who has lost her way, and I hope she can be found again.

I get dressed and return to the living room. Litze gestures me to the old, crumpled, brown settee on the right of his living room, then leaves for a while. He reappears and covers my shoulder wound with a fresh bandage. A graze, nothing more. I was very lucky. I had no right to make it out of there, as the sniper was excellent. Their professional pride must have left them irritated at not making it five out of five kills. Litze disappears into his small galley kitchen to make some coffee. While I wait, I look around and reacquaint myself with the surroundings to see if I notice any changes. It's been a while since I've been here, so it's hard to tell. I think there are some new pictures, and some of the furniture has been rearranged for freshness. But just like its inhabitant, this place feels like it's frozen in time and operates on its own terms. I can't remember whether Lothar has a spare bedroom, which means that I'm probably sitting on my bed for at least the next few days, as I don't expect Litze to give up his bed for me. The fact that he's agreed to help me is enough.

Litze returns carrying a wooden tray with two white, thin china cups and a coffee maker and places it on the table. He sits next to me and pours my cup, then his. He hands me my drink. Then he takes a small sip.

'OK, Sam, I want you to start from the beginning.'

I tell Litze about the botched mission in detail. I start with the target, Karl Yumeni, and how he's on the most-wanted lists. I tell him that the agency rushed this job and put this together in quick time because of the short window of opportunity. This isn't unusual; as a contractor you aren't always given much time to do jobs. They don't tell me who the client is, as it's on a 'need to know' basis. And as a team leader, they apparently didn't think I needed to know, which irks me. They say that I'm a mercenary and a well-paid one, and I have no right to complain. That's the downside of being a private military contractor, freelance assassin, or whatever name you call it. It's called deniable for a reason. Our kind is looked down on by some, but we perform a valuable service, filling in those ever-widening gaps created by the strain of terrorism. Outsourcing is inevitable and happening in nearly every industry. Why should we be any different?

He listens and nods attentively as I tell him of how I got the contract and the agency itself, which is a London outfit with pan-European affiliates. I tell him what little I know about the other team members, how they were wiped out and that I'm lucky to have gotten out alive, of my anger that my team has been killed and my regret that I couldn't save them. I'm confused, as I'm not sure whether my anger or feelings are due to survivor guilt or whether I'm just embarrassed because I failed so spectacularly. Also, I tell him about my regret at ever taking the job and that I probably took the assignment for the wrong reasons. I don't tell him about the little girl in the barn. He might think I was crazy to leave any witnesses, but that's a risk I'm prepared to take. I've crossed so many lines that they've become blurred, and I think it's a burden I prefer to keep to myself. Litze nods as I talk, without interrupting me, as if he's taking mental notes, committing the most significant bits to memory. The conversation lasts long enough to warrant a second pot of coffee as I deviate and tell him about other assignments. I guess I want to offload, but again, Litze just listens and nods quickly with the occasional 'yes' or 'OK'.

Litze puts the cup down on the tray, finally gets up from the couch, and walks over to the defunct fireplace opposite. He puts his elbow on the mantelpiece and stares out the window overlooking his medium-sized garden. He puts his hand over his mouth, suggesting he's in deep contemplation, trying to assimilate all the information. This lasts for around three minutes. I want to ask him a question, but I afford him the same courtesy as he did with me and wait. Then he turns and looks at me.

'This job had "setup" all over it. You should never have taken it', he says without a trace of anger. Litze seems detached, almost cold. My lack of response confirms to him that I'm in agreement.

'Why don't you walk away?' asks Litze. But this is a rhetorical question. He knows the answer.

He knows me.

'It's not my style, but you knew I would say something like that.' Litze smiles at my response.

'This would be the perfect opportunity to disappear. It's not like you knew your team that well', replies Litze, without a hint of callousness.

'But I led the team. I feel responsible.'

'For what, Sam? Is that just pride again, or is it that you're trying to prove yourself?' asks Litze. He was always good at asking the probing questions. He was like that before: he left no hiding place, which made some uncomfortable, but I found it refreshing. Now I'm having doubts. I don't know why. Maybe Litze is right: I could walk away and disappear. I have more than enough money. I have places I could run to and numerous false identities I could adopt. But this feels personal. I want to take the fight to them. That's my way; that's always been my way. I know one day it'll get me killed. I know I need to choose my fights carefully.

'I take someone trying to kill me very personally', I reply, trying to convince myself.

'If everyone in our profession thought like that, they'd never get anything done', replies Litze. 'Don't you see that for some people, killing isn't personal or even emotional? It's just business. Some see it as a sport. A job to be done. Taking the emotion out of it keeps some people alive', says Litze as he walks away from the mantelpiece towards me and resumes his seat on the settee.

'I know this, but something about this job tells me there's more to this. Call it intuition', I say.

'I'm glad you didn't say "woman's intuition"; I hate it when females think they have exclusive rights on feelings', Litze replies as he empties the last drop of coffee from the pot.

'Point taken', I say.

'But, Sam, I agree with you. Something smells off. I don't know why either but looking at it objectively, you shouldn't have made it out of there.'

'Meaning?'

'I mean the shooter. Four from five isn't bad. It doesn't feel like it was from a ridiculous range.'

'Or you could accept the fact that you trained me well', I say to Litze, trying to avoid smugness.

'But you would've been even better if you'd completed the training. You may even have avoided this mess in the first place', replies Litze. I guess I deserve that. 'Anyway, you seem determined to go after whosoever betrayed you, so you'll need to recover properly.'

'But—'

'No buts, Sam', interjects Litze. 'This is what we're going to do. You're going to rest. You will need it, believe me. After that, we will resume training, starting with close-quarters combat and then weapons. Are you sure you want to go after him?'

'Yes', I say.

'Then we'll need some help taking this Yumeni down, hard. Because if you do, we do this right. Remember my saying in German?'

'You mean "Mach's gut"?'

'Perfect. Make it good. Although that's the literal meaning, these days, the Germans say it to mean "Take Care". But first, a toast', says Litze. He walks over to the glass cabinet, takes out a special edition of fifteen-year-old Asbach brandy and a couple of small glasses. He sits down and pours one at a time. He hands me mine and takes his in his right hand.

'Prost', says Litze as we clink our glasses. Litze downs his drink in one go. I don't.

'This stuff is good, no?' he says, and has another. 'This will put hairs on those false chests of yours.'

'Litze?' I say, cupping my breasts with my left forearm. 'These are not false. These are real. I'm wearing a sports bra', I snap. Fucking dinosaur!

TWENTY

LITZE ALMOST SPITS out brandy when I mention the agency I work for. It wasn't a conscious decision to omit it in my conversation. But his reaction makes me wish I'd lied. Litze laughs, then looks skyward and curses in German.

'Jesus, Becker, everyone, apart from you it seems, knows that Coba is one of the worst security agencies out there. What on earth were you thinking? What sandpit did you have your head buried in? Coba Security are the scum of the earth. That's the thing with bad news: it's like a virus and can spread with not much help. These are bad, bad people, Sam. This life is hard enough as it is without working for the likes of them.'

'The contract was lucrative', I say, but that won't wash with Litze.

'And your point is? Yes, Becker, it's lucrative for a reason: it's because it's so high risk, nobody will touch it. A long line of people probably turned it down before you came along. When you accepted, they thought their Christmases had come all at once. It's danger money that you weren't meant to spend. This has "shit" written all over it. If the money is great, it's usually because it's a one-way ticket. That agency doesn't value human life.'

'They seemed OK to me', I say, trying tamely to defend myself.

'"OK" is never good enough in this business. And you flatter them with an "OK". They are far from OK!'

'OK, so I fucked up big time it would seem, but it was my choice.'

'Yeah, and look where your decision making has gotten you', he says, staring through me. 'Not only are they a truly lousy agency, but they also can't spell.'

'What's spelling got to do with anything?' I say.

'They left out the *r*. They should be called "Cobra" because they're snakes. You get into bed with snakes, don't be surprised when you get bitten.'

'I'm sorry you feel that way', I say. Litze can reduce my chronological age in a heartbeat. It brings back uncomfortable memories of childhood and the brutal training sessions where I'd always try to prove myself to him, and often try too hard. It seemed that I could never get anything right then. And nothing appears to have changed.

Litze continues. 'Coba has one of the worst safety records of any security agency. These lowlifes take contracts without thought and promise the client the earth. The problem is that they cut corners: on intel, on equipment, on anything they can. You're just a number to them. Security agencies have a bad enough time without these scumbags being in the market. We have a limited life span in this business. When I was still in the game, I played the odds in my favour. Which meant that I made my luck. I do my due diligence for one reason: so I can see the sun come up once more. There are times when I don't want to see the sun at all, but I'm grateful for the times that I do. It seems that you've forgotten to use the very thing that will save you, which is your intuition. When we were training before, we used to talk about that, remember?'

'I suppose, but it was a long time ago.'

'And whose fault is that?'

I say nothing.

'What happened to you, Becker?' Litze says, glaring at me. 'I know what happened. Someone once said: "When you think you're tops, you don't do much climbing." You stopped climbing all those years ago, and your ego got in the way. You forgot to be still and listen to the voices in your head. But worse, you thought you were ready before you were.'

'Thanks for the vote of confidence', I say curtly.

Litze turns to look at me. 'Remember what I said to you all those years ago: if it's too good to be true, it usually is.'

'Is this lecture over?' I say.

'For now, Sam, for now. But remember: when you can't tell the difference between the client and the target, it's time to reconsider your choices.'

TWENTY-ONE

AFTER BEING WELL and truly put in my place, I decide to rest. My shoulder is still sore, but my pride hurts the most. Money blinded me so much that I've become reckless.

Litze's modest living room is luxurious compared to sleeping in the vehicle, as I can stretch out my stiff back. Our talk means I won't be contacting Coba. If they're as bad as Litze says, then I'm in a whole world of shit that my greed stopped me from smelling. And in the unlikely event that Coba is innocent, then they're compromised. Either way, I can't risk it. Not until I get to the bottom of this. It feels like I've been handed a large box of tangled wiring to unravel, with all the leads being the same colour, and I don't know where to begin. But something that Litze said makes me think about the ambush and the fact that I'm the only survivor. Was I lucky, or was it down to my survival instincts? Or was it something else? The shooter seemed pretty determined to me, so I dismiss any other ideas I have. My mind is too fried to dwell on it now.

I've been trying to meditate for some time but without much success. And that's part of my problem: trying. I've learned from various people that you can't stop yourself from thinking. That's impossible. The trick is to not engage your thoughts. A bit like looking at road traffic or clouds in the sky and just watching. My problem sometimes is that I want to run into the middle of the carriageway and cause a pileup. Only the inhuman or delusional think that being an assassin for a living doesn't affect you in some way. Our trick is to justify the unjustifiable. But some are better at squaring the circle than others. I guess you call that kidding yourself—the land of the lost souls. I've taken so many lives that I don't remember the value of it. And even I'm not deluded enough not to know that's a scary place to be.

Litze doesn't seem the same as he was all those years ago. He appears calmer and at peace with himself, but he's still a mystery. There are questions that I would ask him now that I wouldn't have dreamed of asking eight years ago. Maybe that's a sign of my maturity or my confidence. This evening, we're having a fish curry, one of his specialities, he tells me, comprising salmon, cod, and hake pieces he bought from the local fish market. Litze has cut down on his meat intake over the last years, which is good as I don't eat much meat these days.

I look around the living room and check out his rather modest bookshelf. I know he's read more than what's on display and figure that he's given much away. There's an array of art books, and World War I and II books, and I notice he has *The Art of War* on the top shelf. Then I look to the left and see books by Friedrich Nietzsche, Rumi, Socrates, and a few from Paulo Coelho. He has a small thriller section; there's *The Day of the Jackal* and a few Alistair MacLeans, as well as John le Carrés. Then I see something that makes me re-evaluate my belief that he's such a dinosaur. There's a brown leather case on the side of the TV table that looks approximately A5 size. The cover encases something black, and opening it confirms my suspicions. Litze has succumbed to the lure of the Kindle. That explains why his bookshelf is so bare. I open it and press the side button, and it slowly loads up. I scroll to the library icon, and there are hundreds of titles on the device, possibly more. As I brush my right middle finger across the touch screen, I see he has a very naughty side too, with erotic literature. He must have hundreds of titles on this device. I notice he also has a disc on the shelf labelled 'e-books', which contains enough books to fill his living room twice over.

***

The smell of curry from the kitchen fills the flat as Litze shouts instructions from the kitchen to lay the table and tells me where everything is kept. Then he carries in a large Pyrex dish, bubbling and crackling with its contents, with his oven-gloved hands and places it on the table. I'm already seated, and I start to get up to help, but he puts his hand out to stop me like a traffic cop as he returns with the steamed rice. Litze tells me that it makes a change for him to cook for someone, and that although he likes his own company, it's nice to cook for more than one. He feels you put more effort in when you think of others. I know how he feels. When I can't be bothered to cook for myself, it's guilty takeaways or odd stares from people when I turn up alone in restaurants and cafés.

My stomach has fallen in love, as the curry is delicious. Litze is a far better chef than me. As my mentor, he's better at everything than me. He pours us some Pinot Grigio and we toast. We eat and talk about our respective lives since our last meeting. Not much has changed for him, and the training has tailed off. He does private work as a German language teacher, which he thoroughly enjoys because it means interacting with students from different backgrounds. I tell him about the near misses I've had and show him the scars that I'm able to as if they're trophies, which he isn't impressed about, and he scowls at me. Litze asks me about my love life and whether I'm single. I remind him that I've always considered myself single but neglect to tell the people I'm seeing. He laughs, saying that cardiac hospitals across the globe must be full of my victims.

Litze doesn't talk much about the Facility, and I wonder why. I suspect much has changed and since it's a sore subject, I don't ask. Over the coming days, we often sit in his garden, which he's paying more attention to lately. I sense that Litze gets great pleasure from gardening, like it's a form of meditation. He effortlessly reels off the Latin terms for various plants. I can appreciate why he loves to garden. It's a good analogy for life: you can't force things against their nature, and patience is the key. The fact my mind even entertains an idea of being calm shocks me into the realisation that at least some of Litze's teachings have rubbed off on me.

I study my mentor for a long time, and it dawns on me how much I've missed him over the years. I'm not sure he feels the same way about me, but his actions speak louder than words and he came to my aid, despite everything, which tells me a lot. I realise that should I get out of this one alive, things will have to change. I must remind myself that I deserve a life and that it's up to me to find the good in everything.

There's one thing I need to do, something I've been putting off for a long time, and that's contacting Donny Walsh, something I'm not relishing the idea of at all. But it will have to be done, even if it's just another way to cross someone off my list. Spending time here has made me realise that I made a massive mistake, and my challenge now is to prove to Walsh that I'm sorry. That will take some doing. If it were the other way around, I wouldn't give me the time of day.

TWENTY-TWO

I EXPLAIN TO Litze about my friendship with Donny Walsh and how I tried to save him by arranging a botched abduction, but instead, I ended up nearly getting him killed and lost him anyway. Litze doesn't react one way or the other. And why would he? After all, I took a shot at him eight years ago, so this would hardly surprise him. I tell Litze that Walsh would be useful if we want to track down Karl Yumeni. Litze tells me to move on. But the only way I can is to confront Walsh, even though I have no right to. As much as I've tried, I can't shake this desire to see him. He's one of the few men I've genuinely cared for. And the passage of time has heightened these feelings. I miss our friendship, even though I destroyed it. I've gone through my life with a wrecking ball, wreaking havoc on anything good that came into it. I don't know how to sustain a healthy relationship with anyone. Maybe it's because deep down, I don't believe I deserve one.

'What should I do?'

'Why ask me?' Litze shrugs. 'I can only help you with one mess at a time', he says. I'm already regretting asking Litze for help. 'You know that saying "Let sleeping dogs lie"?' he asks.

'Yes.'

'Well perhaps you should take the dog into the yard and shoot it in the head.'

'I'm not ready to do that', I say.

'Sounds like he matters to you.'

'He does.'

'Then do what you must', says Litze. 'But you should rest now', he continues. 'You'll need it. Change of clothes for you would be a good idea. We can get some in the town tomorrow. Also, I have some contacts we should visit from the old days. Many people are interested in Karl Yumeni. I want to find out more. If you're going after him, you should be prepared. Tomorrow, we'll go to the gymnasium. I will hire out one of the studios, and we'll train there. They have punching bags, but I want to see if you've remembered anything I taught you all those years ago. You have been practising, haven't you?'

'When I can', I say without any real conviction.

Litze shakes his head and curses to himself in German. He is one of the few men who can still make me feel like that little girl he met all those years ago. He needn't have asked that question, as he already knew the answer. Litze is one of the most perceptive individuals I've ever met. That's why he is such an excellent coach and fighter. He could tell within a few seconds whether you were going to win a fight by analysing your body posture. Litze was also very into biomechanics and how you could perform more efficiently in combat. He could improve your technique and skill just by altering one thing that made a big difference in your technique and was dismayed at the way some instructors taught fighting without any regard to well-being.

I tighten up at the thought of fighting Litze tomorrow. I've fought and defeated opponents younger and half my mentor's age, but it's different with him. It seems that he has the Indian sign over me. I'm younger than him and should be fitter than him, or even faster, but I'm not. Litze seems to defy all-natural law. During our time together, I've watched him practice his Tai Chi drills in the garden or sometimes the living room, drawing invisible shapes with his feet and hands. He does it with such grace, which would test most people's patience. Although its health benefits are well documented, Tai Chi is supposed to be the most dangerous form of martial art because of how it works on developing external and internal power, helping to harness 'chi', or life force. These moves are practised slowly, but the techniques delivered at speed can kill an opponent with one blow.

It dawns on me why Litze practises so much. It helps him develop awareness in all situations. Whether that be in a fight, or to improve his decision making. I'm the sum of the decisions that I've made. We all are, it's just that some of us don't get that. We somehow think that it's out of our control. And maybe much of it is. But our decisions can alter our destiny. I've opened a succession of doors and taken numerous wrong turns that have brought me to this place in my life. I feel tangled up in fear and indecision. But this situation has forced me to admit defeat. And I often wonder why when I've been offered help, I've refused sometimes. I think I know why: I've mistakenly thought that somehow accepting help or admitting fallibility is a sign of weakness. I know where that comes from: my father. I spent the best part of my childhood defying him after I finally gave up on trying to please him. I accept now that I can't keep going on about the past. He was a bastard, but I have a choice to make: people are only as powerful as you allow them to be and the thought that I, even now, still hand him that power would give my father immeasurable pleasure.

And it's a feeling that makes my stomach turn.

TWENTY-THREE

AS I LIE on my back, Litze stands over me and extends his hand to pick me up from the floor. This is a regular occurrence during our training session. My timing is off, and my energy is low. I'm not going to use my injury as an excuse. Litze could beat me with both hands behind his back with a paper bag over his head, standing on one leg. This is embarrassing and humbling at the same time, and what I feared. I just want to go back to sleep.

'Just as I thought, Becker. You move like an elephant on ice skates. You should be much better than this if you've kept up the training.'

I listen to him because I know he's right. I don't know what's worse: Litze giving me a kicking or the words. Either way, I have no answers. I've never had problems with most I've fought, but Litze is on another level altogether.

'There's another reason why you're not on top of your game. It's usually to do with something you haven't dealt with', says Litze as he takes off his boxing mitts and points to his head.

We're both in tracksuits. He looks like he's barely broken a sweat, whereas the perspiration falls off me and soaks my clothes. This doesn't seem like the natural order of things given our respective ages.

'Now you're back, there are things that you should resolve. That may help you move on', he says.

'Like what?' I say.

'You know what', he says.

'I don't feel ready.'

'You always say that, Becker, but that's just another excuse. Sometimes you just have to do it.'

'Some worms are better left in the can', I say, but Litze is having none of it.

'It's funny. People like us find it easier to take a life than to face up to our own. A good friend of mine once said that it's the conflict within ourselves that is the hardest. Even Superman can't outrun himself. If you don't deal with it, this will hold you back.'

I know Litze is right. Maybe he's talking from experience. He's seen many things in his life. He's lost someone he loved and good colleagues. That takes its toll. There was a time that I used to like my mind. But that was a very long time ago.

'OK. When should we do this?'

'There's no time like the present, Becker.'

I was afraid he would say that.

TWENTY-FOUR

IT WAS LITZE'S idea that I should visit my family. So now I'm here. And there's nothing to say as we stand together on a cold April day. It looks like it will rain soon as the clouds darken over me in an empty sky.

It's the afternoon, and I look at the six grey tombstones of my family. I didn't tell you before, but they all died fifteen years ago. I don't talk about it much, and this is the first time that I've come back to the Bad Kreuzberg cemetery. Now I'm here, I don't know what to say or feel. As you know, I didn't have the best relationship with my parents, especially my father. But as for my brothers, it seems like a blur. Hazy recollections that look like someone has used an eraser on an imperfect picture and left faint imprints. Even though I was in a family, I never really felt part of it. I always felt like the outsider. Like an unwelcome guest or an inconvenience. So I don't quite know what the hell I'm doing here.

My mentor thought it would help for me to get some closure. That word. It sounds like American psychobabble that you read from a self-help book or hear on one of those TV shows. But what do I need to close? Can you close something that was barely open? Let's not kid ourselves. We didn't do the happy family stuff. That wasn't our style. I felt like I was just trying to survive, competing for attention and eventually giving up. There are few family photos of us smiling. Well actually, that's not true, strictly speaking. If you see any pictures of us, it's me who isn't smiling. You can tell that I wanted to be anywhere but there. You can tell a lot in a picture. A photo can tell many things, but mainly it captures an essence, a moment in time.

I shut down emotionally just to survive. I don't want to go into it, but it was my way of dealing with things. I do remember I used to draw a lot, and I got into trouble for it. I had books full of doodles, sketches, and cartoons. That was my way of escaping. I could enter my virtual world. I was a recluse before I knew the meaning of the word. And would I have turned out to be any different had I been in a different family? It's hard to say, but I don't believe so. I think that I would have turned out like this regardless. Maybe not quite like this, but close enough. Like a parallel-universe version of me. I've always had a strong sense of myself and who I'd become from a very early age. Like I'd been here before. A very long time ago. Sometimes I feel echoes from the past that drive me, influencing me like an invisible puppeteer. I look at the gravestones again and study them. My mother and father are buried next to each other at the head of a lengthways rectangular plot. Together? That's a joke for a start.

Below are my brothers, all together: two by two. I'm supposed to feel something, aren't I? I wait for any emotion to resurface, but nothing. Like a tumbleweed moment. This seems to confirm others' opinion that I am a cold-hearted bitch. But to be honest, I don't feel guilty.

I didn't bring any flowers, just buried memories that one day will choose to resurface when I least expect them to. But for the time being, they have been quarantined. I hope I don't embarrass myself when that happens. The thought of losing control terrifies me. I can feel Litze on my left as he says nothing. Like he knows what I am thinking or even feeling. I don't know whether he was hoping that I'd break down in a crumpled heap. Maybe he feels that this is what's holding me back: repressed emotion. Maybe he cares about me but doesn't always show it. And maybe that's the point: he understands what it's like to keep things locked up and the cost of doing that, and he wants to, in his way, help me. But that time when I must face my feelings will surely come, and that will be of my choosing. I haven't told you their names for a reason, I realise. It's because they're not important to me. You already know I have a thing about names. Like I've blanked them out. Of course, I haven't erased them. That would be impossible. It's just my way of remembering them or not.

I turn my attention to my father's grave and my mood changes. And not for the better. It matches the clouds above me. Even though he's dead, the bastard is still with me like a poltergeist. He's my constant inner critic that I've spent my life trying to keep under control.

Litze can feel my shift of energy as we stand here. He can sense my agitation. He always has. Litze has always been empathetic like that, and he can tell what I'd like to do right now. And you'd probably think I was disgusting, but I don't care. But it's too open here, and it's too public. I guess I could come back at night, but to be honest, I don't want to come back at all. I thought that maybe I would like to smash his gravestone to pieces with a hammer. But that would be too much effort, and he's not worth that. Instead, I would like to piss on my father's grave. Right now. Empty every drop of urine into the soil where he's buried in the hope that it seeps deep down through the coffin and into his rotting corpse. I would. It takes all my strength now to stop me from doing it. You're probably thinking, what kind of daughter would want to do that to her father's grave? But you don't know the half of it. You don't. And maybe you never will. I haven't decided yet. Forgiveness is for the enlightened, and I'm not ready to be enlightened. But I know what Lothar Litze would say: that even he would not be worth losing my dignity for.

Pissing on his grave would be undignified but satisfying at the same time.

TWENTY-FIVE

LITZE HASN'T EASED up on the training. I've lost track of time, but it has been many days since we resumed. It's relentless as usual, just like the old days. I'm doing fitness drills, circuits, and punch bag work, plus stretching and Pilates in the gym to improve my core strength. I, at last, dare to look at my stomach as my six-pack starts to take shape. I don't understand where Litze gets his energy, but at least my shoulder is healing well. I was very lucky. It could have been a lot worse. I don't even want to think about how close I was to dying.

I'm enjoying spending time with my old mentor. He seems less distant and more personable than before. That might be because he's not at the Facility. I also notice that Litze still doesn't speak much about the organisation. My natural curiosity makes me want to ask questions, but I sense something. Like it's a sensitive subject now. So I trust my gut and resist the temptation to ask.

I wonder about the people I used to train with and what they're up to. It's only come into my mind now I'm back in Germany. It's not like we were close or formed strong attachments. After all, we were competing for most of the time. The probability is that some of them won't still be alive. That's a given. The dropout rate was high. And anyway, I never really understood the ethos of the Facility. Or more to the point, I wasn't open to understanding. The organisation was set up to help people. It was neutral. But my behaviour eight years ago went against all that. Given their code of secrecy, I'm surprised that I'm still alive and that I could get back into Germany. I often wondered about the agents I've killed in the past and whether they were Facility operatives but thought that if they were, they would have been much harder to kill. Litze warned me about my arrogance and said that I should show just enough respect, but not too much. My problem was that fighting came easily to me. It was as natural as breathing, but I think I took that skill for granted. Litze knew it. So did many of my trainers. But I'm someone who can't be told, and I have to learn the hard way.

Certain behaviours lead you down a path, and my big head has gotten me to this dead end. And I wonder how Litze was so sure that I'd return to seek his help. I think he realised soon enough that I'd run into trouble. I guess there was a certain inevitability about me. Some would say I was predictable. An accident waiting to happen. My reckless behaviour would guarantee it. I would test most people's faith, as often many would give up on me. I also think that I chose people or situations that would confirm to me that no one could be trusted. It was my way of needing to be right. Like a self-fulfilling prophesy. But I realise that's a cowardly way to live. It was my way of staying in my comfort zone. So much for my thinking that I'm some sort of risk taker.

Litze had a good handle on human behaviour most of the time. And I think he understood me, which is why he wanted to help. He also knew that the best life lessons are learned through making your mistakes. Litze would say to me that a man who never made a mistake never made anything. He also said that a mistake is only a mistake if you've done it twice. That's one mistake that I haven't yet managed to correct.

TWENTY-SIX

LITZE LOOKS SAD now as he rests on the settee, scrolling through the contacts on his mobile phone. He switches his gaze ahead and stares into space, contemplating his next move.

'I know a man that can help us', he says, turning to me.

'Who?'

'Udo Fleischmann', says Litze. 'A former colleague from the Facility. We were a great team, and we saved each other's asses many times. He's the best agent I ever worked with. We were brothers in arms. Fleischmann was well respected and what he doesn't know isn't worth knowing. If anybody can help with this mess, it's him.'

'I sense there's a "but"', I say. My mentor doesn't seem enthusiastic about contacting Fleischmann.

'You're perceptive, Becker. Asking for anything might be a step too far after the last time'.

'The last time?' I ask.

'Yes'.

'Did you lose touch?'

'Years ago.'

'What happened?'

'It's complicated, Becker.'

'Then uncomplicate it'.

'I'd rather not go into it.'

I decide to back off. But it sounds personal.

'You know how hard it was for you to ask me for help after all these years?' continues Litze.

'Yes.'

'Well, I have a similar feeling. That's how hard it's going to be for me to face Fleischmann.'

'Do you think he will help you now?'

'I honestly don't know, but I will give him a peace offering. We used to do this as a joke when we fell out, which wasn't often. Not sure this will work now, but it's worth trying.'

***

The drive to Idar-Oberstein takes only forty minutes from the safe house on the autobahn travelling south-west through Germany. It would have been easier and faster to get a train, but Litze's Fiat is the best option. I forgot how good my homeland looks in April, despite the descending gloom. We don't speak much in the car, and I decide against putting on the radio. Litze doesn't usually listen to music while driving, and I also feel he doesn't want any distractions. He probably wants to rehearse what to say to Fleischmann. Much like I did before I contacted my mentor.

We turn off the autobahn and then join a minor road that seems to circle back on itself. The mid-afternoon traffic is surprisingly light, which suggests we've just beaten the rush hour, or we've avoided heavy traffic earlier. Then we pass through a set of small villages. I count about three in total. These places are sparsely inhabited. My nose has been re-educated as I can smell the country air. It's a reminder that I've spent too much time in the city of London. Then we hit a great expanse of land, which looks private. Rows of golden wheat fields as far as the eye can see, with a sprinkling of outbuildings.

Litze then takes a left turn up what looks like a dirt track to some more private land. The Fiat isn't built for these kinds of roads, but Litze is determined to continue.

In the distance, there's a medium-sized cottage. The image of the building sharpens as the car eats up the driveway. I see six windows. Four across the top, two either side of the large wooden door, which looks like it's been made with vertical beams. The Fiat grinds to a stop on the gravel path and we get out. Litze goes to the door first. He knocks, gently at first. Waits. Then he knocks again, more forcefully this time.

Still no answer.

Litze is about to try for a third time when his knuckles hit air as the door finally opens, and a burly man appears from behind it. He seems about six foot four. He has short brown hair and is wearing a thick denim shirt, which is open at the neck and reveals traces of his brown chest hair; brown corduroy trousers; and boots to match. I assume it's Fleischmann, although Litze did not describe him to me. He's not looking pleased to see him.

'Hello, old friend, I've bought you your favourite brandy as a peace offering. I was wondering if we could—' And before Litze can finish his sentence, Fleischmann slams the door in his face.

Litze looks back at me, slightly embarrassed. Then he knocks again.

'Udo. Don't be like this. Come on, let us in.'

The door opens. 'What did you expect, Litze? You shouldn't have come here. That bottle of Asbach brandy may have worked before, but that was then, even though it's a very expensive special edition.'

Then he looks at me. It's more than a look. It's like a serious examination. His eyes squint in an unfriendly manner. He seems confused at first, then his face breaks into recognition. His expression tells me that I'm not welcome here either.

'And I can't believe that you brought the girl here. Still crazy as ever, Litze? Still living on the edge? Trying to live in the past? Why did you bring her here? Of all people. You obviously like to do things the hard way.'

'But—'

'No buts, Lothar. I told you that last time. We're done! Now get off my land before I shoot you and that death trap you brought with you.'

'Five minutes, Udo. Just five minutes', pleads Litze.

'It's never five minutes. I hope you have a watch, Lothar, because I don't want to give you the time of day. I should have listened to the others.'

'Just five minutes', pleads Litze again.

Fleischmann pauses for a long time. He looks at Litze; then he looks at me. The stare of disdain from his eyes burns into me like a laser. He holds the door, but I sense he's torn.

He looks at Litze and finally says, 'OK, but the girl stays outside.'

My feeling was correct: he hates me. But for once, I don't know the reason why.

TWENTY-SEVEN

I WAIT IN the car. It should only take five minutes if Litze is true to his word. Now it comes back to me: I remember Fleischmann, and I'm surprised at the animosity he has towards me. I didn't have many dealings with him in my time at the Facility, but I knew he was important and worked closely with my mentor. That's all I know. Whatever happened with them was serious. But he's angry with the both of us. Especially with me. I'm someone who can evoke those feelings even amongst the most patient of souls. I'm no diplomat. Instead, I revert to type and like to put gasoline on fires. I stare blankly through the windscreen and meditate to help me relax. I can hear the faints sounds of country life, but nothing from Fleischmann's farmhouse. I can see a small outbuilding in the distance and focus on that. When I meditate properly, I'm not even aware of my surroundings, and it's a great feeling. It's like an out-of-body experience. My problem is that I don't do this enough.

My trance state is interrupted by a knock on the passenger-side window. It's Litze. He waves me in with his right hand. Whatever my mentor said seems to have worked, as somehow, he got more than five minutes. Litze closes the door behind him and points to a chair opposite where Fleischmann is sitting. The inside has pine ceilings, stone walls, and mostly wooden decor with matching tables and chairs. The surroundings feel stuck in a time when the world was a friendlier, better place. A time when you could leave your front door open, without fear of being taken advantage of.

'You may come inside. Litze has bought more time, and I don't want to risk you being seen outside', says Fleischmann, maintaining his unfriendly tone. 'Before I help you, Lothar, there's something that I need to say to this whore.' Litze looks at me, shocked and embarrassed.

'Who are you calling a whore?' I say. I feel my anger rising.

'That's what you are. A mercenary, isn't it? You're worse than a whore. The world's two oldest professions and you're the worst of them. At least some whores care and are choosy about who they fuck.'

'I don't have to take this', I say, and walk towards the door. I don't want to walk away, but I must. Me walking away from confrontation. I must be growing up.

'Sit down!' shouts Fleischmann.

I turn and look at him for what seems like a long time. I forgot to say that I don't like being shouted at. My hands tremble. Litze knows I'm about to blow.

'Please', says Litze.

I remain standing. I want to remain defiantly on my feet.

'There's something that you need to hear, Becker. Do you want to know what happened after you went rogue?' says Fleischmann.

'Leave it, Udo!' says Litze.

'I won't, Lothar; she needs to hear this. Someone should tell her. She needs to understand why you stayed at the Facility longer than you wanted.'

Fleischmann has gotten my attention. I decide to sit down.

'What are you talking about?' I say to Fleischmann. Then I turn to Litze. He looks uncomfortable.

'In the Facility, we had a joke about you: "How many Beckers does it take to change a light bulb? None. She stands still and expects the room to revolve around her"', says Fleischmann. 'You thought you were some big shot, but you were a pain in the ass. We hated your guts.'

'So I didn't win a popularity contest. So what?' I say defiantly.

Fleischmann continues, 'Becker, the Facility was started in the sixteenth century by great men and women. A secret society. We had a noble tradition. The idea was that we were not influenced by governments. We wanted to help people. We were supposed to be above the temptations and the excesses of other covert organisations. But your behaviour, Becker, was shameful. You were like an open wound, and everything around you seemed like salt. Self-centred, angry, reckless, a lousy team player. Not qualities we look for in the Facility. Yet Lothar never gave up on you. Even when you shot him, he forgave you. He saw something in you. I can't see what myself. You think the word discreet is some island in the Mediterranean. Also, it didn't help that some thought that Lothar favoured you. That created a lot of resentment with the other recruits.'

Favoured me? That's news. Most of the time I thought Litze was a bastard. If he favoured me, he had a strange way of showing it.

'When you went rogue all those years ago, we had a vote, though it wasn't unanimous. We voted to kill you. You can guess who didn't vote to have you burned', says Fleischmann, looking at Litze. 'You were a liability and a disgrace to the organisation. But Lothar pleaded with the Facility to spare you. He sacrificed himself.'

'Enough, Udo!' says Litze. He looks uncomfortable.

'I'm not done', says Fleischmann, who glares at Litze. Then he moves closer and fixes his gaze on me. He knows what I'm feeling now, but he doesn't care. It's as if he's trying to provoke me into a reaction. But I want him to goad me; I really want him to.

'You always thought you could walk before you could run', says

Fleischmann. 'You always were ahead of yourself—thought you were better than everybody else. You wanted to sit at the top table, but you couldn't even use a fork. Years of tradition, which you broke because the going got tough. You ran instead of facing up to your responsibilities. You seem to be so angry and want to fight the world. But you should be mad at yourself. You're a liability, Becker. A team of one. You should be thanking Lothar for saving your stupid whore ass. In fact, you should kiss the ground he walks on. He stayed six years longer than he wanted and he promised not to pursue his life's mission: discovering the reason for his wife's death. The Facility agreed, and I was also part of the deal to stay, because, on balance, Lothar was worth more to the organisation than wasting valuable resources killing you. So instead, we decided that you were to be disavowed in your absence for life, while you were selling your soul. The word gets around. I even heard that you work for Coba Security. My God! I'd laugh if that wasn't so pathetic. This deal, amongst other things, put a strain on our friendship. But after our talk earlier, we both concluded something: We've already let one woman come between our friendship. You won't be the second. In fact, no woman is worth losing my dignity for. And especially not you.'

I sit in silence. The room feels cold, and I look at Litze. He can't look at me. Instead, he looks at the floor. I feel heavier, and my debt to him increases even more.

TWENTY-EIGHT

IT'S CLEAR NOW why Litze was so evasive about the Facility. I wish I'd never contacted him. I want to say sorry, but I feel it would be pointless now. I can't look at Fleischmann. Not because I dislike him. I know he's right about me. It's just that nobody has ever said it to me like that before. Nobody dared. And that's the trouble with anger: either you attract trouble, people tell you what you want to hear, or you push people away. I understand now. I've been the author of my downfall. All those missed opportunities. All those good people were trying to help me, but I repelled them with my anger combined with a wall of ego and pride. I don't like what I just heard, but this is what I needed to hear.

Fleischmann and Litze don't look like brothers in arms to me. They seem tense and heavy. I don't exactly know why they fell out, but I know that relationship will never be the same. I rise from my chair and walk to the front door without looking at or saying a word to Fleischmann. Litze follows me.

'Becker's bad news, Lothar. Only a fool would associate with someone who kicks a hornet's nest when they're naked', says Fleischmann.

'You take care', says Litze as he turns around and faces Fleischmann. They don't shake hands, as these former friends are now strangers.

'Goodbye', says Fleischmann. Then he closes the door on Litze for the last time.

***

We drive to Litze's place in silence. I know he didn't want me to know about the sacrifices he made. He doesn't expect me to feel beholden to him. He knows I'll try even harder to repay him. Perhaps too hard. The fact that we don't talk makes the journey seem even longer. I don't know whether Litze is quiet because I know he cares or because he feels more vulnerable. I tried for years to smash down that wall between us, but Fleischmann did it in one afternoon. The bastard!

I want Litze to say something. Anything. But he stares ahead, driving, in deep thought. I look at my mentor differently now. And I look at myself too. But not for long enough. That's always been the problem with me. I looked outward for too long because it suited me. They say hypocrites think others do misdeeds.

I decide to break the ice and say thank you to Litze. But he doesn't respond. He keeps his eyes on the road and instead he changes the subject.

'Are you hungry, Sam?'

'I'm not feeling hungry', I say. The time with Fleischmann has killed my appetite.

'You have to eat something. We'll need to. We have a lot to do.'

I don't reply. It's not like me not to eat, but I'm not hungry.

'I know he insulted you. He can be very direct, but Udo is a good man', says Litze.

Now it's my turn to change the subject. 'What did Fleischmann say?'

'It's what he didn't say. When I mentioned Karl Yumeni, I noticed a sort of reticence, a shift in his energy. Like he was hiding something.'

'Hiding what?'

'I don't know. Fleischmann doesn't frighten easily, so if he's worried, that's a sign that we are onto something. Fleischmann said that he knew nothing about Karl Yumeni.'

'And do you believe him?'

'No. Remember, I worked with him for years. I know when he's lying. Also, the last thing he said to me was goodbye. Like he'd just looked at a dead man.'

TWENTY-NINE

MY MIND YEARNS for some levity now, as I'm itching to find out why my mentor and Fleischmann fell out. It's as if Litze can read my thoughts when he looks at me and says, 'And don't even think about asking.'

He leaves me to ponder. I was the second woman they fell out over. Who was the first? Was it Litze's ex-wife? Was it some femme fatale who played them like violins? Litze used to say that he was like a Stradivarius violin: difficult to play. Unfortunately for him, not impossible. Men fighting over a woman sounds like a romantic idea, if you're into that sort of shit. But one thing that I agree with Fleischmann about is that nobody is worth losing your dignity for. When that's gone, it's game over.

***

I decide I will eat after all, even if I am not that hungry. It's my attempt at distracting myself, so we stop at a local café off the autobahn heading west towards Frankfurt to have black coffee and stollen cake. Instead of taking sweetener with my coffee this time, I decide to not have any. It tastes surprisingly good. Like I'm tasting the flavour for the very first time.

'This isn't going to be easy, Sam', says Litze as he raises the coffee cup to his lips.

'You should know me well enough to know that I'm the world's expert in taking the path of most resistance.'

'It doesn't have to be this way. You can still walk away from this mess.'

'Do you have a reason why you want to warn me off?'

'I hope you're not implying what I think you are.' Litze fixes me with one of his 'you're about to cross the line' stares.

'Sorry', I say sheepishly. 'You know I have trust issues.'

'No problem, Becker. I'd be worried if you didn't in this profession. You're right to question everything. I've gone to some dark places, but even I'd draw the line at scum like Yumeni.'

'I need to find out what's behind all that. And I owe it to my team to pursue this.'

'Team? That's a first coming from you. The ultimate lone wolf.'

'Yeah, I know what you're getting at. Maybe it's just ego then. It's not exactly like I knew them, or we were close. But I was the team leader, so I feel responsible. This feels personal.'

'Your need to prove yourself again? You father did an excellent number on you, didn't he?'

'And I've tried to prove myself to every man ever since like it's some default setting.' I look at Litze, and he knows I include him on the list of males from whom I've been trying to seek approval.

'Are you sure you want to go ahead?'

'I do, even if I have to do this alone', I say. I feel guilty asking Litze for help. Especially now.

'You're not alone.'

'Are you sure?'

'I promised, Sam. I try to keep them when I can. Do you keep your promises?'

'I try not to make promises I know I can't keep', I say, which is partly true but is also an excuse.

'I understand. I guess it's even harder to keep promises in this profession. We may not be around long enough to fulfil them.'

I take a sip of the cooling coffee and pause for a moment.

'It seems that everything I touch turns to shit.'

'Then don't touch anything.'

We look at each other and laugh.

'What a fucked-up life, Sam. It's why we understand each other. We're outliers. Part-time extroverts who are trying to function in a world that we don't belong to.'

'I meant what I said earlier', I say to Litze in between sips of coffee.

'What do you mean?' he asks me.

'Thank you and sorry.'

Litze says nothing.

'Is it true that everybody hated my guts in the Facility?'

'Not everybody. Even I liked you some days when you weren't the bitch from hell, which wasn't that often.'

'I hate to admit it, but I'm glad Fleischmann said what he did, even though it was hard for me to hear.'

'It's a shame because he's the kind of friend you'd want. The best kind. I used to call him a "front-stabber" because I always knew when the knife was coming. People like him are rare. To be honest, I miss his company. And he has a vicious tongue.'

'I noticed', I say.

The mood between us has lightened somewhat, which I'm glad about. And I start to think that everything happens for a reason. Despite the circumstances, I believe I was meant to meet Litze again. At least I can die with the knowledge that I made peace with one of the two men in the whole world that I've cared about.

THIRTY

IMAGINE SOMEONE IS holding a remote control and can speed you up, slow you down, make you pause, make you go backwards, or stop you altogether. That's what it's like fighting Lothar Litze. And he seems to have gotten better over time, whereas I seem to, at best, have stood still. But I'm a trier, and I go again and again and again. The mat might as well be stuck to my ass, as I spend much of my time on it. But I'm not going to give in as I know this is making me better. At least that's what I tell myself, despite evidence to the contrary.

When we spar, his footwork is fluid. Exquisite. Like he's skating on ice. His facial expression is impassive, like a man at ease with himself and the physical environment. Almost like they're one and the same. Compared to him, I look ponderous, awkward, slow, a comedy, like a Keystone Cop. Maybe I'm doing myself a disservice as I've fought and killed some excellent fighters in my time and had some close calls. But nothing quite like this. Litze is playing with me, which makes this even more embarrassing. He's so lightning quick that his punch ratio is sometimes three to one in his favour. I imagine what I must look like to him: he's set his remote to slow motion, and I move like I'm doing a spacewalk in zero gravity. That's what they say happens when you fight for long enough: you slow everything down, and you seem to have more time than your opponents. Like the great sports people of our age such as Lionel Messi or Roger Federer. They read time and space so well that they are always four or five moves ahead.

In the evening, my muscles ache and so I have a soothing bath. I reflect on the day and wonder if I could've done anything more, but at least I gave it my best shot. But that thought doesn't console me. Litze gets a takeaway from the Chinese, which is preferable to my offering to cook, because judging by the sparring sessions, cooking him a meal would be my best chance of killing him. Litze says nothing about the sparring today. He doesn't have to. Unlike him, I haven't been practising my basic techniques, the importance of which Litze has tried to drum into me. If he's disappointed, he hasn't shown it. The fact that he's kicking my butt is punishment enough.

**

I'm getting used to the early morning starts, though I'll never really be a morning person. I make sure I have a good breakfast because I'll need the energy. And coffee will keep me going. Another long day ahead of training, and I hope that I'll make a breakthrough. Get a sign that I'm making some headway. Even a small one. Then I remember when I had the most success. It was when I was detached from the outcome. The problem now is because I'm fighting my mentor, I care too much. Instead of being, I'm proving all the time. A legacy of feeling inadequate and never being good enough. Somehow, I must muffle my critical voice so I can fight more freely.

After our warm-ups and stretching, we resume training, and Litze stands in front of me in a fighting stance with his guard up. We do drills where we each take turns attacking and defending. He starts and picks me off, hitting me with a flurry of punches and kicks. I try without much success initially, but I remember to pay attention to my breath and tell myself to relax, even though my instinct is to tense up.

I try to trick my brain into relaxing, thinking that it's going to be OK, but at first, my mind doesn't believe me. I focus on my breath, and it's better this time as I manage to block some of my mentor's attacks. Some success. I won't start celebrating yet. Litze reads what I'm trying to do and speeds up, increasing the intensity and putting on the pressure. I try to override my fear and breathe; relax; breathe; relax. I don't want to feel any unnecessary tension until it matters. I seem to be blocking more of his techniques. It's working. Litze says nothing. He just nods in quiet approval. It's my turn to attack and his turn to defend.

I throw the first punch to his face, but he reads it easily, swatting it like he would a fly. I dummy but he reads it again, and I know I must be conscious that my body and my facial expressions don't make it easier for him. I know I'm tensing up. I'm not trusting myself, and that's always been my problem: I'm not good at being in a state of flow, and it's my lack of faith that is the reason I'm tensing. I go again. Two punches. He reads them like he has an early warning system. But I know at this moment it's his experience against mine, his relaxed demeanour against my relatively tense frame. I visualise myself being calmer, like I'm on a beach or somewhere hot, on a holiday without a care in the world. I want to bring this state to the here and now. I'm lighter on my feet. I move around, shuffling. I slow down and speed up, trying to turn the tables on my mentor. I don't want him to have the remote control this time. I want to wrestle it from him. It's my turn to take care as I slow my mind down some more and see an opening in Litze's chest. I throw a reverse punch without tension, fear, anxiety, and with only with one intention: to make contact. He blocks it just in time, but I'm getting closer. I feel it.

I try again, and I miss, but still I'm getting closer. It's marginal, but I'll take that. Then for a moment, I don't see Lothar opposite me. His form changes into that of someone else. I see a very familiar opponent. Someone more awkward than my deadly mentor. Someone who has been the bane of my life so far. This figure laughs at me in a mocking tone, like a bully. It taunts me constantly. 'You can't do it, can you ?!' 'What are you scared of?' 'You should quit now.' 'Are you serious?' 'Stupid bitch.' 'You've always thought you were ahead of yourself.' 'Loser!' 'You're ugly.' 'Isn't it time you lost weight?' 'You can't even maintain a proper relationship.' 'Are you wearing that?' 'Watch out for that cellulite!' 'You're not very good at this, are you?' 'Misfit.' 'Isn't it time you got laid?' 'You're cheap, selling yourself like this.' 'Slut.' 'Whore.'

And it's not my father this time. I can see her clearly now. I thought I'd killed her, but she keeps coming back. Fuck off, Sam Becker, I say to myself. I throw a lunge punch and as soon as I make contact, my startled mentor reappears, and he's sent backwards. We both stop as if we've just witnessed a eureka moment. Litze says nothing. He just nods in quiet approval. He's not big on praise, but it's his way of saying I've done a good job. It may not be anything to you, but for me, this is a big thing. It means that I'm beginning to face up to the things I've been running away from.

I'm elated and relieved, and Litze knows it. My rare success against him has given me the courage to phone Donny Walsh at last. I've been putting it off for some time, but this buoys me. Litze decides that we should take the afternoon off, which is unusual for him. I think it's a reward for my breakthrough, but I'm not sure. We decide to walk to the old town in Bad Kreuzberg, which has much more character than the new areas of the town but has of late been invaded by modern stores, still in period buildings which don't look too out of place. We order lattes and some homemade black forest gateau at Litze's favourite local café. The owner greets him warmly, and my mentor introduces me as one of his old students from way back.

Even though I never came close to beating Litze at any time, you should be grateful for small victories. Especially against him. He still practices his fighting with clockwork regularity and has the self-discipline to do it by himself. But I sense there's a more profound reason why he does it: it's to keep his demons at bay. We all have our methods. Some prefer drugs, sex, drink; but for him, it's martial arts. He's also much more at peace with himself than when I last saw him eight years ago. I guess that's what they call reaching enlightenment. I sometimes wonder whether he looks back and recognises the person he is now, compared to the person he was. And this is a lesson for me too. I've still got a long way to go before I get there, wherever 'there' is. Knowing my luck, I'll reach enlightenment just before a bullet enters my brain. But better late than never.

***

After a few more lattes and another piece of gateau, we walk back to Litze's apartment through the old town, across the bridge under which the river Rhine travels peacefully. The orange sunset gently tints the landscape like a skilled watercolour artist. As we enter Litze's place, I throw my jacket on the sofa. Litze goes into the kitchen to prepare something to eat.

I find my personal mobile. I scroll down and see Walsh's number. If he's a creature of habit, and I'm hoping he is, then he has the same one. I believe it's his office number. What would have been a simple thing to do before isn't so simple now. I feel my throat dry as I highlight his number and press the phone icon on my Nokia touch screen. I let it ring for a few minutes, and I hear a female voice which is unfamiliar to me. I ask for Donny. The voice hesitates and asks if

I'm family, and I say no, an old friend. Then the woman stutters and tells me that she's terribly sorry. I feel like I've been punched in the stomach. I know what she's going to say before she says it, but I let her continue. At which point, Litze comes back into the room and reads me. Apart from my mentor, everything seems to disappear from view. All I see now is the phone in my hand, like everything has faded to grey. My stomach starts to tighten, and I feel sick. My body starts to tense. I can see in Litze's expression that it must be written all over my face. He looks quizzical. But I can tell he's seen this look before. It's the look of someone who's heard something awful. He's been both the recipient and the bearer of bad tidings, so he knows. I try to compose myself as I listen to the news, but I don't. Not really.

Walsh has been dead for the last two years.

THIRTY-ONE

'ARE YOU OK, Becker?' asks Litze as he moves closer.

'Walsh is dead', I say after a brief pause, staring through Litze.

'How?'

'A gas explosion apparently.'

I try to take it all in, but my brain is scrambled. I don't know what to think. And it's like my feelings are waiting to catch up with me. I know they will, no matter how much I try to outrun them.

Litze says nothing.

'Good. Well at least that's one less thing to worry about', I say, as if being callous will nullify my loss.

I need to focus.

Focus.

I tell myself that as I think about my next move.

But I can't outrun myself. The emotion comes over me like a tidal wave that I can't beat. I don't want to cry, but my body has different ideas as I struggle.

Litze looks at me, unconvinced. It's the look he used to give me as a child when I lied to him. He knew I wasn't truthful then. He knows now. He always knows.

Walsh is dead. End of story. There's nothing I can do about it. I can't afford to care now. I've work to do. There'll be time for grieving later if I can be bothered, but now, I must deal with the living. I'm lying to myself now. That's how desperate I've become, but you can only do this for so long. Denial is only temporary. It may last months or years, but never forever. The truth is like a thorn that gets stuck under your skin but eventually, it will find its way to the surface.

'Would you like something to drink, Becker?' asks Litze, as if he's asking for the sake of asking.

'No', I say.

'Food will be ready soon', says Litze, which seems pointless and inappropriate, but he feels he should say something.

'I'm not hungry. I'm going out to get some air. I'll be back later.'

I leave Litze standing there as I grab my jacket and walk towards the exit. I don't know where I'm going. All I know is I want to be left alone now. My grief is chasing me, and I've got to outrun it.

***

I walk into the main town centre, and it's starting to fill up. Thursday evening and people are already out eating and drinking. The smells of food waft through the cold night air as I feel even lonelier than ever. I can't cry now. All I feel is a tightness in my body, and I need alcohol to loosen me up. It's been a month since I got hammered, and according to others, it's not a good idea. I apparently change, and not for the better. Or maybe alcohol just reveals my true nature, which is worrying enough. I've never been a big drinker, but when I go for it, I go. Litze would be unimpressed with my ill-discipline and would think I'm taking the easy way out. Maybe I am. But tonight, I don't care.

I have no problem going to bars on my own, despite the looks I get being a single woman. And some don't know how to approach me. A woman on her own can elicit sympathy, curiosity, or unwanted attention. And I'm used to dealing with all of those. I'm a people watcher, so being alone suits me. I like to observe behaviour, and in my business, that's an occupational necessity. I can usually tell things about people just by the clues they give off. I was taught to watch people as it would come in handy; there are little telltale signs that everybody has. But body language isn't an exact science, and you can be easily fooled.

I walk further down into the old town in a daze. I'm going through the motions of window-shopping as I move my legs one step after another, aimlessly. I consider a local bar, but it doesn't seem like the clientele that I'd feel comfortable with. Too busy, too conservative. I would stick out too easily. I just want to drink. No company. Just my thoughts as my companion as I try to take stock of my news. At least death is final. There's no way back.

I head towards Die Klasse bar in the town centre. It's a vibrant place with a young clientele and minimal decor. The lighting is cool blue and low. There's a combination of black leather seats for the lounge areas and matching black bar stools. I approach the bar and immediately get the attention of an attractive ponytailed blonde woman with a pierced lip. I order a rum and Coke and down it quickly. I order another. And another. I don't know how many I've had. The alcohol courses through my veins like a transfusion. I look around me and see that the bar is not quite full, but it's early, around 8.00pm. But there's still time. I'm not sure there's enough alcohol in here to drown my sorrows, but I'm going to damn well try. As the night blurs, I have foggy conversations with a succession of men, and I smile sweetly. I'm a happy drunk sometimes. I'm becoming less inhibited and more flirtatious. I like that side of me and should show it more often. I realise I've become uptight and stiff and wonder if that's my German genes coming out: too serious, everything too correct. I feel my body relax and wonder what signals I'm giving off now. I'm not too drunk to know that Litze would be furious with me if he was here to witness this. Each drop of alcohol is making me even more relaxed, but tonight, I don't care about myself, as I can be reckless at times.

I'm accepting drinks from strange men who look at me as if I'm some novelty act that's walked in, or that could be the drink making me paranoid. Isn't that what I'm supposed to do? I might even get lucky. I'm not a tramp, if that's what you're thinking. But what's wrong with being a tramp once in a while? The drink is working. I push Walsh to the recesses of my mind, and I tell myself that all is right with the world. I'm OK. I am. Just another drink should do it. And if I can still remember what I did the night before, I can't be doing it right. I raise my hand to the blonde woman behind the bar, and she lines up another one, and another, until the room fades from view.

***

My vision emerges from the darkness as I start to refocus. For a split second, I think I'm at Litze's, but I don't recognise this room or this bed. I try to raise my head, but it's heavy and hurts with every move. My stomach feels sickly. There's a stale smell of cannabis residue in the room. I'm lying next to a man's head, and I can see the back of his skull. He has short black hair, and I notice a tattoo of a barcode at the nape of his neck. His body rises and falls as he snores monotonously. I lift the duvet cover just enough to realise he's naked. He's got a good body. Well built. Lean and muscular, just how I like my men. I raise the cover some more and look at my naked body. But I don't remember anything. In the corner of the room, I see my clothes draped over a small wooden chair. I turn slowly to the right, and there's another man next to me, also naked. He murmurs and reaches across with his outstretched right hand, and I push him away. The last thing I remember is the bar. After that, I don't remember anything. It's a long time since I've been in a situation like this. A long, long time. My head pulsates with pain, but I'm determined to get up.

The man on the right of me is a white male, with dark brown hair and stubble that is just a few days from forming into a beard. I can only see the top half of him, but he's skinny. His muscles are sinewy, but I can tell he's stronger than he looks. My legs struggle to carry my head as I walk towards my clothes and begin to dress. I look around to see if I've left anything behind, and I check my pockets. Nothing seems to be missing, but I want to fill in the gaps of the last few hours. But part of me thinks maybe I shouldn't.

I sit on the bed and shake the man.

'Where am I?' I ask.

The man sits up on his side of the bed and rubs his eyes. 'This is my place. I live here in town, not far from the bar where we met.'

'What happened?'

'You don't remember?'

'I wouldn't have asked if I did.'

'You asked me if I wanted to buy you a drink and I said yes. But to be honest, you were out of it, so I asked the barman to go easy. He's a friend of mine.'

'Who's the other guy?'

'A friend of mine, we go out together.'

'I see.'

'I know how this must look, but it's not what you think.'

'What do you mean?'

'You're in bed with two guys. I'm surprised by your reaction.'

'What are you talking about?'

'You haven't freaked out.'

'Freaked out?'

'You don't remember, do you?'

'Remember what?'

'When you were in the bar, you picked us up. You were drunk, but you knew what you were doing. You were very assertive. We liked this; it was unusual for us. It's not often we see a woman behave like this.'

'Behave like what?'

'Like she's in control of what she's doing: picking up strange men in bars. You were very insistent. We all went home together. We knew you were drunk. But you can be quite aggressive. You started to do a strip for us, but you were laughing and falling. Then you tried to take our clothes off. We were unwilling because you were drunk, but you wouldn't take no for an answer. So we played along and took our clothes off. Then you led us to the bedroom.'

'And?' I ask, not entirely sure I want to hear this.

Then you started to kiss me, hard, and then you pulled my friend over and began to kiss him too. In the same way. You were getting into it.'

'Did we?' I say.

'No, we didn't. You were too drunk. We may be horny men, but even we have standards. We're not desperate.'

'Thanks', I say.

'I don't mean that you're not attractive. You are. Very. It was just that you were too drunk to do anything. We're not the type of guys who would take advantage of someone like that', he says as I feel a wave of relief, despite my headache.

'You say I was doing a striptease. Really?'

'Yes, I tried to stop you, but you kept hitting us. You got quite violent at one point.'

He turns and shows me deep scratch marks on his left side.

'I did that?'

'Yes, you did.'

'And you did this', says the other guy as he points to a small bruise on his left side.

I pause for a moment. Then I go cold. I've had a close call. I curse myself in my head for being so stupid; I thought I'd grown out of this.

'I'm only naked from my top half', the man continues. 'I preferred to keep some of my clothes on', he says as he pulls the covers aside to reveal his pyjama bottoms. 'We were going to sleep on the couch, but it's not that comfortable. My friend was going to sleep on the air bed. But you didn't want us to go. You kept asking us to stay. You look like someone that most people wouldn't want to argue with. And you don't seem to take no for an answer.'

'I see', I say. That does sound like me. I feel like an idiot.

'Anyway, I doubt there's a man on earth who could compete with your imaginary cock!' says the man. That's not the first time I've heard someone say that to me. At one time, I may have taken that as a compliment, but not now.

'And we prefer women with less testosterone than us!' says the other man.

I've been told that before too.

'And by the way, you talk in your sleep', says the other man.

Oh, great! I think.

'What did I say?' I ask.

'Mostly incoherent stuff. Nothing I could understand or that made any sense.'

I sigh with relief. He seems like a good guy. They both do. I'm relieved and grateful that they didn't take advantage of me. But I'm a fool. I got lucky, again!

'I heard you say this person's name over and over.', says the first man. 'It sounded like—'

'Donny?' I interrupt.

'Yes, it sounded like that.'

So much for drowning my sorrows.

THIRTY-TWO

MY LEGS MANAGE to carry my head out of the flat in silence. My recklessness, which I thought I'd reined in, was always there beneath the surface like molten lava under a volcano, ready to erupt any second. Someone was smiling down on me when I hooked up with those guys. Why do I believe them? Because the person they described to me in uncomfortable detail is all too familiar. A Mrs Hyde character: someone whom I thought I'd buried and comes back to mock me as a reminder that we're not through yet.

The grief I'm trying to hide comes right back and buries me instead. Last night was my attempt to find some respite, but I know deep down it is ridiculous. And I know why I still can't cry: when your father tells you that crying is a weakness, that shit stays with you. Sure, I've cried since, but I mean the type of tears that leave you drained. Not just crocodile tears. And I don't want to think about what not crying has cost me. All I know is that it can't be healthy. It's going to come. I feel it. At the moment, I feel numb. The sad thing is that I find it easier to lose my temper or pull the trigger than to shed a tear. All these years, I've been confused as to what I think real strength is.

I walk down the steps of the apartment block and onto the cobbled streets of the old town of Bad Kreuzberg. There's a chill outside, but the rising sun will soon change that. I check my mobile, and it's 5.45am. I'm glad I didn't check the mirror as I don't think any glass would withstand the horror show of my face.

The old town feels peaceful this time of morning. I'm not far from Litze's, but I wonder if I should leave it a while before I go back. He will not be impressed. Maybe that's why I feel I need to prove myself all the time. With my father, it was about defiance. With my mentor, it was always about approval. I didn't want to let him down. You'd think I'd have grown out of that by now, but it stays with me. Maybe that's why I've had some success so far in my profession. And maybe that's the point of Litze's methods: he wants to keep me on my toes. I also sense that his upbringing was uncompromising. If it was good enough for him, I guess it's good enough for me.

I check my phone, and there are no messages on my voicemail. I walk down the empty high street. The sunrise dazzles the scenery as the light bounces from the pavement to the shop windows, reflecting and refracting everywhere. I walk towards the bridge in the town centre and stop awhile. I peer over the bridge and notice how the rays make the river sparkle like an endless jewelled bracelet. And I wonder how many people have been here before me, watching and waiting. I wish I was like a river sometimes and could go with the flow. But I've been swimming against the tide. That restlessness that I've always felt has never really gone away. And I don't delude myself into thinking otherwise. I look at the river again and realise that I have to be like water. It's the only way I'll be able to cope.

I stare into the distance and see the houses on the riverbanks, and I think it must be a good place to live and feel connected to nature. Another reminder of the fact that I lost my way a long, long time ago. And I need to get it back soon. At this moment, the fact that I'm the only person on the street feels appropriate, like an adequate metaphor for my life. It doesn't have to be this way. Not always. Not forever. But the fear in me won't let me get close to anyone. Maybe that's why I fell out with Walsh. I used the abduction as an excuse. Maybe subconsciously, I sabotaged our relationship. I wanted to drive him away, not believing deep down that I deserve anything good in my life. Now I'll never get the chance to find out. Something, along with a long list of other issues, I'll have to deal with.

As I walk back to Litze's flat, I hear footsteps in the distance. And I'm not too hung-over to notice an urgency in their sound. Like they're after someone.

You don't need three guesses as to who that person is.

THIRTY-THREE

I SEE THREE women in the distance on the other side of the bridge. And they don't look like they're about to ask for directions. They look angry. Bad news. I've seen that bulletin before. They walk as though they're ready to fight someone. Not calm but assertive and purposeful, like they're primed for action. I continue to walk and adopt a confident pose. Just in case. I may have got this wrong. But my paranoia won't go away.

As they get closer, I can see the women. They're all dressed in biker jackets and wearing denim jeans in varying shades of blue. They're walking side by side now, and my instinct doesn't feel wrong. While I don't sense an immediate threat, I'm on my guard and already watching, calculating and assessing my next move. Three isn't a problem for me. They look handy, but not badass handy.

'So you like stealing other women's men?' says the girl at the front. She's very curvy and dressed in a biker jacket with chains, skin-tight jeans ripped at the knees, and short black boots. Her hair is dark and below-shoulder length. She has hard, strong features and looks like someone you don't mess with.

'I'm talking to you', she says, raising her voice slightly to make her point, and partly to intimidate me or to make it clear that she's talking to me. The woman is more brazen now and comes closer, with her two girlfriends behind her. She stares at me and through me. It's one of those looks that you give when you've smelt something bad or have stepped in something. I stare back at her impassively. She pokes her index finger at my collarbone. I don't flinch, which surprises her. Then she does it again, as if I didn't get it the first time. I grab her index finger with my left hand and lever it towards her face, which results in her dropping to her knees in pain. I've just done enough to make my point.

'Leave her alone', shouts one of the other women as she comes closer. I exert more pressure on the woman's finger and gesture with my right hand for her to stop.

'If you don't want your friend to have one less nail to varnish, back off!'

The other women are thinking whether they can take me. I can see it in their eyes. They both move closer, and I exert more pressure on the leader's finger.

'I won't ask you a second time. And she won't be the only one picking her fingers up from the ground.'

The two women back off.

'What's this all about?' I ask calmly.

'You were all over my man last night', she says, grimacing. I'm trying to remember but I can't. I kissed lots of men last night. 'So you like stealing other women's men?' she says again.

'In my experience, nobody steals anybody', I say.

'So you've done this before?' she says.

'You're asking the wrong question', I say.

'How do you figure?' says the woman on her knees.

'The question you should have asked is: why does he feel the need to go elsewhere in the first place?' I say.

'Is this your way of justifying it to yourself so you can feel better?'

I apply more pressure on her finger, as if it's a reflex, and she lets out a scream. She hit a nerve. The others move forward instinctively, but I give them the look that says back off.

'Nobody steals anybody. He knew what he was doing. He was aware that he had a girlfriend. I wasn't.'

'Would that have made any difference?' the leader asks as she stares with hatred. through her pain.

I say nothing.

'I cook, I clean, and I wash his clothes. I look after him well.'

'And your point is?' I say.

'I expect something in return.'

'So you give to receive?'

'Yes, doesn't everybody?'

'Maybe. But if you give freely, then that's a gift. If you give things to receive, then that's called a bribe. Anybody worth anything won't accept a bribe.'

Confusion distorts the woman's face as I look at her. 'Why does he want more sex?'

'It's not about more sex, just different sex', I say.

'Is that supposed to make me feel better?'

'No.'

'Then what?'

'Relationships are like bridges: you never really know how strong they are until they've been tested. If a juggernaut destroys the bridge, don't blame the juggernaut.'

'Way to go, Oprah', says one of the women as she gives me a slow hand clap. If you need relationship advice from me, then you're in deep shit.

'Look at us', I say. 'The only person who would be enjoying this moment is your so-called boyfriend. It would boost his ego to know that women are fighting over him. All that's missing is us wrestling naked in a mud bath with our tits out. He'd love that.'

'Bit late to play the sisterhood card, isn't it?' says the woman on the right of me.

'Wasn't trying to', I say. 'Don't believe in sisterhood. Never had a sister, real or honorary. Sisterhood doesn't exist, especially when it comes to women competing for men. We're worse than men in that regard. The only difference between you and me is that I'm honest about it.'

I look at the woman on her knees. Then I see a flicker of realisation on her face, like she's remembered who she's really angry with. I release her from my finger lock. The woman rubs her sore digit with her right hand and gets up slowly. She gives me a cold, hard stare. She then turns to her friends, and they walk away.

I wasn't the juggernaut in this case. But I have been. More times than I care to remember.

THIRTY-FOUR

I LET MYSELF into Litze's place like a woman who's returned from having an illicit affair. I worry about waking him, but he's usually an early riser. He could be eating breakfast. I enter the living room and it is as I left it: unmade and with my things scattered on top of the couch. I walk into the lounge and smell coffee coming from the kitchen, which means Litze is up. But I can't hear him, so he's probably already down at the gym. I'm in no fit state to join him. I go into the kitchen and feel the coffee pot. It's warm enough to drink. Just what my head and my stomach can manage. I don't think this sick feeling is due solely to the alcohol. Since I heard the news of Donny Walsh, my body has been tense with shock. That's what I think. Like a grief default setting. I return to the living room with my beverage. Coffee is probably the last thing I should be drinking if I want to relax, but I don't care. I lie back on the sofa in yesterday's clothes and stare pointlessly at the ceiling as if I want it to give me some answers that will never come. And I'm too tired to sleep, so I decide to lie here, paralysed with indecision, until Litze returns. I can imagine what he'll be like. He won't go easy just because my closest friend in the whole world has died. In fact, he might be even worse than usual.

***

I haven't slept that well in days, and the news of my friend's death hasn't helped. I've trained for sleep deprivation, and I'm used to it. That's part of the life of an operative, but it's unnatural to me. But despite the coffee and my grief, I'm succumbing to tiredness. I'm not sure how much quality sleep I'll get, but I embrace the chance to rest. I can't face Litze. I can't face anyone. I don't even know if I can face myself. This sounds ridiculous now as I try to force myself to cry, but still the tears won't come. And Donny would be insulted if he knew I tried to induce tears. I wonder what the others have thought of me during the years. I never really cared before, but I'm starting to think about it. Probably that I'm a cold-hearted bitch who is too busy feeling sorry for herself. They said I lacked awareness when I was younger. That's what I overheard while I was at school. But they didn't know I was listening. I was too young to understand what that meant, but I realise now. I guess anger and awareness don't go hand in hand. Anger blinds you, and I've learned that the hard way. While I'm nowhere near as bad as when I was younger, that's never gone away.

I don't just want to sleep. I want to escape to dreamland and think of happier times, remembered or imagined. This is the only time I'll reunite with my friend Donny, in my dreams or through my memories. They say when we dream, we leave our bodies and travel and then return before we wake. I wonder whether we are awake at all and this isn't part of some dream or nightmare. Society is good at making us think what we see is real. But it doesn't fool everyone. I'm starting to think the unthinkable: that ignorance is bliss. But I put that down to how I'm feeling now. It's like a defeatist attitude. I don't believe that. Not really. Desperation has a way of making you question your values. That's been my problem over the years: I question and think too much.

I'm starting to get frustrated because I can't sleep. I want Donny to fuck off out of my head. He's draining me. I've got to put him to one side while I sort this mess out once and for all. Then I'll have time for him. Maybe then, I'll start to cry.

***

I can't even tell whether I slept properly or remember if I've dreamed anything. I check the bedside clock, and it's 10.30am. Two hours. Not a great amount of sleep but it's better than nothing. I still can't hear anything, so Litze is out. I feel like shit, though. My head is pounding and my stomach nauseous. I should try to eat something, but I think my gut won't thank me for it. I'm about to get up from the sofa when I hear the front door. Litze's back, and I decide not to call out. I'll stay put until I'm ready to face him.

THIRTY-FIVE

THERE'S BEEN THIS invisible wall between us during the last few days since Litze and I resumed training. And I accept that's my fault, as I've completely shut down. I haven't said anything about when I disappeared the other night or about Walsh. I'm trying to bury it, but I know that's not possible, so I withdraw. I see what they mean about trying to shake a monkey off your back. Every time I try to rid myself of it, it seems to tighten its grip. Like it's part of me now, fused or welded to me. Something I must carry for the time being until I have the courage to face it. That's right: courage. I know I'm running, and I'll admit that. Litze knows it.

We're in the woods today for firearms training. Litze has made some makeshift targets out of wine bottles. It's pretty basic, but for what we need, this is good enough. He places the vessels on a sideways tree trunk. And he's brought a couple of handguns and a sniper rifle, though I don't recognise the model. It looks similar to a classic Winchester rifle. But judging by the lack of markings and serial number, this looks custom-made, which makes sense. In our game, more and more assassins are paying top dollar for bespoke equipment. And it makes a difference. They do the same for golfers, soccer players, tennis players, and Formula 1 racing-car drivers. The belief is bespoke equipment gives you the competitive edge, and success and failure can be caused by the finest of margins. You're booked for a fitting, much the same as when you go for a new suit. They consider the person's particular body weight, biomechanics, and personality traits to ensure that nothing is left to chance. They even make moulds of your hands so that you feel that the weapon is part of you, and use biometric recognition which personalises the weapon.

Litze will have the advantage because his rifle is custom-made for him, but I can soon get used to a new weapon. I've had a natural flair for guns from a very early age and manage to calm myself down long enough to shoot accurately. I'm also good at crossbow shooting and knives, but I prefer guns. I've never really been interested in all that technical jargon concerning guns. That stuff usually bores me. I find it very easy to get into the zone, and maybe that's not a healthy thing as a child growing up. The weapons guy at the Facility all those years ago used to reel off what this gun did, its speed and number of rounds per second, and he would get annoyed when I paid him no attention. He took it as a personal slight, but he was old school. When he lost his temper with me, I told him that there are only a few things I need to know about toys: so long as they're well made, feel good, or vibrate, that's all I care about. That did the trick and shut him up.

'You need to relax more, Becker', says Litze tersely as I cock the handgun. He's trying to provoke a reaction from me. But I'm not going to bite, I hope. He's been like this all morning. It'll take more than this to tear this wall down. 'Need to be steadier on your feet. Shoulders down, relax, focus on your breath', he says curtly. I still don't respond as I squeeze the trigger and shatter the green glass bottle in the distance. My lack of reply makes him even madder, but I don't care. And he knows it.

'OK. Let's go again', he says sternly, but he's just reacting to my indifference, so I only have myself to blame. I don't want to let anybody in. That's been my trouble. I shut people out. Usually the people closest to me, which explains a lot.

'You have too much tension in your body, Becker. Remember what I told you, or do you still think that you know it all?'

I don't respond.

'What's the matter, Becker, got nothing to say?'

Still no response.

'Give the gun to me; I'll show you how it's done.'

He snatches the Glock 17 pistol out of my hand and shoots the remaining bottles in the distance. Quickly, cleanly.

'That's what I did', I say.

'No, you didn't', he replies. 'Your targeting is way off.'

I take the pistol again, reload, and shoot. 'I think you need glasses, old man; there was nothing wrong with that.' I know as soon as I say old man that it's a big mistake.

'Yeah, this old man kicked your ass in training. You got lucky the other day. Do you think I was trying? I was just warming up. Your techniques were embarrassing.'

'If you say so.' I turn and walk away.

'Don't turn your back on me!' shouts Litze.

'I don't have time for this shit.'

'That's you all over. You can't take criticism. You just run or you blame someone else. You never take responsibility for anything.'

I turn and glare at him. He glares back.

'Oh, a reaction, Becker, truth hurts, doesn't it? I'm surprised you can stand upright with that chip on your shoulder.'

I feel my neck tense, but I'm trying hard not to react.

'Poor Becker, feeling sorry for herself again. The way you behave, you think you have exclusive rights on pain.'

'What the—'

'I haven't finished yet. You need to get over yourself; that's why you're in this mess. You want to walk before you can run? You are in over your head.'

'Fuck off, Litze; it's got nothing to do with you.' I know I've gone too far now.

'Fuck off? Nothing to do with me?' He pushes me with both hands on my shoulders and sends me crashing to the ground. 'Nothing to do with me?' he repeats. 'I should kick that soon-to-be-cellulite-ridden ass of yours.' Now he's going too far. 'You'd be nothing without me, you arrogant, ungrateful little shit. You'd be dead too if I wasn't there in the past to watch your back.'

'I'm surprised that you had time to watch my back. You've spent enough time on it', I reply angrily.

'Fleischmann was right. The others at the academy hated you. In fact, they couldn't stand you. You were a liability. A lousy team player who was more interested in her glory than working for the team. Your head was so far up your backside, they had to send air, land, and sea rescue to find it. I had to beg them not to kill you. Now I think that was a waste of time!'

I feel my anger rising. My glare burns into Litze. He's playing a very dangerous game, but he is past caring. He's pushing me into that dark place. I look at the gun in my hand. Litze watches me. I get to my feet. It takes all my willpower not to aim it at him. It's like there are two opposing forces: the one that pushes my arm up is battling with the one pushing it down.

'You want to use it again, Becker? You want to shoot me like last time?' Litze pats his chest. 'No bulletproof vest now. You can make sure this time, or what about a head shot?' Litze points between his eyes. 'That would do it. What's the matter, Becker? Got nothing to say for yourself?'

He's in my face now and glares at me. The last time I saw him like this was years ago during our training sessions. Litze's anger rises.

He pushes me, but I don't react. Then he slaps me hard across the face.

'You didn't see that coming, did you? You should be used to that.'

My left cheek stings and the blood tastes like copper in my mouth.

He goes to slap me again. This time, I block. I don't want to fight him. He tries to hit me again, and I block, but I'm still holding the gun. Then a flurry of blows. He hits me, and I don't respond. He hits me again, this time sending me to the floor. I get up slowly. I still don't want to retaliate, but there's a limit to what I can take. He pushes me again, taunting me. I feel like an elastic band that's being pulled to the point of no return and about to snap. Then I point the gun at him.

'Back off!' I shout.

'Shoot me, Becker!' he says, pointing to his head. 'What are you waiting for? You want to do it, I know. I can see it in your eyes. Poor Becker. Mommy didn't love you because she was too weak and didn't protect you from Papa', he says mockingly. 'Well, let's play the violin. The metal in your hand is warmer than you. You want to shoot me? Do it! Do it! It's your answer for everything: you fight without thinking. Not that you're any good at that anyway. Thinking isn't your problem, Becker. The problem is that you don't feel. You told me once that you were afraid to die, but that's not true, Becker. The trouble with you is that you're afraid to live. No wonder nobody gets close to you. Walsh was lucky. Even dead, he's more alive than you. You don't give a shit, Becker. You act all tough, but you're a coward, Becker. Walsh was nothing to you. He was just one less thing to worry about.'

I raise the pistol and aim at Litze's head.

'What are you waiting for?' he screams. 'Shoot. Get it over with. You want to. That's all you'll ever understand. You're a killer. Don't just stand there feeling sorry for yourself. Do it!'

I look at Litze one last time. He has no fear. He's not bluffing. Men like him don't. He accepts what's going to happen next. I raise the pistol and aim at his head. He's completely impassive now. His cold, blue, nerveless eyes fix on mine. I release the safety, aim, scream from the bottom of my lungs, lift the weapon above Litze's head, and fire the last rounds into the sky. The birds scatter at the sound of echoing gunshots. I drop the gun on the ground and fall to my knees, exhausted.

Litze walks over to me and picks up my gun. He puts his left hand on my shoulder, looks at me, and says in a soft voice, 'At last, we're getting somewhere.'

THIRTY-SIX

'I CAN'T CRY', I say, struggling to catch my breath. I'm wheezing like an accordion. My chest is tight. All the emotion of the last few days has caught up with me. I feel like shit.

'I know, Sam', says Litze. 'The time will come. I'm sorry I provoked you. It was the only way to get a reaction. Remember: I know you too well. I know you're trying to bury it. But it's not good. You have to deal with it.'

'I know, I know. I'm just frustrated. I never got the chance to make it up with Walsh, and now he's dead, and I have to live with this. It was my fault. I fucked up. I look back and replay all the times I could have said and done things differently and the things I wanted to say to him, but I was too proud.'

'You mean scared?'

'Yes, Litze, you're right. I was.' I turn and look him in the eyes. 'How do I live with the guilt?'

'You just do, Becker. Guilt is good, used in the right way. It keeps you focused. It stops you from being lazy. It helps you to remember that you're only as good as the last thing you did. But guilt is like a bath: you stay in it, but not for too long. It's there as a reminder and not for you to wallow in. Remain in the bath too long, and your skin wrinkles.'

I laugh. 'All that stuff you said earlier. Was it true? Did you mean any of it?'

'You'll be pleased to know that the bit about your ass isn't true.'

I laugh again.

'That's better, Sam. You should laugh more. It suits you. You don't do it enough.'

'Litze?'

'Yes?'

'I'm—'

He gently puts his finger over my mouth. 'No need', he says. 'We have work to do. People to kill.'

***

That incident in the woods did the trick for now. It released some pent-up anger. I still can't cry, but there's no point in trying to force it. That would be like sitting on the toilet when you're constipated. It'll probably come when I least expect it. And there will be more days like these, but that's part of the process. Now I can refocus on Karl Yumeni. If I'm lucky enough to get out of this alive, I'll visit Walsh's grave. It's the least I can do.

Coming back to Germany and meeting Litze has made me realise that I have to sort myself out. But I know this will catch up with me in the end. Few people go through this life without a cost. And to pretend that somehow that killing doesn't affect you is bullshit. Assassins are in a unique position of power, and many of our kind don't have an allegiance to any ideology. We are natural predators. But even I know that to have no moral compass is scary. My emotional guidance system has been fucked up for years, and Litze has reminded me that running away from your feelings is a sign of weakness. Emotions are a way to tell us what we need to change. I've just hit the tip of the iceberg. I'm not looking forward to facing my feelings, and I regret hurting the people who thought that because I didn't show emotion it meant I didn't care. It was just that I didn't know how. I was trying to protect myself. Cowardice has many impostors.

THIRTY-SEVEN

WE RETURN FROM the woods to Litze's flat in silence. I sit on the living room sofa, still in a daze. He claps his hands as he notices me wandering again.

'Becker, snap out of it', says Litze as he holds my head in his hands. He stares back at me with his blue eyes. There's a delay between when he utters his words and when I register them. 'What's done is done. You need to concentrate on the mission', he says. His expression is quite stern, but not entirely unsympathetic.

'I'm OK', I lie. 'You said that you had someone that can help us?' I say, trying to change the subject.

'Yes, their name is Purple Dawn. They are a white-hat hacking group. I came across them by chance.'

'How?'

'Sometimes they post puzzles which seem innocent, but they are designed to assess particular qualities that they are looking for.'

'Like a recruitment technique?'

'Exactly. I came across one of these puzzles while I was surfing. I was intrigued. These techniques are often used by the CIA, NSA, MI5, and other groups such as secret societies. These people sometimes use physical locations, online locations, or a combination of both. In my case, it was online.'

'Weren't you worried?'

'About what?'

'About your safety?'

'What do I have to be worried about? I couldn't care less now that I'm older. Maybe that's good. Maybe it isn't. I've lost so much. Some good colleagues, friends, the love of my life. This looked like an adventure for me. I thought I should live a little.'

'So when you solved the puzzle, what did you do next?'

'I just waited, and then I got a message days later on my computer. In was an encrypted email that congratulated me on my score so far and gave me a link to a website.'

'That was still a big risk.'

'True, but I had a good feeling about this. As if someone was looking for people like me. They've been very helpful. They know a lot about me, but I know nothing about them. I have a contact that I use. I don't know who it is, but he or she has been very useful. They've given me information that I wouldn't have access to normally.'

'But as you said, you know nothing about this group. How do you know that they're not cyberterrorists or a government agency posing as an online terror group?'

'Your concerns are warranted, but I trust my instincts on this one. And your mission will be another test. Trust is a two-way thing.'

Litze is right, of course. He would have been laying traps of his own. Someone like him wouldn't be intimidated by an online hacking group. Like he said, he has nothing to lose.

'I'll leave you now. We'll go to the Internet café tomorrow to make contact', says Litze as he walks towards the kitchen. 'They don't always get back to me immediately, but they are pretty swift.'

I sit here now trying to take in the news of Walsh's death. Aren't you supposed to cry? And I feel sorry about that. But apparently not sorry enough, as at the moment I don't seem to feel anything. I guess it's shock, and my reaction makes me look callous to Litze, but I think he understands. That's why he leaves me. He wants to give me time, and this is a compassionate side to him that I haven't seen before. But I do notice that my body is tense, and I don't think it's to do with the discomfort of the last few days. I think it's adrenaline. Even if I don't show it through tears, my grief has manifested in another way, and I realise that I'm trying to trick my brain and tell it that everything is OK, but my body doesn't lie. It's proof that I need to listen to it a lot more than I used to. When I used to have an illness, my father would say that I was faking it and there was nothing wrong with me. Whenever I've had an injury since, I've told myself to get on with it. But I believe I've done myself more harm ignoring injuries than dealing with them.

I go to the living and rest for a while, which seems futile. Too many things are going through my head. Many, many regrets, and frustration that Walsh and I didn't manage to make peace. The fact that I didn't try hard enough or didn't say what I meant when he was alive. This is a lesson I didn't want, but one I needed. I'm not the best communicator. I cringe at the thought of the way I've been and realise that I need more finesse. I can't use the fact that my parents were shit teachers anymore as an excuse. I have to take charge and make changes. I'm just sorry that Walsh is no longer alive to see them. You shouldn't wait for people to die to do that.

THIRTY-EIGHT

WHEN DONNY WALSH and I were last on speaking teams, he tried to explain to me about the dark net. I went around to his Camden flat early one morning after I picked up some chocolate croissants from a local Co-op. This wasn't a regular thing, but it was something we liked to do together from time to time. Donny would make fresh coffee in his percolator. That's one of the smells that would hit me, along with the cannabis that stank out his apartment. Although I did like to take some from time to time, I didn't want to lose my edge. I liked the fact that it made me hungry and enhanced sexual arousal. But after a while, I realised that I didn't need it for the sexual stimulation. I'm not exactly inhibited and my brain, which is the most important sex organ, has more than enough stimuli to arouse me.

I like to push boundaries, and to be honest, I don't think I've reached my limit. As I've gotten older and more relaxed, I've cared even less about how society says women should behave. I think I was rebelling against the shitty blueprints provided by my parents. Especially my father. He didn't mind if you had an idea, so long as it was one of his. I'm not going to go into graphic detail here; maybe that's for another time. But I've enjoyed most of my experiences. To describe them now would be pointless. What a good sexual experience is, is subjective, and I don't want to get into a pissing contest, metaphorically speaking, anyway!

After our coffee and croissants, Donny took me outside his flat, and we walked down the high street. He told me just to look at the scenery. So I did, but I didn't quite know what I was supposed to be seeing. I'm good at observing things. Litze had trained me in observation techniques, to look at things that were out of the ordinary. He said that little details could save your life. It was the same as I saw from the view outside Walsh's apartment: the brick buildings grimy with years of pollution but that would have cost a king's ransom. The sprinkling of vegetation coexisting with the brickwork. The strange-shaped clouds with Latin names against a vibrant blue sky. It was early, so people were milling about, taking their usual Sunday stroll. But I still didn't understand what I was supposed to be seeing. He said that what I was looking at, which was the outside world, was just the visible part. That this was an illusion and we live in an illusionary world. And that what we see is a small fraction of what is there. Just like the dark web. He said that when we go online, that's only one five-hundredth of what is available on the Internet. And what we experience is the tip of the iceberg. I asked him what was there. And he said that I didn't want to know. But when someone says that to me, that's practically an invitation to find out. And anyway, Donny didn't know of the world I was part of. At least I assumed so. I'd seen the worst of humankind in my underworld, and I think you need a bit of depravity yourself to be able to function in it but at the same time be able to detach yourself from it. For the most part, Litze manages to do that, but that's after some years of experience and self-reflection. We're both on different stages of our journey.

The dark net, aptly called, expresses the best and the worst of us. Some parts of which are too graphic to mention. Think of your worst nightmare and multiply it by a number with at least fifteen zeros, and you'll get the picture. Not only is the devil in the details, but he's already set up shop on the dark web. But it made me realise that my depravity is relative. And compared to some of the things I've seen, I'm a fucking amateur. It's as if the dark web is a canvas, a Pandora's box where dreams and nightmares can occur at the same time. And part of me was grateful for this virtual world, as it helped recalibrate the thoughts I had about myself. It made this assassin look like Bambi in the woods.

Looking back, I wonder whether Donny knew that I would investigate, despite his warning. In all probability, I think he did. Maybe he meant, 'You don't want to know, but maybe you should.' They say ignorance is bliss. If that's the case, then why are some people still unhappy? Some things I discovered on the dark net could be useful to my business going forward. I figured out that there are assassin sites available. You can offer your services for a price, and all the payments are untraceable. And you could be paid in bitcoins, though to this day, I still don't understand what they're about.

And you could state your terms. Some people drew the line at children and world leaders.

Others didn't.

They didn't know what the line was, and that disturbed even me. But it got me thinking: the dark net is open to everyone, so there was more than a strong possibility that this would be perfect cover around the world for governments to do off-the-books operations. This would be ideal, as there would be no blowback. The dark net is a virtual Wild West, where literally anything goes. And maybe I was naive. I wondered how many of the contracts that I'd been involved with came through the dark web. I was an off-the-books assassin, so it would make sense. Clients don't want to associate with us. We wouldn't exactly be on most people's Christmas card lists.

Whether I like it or not, we're all connected to this, one way or another.

The dark web is just an analogy for what lies beneath in most human beings. What we see, the visible, is an illusion. We think we know, but the more you know, the less you know. But maybe that's the point: the invisible is the part we keep hidden from most people, and we operate in superficiality. Who, after all, wants to know that their husband has been secretly banging their best friend, his secretary, or black-book assassins? Or what governments do behind the scenes, in our name? Or the little white lies we tell each other and ourselves to pretend that everything is OK? Whoever said honesty is the best policy didn't live in the world and came from an admirable idealism that would melt as quickly as a snowdrop in hell.

And I worried about Donny. How dark had he gone? What had he gotten himself into? Was my concern misguided? He was a grown man, and he could take care of himself. I knew it was none of my damn business, but I was a meddling bitch and my ego got in the way. I didn't want to lose him, but my dysfunction prevented me from telling him how I felt. Yes, I could play that old record and say that it was my upbringing. But my remnants of honesty just mocked me.

I was just a chicken shit who killed people.

THIRTY-NINE

FRANK'S INTERNET CAFÉ is one of two in the city of Bad Kreuzberg that we visit to contact Purple Dawn. We leave Litze's flat around 9.00am. Three days after I learned of my old friend's death. I'm still not with it and I'm having trouble focusing, and I'm still not eating or sleeping properly. Litze doesn't have a full-sized computer at home, just his Kindle. So here is as good a place as any. To access the cyber-hacking group, we have to go onto the dark web. From what I remember from my late friend Walsh—and from what I could follow, because he could get overly technical—the dark net can be accessed via specific software, configurations, or authorization.

We park outside the yellow Postbank building, and Litze puts change into the parking machine for an hour of time. But I can't think we'll need that long. I look ahead and see the sign for Frank's Internet Café in red on a faded off-white background, written in a retro-futuristic computer-style typeface, which looks like something from the seventies. To the left of the building is Bad Kreuzberg's main train station, which dominates the foreground with its glass and grey-brick exterior, which expels and ingests commuters at a steady pace.

We approach the café and walk into the dimly lit interior, illuminated by some of the computer screens and soft lighting. What hits me first are the smells of coffee and the residual body odour of previous customers. Maybe that's part of its appeal, in that it's earthy and not too clinical. Litze nods to Frank, the owner, who has a full face with huge stippled red cheeks and looks like he could be a member of ZZ Top, with an enormous greying beard, which reaches to and rests on the counter. He's wearing a baseball cap and sunglasses. They exchange a few words; Frank gives me a cursory glance, then Litze and I walk to a private booth with a flat-screen computer. The space is a rectangular shape with, I estimate, about twenty-eight flat-screen machines hung on the centre partition.

I pull up another chair and sit next to Litze, and he moves the mouse, which lights the screen. Litze goes to the Tor website and downloads the software, which will enable him to contact Purple Dawn and protect his anonymity. It's slow today, but this isn't that unusual for this software, so I've been told. He finally gets to a white screen with a purple horizontal rectangular panel, which is landscape and two-thirds up the white background; I assume this is the Purple Dawn website. Litze types in his user name, 'SilverFox', without spaces, and his password on the top right of the screen. After a short pause, a message saying, 'Welcome back, Silver Fox', appears above the purple panel. The chat adviser introduces themselves as 'Maverick Spirit'. Then a message appears asking how they can help. Litze types in the words 'What do you know about Karl Yumeni?' After a pause, the screen goes into 'think' mode as a purple dotted circle appears, rotating clockwise. This seems to me to take ages, or that could just be my impatience.

Litze tells me to grab some coffees, so I go to the counter, where I see a couple of scruffy-haired young boys dressed in ripped jeans and baggy jumpers, who look like students. They're paying for Internet access and some drinks. After Frank finishes with them, he asks for my order, which is two black coffees. He puts some beans into the machine and soon it gargles, spits, and hisses. Frank says he'll bring it over, but I prefer to wait for it. He serves the drinks in medium-sized white mugs. I offer to pay, but Franks tells me to settle at the end, once we've finished on the computer.

I return to the private booth and place Litze's coffee to the right of the keyboard. The computer is still slow. Litze says that it isn't usually like this, Purple Dawn have usually been more reliable, but he assures me that there's nothing to worry about. At this rate, I'm starting to wonder whether an hour for parking will be enough. I ask him why he doesn't go onto the site that looks like a fake Wikipedia page or the other sites on the dark web. Litze says that he trusts his source and that even on here, his enquiry might be too risky. There are many, as he calls them, opportunists, scammers, or whack-jobs claiming to know stuff or selling false information. It seems that the real and the dark web have at least one thing in common.

I hear the front door open as more people enter the café. I'm glad we're in a private booth. And I start to think, why would Litze do his search here, in an Internet café? It doesn't seem that discreet to me. The owner must know Litze very well, hence the private booth, and his communications are encrypted, so there'll be no comeback. Since Litze has no computer at home, this is his best option. But I'm assuming here as my tech knowledge is limited, to say the least.

Litze frowns at the computer as the screen goes purple. It seems like my impatience is catching as he fixes his gaze on the machine like he's willing it to speed up. I sense this hasn't happened before and that something is wrong. Litze moves the mouse a few times in a vain attempt to refresh the screen, but there's no response. We just watch and wait. I check the time; we've already been here thirty minutes. Litze tells me that this hasn't happened before and is now worried that he's gone too far with his request. He felt that he'd built up some trust with Purple Dawn but now feels he may have jeopardised it.

Eventually, the purple screen dissolves and a message in bold black writing appears which simply says: 'Sorry, this is not our fight.'

FORTY

LITZE SLUMPS BACK in his chair. He pauses for a moment and takes a mouthful of black coffee. I look at the screen, not in disappointment, but in confusion.

'But this doesn't tell us anything', I say, not hiding my frustration.

'You're wrong, Becker, this tells us everything', says Litze as he types 'Thank you' into the purple panel, then logs off.

'I don't understand.'

'Whatever you're involved in, Becker, you're already in way over your head.'

'I suspected that when I got ambushed.'

'You don't get it, Becker. If this cyber-hacking group doesn't want to get involved, there's a good reason.'

'Could it be self-interest?'

'Maybe, but I don't sense they would have much to fear. Purple Dawn can take care of themselves, I'm sure. This is about something else.'

'But what?'

'Purple Dawn's message confirms that Karl Yumeni is not bad news, he's the worst news.'

'But if he's bad news and if Purple Dawn are the good guys, why won't they help you?'

'It's about choosing your battles. Becker, contrary to what some people believe, not all hacking groups are as reckless as some think. What they release to the public has ramifications for years. They said it's not their fight for a reason. They didn't warn me to back off, although most people in their right minds would. They've left it down to my choice, but they're staying out of it.'

'What do you think Purple Dawn know?'

'To me, it looks like they've spotted some pattern of activity that doesn't sound right. If Yumeni is into terrorism, then we don't know what his network is. This could be anything.'

'You think that Purple Dawn want to stay out of it because they're afraid that they'll make things worse?'

'I have no idea. Maybe they did this before and got their fingers burned. Who knows?'

'You seem reasonably calm about this.'

'What do you expect me to do, jump up and scream? Becker, my relationship with Purple Dawn is a new one. I'm grateful for the fact that I've got this much information as it is. In the early days, it was a few minutes. Then the amount of time they spent with me got longer. It shows that they are beginning to trust me. But as with any relationship, trust has to be earned. Purple Dawn drip-feed me information for a reason. They want to know what I'll do with it. This is about trust. In a way, you could say this is a test. I just hope I haven't undone our relationship by making this enquiry. But I had to try.'

I say nothing.

I take a sip of my cold coffee as my mind spins, trying to work out how far this rabbit hole goes. I replay the last few days before the mission. The training, the briefings, and what we weren't told, as it turns out. This was no simple snatch operation, and I wish my greed didn't get the better of me.

'I feel like we're working blind', I say to Litze.

'I know what you mean, but I don't think it will be too difficult to figure out. We are aware that Yumeni is a high-priority target. And from what I can tell, he knows stuff. So he's useful and dangerous at the same time. Is there anything in your Coba briefings that could help us?'

'No. Coba was very minimal when it came to information. I thought they were holding back, but now I feel that they didn't know much about the target either. I don't even believe they knew who the real client was. Coba's eagerness to please and their greed got the better of them too.'

'This goes back to Karl Yumeni', says Litze as he sits upright in his chair and finishes his coffee. 'Whoever he is, he's being protected, and we've been blocked at every turn. He's too hot at the moment, and your ambush proves that. So we need to find a way to draw him out.'

'How?'

'If he's on the most wanted list, someone will know something. We just need to shake enough trees. Word will get to Yumeni that we're after him. And judging by what's happened so far, self-preservation will be high on his list. When all else fails, you can't beat good old-fashioned intelligence on the ground. I know just the person.'

'Who?'

'Someone whom I don't usually deal with.'

'Friend or foe?'

'Neither. He's a businessman. He trades in information.'

'Who is this person?'

'His name is Wenzlov Holz.'

'And?'

'And if you're visiting a man like him, then things must be really bad.'

FORTY-ONE

EVEN THOUGH BAD Kreuzberg is so quiet, you'd have to make an appointment to get mugged, Litze decides it's no longer safe to return to his flat. Especially now he knows that we're in deep. He won't risk bringing a shitstorm to the place that's been his home for many years, so we drive to a safe house a few miles away. We leave the Internet café with more questions than answers. And I have a hard time switching off. The redacted files from Coba should have told me everything I needed to know. Which was not to walk, but to run! I'm facing an enemy that's bigger than I can comprehend, and my underdog status is now becoming annoying.

The new location is basic. It looks modern compared to Litze's apartment. It has dulled grey walls, without pictures, and a fresh smell, and it's situated in an even quieter suburb north of Bad Kreuzberg. Litze comes in from the kitchen with a tray of freshly made coffee. He likes it strong, so the caffeine surge isn't going to help my agitation. But some things are worth sacrificing for the taste of good coffee. He sets the tray on the coffee table and pours coffee into the delicate, white china cups. We take small sips almost simultaneously. Litze places his cup back on the tray and takes out his phone from his inside pocket. He scrolls through the contacts in his phone book. Then his eyes settle on his phone for what seems a while. And now I'm intrigued about Wenzlov Holz, so I press my mentor for more information.

Litze tells me that Wenzlov Holz is the guy you go to if all else fails. Like going to a loan shark who charges stupidly high interest when the banks won't touch you, but worse. Holz is around fifty years old and has been in and out of prisons since he was fifteen. He honed his skills as a trader at school, where he used to be bullied. The kids liked the fact that Holz knew things or could get information. That's how he developed his organisation. Over time, he employed a team of researchers for the sole purpose of getting information that people would want. Like a Google for the criminal underworld. And none of his researchers ever knew or met each other. This kept his organisation focused, and he was the common denominator. People come to him. You ask for information; he decides what it's worth. It could be guns, girls, boys, drugs, or selling someone out.

If you displease him or insult his intelligence, he can get nasty. Some have gone into his organisation wanting to trade information, and what they've offered is so laughable, they've come out minus a limb or an organ, or not come out at all. So you must be desperate to see him. But are we? Litze seems to think so. And I'm beginning to agree with him. Yumeni is protected by walls within walls, and we need a Trojan horse to get in. You'd think that a man like Holz would be in extreme danger, but that's not the case. Not only is he heavily protected, the thing that protects him the most is information. He knows everything about everybody, which makes him dangerous.

Litze tells me that he's only visited Holz twice before. You visit him when pragmatism kicks in. Some would say you see a guy like Holz when you've lost your mind, or you have your heart in your hand, or when your soul is worth nothing. Litze looks at Holz's number one last time before he sends a text. He gets a reply soon after, and we're in. And I wonder what we have to trade.

***

The next morning, we leave the safe house and drive north to another town called Traisen am Main. We park on the outskirts of the city. The landscape has the bland, bleak, metallic quality of heavy manufacturing about it. Litze drives to an industrial estate, stops, and studies the colour-coded map at the open-gated entrance. The warehouses vary in colour and size. Some are pristine. Others not so. We drive through and finally arrive at a unit at the end of the industrial estate and park just outside. It's too secluded for my liking. I would say it's even risky, but I have to trust that Litze knows what he's doing. The fact that he's come out of this place twice before proves that he does. I'm hoping that it's not third time unlucky.

We walk up to a blue metallic door, rusted at the hinges and the edges. Litze presses a button on the intercom, which squawks like a high-pitched crow as a muffled voice asks us to identify ourselves. Litze responds, and after a long pause, the door buzzes open. A giant man with a sandpaper-textured beard and short dark hair appears behind it. He's dressed in a black suit and open-necked shirt, rather like a nightclub bouncer would wear. He waves us through a dimly lit corridor and into a small side room. We both have our arms outstretched as the big man searches us. I don't like being unarmed. I think that I should be worried, but Litze doesn't seem to be, which reassures me to a point. Apart from two blue plastic chairs and a white table, the room is bare. The big man gestures to us to sit down and leaves the room. I look at Litze and wonder what this is all about, but his expression gives nothing away. He did say he had had dealings with Holz before, but I haven't, so you can forgive my apprehension.

We've been in the room for about fifteen minutes when the big man returns. He takes us back outside to an awaiting black SUV and produces two canvas hoods for us to put on. Litze senses my discomfort. He looks at me and nods reassuringly, so I decide to trust him. Litze hasn't let me down before. If anything, he has more right to distrust me than the other way around. We sit in the rear of the SUV and place the hoods over our heads; they smell used, but at least I can breathe. I guess I can understand the caution. It's kept Wenzlov alive so far, but some people will want to kill him for the hell of it. He's made many enemies, and nobody is exempt from karma.

***

I feel the car's undulations as it drives on different surfaces, and I can't help trying to work out where we're going. We're not speeding; I can tell that much. I can sometimes hear light or heavy traffic, but nothing about the route seems out of the ordinary. No telltale signs of train noises or factory horns. I don't even have smells to rely on, apart from the hood, which feels itchy on my skin. The SUV isn't exactly soundproof, but it masks most of the exterior noises which I guess is the point. It's also hard to work out how long the journey takes, but my internal clock is usually quite good. In the end, it feels like it's taken at least forty-five minutes to an hour.

The SUV eases to a stop, and we are led out by the big guy. We remove our hoods. The light assaults our eyes, causing us to squint before they eventually adjust. I can see another industrial warehouse estate just like before, but with fewer units this time. We follow the big guy towards a white building that looks like a row of sugar cubes stuck together, with neatly arranged, pristine windows and a double door in the centre. The keypad sings as he presses it four times, and we then follow the big man.

We walk up one flight of stairs, through another key padded door, and into an office complex.

Behind the reception counter, there's a stunning-looking girl dressed in a school uniform. And she's chewing gum, as if somehow that's part of the act. She has spiky purple hair and angular features. You could say she has an androgynous look. Her eyes, highlighted with black eyeliner, stand out against her white skin, making her look like a panda. Her open white shirt reveals traces of her black bra struggling to contain her ample breasts. And her short sleeves show tattooed arms that have forgotten they once showed any bare skin, which suit her look. Her black-and-gold striped tie is knotted thick and worn as a medallion around her neck, and I can see one of her ripped-fishnet-stockinged legs poking out from the side of the counter. She's wearing gloss-polished black platform boots that are so high, you would need altitude training just to wear them.

She looks at us, then picks up the phone to inform her boss that his appointment has arrived.

The big man takes us through a busy open-plan office with workers fixed at their computers. Then we walk towards a tall, thin man wearing a grey suit that hangs off him like he's made of wire. His thin skin looks taut against his hard face. His eyes are sunken and menacing at the same time. He smiles at Litze. But it doesn't look like the greeting of an old friend. It looks like one of smug satisfaction. As we reach the thin man, he shows us into his office, where two of his black-suited associates are standing at the rear. Then he kneels and puts his right hand on the floor. He pretends to shiver as he says, 'I'm just checking the temperature, Litze. Hell must have frozen over for you to come back to see the likes of me again.'

FORTY-TWO

WENZLOV HOLZ GETS up from the floor and nods to the big man, who leaves the room.

'Sit', says Holz.

'I prefer to stand', says Litze, and I instinctively stay on my feet.

'As you wish', says Holz, who sits behind a large wooden table. His associates remain standing either side of him. The office is neat-freak clean. There is a phone and a big scribble pad on the table, along with a self-contained flat-screen computer; two grey, medium-size filing cabinets are on either side of the table, and there's a black leather couch on the left.

'So Litze, what can I do for you?' asks Holz. He doesn't acknowledge me.

'Karl Yumeni.'

Holz looks at Litze impassively. 'Is that supposed to mean something to me?' he asks.

'Cut the shit, Holz, you're the go-to man. What you don't know isn't worth knowing.'

Holz pauses for a moment, then replies, 'OK. You're right, Litze. I am the go-to man. What do you want with him?'

'We want to bring him in.'

Holz looks at Litze for a moment, then laughs. So do his

associates, as if it's part of their job description.

Litze says nothing. He just looks at Holz, who stops laughing, and so do his men, right on cue.

'Why?'

'We have reasons to believe he's the head of a terrorist cell and planning an attack in Europe, maybe here in Germany, but you already know that.'

Holz says nothing.

'So you want me to tell you where he is?'

'Yes.'

'Do you have any idea what you're asking, Litze?'

'Enlighten me, Holz.'

'You can't just come walking in here asking for a guy like him.'

'I know, which is why I'm here in the first place. If there were any other way, I would've tried it. We can't even get anything on the dark web on this guy. You're the last resort.'

Holz pauses for a while, drumming the table with his fingers and swivelling on his chair.

'OK, Litze. Just suppose for one moment I know something about this Yumeni guy. What's in it for me?'

'That's something you normally decide, remember?'

'Yeah, you're right. I do, and it isn't always something of monetary value.'

'I remember, Holz. You can do some sick, twisted shit.'

'Now, now, Litze. Please modify your language, especially while there's a lady present.' He can't possibly be referring to me. 'And who is this?' asks Holz, staring at me for the first time.

'A trusted associate of mine', says Litze. Again, he can't possibly be referring to me.

'This associate has a name?'

'Sam Becker', I say.

'This is the point where I feign surprise.' He smiles. 'But I deduced that. I'm glad you didn't lie, which I appreciate', says Holz as he asks one of his associates to hand him a brown folder from one of the cabinets. 'I took the liberty of checking on you, Becker. I read your file. You couldn't make this stuff up. A walking tornado. You trained her, is that right?' he says, looking up at Litze.

'Yes', he says.

Holz looks down and thumbs through the file. 'You went rogue eight years ago? Hmm, that would explain everything. The recklessness, the fuck-ups. And you still call her a trusted associate?' he says, looking at Litze. 'I like your optimism, misguided though it is. There's a rumour that she shot you once, is that right?'

Litze says nothing.

I don't like the fact that Holz knows so much about me.

'This leap of faith is touching. But coming here asking for Karl Yumeni when many would hesitate to mention his name . . . You have some balls, Litze. Especially as you know that this motherfucker is as bad as it gets', says Holz, closing the file.

'You love a challenge, Holz. That's why you run this operation. You like the buzz. If you can't or won't help us, then we'll be on our way', says Litze as he turns to leave.

'Not so fast, Litze', says Holz as he rises from his chair. 'You're here now. So let me see if I've got this right: you want me to get you to Yumeni so you can get him?'

'Something like that.'

'To kill him?'

'If we have to.'

'Do you realise what a shitstorm that could bring?'

'I think we're getting the idea.'

Holz looks at Litze for a beat as he clasps his hands. 'So what are you going to offer me?' he asks.

'Like I said, you decide. You always have.'

'It's hard to put a monetary value on something like this. I know people who would pay a fortune to get their hands on Yumeni. And I don't think that you have that kind of money. So I'm wondering, what do you have to trade if it isn't money?'

Litze says nothing.

'This is different. This is Yumeni you're talking about. You're the one who wants him. There must be something you're willing to trade. Something that is priceless to you. Litze, you wouldn't come in here if you didn't have some idea of what you're willing to risk. I know you too well. Are you expecting me to work out what that is? Or are you afraid to tell me?'

Litze says nothing.

Holz looks at Litze for a long time, trying to read him. Then he looks at me and smiles. Now I know why Litze didn't say anything before. I have a sick feeling in my stomach.

FORTY-THREE

'BECKER IS THE trade', Holz says, smiling, as Litze looks at me. I hope he has a plan. I hope this is a joke, but I don't see him or anyone laughing.

'Yes', says Litze.

'I bet you didn't see that coming, Becker', says Holz. 'But from what I hear, that's an occupational hazard.'

My palms are sweating. My heart is racing.

'Remember the last time we traded? I offered you one of my best agents.'

'Yes, I remember. It was a cage fight that time. You put him up against one of my best fighters. That was unfortunate. Very unfortunate indeed. Is he still eating through a straw?'

Litze says nothing.

'So you think your girl can go one better than the last time?'

'Yes, I do', says Litze. 'I say that Becker will beat anybody you put in front of her.'

'Really?'

'Really.'

'You said that last time.'

'This will be a different outcome.'

'You think so?'

'I do.'

'I didn't think less of you, Litze, when you lost. It was just one of those things. This isn't your way of getting payback?'

'No. If Becker wins, I get the information that I came for. If she doesn't, I get nothing.'

'It won't be nothing, Litze. You could get your girl back eating through a straw, or worse. Our people will play with her for a while; as you know, Litze, I'm a voyeur. I like to watch. And we'll film it. I might even add her to my private collection of X-rated videos. Or I might decide to sell it. I know clients would pay a fortune for that. Do you really want to do this?'

'Yes', says Litze, not looking at me.

Holz pauses for a moment, then continues, 'If the rumours are true, she did try to kill you once before, so you don't exactly owe her.'

Litze says nothing.

I now understand why Litze has done this without telling me. I may not have agreed to this, and it has to be convincing enough for Holz to believe that I've been set up.

I look at Litze, and he looks at me. If there's a trace of remorse in his eyes, he hides it well.

'Can you excuse us for a minute?' says Holz as he goes to the rear of the room to talk to his associates.

Litze and I don't look at each other as Holz and his men huddle and whisper conspiratorially. After a while, they break and resume their original positions.

'OK', says Holz. 'You know I like a good contest. You're a man after my own heart. Yumeni is priceless. The fact that you're prepared to offer Becker proves you're serious. We like your proposal very much indeed. But owing to the extreme circumstances—the fact that this is Karl Yumeni we're talking about here, and not some low-level criminal, and the fact that this is Sam Becker—we're going to up the stakes.'

I look at Holz; then I look at Litze.

'Becker will fight three of our best people, at the same time', Holz says with a smile.

'Deal!' says Litze.

FORTY-FOUR

LITZE AND I don't speak to each other. There's no point now. I understand what he's doing. And to be honest, in his position, I might have done the same thing. Karl Yumeni is a high-value target, and Litze doesn't have enough money to offer Holz. But a man like him has so much anyway, what else could you offer him? Apparently, Holz is a big fight fan and has always been interested in boxing and mixed martial arts, more as a voyeur than a participant. He owns one of the largest collections of sporting memorabilia in the world. Holz beams with pride as he shows us his private collection in a special vaulted room in his warehouse facility. His haul is stunning. It must have taken years to amass this collection. He has baseball, American football, golf, and soccer items, which span at least nine decades. But his thing is fighting. The room looks like a who's who, with all the good and the great from among fighters of all styles, male and female. He has boxing belts; early archive films of Muhammad Ali; interviews; magazines; black belts; samurai swords; Gracie brothers posters; Bruce Lee's nunchakus; photographs, some framed and autographed; early fight contracts; trophies; scorecards; some of the original boxing gloves; fight programmes; and rare tickets. Holz tells us that he never attends these auctions and prefers to use an agent to act on his behalf.

He organises some of the best underground bouts in the Rheinland-Pfalz region. All illegal. All off the books. And I start to wonder what happened to the agent Litze sent in before, whom they crippled. Litze can be ruthless when he has to be. Yumeni has to be put down like a dog, and we have to take him down, even if it means sacrificing everything, including me.

Then I wonder about his late wife and the sacrifices they made. And the cost to him personally. I sometimes felt he took out his grief over his late wife Silke on me during my training, though he'd never admit it. When you're backed into a corner, use any leverage you have. He taught me that. He said that everybody has a weak spot, and for him, it was about getting the job done. It must be hard for Litze to get his hands dirty while keeping his soul clean.

Holz ends his guided tour, and we return to his office. Litze looks at me and nods gently before I prepare for my fight. It's his way of saying good luck. He doesn't want to say too much. This is what I'm trained for. And I don't have the time or luxury to think about how I feel about this right now. The big man comes into the room and shows me into another, smaller office. He tells me that the fight will be in an hour, which gives me enough time to meditate. Plenty of time in fact. I sit on the chair and close my eyes. I focus on my breath and allow whatever thoughts I have, good or bad, to come into my head, like a detached observer. Many of my instructors have told me that if you're attached to the outcome, you've lost the fight. I know that my best chance is to fight regardless of the outcome. The last guy let Litze down; maybe it's an opportunity to redeem some of his reputation, and for me to repay his faith in me.

***

The big man returns to the room and says that everything is ready for me. I silently follow him downstairs. We walk through a series of corridors, through two sets of double doors, and into a custom-made space with mats on the floor bathed in the glow of the yellow light from above. I thought it would be a ring, but it isn't. I've been taught to fight in open and confined spaces, but given my numerical disadvantage, an open space is probably better. I see Litze and Holz emerge together from the dark perimeter. I look at Litze, but he just looks through me. Then I see the three fighters. Two men and a woman. They swagger confidently towards me in a line, shadow-boxing at the same time. They certainly look the part. The men are tall and action-hero bald, like clones of each other. Both are wiry, dressed in grey sweat tops and bottoms, wearing trainers. The girl, who is slightly smaller, looks like she could feature on the cover of one of those fitness muscle magazines, with her black Nike top and matching tight bottoms. She has cold, peephole eyes, and her hair is tied back, which accentuates her hard features.

This isn't a fair fight.

Litze knows it.

Holz knows it.

I know it too.

But that depends on which side of the fence you're sitting on. If you believe in numerical advantage, then it's unfair. If you believe in numerical advantage with competent fighting skills, then it's unfair. If, however, you have superior fighting skills, despite having a numerical disadvantage, then that's a completely different story. Like the stories some of my SAS contacts used to talk about where there were eight of them against three hundred in Afghanistan and they still managed to fight off the enemy. It wasn't the dog in the fight, it was the fight in the dog, as they say.

The fight lasts fifteen seconds. I feel sorry about that. One, because I expended more energy than I wanted to, and two, because it proves to Litze that I've gotten rusty. And I don't want him to tell me 'I told you so.' A better-prepared Sam Becker, who'd kept up her practice, would have finished it in less than ten seconds. I remembered everything that my mentor taught me and went to work. This time, I was the one with the remote control. I slowed them down and sped them up when it suited me. I've been told that when I fight, I have this cold, glazed expression in my eyes. Like a lion that's looking forward to supper. And these three saw it too. I could tell in their faces. Despite their numerical advantage, there was doubt in their eyes. And I put it there. That fed me like coke feeds an addict.

Like I said before, I'm not an aesthetic fighter. I'm a dirty, ugly fighter who wants to get the job done. Holz thought he was clever when he got his so-called three best fighters up against me. All he showed was his desperation to win at all costs. And if he were that confident, he would have put up his best fighter, not all three. For all his fighting memorabilia and so-called knowledge, Holz knows jack shit about fighting. He wasn't to know that having someone like me fight more than one person is like inviting a porn star to an orgy. He also wasn't aware of the reason why Litze was impassive earlier. But I was. It wasn't because he was worried about the outcome. He was trying his hardest not to laugh.

You could say that I've gone soft or I've changed in some way, because although I beat up these three pretty good—broken bones mainly—at least they're not eating through a straw. I showed mercy.

What's happening to me?

FORTY-FIVE

HOLZ GIVES US the information we want, even though he does it begrudgingly. The fact that we're allowed to walk out of his warehouse alive shows how much Holz respects my mentor. Even though he lost, a deal is a deal. Very old school and quaint. I like that way of doing business. If only I could find more people who do things that way. It isn't much of a lead, but given we were drawing blanks before, it's better than nothing. It's better than what we got from Purple Dawn, which was nothing.

Karl Yumeni has been on Holz's radar for some time. But even he had trouble getting information, which makes me more curious. Sometimes what people don't say can tell you more than what they do. Nothing of any worth came up on the usual databases. Breadcrumbs. But you got the feeling they were laid there deliberately to mislead rather than inform. Which seems to suggest that an unknown entity, with unlimited resources, is protecting him. But why?

The lead Holz gave us is a location ninety kilometres north of here near a town called Idstein. There's no guarantee of Yumeni's whereabouts. It could be another dead end. But it's the best bit of bread we could find. It's the last known information about someone who looks like him. This was picked up from one of the satellites that

Holz's organisation has been monitoring. There was some activity over an eight-month period. Lorries have been travelling to this place about once every two weeks from various places, but other than that, it's vague. But what is interesting is the location. The trucks have been parked outside a secret warehouse facility which is listed privately as AXAS Gmbh, which means absolutely nothing to me.

Holz found a back door into their security system, which allows him to trace the people behind AXAS. Because whoever they are don't want to be found. They did a good job hiding their tracks, as Holz tells us that it took one of his spotty tech wizards more than half a day to break through the encrypted files. He eventually discovered that AXAS is a shell company for pharmaceutical giant Huxcor, a US-based company that is over a hundred years old and manufactures all types of cancer drugs and migraine tablets. From what I know, they have a clean record. But what do I know? Big bad pharma has a habit of doing things. And I'm wondering what's the connection between Yumeni and a major drug company. If they're connected, then Huxcor won't want to advertise the fact; that's clear. This won't be the first time that a big drug company has gotten itself into shit, and I guess it won't be the last. But links to terrorism?

When you get to the point where nothing surprises you anymore, that's scary.

FORTY-SIX

'YOU DO UNDERSTAND why I couldn't tell you earlier about the fight?' says Litze after the big guy drives us back to our car. Litze takes the wheel and we head north.

'Yes. You were trying to give the impression that you were ruthless. I think you succeeded.'

'Holz feeds off mind games. He's twisted like that. If he got any idea that this was prearranged, that could have blown the whole deal, and we would have got nothing. You do know that?'

'I do. And he read my discomfort, even though I tried to hide it.'

'I think you did well under the circumstances. If it's any consolation, Becker, I had complete faith in you.'

'Thanks. I think.'

'You don't believe me?'

'To be honest, with someone like you, I don't always know what to believe. But I understand it's your way of keeping your agents on their toes.'

'Well, I'm glad you understand that. It's a shame the other agent didn't.'

'You mean the man you sent in before me?'

'Yes.'

'What happened?'

'He got cocky. He thought he was at the top of the mountain, but there's no such thing as the top. He needed to be taught a lesson.'

'So you threw him off the mountain and into the ravine?'

'Something like that.'

'Where is he now?'

'He's receiving the best of care. But he won't be climbing mountains any time soon.'

I look straight at my mentor for a while.

'What?' he says.

'Is that what would have happened to me if I'd stayed at the Facility?'

He says nothing.

***

We've been driving for a while before I register my aches and pains. That's what being pumped up does to you. I look at my bruised and shaking hands. The nerves are something that I've experienced more as I've gotten older. And my drinking doesn't seem to help much.

We turn into a service station with a shopping complex. Litze must have read my mind, or heard my stomach, as I'm now hungry. We walk into the café at the rear of the building and order two tuna melts with black coffee. We talk about everything and nothing. Something we've never done before. I was young when I left the Facility and probably didn't have anything to say then. But eight years is a lot of conversation material for both of us. And we people-watch, one of my favourite pastimes between assignments when I go out on my own, which is more often than not. The clientele comprises everything from truck drivers to families to office workers. The tuna melts don't sate our appetites, so we order more coffee and cake, which Litze will make me work off in our training sessions, that's for sure. He tells me about how he's kept himself busy over the years by teaching German and English to international students. It's not great money, but Litze likes the mental stimulation. I'm about to ask him something, but he is momentarily distracted. He looks out of the window of the café behind me. Then I turn around and see four men in the car park. And they don't look friendly. They look like bad news. The worst kind of news. It's starting. I just hope I'm in good enough shape so that I can do my mentor justice.

FORTY-SEVEN

THE FOUR MEN walk across the forecourt and head our direction.

'Easy', says Litze as I instinctively prepare myself to fight, and he gently squeezes my arm, pulling me back to my seat. The men are walking in a line and wearing suits and open-neck white shirts. They look nondescript with their crew-cut hairstyles in various shades of blond, except for the one in front, who I assume is the leader. He has dark hair. Medium build. Just short of six foot. He gestures for his men to wait with his right hand as he walks towards the café. Then other men stop and walk back in the opposite direction.

'Do you think they're for us?' I ask.

'Certainly', says Litze. 'I can't see anybody in here that would attract such a visit. And that's not me being paranoid. I've done this long enough to know. I told you about reading people. The telltale signs. It's the little things you should worry about, not the big stuff. They're too visible to be a kill squad.'

He's right. The café has few customers. Some couples and a family; nothing that would attract this kind of attention you would think, but nothing should be taken for granted. Not in this business.

I feel for my Glock pistol under my jacket. Litze does the same. It seems like a ridiculous routine as we know we're armed, but you know what they say about old habits.

'They may not be a kill squad, but they're not good news', I say.

'Yes, you're right, but I don't sense any immediate danger. Not yet.'

'What now?' I ask.

'We wait.'

The man with the dark hair sways through the main entrance. I get a closer look at him. I reckon he's in his late thirties with a skin colouring that suggests that it's not tan, but that he's got Spanish or maybe Italian heritage. He has a quiet confidence about him. He has a healthy head of black hair that appears to have defied the greying process so far, and sharp facial features, clean shaven with a square jaw and a nose unharmed by violence. He has a classic look that transcends time.

I scan the café to make sure it is us he's after. To the right, there's an old couple drinking soup. They seem harmless, but not prejudging is easier said than done. To the left, I see a very attractive younger couple who I'd say are in their mid-thirties, with a pram. They wouldn't look out of place on the cover of *Sports Illustrated* as they appear insanely fit. No doubt due to the combination of the gym and bedroom athletics. Either the baby is well behaved, or it could be a cover. It wouldn't be the first time a young couple with a kid has been used. I shot a similar couple on an assignment three years ago in Mexico. They smelt wrong. Like they were ham actors in a bad play. They were overacting, trying too hard. And luckily, as it turned out, my hunch was correct; there was no baby in the pram. Litze taught me to trust my instincts. If it seems too good to be true, it usually is.

The man turns his gaze to our table and walks towards us. 'Mind if I join you?' he asks.

Litze looks at me for a moment. I nod, then he nods an affirmative to the stranger. The man takes his seat with his back to the entrance opposite us. He gestures to one of the waitresses and orders a black coffee. He asks if we would like a drink, but we decline.

'You must be Herr Litze, which must make you Frau Becker', he says, cutting to the chase. He doesn't offer his hand.

'Who's asking?' I say. 'Let me guess, government agent?'

'Am I that obvious?' he asks.

'Not really. You dress better than most government agents I've known, but this isn't a social call, is it?'

'No, Frau Becker, you're right about that.'

'Why are you here?' Litze asks.

'To deliver a message.'

'Did Fleischmann send you?'

The man says nothing. Maybe because he's a bad liar, and Litze would know if he were lying by a mile.

'If you only wanted to deliver a message, why did you bring your boyfriends?' asks Litze.

'Well, you can't be too careful', laughs the man. 'You of all people should understand that.'

'Maybe I do. But are those goons outside to reinforce the message?' asks Litze.

'If I wanted to do that, do you think I'd come into a café with people in it on my own to meet two of the most dangerous people we have on file? This, of course, could be a double bluff to lull you both into a false sense of security, but I left my boyfriends outside as a show of good faith. We wouldn't want them to scratch your eyes out, would we? Some of us prefer force as the last option', he says, looking at me directly. What he's implying isn't subtle at all.

'Who's talking?' I say.

'Paul Sabatini', he says.

'But you are a government agent?' I ask.

'Yes.'

'Who do you work for?'

'I work for an organisation called D19.'

'D19? Never heard of them', I say.

'Nor have I', says Litze.

'That's the idea', says the man. The waitress brings over his coffee.

'So why are you here?' I ask.

'I'm aware we have a mutual interest: Herr Yumeni', he says. Litze and I look at each other momentarily, then I turn to him.

'And?' I ask.

'And we want you to back off.'

'Who's "we"?'

'I can't tell you', he says.

'Why?' asks Litze.

'I'm sorry, but that's classified information. I'm asking you to stay out of it.'

'Asking?' I say.

'According to your file, Becker, you don't like to be told. Asking sounds nicer than telling.'

'But you really mean telling, don't you?' I say.

Sabatini says nothing.

'You can't polish a turd, and you insult our intelligence by even trying', says Litze. 'You're not asking us, this is a threat, right?'

'OK, I prefer to call it a request, or if you want me to polish it a little more, a friendly warning, which sounds like an oxymoron, I know, but that's the best I can do', replies Sabatini.

'You don't look like a typical errand boy.'

'Thanks for the compliment. You're right; I'm not.' Sabatini takes a sip of coffee. 'I know all about you, Herr Litze. I requested this assignment personally. I'm a big fan of your work. Many of my colleagues are. Some consider you a legend. I came to see you out of professional courtesy.'

'You shouldn't believe everything you hear about legends', says Litze.

'You're too modest. The German government are grateful for what you've done for our country—the lives you've saved, the wars you've prevented.'

'But you're not here to give me an ego boost. You could've just sent a letter on that expensive government paper or given me a long-service medal. Why do you want us to back off?'

'Yumeni is politically sensitive at the moment.'

'How?' asks Litze.

'I can't tell you.'

'So that's code for if we expose him, the German government will be embarrassed?' asks Litze.

'If you want to look at it like that.'

'Is there any other way?' says Litze.

'I suppose not.'

'And if we don't back off?' I say.

'I'm trying to help you out here. You know how this ends. This will turn from friendly to unfriendly', says Sabatini. He faces me. 'I know about you too, Becker.'

'Then you know I won't back down.'

'Yes, I know. You have this reputation for being like nitroglycerine.'

'News travels fast', I say.

'Yes, Becker. Some people leave a carbon footprint, whereas you leave a chaos footprint', says Sabatini.

'But what if I agree with her? What if I don't want to back down either?' says Litze.

'Then I would be very, very disappointed, Herr Litze. Disappointed that you'd align yourself with Frau Becker. I'd think: How the mighty have fallen', says Sabatini as he drains his cup.

'Maybe your mistake, Sabatini', says Litze as he takes another sip of his coffee, 'was to think that I was mighty in the first place.'

'I'm asking you as one professional to another', says Sabatini.

'I'm telling you that we can't do that', says Litze.

Sabatini pauses for a moment, then continues. 'There's much more at stake than you can comprehend. Think of it as in regard to protecting national security.'

'Bullshit!' says Litze. 'National security is a convenient term. A guilt trip. Brainwashing. An attempt to make people feel unpatriotic and think they should be loyal puppies. That's the trouble with government: they believe that misdeeds are done by others. Do I look like I'm on a leash to you?'

'No', says Sabatini.

'Some things transcend so-called national security, like doing the right thing. The problem with you, Sabatini, is you've been too long behind a desk to know what that is', says Litze as he drinks some more coffee.

'I don't have to be here', says Sabatini. 'I'm trying to help both of you.'

'No, you're not. You're trying to save the asshole that sent you here in the first place, so let's be clear on that. If you want to help, you can assist us with our investigation. Yumeni is bad news, and he's up to something. Something big. I can feel it. And he's being protected. That's the really sad part. And if that's the case, then I'll bet my euros that money is behind it. Becker was getting too close. That's why she's in this mess. The fact that you're here proves that we're onto something. And whoever sent you clearly didn't read my file properly. If he had, you and he would have known that this would be a wasted journey', says Litze.

'I requested I speak to you personally. Herr Litze, walk away. You too, Frau Becker. You're both in over your heads', says Sabatini.

'But you've not told us anything. Nothing. If we ask questions, you'll say it's classified. You haven't given us a good enough reason to drop this. We know how this works: if we don't back down, you or some other interested party will kill us. But that works both ways, Sabatini. I know the game. If you want us to back down, you've got to do better than this false-charm offensive you've attempted.'

'What am I supposed to say or do?'

'You could tell us what this is really about', says Litze.

Sabatini says nothing.

There's a lull as the cute waitress comes over and asks if we want any more coffee. I shake my head and ask for the bill.

'I know why they call government officials paper pushers', says Litze. 'They use the documents as toilet paper for when they shit themselves, while people like us do the real work.'

Sabatini slowly gets up from his chair and looks through us like we're ghosts. He gets some money out and leaves it on the table.

He nods politely to both of us and walks to the exit.

'Litze, what now?' I ask.

'We're on high alert, that's what. But his visit is a sign.'

'How so?'

'Despite overwhelming odds, somebody out there is really worried about us. And that, Becker, isn't necessarily a bad thing.'

FORTY-EIGHT

I HOPE LITZE is right about Sabatini's boss being worried about us. But this can work in two ways: either the people after us will act with extreme caution, or they will be going in guns blazing regardless, without consideration for collateral damage. It depends on how badly they want to cover it up. Either way, this won't be a foregone conclusion for them. And I hate the idea of people thinking that they can take me down with a click of a finger. It's a lack of respect, and respect is something I've had to earn all my life. That Sabatini was here at all shows that they want to avoid confrontation. And they must have known that they don't have any leverage on either of us to make us change our minds.

If you're wondering about the 'boyfriend' comment that Litze made to Sabatini, he isn't homophobic. Litze is provocative. It's his way of getting a reaction. He used to do that with me all the time, and it was a way of trying to find out where someone was in their mental state. Some people would've reacted defensively, but to his credit, Sabatini laughed it off. Which could be a sign that he's comfortable in his skin, that he doesn't need to prove his so-called manhood. Which means that Sabatini is someone we have to take seriously. Even though the conversation didn't end in the way he hoped, I think Litze was secretly impressed with Sabatini. To be honest, I liked him too, but we may have to kill him, and it isn't good to get emotionally attached.

'How long do we have?' I ask.

'Difficult to say, but not long, I imagine', replies Litze.

'Do you have any leverage?'

'Yes and no, Becker. Remember I told you about that book *The Art of War*?'

'Yes, I remember.'

'Well you'll recall one of the main quotes, "All warfare is based on deception". Making people believe what you want. It's not necessarily about being a monster. It's about making others think that you are.'

'So you're telling me that for all these years I thought you were a mean sonofabitch, you were a pretend sonofabitch all along? If you were acting, I'd hate to see you when you were doing it for real.'

'Hilarious, Becker. I can be what I need to be. That's the point. A lot of my reputation has been built on myths that I've allowed to go unchecked because it suited me, and it made life a lot easier. Especially when getting cooperation. You should try it sometime.'

'I can be easy, don't you worry about that, but that's usually on a second date. Sometimes on a first, if they're lucky. I might even skip coffee if they're exceptional.'

'As I was saying', Litze says, shaking his head and trying not to laugh, 'the illusion is part of the reason why I've managed to keep this face from developing even more wrinkles. In the event of my death, I have an insurance policy in the form of audio and video tapes, papers, microfilm, illegal transactions.'

'But that won't necessarily stop them from killing us.'

'No, but it will give them something to think about. It's nice to know that sometimes you're worth more alive than dead.'

'Well, I hope for your sake that this information has been left with somebody reliable.'

'Becker, I've planned this for years, amongst other things.'

'Like what?'

'I've made a will for instance.'

I go silent at this stage. I haven't made one. It's not that I'm afraid of my mortality. That's part of an assassin's life. It's just that I have no one to leave my money to, and it's not something I've ever thought about. Maybe it's time I did. But that would mean making friends, getting close to people, being sociable, which feels like too much effort. Maybe I could donate to charity, but I don't even have a cause I believe in. The days when I did seem a long, long time ago.

'But we have to deal with the here and now', says Litze as he points to the window behind me. I turn on my seat and see Sabatini with his four men still waiting in the car. They look like they're talking amongst themselves. I wonder whether they are going to kill us here. I check out the entry points to the building. There'll be one at the rear of the building, and there'll be another in the kitchen area, which they will also know. But this is too public. It would be very embarrassing and difficult to explain.

They could claim that we were terrorists and fabricate a hostage situation. Easy enough to do and current. They have the resources to do it, but it depends on how badly they want us stopped. They have to balance the need to do this job efficiently with minimum comeback. That's never easy, and that's something that I haven't always been able to do. But that's why people like me are hired to take the fall when things go belly-up. The best individuals in this line of work are the ones you don't notice.

I watch them for a while longer and try to read their body language. I visualise myself in their car, trying to gauge the mood. I can tell they're contemplating something, but our chat with their boss seems to have done enough to deter them, as they drive out of the forecourt.

'The next time we see Sabatini, we won't be sipping coffee', says Litze.

'You can back out of this anytime', I say.

'And miss all the fun?' says Litze.

He doesn't bluff. When I was younger, I always thought that he had nerves of steel. But he did try to kill himself once. He's already reached his rock bottom. Losing his beloved wife would have altered his perspective. What else did he have to lose? That's why Sabatini wanted to talk sense into him. Whoever sent him knew of Litze's reputation for stubbornness. And mine for that matter. My mentor has powerful friends in the government, which is why he still has some influence. But I'm a nobody compared to him.

I'm lousy at cultivating relationships and have not exactly had the best role models. I used to think that diplomacy was elaborate bullshit or a sign of weakness. I now realise that it is an essential way of surviving in the world. Egos need to be stroked, and Litze is very charming at times when he wants something.

But I'm his blunt instrument. What I need to learn is that it isn't about being a stick. I have to offer the carrot. The problem with me is I'd still want to stab someone with the pointy end of the stick.

We look out of the café window. There are still cars and trucks parked on the forecourt. The flow of customers has slowed momentarily. So we wait until more customers come into the café. This won't make us such open targets. We order two more coffees and wait for about forty-five minutes. We discreetly check our weapons and decide to chance it and leave. It occurs to me that we could be cut down by a sniper, but our deaths would still be difficult to explain. And Litze is banking on his insurance policy. My gut tells me that the attempts on our lives won't be here.

'The thought of killing government agents doesn't fill me with great joy', says Litze. He looks serious this time.

'It's not a problem for me', I lie, 'especially if they get in the way.'

'OK, Becker, but it's a line we've both crossed before. Not that it's any consolation for me at least', says Litze as we leave, and I'm dizzy as I try to comprehend what kind of shitstorm I've gotten us into.

FORTY-NINE

I FEEL LIKE we're on a countdown and the clock is ticking. The clock has always been ticking, but it sounds louder than usual. Other times, it's like a subliminal murmur. But it's always there in the background. That's probably why I've been so reckless in the past. I live each day as though it is my last, because one day, it will be. And I wonder how Litze has dealt with this uncertainty. Then I realise uncertainty becomes your norm. You get comfortable with the uncomfortable. That's the life of an assassin. But our kind doesn't have exclusive rights to uncertainty. I've never really known anything different, even before I was a trained killer. I've had a sense that others can feel my restless energy. My soul tosses and turns like it's on a bed of rocks, never quite settling for any length of time.

Getting used to the uncomfortable is my way of dealing with the thought that a sniper tried to kill me sixteen days ago. Those are the tricks you play on your mind. But I realise I'm just delaying the inevitable as it will come to the surface. It's just another day in the life of Sam Becker. Coba will be after me too. I haven't called in, followed any of the protocols, and I've abandoned any idea of going to their safe houses. In this situation, we'll have the same objective, which is self-preservation, but we'll be on opposite sides now. How things turn so quickly.

We head towards Idstein to follow up Holz's lead. The midday sun illuminates the countryside as we weave through the traffic. Litze's Fiat isn't quiet, but it isn't too noisy. It makes a masculine; guttural sound and I can feel its vibration inside. Litze is a steady rather than spectacular driver, which is in stark contrast to me; I sometimes drive with reckless abandon. The afternoon traffic flows smoothly, and I'm glad that Litze is driving, so I don't have to readjust to travelling on the right side of the road as I've been so used to travelling on the left side, having lived in the UK for so long.

'You OK?' I ask Litze.

'Never felt better, Becker.'

'You still have time to back out of this if you want.'

'Not a chance.'

'I can think of much safer and more fun ways of getting my excitement.'

'I bet you can. At my age, Becker, I'll take all the excitement I can get. Anyway, I like being back in the game. It's good to feel useful again.'

'What did you think of Sabatini?'

'I liked him.'

'Do you think that he's torn?'

'Maybe. He said it's in the interests of national security. When I told him that was bullshit, I felt he agreed with me but couldn't say. He was toeing the party line. People like him, company men, are good at working for assholes because they know how to play them.'

'I couldn't stand being so politically correct and so self-contained. It would give me constipation.'

'I hear you, but like it or not, we need people like him in the world. I almost regret that comment about paper pushers. He was the messenger, and we shot him. The thing is, he knows he needs people like us too. That's how the world works.'

'If he knows your history, and he's aware of my reputation, then why bother making contact?'

'That's what I was thinking. He could just be the eternal optimist, or there could be another reason. We'll find out soon enough.'

Litze looks at me momentarily; then he glances at the rear-view mirror.

'Becker, have you been paying attention?'

'Attention to what?'

'Before we started talking. The last eight kilometres, a black Mercedes has been following us. We've got less time than I thought.'

FIFTY

I SEE THE black vehicle, three cars back, trembling in the right-hand wing mirror as it travels the autobahn. Then my eyes return to the road ahead. In my peripheral vision, I can see Litze discreetly checking the left and rear-view mirrors.

'Did you see the car?' he asks.

'Yes', I say, looking again to my right. The car hasn't closed the gap between us. 'How do you want to do this?' I ask.

'There are two cars between them and us. We'll maintain our pace before we move. Have your gun ready. And, Becker?'

'What?'

'Don't mess this up.'

We travel for about three kilometres, maintaining the distance between ourselves and the black Mercedes. It gleams as the rays of the sun caress the body. I didn't spot it, but Litze did. He was always good at noticing stuff like that, even when you thought his attention was somewhere else. He has a situational awareness that comes only from being a wise soul and from years of honed experience. It's the very same awareness that's kept him alive. We can't outrun our pursuers, but Litze will look to outwit them. He's always been a master at lulling others into a false sense of security.

Litze overtakes a large, orange haulage lorry. And I see through the passenger window that the black Mercedes has reacted; it's like a call and response.

Litze repeats the same move again, this time overtaking a blue Vauxhall sports car.

The result is the same.

Then Litze decides to up the speed. The old Fiat seems to offer more than it looks capable of. Just like its owner. We speed past some more cars in another slick overtaking manoeuvre. But Litze does nothing out of the ordinary. Nothing that suggests we know that we're being followed. I look in my mirror and the black Mercedes speeds up. I can't tell exactly what the distance is, but it's closer. It's hard to tell how many passengers there are without looking round, but I think there are maybe three in the car.

Litze tells me to get my gun ready. His hands glide over the steering wheel and gearstick, and his feet press the pedals, all in effortless syncopation, as the engine roars in response to the increased speed. He accelerates behind another lorry, then overtakes. I can feel the car's vibration transmit through to my body. Then Litze goes faster as he repeats the same moves. The engine revs and the red needles blur around the dials, twitching like nervous wrecks. Like he wants them to know that they've been spotted. He's taking the fight to them.

That's typical Litze.

The black Mercedes responds in kind, as if to say: We know you know.

We're using other vehicles as cover as we weave our way through the traffic. There's no point in either side keeping up with the pretence. We're both playing a dangerous game as Litze wants to know how far these hunters will go. There is potential for collateral damage on this autobahn. I'm sure we'll find out soon enough, as the black Mercedes accelerates. It wants to come alongside of us and attack, but Litze won't allow this to happen; we'll use other cars as cover. Also, we have some advantage being a few cars ahead.

But zero advantage with speed.

Litze's gaze is focused as he relaxes and gets the car into position. As we head for an exit on the right of the autobahn, the black Mercedes closes in.

I said that Litze was steady rather than spectacular. But he is skilful. This move will take all of his nerves. But if he gets this wrong, it's game over. Litze speeds up towards the slip road.

The black Mercedes responds.

The car tyres screech and our bodies whip violently to the left as Litze throws a sharp right on the steering wheel.

Litze takes a sharp left turn, throwing us to the right in our seats. We speed down the country lane illegally fast, but Litze is always in control.

We turn again, a hard right onto another lane as a white van comes unsuspectingly out of the junction; startled, the driver abuses us with his horn.

Then we hit another road. This time, it's relatively straight. There are no turns and nowhere to go. I look behind, and I can see a black figure pop out from the right side of the Mercedes, aiming a gun. I see the muzzle flash, and I can hear the sound of gunfire above the noise of the car. He misses, but their car is faster than us.

They're closing.

The man fires again but misses. Given their advantage, I doubt they'll miss again.

Our bodies swing to the left, and the car screams as Litze turns the steering wheel full to the right on a hairpin bend and seamlessly executes a handbrake turn, so we're now facing the black Mercedes.

Litze wants to play a game of chicken.

He doesn't care about the outcome.

He wants to find out if they're as determined as him. He used to say to me that he didn't bluff, and it's as if he's trying to prove it to himself. If this is his way of creating the element of surprise, then it's too late for me to complain. That was part of the training: Don't do what they expect you to do. It makes your enemy think. He's turning this situation on its head.

He wants to be the hunter.

This is what Litze planned for. His trap. He'll risk everything to prove a point.

The two vehicles devour the road between them.

Two hundred metres before impact.

One hundred and fifty metres before impact.

Seventy-five metres before impact.

Neither of us is backing down.

Everything seems in slow motion. My reptilian brain takes effect like a survival mechanism. I get into my peaceful space and feel a weird sense of exhilaration as I smell death in the air. I lean out of the passenger window, and my eyes water instinctively against the wind as I feel the G-force created by the car's momentum mutating my face like it was plasticine.

I fire several shots into their windscreen. The man returns fire. I don't think the bullets hit us. Either that or we're already ghosts. An unnatural calm descends on me as I shoot again into the windscreen.

It cracks.

Exactly as I hoped for, as visibility in the Mercedes is compromised.

Then I shoot the front tires of the black Mercedes. The car sways like it's being driven by a drunk, rubber disintegrating on the tarmac and flying off in all directions, along with the sparks from the tortured wheel rims.

Thirty metres to go.

Litze speeds up. I should be worried because he's risking my life as well as his own. But I don't have time to care as this is turning into a death orgy.

The clock ticking is an irrelevance.

Twenty metres to go.

Ten metres to go.

I relax even more and momentarily think about closing my eyes but decide I want to see this coming. It's like my brain has tricked me into thinking that I'm no longer in my body as I float and watch myself and my mentor in the car, like an observer. Litze holds his nerve as the black Mercedes loses traction, skids, and slams into a thicket of bushes. Our bodies thrust forward, stopped by our seat belts, as Litze screeches the Fiat to a halt a few metres past the place of impact. I look across at him and he looks as though he's just stepped off a beach somewhere. I wait so that I can return to my body. I unclip my seat belt and look over to Litze again.

I know him too well. He won't say that he planned for this outcome, because he didn't. He wasn't attached to the outcome, which made him more dangerous than ever.

FIFTY-ONE

WE ADVANCE TOWARDS the black Mercedes with our guns drawn. The mangled vehicle is contoured against a tree and encased in a hedge but at an angle, lifted off its rear, its wheels still spinning. I smell burning rubber and see steam coming out of the car as it hisses its last defiant breath. The driver and passengers are slumped and obscured by white airbags, which are now laced with blood. I open the passenger door, which takes a few attempts as the crash has distorted the frame. There are three occupants. All male. Two in the front, and one rear-seat passenger. I can see blood on the unconscious driver, but I think he's still alive.

The others are fading. I check for a pulse on one of the men as I point my gun and can't feel anything. I check another person. I look at Litze, who has his gun raised, and I shake my head, telling him it's unnecessary for him to shoot them.

I check for a pulse on the driver, and I can still feel it, but it's very faint.

Litze takes their weapons and goes through the dead men's pockets. He finds a wallet and throws it at me to check. The wallet smells new and looks expensive, which seems to suggest that it was bought specifically for this trip. It's rare to see men with brand-new wallets in my experience. Normally, the guys I've known have their money in battle-worn leather, stuffed with currency, coins, various dog-eared business cards, and old receipts. If they don't want to incriminate themselves to any significant other, keeping receipts is a bad idea. I open the black leather pouch: Some credit cards with different names. Almost certainly fake IDs. I also see a mixture of euros and American dollars in the money section. It's a lot, and I don't bother to count it as I put it in my inside jacket pocket. Litze does the same, as I see him stuff the retrieved money from the other wallet into his back pocket. He also has multiple IDs in his find.

The driver looks completely out of it, but we can't hang around because the polizei will be here soon.

Litze throws me a mobile smartphone which has no brand markings on it. Which suggests it's mission specific. I press a side button, and the screen lights up with the time and date, but it's locked. I throw the mobile on the ground. My first instinct is to smash it, but this is pointless as it can still be traced.

The driver is still out of it, but we can't leave him alive. And I don't think we have enough time to make him talk. So I aim. Litze tells me to wait. He slaps the driver's face, but still no response.

'We should go, Litze', I say. 'The polizei will be here in minutes.'

Litze ignores me and slaps the driver around the face one more time. The driver groans a response.

'We should finish him off', I say, and aim my gun.

'Wait!' he says. 'I want to find out who they are.'

'We don't have time for this', I say.

'I need him alive for now, Becker.'

'Have you lost your nerve, Litze?' I say. I have a big mouth and regret saying it. Litze looks at me as if to say: Who the hell do you think you're talking to?

'No. I think we should just wait for a moment. Just until he regains consciousness, and then we can decide after.'

'But it's not safe here.'

'A few more minutes, Becker.'

'It's not as if they would afford you the same courtesy.'

'That's not the point, and you know it. I want to know who they're working for. Given that this is your operation, I guess you'd like to know too. Who killed your team? Who set you up? Remember? He probably won't talk anyway, but while there's a chance, I think we should take it.'

He's right of course. It's my hot-headedness that got me into trouble in the first place. I say nothing. The man looks like he's coming to.

'What did I tell you about patience, Becker?'

I let it go. I'm too tired to argue with him because I concede that there's no point. My thought now is to get us off the road before any cars come or the police show up. The driver shouldn't be moved, but I check him again. He doesn't seem to be seriously injured. Some bruising and whiplash from what I can tell.

Litze and I struggle to drag the men out of the car one by one and lay them out on a patch of grass, which looks like it belongs to a nearby farm. I go back and search the car. It's spotless inside and smells unused, which suggests that the vehicle is probably an off-the-books rental. Which means that it's untraceable. Then I begin to wonder who sent this hit team. My agency, Coba, is the first that comes to mind. The first thing they would want to do is to clean house. And the fact that I haven't called Coba makes me look guilty of sabotaging this operation, even though I almost got killed. Or Yumeni's men are behind this. And there's the small matter of the sniper who's still out there. I feel out of my depth. I'm definitely out of my comfort zone now. I'm up against an enemy that I can't see, feel, or smell. And I look at my mentor again, and even though he gives me shit for my failings, at least he's here, despite everything. Most would have deserted me and most have.

I go back to the driver and see that Litze must have found some plastic cuffs in the car, because he's bound him with his hands tied behind his back. He checks him again for vital signs.

'How long do we wait?' I ask.

'I'm going to give him three minutes to talk.'

'And if he doesn't?'

'Then you do what you do best. I almost feel sorry for him.'

FIFTY-TWO

WE WAIT FOR a moment. The driver is slipping in and out of consciousness. We've sat him upright against a tree. His eyes look glazed over, like brown marbles, like he's coming to life for the very first time. He makes low groans, then he sees us pointing our guns. Then I see realisation followed by fear in his eyes as he instinctively tries to wrestle his hands free from the plastic straps.

'Who sent you?' asks Litze.

The driver says nothing. He doesn't have to. His eyes betray him.

'Again, who sent you?' asks Litze.

Still no response.

'My colleague here is a bit impatient. She wants to kill you. Are you listening?' says Litze as he slaps him around the face.

'Tell me what I want to know', I say.

The man looks at me, trying to hide his fear. But I can smell it like a feral animal.

'And if I do?' he says. I can't place his accent, but he sounds Eastern European.

'I'll make it quick, I promise.'

'So there's nothing in it for me?'

'Are you saying you'd prefer a slow, agonizing death?' I ask.

The man says nothing.

He doesn't look like a believer or some fanatic. These look like mercenaries, just like me. Which means that survival should be top of the list.

Litze points his gun at the driver. The man looks on, resigned.

'Two minutes', I say.

The man says nothing.

'Think of it as your last good deed', I say. And I try to remember what my last one was.

I could've promised that I would spare him like I've done with my other kills. But that's a lie, and there is no point in bullshitting him. That would be crueller than killing him. Giving him false hope is like death by a thousand cuts.

No one should take pleasure in ending another's life. But sometimes, I've enjoyed it more than is healthy. After so many kills, you become almost desensitised. That's when you should worry. That's when your judgement and any moral code get lost in the haze.

I take the gun and point it at the man. Terror paints his face.

'Who sent you?'

'We're just contractors. We never know who the real client is.'

'Who are you working for?'

'You're not going to let me live.'

'Do you have anything else to say? Anything that might buy you some time or even convince someone like me that I should spare your life? Even in the minute and a half you have left, even someone like me could be convinced. If you believe in probability, then there's always a chance, so make it count. Give it your best shot. No pun intended.'

The man hesitates for a moment, a luxury he cannot afford as we're running out of time. I sense his deep thoughts. Maybe it's his life flashing before his very eyes. Memories, good and bad; missed opportunities replaying in his head. Then finally, he shows some genuine emotion.

'Please, please don't kill me. I have a family', he stutters. His voice sounds dry and painful.

The man is right. I don't have a good reason to keep him alive. He won't get the sympathy card from an assassin. His plea won't work with this bitch. What does family mean to someone like me? Of course, he isn't to know that. That word, family. It irritates me. It's like he's speaking a foreign language. A three-syllabled noise of nothingness. When people use that word family, it registers other feelings. Not of warmth, connection, or belonging. For me, family means misery, pain, abuse, conformity, disconnection, alienation, duty, bullshit. For me, his last sentence was a so-what. I can tell by the look on his face that he knows I'm not at all swayed. As if I've been insulted in some way.

I shoot him twice in the head.

'We should get out of here', I say.

'You did the right thing, Becker', says Litze as he walks over to me.

'You think so?'

'Yes, I do. Look, I found these on them', he says, and shows me two plastic bottles in his right hand. I recognise them instantly. These are bottles you use to collect DNA samples. They would probably have cut a chunk of hair, or more likely they would have cut off my finger. Proof-of-death bottles, we call them. This was a kill squad. But I don't know who sent them. I suddenly feel cold.

FIFTY-THREE

WE DUMP THE driver's body in a ditch and leave the scene before another kill squad arrives, no doubt tracking their mobile device.

We're no closer to finding out who we've just killed. But our actions have just upped the stakes. A Coba hit team would make sense. But from what I've seen, there's no one on Coba's team that would keep me awake. Litze always warned me about my arrogance. He said you should respect your opponent. Too little or too much respect wasn't good, but the right amount was needed. The problem with me is that I didn't get that balance right. He said that it was the people you thought were the least likely to trouble you that you should be wary of. But Litze knew me better than anyone and realised that my hubris was insecurity in disguise.

Have we killed German government agents? That's a possibility, but if the shitstorm we've found ourselves in is as big as we think it is, then they could outsource the solution. That's what I'd do. It would be in their interest to form alliances with those who benefit in getting us out of the way. Maybe that's what Sabatini was implying when he paid us a visit in the café: he wasn't necessarily going to be the trigger man, but he would look the other way. In other words: we were on our own.

But that's the way Litze and I like it: us against the world.

Seemingly impossible odds, so this is a breeze. This situation reminds me of a time when I was at school and a girl had me in a headlock because I refused to give her my dinner money. She was a fat bully of a girl who terrorised the kids in school. She had me good but even then, I wasn't going to back down. I was going blue, and my stubbornness overtook my common sense. But that was one of the few times that I could thank my father. I would always defy him and never back down. I was surrounded by a group of girls that day, and I could hear them roaring on the fat girl. She'd asked me to give her my money, and I'd said no. My favourite word in the whole world: no. She repeated the request while squeezing tighter, and defiantly, I gave her the same answer. I don't think she was used to this, which confused her. Her tactics worked ninety-nine out of a hundred times. I was her one-in-a-hundred bump in that particular road. The thing you've got to realise about bullies is that they are cowards who can't deal with their pain and try to give it to someone else.

I could feel the fat girl's confusion in the way she shuffled. The baying crowd started to realise that I wasn't going to back down. The psychology changed. They started cheering for me. Me! Most of my young life, I'd been shouted at, but cheered? This was a new experience. In the end, the fat girl let me go. I looked at her with my blue face, and she looked back at me, bemused. With a grudging respect. What was even more amazing was the next day, everybody knew my name. They spoke to me like I'd only been noticed for the very first time. And I remember thinking that it was sad that this was the only way to get friends.

As you can probably tell, I hate bullies. So whoever is after me can get me in this headlock and squeeze as tight as they want. Because they'll have to turn me blue first before I give an inch. And I wonder, what was Litze's headlock moment? Maybe he didn't need one. But there's something about him which says, I don't give a damn either.

That's why we like each other. Not all of the time, I'll admit. I'll qualify that: get each other. Litze understood my stubbornness because he has a similar character. The more they squeeze, the more I won't back down.

Stupid, I know.

FIFTY-FOUR

WE LEAVE THE carnage and drive for a few more miles to the next village. Litze knows Germany like the back of his hand, but even though it's my home, I feel like a stranger here. And that's nothing to do with the eight years away. I've always felt like a stranger in my country. It's a bit like when you don't feel comfortable in your body. I've always been told that I think like a man, but I'm in a woman's body. That could be to do with having brothers, or it could be my nature. I'm not the only person who feels ill at ease in their environment. I've always found Germany too patriarchal for my liking. And my father was the first to try and fail to make me conform.

Litze puts his mobile in his pocket and pauses for a moment. I've seen that look before: he's calculating his next move.

'I know a contact from the old days that will give us guns and personnel if needed', he says.

'But who's protecting Yumeni?' I say.

'It could be everyone and no one. Whatever we think about this scumbag, Yumeni is an asset to somebody. There could be as many people who want him alive as dead. I feel like it's a race against time. My instinct is to find out what he knows before we take him out.'

'You have a different instinct to me, Litze.'

'But your original mission was to take him alive, remember? And you want to deviate from that?'

'The mission changed when someone wiped out my team and nearly killed me. He's probably behind it. Coba is almost certainly involved, so I don't work for anyone now. And to be honest, it was my original instinct to kill him. I was reluctantly following orders. Remember, I'd read his file. People like him don't deserve to live. It would have been hard for me to take him alive. I can tell monsters a mile off. I've had good practice, remember?'

'OK, Becker, but think about this. What if killing him makes things worse?'

'How could it make things worse?'

'Becker, I've had to do deals with people whom I couldn't bear, for the mission. Scum who'd killed good friends of mine. You know how hard that is?'

'No, Litze. I don't have friends.'

'Yes, I remember. That's when pragmatism has to overcome emotion. There were bigger fish to fry.'

'And you think that Yumeni is part of something bigger?'

'Absolutely. Yumeni is a cog in the machine. Purple Dawn won't help us. We get a visit from a government department, then a visit from a kill squad. I don't believe in coincidences, Becker. This smells rotten. Aren't you curious to find out why? Who set you up? Who killed your team?'

'Maybe, but that curiosity isn't as big as yours. We're different, you and I. Remember, I'm your blunt instrument.'

'Only too well, Becker. I hate this world that I've operated in. But what gives me comfort is the fact that there has to be meaning behind this. Killing for the sake of killing isn't good for your soul. We are in a unique position; with that power comes responsibility.'

'Maybe that's my problem, Litze: irresponsibility is part of my DNA.'

'You say that, and I think you joke, Becker. You're a good woman. Maybe not as good as you think you are, but not as bad as you think either.'

'Thanks, I think.'

Litze turns and looks me squarely in the eyes. 'You have to find meaning in this. Otherwise, you'll go crazy. It's not about getting the best payday. When normal rules don't apply, we're the extreme option. And maybe someone higher than us will judge us in time, but until then, we can balance things up behind the scenes.'

'You mean I have to find a purpose?'

'I mean you always have a choice, Becker. You can choose whose side you're on. You can opt to be on your side; you can decide to help those less fortunate than you.'

'You mean like a Mother Teresa with a gun?'

'If you're going to mock me, then I won't waste my breath. Maybe the problem with you is that you haven't experienced real loss. If you did, you wouldn't be so flippant.'

That comment stings momentarily. Loss is relative. Litze is so wrong about me. I've experienced the loss of my childhood. I can't even remember one happy moment with my father. The loss of a mother who took his side when I defied him. The loss of my brothers, who failed to protect me and treated me like an oddity. The loss of any real friendships growing up, which was my fault, because I pushed people away out of fear of rejection. The loss of my friend Donny Walsh (again, my fault!). Loss of identity as I tried to find my way in the world. I used humour as a coping strategy. Also, because I'm deeply cynical. I said one day I'd see a shrink, but I've been putting it off for years because I'm afraid to face the truth about myself. But the past is catching up with me. The biggest challenge I face is to get out of bed some mornings and convince myself that I deserve to be happy.

FIFTY-FIVE

WE TRAVEL FOR a few miles in Litze's car, but know we can't use it for too long. We will have to ditch it. Litze says we'll steal another when we get the chance.

Litze looks at me. 'Are you scared?' he asks.

'No.'

'You should be. Fear, once in a while, isn't a bad thing.'

'Are you?' I ask.

'I manage fear. When I was younger, I was more fearless. Then I grew up, and life had other plans. I miss those days sometimes when ignorance was bliss. Then I got older and got attached to stuff. That's what keeps you fearful.'

'What do you mean?'

'Attachment, Becker. People fear because they have something to lose. Whether that be an object or a person. They identify with that object of desire. So when they lose it, they become lost.'

'Is that what happened to you?'

'Yes, I allowed my value to be determined by external things, so when I lost them, I was fearful.'

'What changed?'

'When my wife was killed. I'd never experienced so much pain before, but it put everything in perspective. It was very humbling. It changed the way I looked at life.'

'What did you mean when you said that you manage fear?'

'You do realise that most of the things people worry about never happen, right?'

'I guess so.'

'In the back of my mind, I always knew that, but I needed reminding of that fact.'

'I guess we're too busy worrying to remember.'

'Exactly, Becker. If you ask most people whether they'd prefer to manage one thing or a multitude of things, you'd think they'd choose one thing, as they'd believe it would take the least effort.'

'I suppose.'

'But what if I said that the multitude of things are events outside of your control, but the one thing is how you respond to these events? That changes the picture completely.'

I pause for a moment. Then I realise what Litze is getting at. 'Because managing the one thing that you have control of, which is yourself, or the way you respond to stuff, is always the hardest thing to do?'

'Right!'

'So, are you saying that I should become an existentialist assassin?'

'If you mean that you create your reality and the meaning you give your life rather than being influenced by external doctrine, then yes.'

'I thought I did that anyway.'

'Yes, you do more than most, but there's always room for improvement.'

'Are you saying you're less fearful?'

'Yes, but my fear hasn't gone away completely. When I feel it, I ask myself what it's telling me. Maybe I need to look at something in a different way or change something inside me. And, Becker?'

'What?'

'I find it very hard to believe that you don't feel fear. In fact, I would go as far as to say that you're lying. At least to yourself.'

'How do you know what I think or feel?'

'Of course, I could be assuming, which is always dangerous. I trained you, Becker, remember? I've seen you display a range of emotions, but I've never seen you cry. But I understand why you deny feeling fear. That's your father's doing, isn't it?'

I say nothing.

'You thought that if you showed fear, especially to him, he would win. But the problem with that, Becker, is that you've suppressed that voice that'll keep you alive.'

'I don't understand.'

'Becker, fear is a survival mechanism. A fight-or-flight instinct. It seems that you've confused fear with weakness. But not admitting to fear is the weakness. When I said that you have to manage fear, what I meant was it's like any emotion: you have to ask yourself what it's telling you.'

'I guess I never thought of it that way.'

'You never stayed around long enough for me to help you.'

'I can't argue with that.'

'Our first instinct when we feel something is to look outside for the answers or blame someone when we should look inside. You made some bad choices, but you don't need me to tell you that. I just hope that if we get out of this alive, you'll listen to the voices that you've been ignoring all these years and look inside.'

'But that's my problem. I don't want to find out what's inside.'

'But sooner or later, you'll have to deal with it. Otherwise, it will eat your guts like battery acid.'

'I see.'

'Do you, Becker? Do you really? I hope so. I'm not as fearful as I was. Sure, it suited me to let others believe that I was fearless. But again, they mistook that for strength. That worked in my favour. I was the leader, and I had a responsibility to set an example. And I was working with a bunch of people who had an antiquated view of leadership, so I played that game, but inside, I was often shaking.'

It's starting to make sense. When you had a father like mine who was such a bad role model, that's all you know. And then it starts to click in my brain. My father was of that generation where you couldn't show fear because it was a sign of weakness. I'm just perpetuating the cycle.

'OK, I feel anxiety', I say. It's the best I can do.

'It's not a contest to find out who feels more or less fear, but if it's anxiety you feel, that's a start.'

'A start of what?'

'The start of your finally looking inside for answers.'

'I think I'm more worried about the inside than the outside.'

'I know, Becker, but little steps.'

He's aware that I lie about my fear. But my denial has become instinctive. So much so that I don't even realise I'm doing it. I should know better than to do something like that to someone like him. He's seen things and done things that would make most people fearful. But he's had to manage his fear or else go mad. I've just run away as I've always done. My way of tackling fear was to keep proving myself. Even lying about my fear to prove to others that I didn't have any. But that made me less human, and people don't hang around with energy like that. I don't take offence at what Litze said to me before. He's trying to help me, even when he's hard on me. It's his way of making me better. I didn't see it then, but I'm starting to now.

I'll confront my fear one day, but now I'm focused on the lead that Holz gave to Litze. Hanover, of all places. This thing just gets deeper. It seems we're just digging in the dirt. And when I find out who's responsible for setting me up in the first place, they'll find out what fear feels like.

FIFTY-SIX

I CONVINCE LITZE that buying a car is better than stealing one. I explain to him that I can use one of my multitude of fake credit cards and accounts, which won't be flagged up by the authorities. Resources courtesy of a few contacts I've made over the years. Not a cheap service, but worth it. My false identities have gotten me out of a hole when I needed them, and if one of my cards has been compromised, I switch to another, just like musical chairs. And as in that game, I lose a card every time. I tend to avoid credit transactions unless I have absolutely no choice. As I have the funds to buy a vehicle outright, Litze agrees that's the best option. But I suspect he's a little disappointed that he can't put his hot-wiring skills to good use.

We ditch Litze's beloved Fiat deep in an enclave of woods so that it won't be found for days. Then we walk a couple of miles and eventually find a second-hand car showroom on the edge of a nearby village. We walk through the forecourt of cars and enter the small office, where a balding man, wearing an open-neck blue shirt, is sitting behind his desk. He gets up and offers a handshake, which we reciprocate. As we take a seat, Litze does most of the talking to the salesman while I zone out of the conversation. Cars have never been my thing. Litze sees an eight-year-old, dark-blue BMW 3 Series. It's in good condition. Litze looks at me in that 'what do you think?'

way. I give him a trusting nod, and he takes the car for a test drive with the salesman. I sit at the desk and wait for a while. The showroom is neat, tidier than the ones I've been in before, though I haven't been in many, to be honest. The walls are sparsely covered with adverts of special deals and credit agreements. The wood desk looks well-worn and has survived most things, it seems, including coffee stains that no longer look out of place.

Litze gives me the thumbs-up as he returns and confirms that we'll buy the car. My mentor haggles and manages to get 15 percent off the price, telling the salesman that we'll pay in cash. I hand the money over to the seller, which seems to surprise him, as he wrongly assumed Litze was paying. I may be considered one of the deadliest assassins in the world, but here, that counts for nothing. I'm just a woman in a car showroom.

We drive to a petrol station to fill up the rest of the tank and buy some water, chocolate, and crisps, and some cheese-and-tomato sandwiches. We eat and drink in the car and head to Hanover. Although he misses his Fiat, I can tell Litze is pleased with driving the BMW.

I think back on the hunt for Yumeni and the fact that we seem blocked at every turn. Or if we try to find out more, there's no clear information. What does he have? The deeper we dig, the more intrigued I am. But I do like to play with fire. It's seductive. More like addictive, some might say. It has a fascination for me; whether it be the danger, taking all sorts of risks, or my lust for bad boys, I seem to be drawn irresistibly to the dark side. It's as if I were once white blotting paper and I've absorbed the black ink. And as we know, you can't get rid of that stain. But my paper has a unique quality: I can't seem to stop absorbing black ink. I don't want to stop, truth be told.

Yumeni seems to be my black ink now, and I have to see this through. But there will be a cost. There always is. Will Litze be one of the costs? I hope not. He's been good to me. Too good. I don't know why he's stuck with me like this, but I'm glad he has. And I think he likes being useful. I came back to him after all these years, and he didn't reject me, even after what I put him through. Maybe I was his ultimate test of faith, because trust me, I would test most peoples'.

The more I look, the more it feels as if we're chasing a ghost and we couldn't stop now even if we wanted to. We've set off a chain of events, which means the momentum is unstoppable. Now it's gone too far. We're now the hunters and the hunted at the same time.

FIFTY-SEVEN

OUR NEXT MOVE is to see an old colleague of Litze's, whom he's already sent a text to. He doesn't say much about who this is apart from the fact that this contact is someone he can rely on and is on the way to Yumeni's last reported location. I resist the temptation to probe him. We take a toilet break and buy more supplies from a petrol station. And I can't resist more chocolate, which I seem to have more guilt about than snapping someone's neck.

I feel the cold more now that I'm back in my homeland, as the temperature drops. Even though I have Germanic roots, my body responds better to the sun. It always has, as long as I can remember. My father used to taunt me about it. One of many in a long list of things with which to get at me. But the heat reanimates me, and I often wonder why. It's as if I have a gene passed down from a distant past that skipped generations and programs me like an algorithm that I've never been tempted to fight. Our family line is very hazy, but I've heard that I have some African and Spanish origins, which may explain things. Origins that would've freaked out my father.

It's only now, when I look back, that I realise that this operation to snatch Karl Yumeni was as simple as trying to give a litter of cats a bath. My agency, Coba, will be mad, but their client, whoever that is, will be even more furious. There'll be penalty clauses for messing up this contract, or the client could pull the work and give it to someone else. That's assuming that this was an exclusive assignment, which isn't always the case. And I didn't even think to ask whether it was. Litze always told me never to assume anything, but I got greedy and complacent. Though I doubt that the client would go multi-agency on this. It seems far too risky, but that's not a given. It wouldn't be the first time a client has lied about exclusivity. Coba's professional pride means that they'll try to salvage the job. Their reputational damage will be huge but not unrecoverable. There's too much work out there. It seems all you need is a gun, an office, and a phone with a fax, and you're good to go. OK, maybe I'm exaggerating to make a point, but you get my drift: that it's too easy to set up a security business. Coba could do what many private security companies have done when their reputations have gone to shit: rebrand themselves by changing their name, get a pretty new logo, and act like nothing happened. It seems that many in the security community have short memories and unlimited budgets.

**

I check my phone; it's a quarter past two.

'How long to go?' I ask Litze.

'About half an hour. Normally it would've taken about an hour, but this route is longer and probably safer.'

**

The car jolts me awake; I unexpectedly nodded off. Litze is still driving

He slows the BMW to twenty miles an hour and turns into another side road; hooks left, then right; then goes straight down a steep slope. I hear the wheels stir gravel, which makes metal percussive sounds on the bodywork as we descend further. I look outside, and there are more trees. I'm not sure what kind, but they look like beech trees. The leaves offer a variation of shade as shards of sunlight cut through them intermittently, like strobe lighting. The road ascends, then levels off as we finally come to rest. In the foreground is a modern white building which seems to have more glass than brick, but I like it. It's a house ideal for exhibitionists, and it reminds me of a Huf house. These can be constructed in a matter of a week and are a marvel of German precision engineering. I saw many of them on my travels, and I love the minimalist design. I promised to buy myself one, but I don't stay anywhere long enough to live in it.

Litze steps out of the car first. Then I leave the vehicle. Litze and I walk a few steps towards the building, and before we get further, an obscenely attractive woman comes out of the front door. She walks towards us. She beams when she sees my mentor. I look at Litze, then look at her. Call it woman's intuition, but something tells me that their association isn't strictly business.

FIFTY-EIGHT

'THIS BETTER BE good, Lothar. I was about to go on a date with two hot special forces guys. And they were happy not to flip a coin for me', says the woman in a deep, husky voice as she hugs him warmly in a way that suggests that her hands have already been acquainted with him. You know that saying 'She had a body made for sin'? She looks like the original prototype. I guess she's in her mid-to-late thirties. She has curves you could ski off, like they were designed in an engineering lab or by an architect. And not an ounce of fat on her either. She's about five foot four. Her breasts, which haven't heard of such a thing as gravity, and her ass balance her body beautifully. She has thick, black, shoulder-length hair. Her face has a sprinkling of freckles; a Mediterranean tan; full, blow-job lips; and a smile that beams like a lighthouse. She's wearing black spray-on jeans and a matching woollen jumper under her waist-length leather jacket, which cups her ample cleavage. A body made for sin? She is sin. This woman exudes a confidence that I've rarely seen in most people. She knows who she is: an orgasm on legs. I do believe that I am in awe of this woman, which is unusual for me.

'So, who's this little cutie?' she says, turning to me.

'Behave yourself, Karla', says Litze as he introduces me. 'This is Sam Becker, a former protégé of mine. Becker, this is Karla Blume.'

'"Protégé"?' she replies, holding up her fingers to indicate quotation marks. She scans me like an X-ray machine, the way us women like to do. 'Hmmm, very nice.'

'She's young enough to be my daughter, Karla', insists Litze.

'Yeah, but she's still old enough', replies Karla, who extends her hand to me. When I shake it, I feel like I've been tasered with sexual energy. 'So Lothar, to what do I owe this unexpected and delightful pleasure?' she asks.

'We need help.'

'What help? You're rather vague. If I'm going to put my ass on the line, it has to be for a good reason, Lothar. And I know how much you like my ass.'

I look at Litze. He feels my stare but doesn't dare look back at me.

'Can we go inside?' asks Litze. 'It would be better than talking out here.'

'Sure, of course. It's so good to see you, Lothar', she says, hugging him again. I sense his embarrassment as he still avoids my gaze.

We enter Blume's house, and it's what I imagined it would be: a Zen paradise. Wide open spaces, high wooden ceilings, lots of glass that makes you feel part of nature, white walls with giant modern art canvases that look like somebody has spilt paint on them. There's a huge L-shaped, six-seater, grey leather sofa with white cotton cushions, which seems to be designed for a basketball team, in the main seating area, with a real fire in a rectangular opening in the wall. Dark, freestanding figurines of African women are tastefully arranged in a line along the walk opposite the seating area. There's a massive flat-screen television. There are no carpets but an off-white rug under the wooden coffee table with a copy of an old *Elle* magazine. The giant L-shaped room extends into a huge dining area around the rear of the house, with a glass table resting on C-shaped chrome legs.

There are also eight white Panton chairs, three on each long side, one at either end. The kitchen area is open-plan with an island for cooking. And the metal appliances are all neatly housed in rich brown oak, with brand names that are so exclusive, I don't recognise them.

We all take a stool at the breakfast bar, and Blume goes to the fridge.

'Beer, anyone?' she asks.

'I'll take a beer', says Litze. 'What do you know about Karl Yumeni?' he asks.

'Oh', says Blume as she takes a drink. She wipes her mouth with her left hand and places the bottle on the breakfast bar. She stares at me, then back to Litze. It's the first time I sense discomfort in her demeanour. 'So that's what this is about?'

Blume takes another swig of beer, then composes herself. Her breasts nestle on the top of the breakfast bar as she relaxes. 'I wish I didn't know anything about him', she continues. 'He's like one of those horrible bedtime stories: once you read them, your mind's never the same.'

'We want to go after him', says Litze.

'What for?' she asks.

'It's easier if I explain', I say.

I give Blume a brief overview of my mission, describing the ambush. My contacting Litze for help after eight years, which she seems surprised at. The visit from a German government official, the Holz visit, and the attempt to kill us by three hitmen.

'You sure know how to show a girl a good time', she says, looking at Litze. 'I'm jealous, Lothar.'

'So what have you heard about Karl Yumeni?' I ask.

Blume pauses for a moment and places her drink on the counter.

'I know that only someone with a death wish would want to go after a person like him. And you seem too young to have that.'

I say nothing.

'He's one bad, bad dude', she continues. 'Whoever Yumeni is, he's being protected by some very powerful people. Nobody has managed to get him or pin anything on him so far.'

'What do you mean?'

'There are rumours—unproven—that he's part of a terror cell in Europe.'

'ISIS? Al-Qaeda?'

'Sadly, they're not the only shows in town, Becker. It's not uncommon for splinter networks to break away from the traditional enemy.'

'You mean factions within factions?'

'That's right. Some think these organisations have become too bureaucratic. That can affect the speed of the decision-making on the ground.'

'So these terror networks form sub-networks?'

'That always happens. It's the history of the world. Not everybody is built to follow orders blindly. Some prefer to go it alone because of differences in ideology.'

'And you think Yumeni is part of a splinter group?'

'I'm not sure about Yumeni exactly. I don't think he's a believer. He's a pragmatist. He'll go where the wind blows. That makes him even more dangerous.'

'You mean he's a terrorist for hire?'

'Yes. Money is their god. There are a lot of people who do weird shit for it. Especially on the dark web. I call it the house of sickos. These hired guns are good for traditional terror organisations, who will happily take the credit because it gives the impression that they have a wide reach, even if that's not true. They're not bothered if someone else's finger is on the trigger.'

'That's even more of a reason why we should stop him', says Litze.

'Forget it', replies Blume.

'Why?' says Litze.

'Have you seen his security detail? It's tighter than a condom on a marrow. You won't get through it. And only a lunatic would even try.'

'We tried, and failed', I say, referring to my botched operation.

'Like I said, only a lunatic would try. Forgive me for saying so, but that's one job you should never have taken. But I guess Lothar has already told you?' says Blume.

'You could say that.'

'Ah, don't sweat it', she says. 'Litze is the best in the world at telling you "I told you so." I've been in plenty of scrapes, but Lothar is always there to save the day. As I said earlier, I figure he likes my ass; that's why he keeps saving it.' She winks at me and smiles at Litze. I do believe he's blushing. I've never seen him so uncomfortable before. And I love it.

'It seems that Yumeni has come from nowhere', I say.

'But you know, there's no such thing as an overnight success', she says. 'Yumeni is utterly ruthless. He would have killed a lot of dogs so that he could become top dog. But forgive me, Becker, you don't strike me as a believer in a cause. You're a lot like me: a gun for hire. This job was for the money, right?'

'Yes.'

'Whatever they offered you wasn't enough.'

'Listen', I say. 'You seem pretty intuitive. You're right about me: I'm not someone who believes in anything. I'm a gun for hire. I don't have a cause, an external one at least. But after the life I've had, maybe it's my chance to do the right thing for once. I'm the world's expert in doing the wrong thing. I took eight years to pluck up the courage to contact Litze. Eight years of missed opportunities and fuck-ups. Eight years of taking wrong turns, false starts, and false hopes. I've killed a lot of people. But I come back to the fact that I returned to the one person I was too proud to listen to. Why, I ask myself, after all this time did I return? Because maybe I'm starting to realise that there's something bigger than me. And if I thought this was it, that would be scary.'

'Nice speech', says Blume. 'It almost moved me to tears.'

'I understand your cynicism; I'd be the same way if I were you.'

'So how do we contact Yumeni?' asks Litze.

'Looks like you've already stirred the hornet's nest, which means that Yumeni will come for you. But if you want my advice, walk away, Lothar. You too, Becker. Kick back in the Caribbean. Remember we used to say we'd do that together one day?'

'I'm serious, Karla', says Litze.

'So am I, Lothar. This guy is not worth the nuclear shitstorm that it will bring. Someone will get him; that's a given. It doesn't have to be you.'

'So, you don't think I'm up to this?' asks Litze. He stares at Blume quizzically.

'Lothar, you're worth a thousand, a million of someone like him. You're the best man I've ever known. I've never met a person like you. A charming and sexy older man. I never thought men like you existed. Do you know why you're special? You've never once tried to control me. Not once! Do you know how rare that is for a woman?'

'That's rare for most people', I say.

'True, Becker, it is rare. I used to tell my exes, if you don't have the courage and the wisdom to leave me alone, then leave me the fuck alone.' She looks at me. 'Lothar is the first man I've met who understands that controlling others is pointless. Anyway, I have no desire to go to your funeral too, Lothar. This assignment is full of shit. You're in too deep, so get out before your head is covered in it. I'm telling you, as your friend. Walk away. Leave it to the universe or whatever you call it. Yumeni will get what's coming.'

Litze stays silent for a moment. He takes another swig of beer and turns to Blume. 'This isn't like you, Karla.'

'What isn't like me? You mean cautious Karla, rather than reckless, I-could-take-on-the-world Karla? Well, I've tied her up, gagged her, and locked her in a cupboard. And when she screams, I hit her. And if she's good, I let her out for water breaks.'

Litze puts his bottle down. 'Who's gotten to you?' says Litze.

'No one has gotten to me.'

'Are you sure about that?' he asks.

'OK, I lied to you, Lothar. Yeah, someone did get to me. I got to me.'

'I don't understand.'

Blume takes another bottle of beer from the fridge, opens it, and drinks a mouthful. 'I had a dream the other night. I was walking in a large park. It was peaceful, but there was nobody there. The sky was cloudless. It was hot too. Just my kind of weather. I kept walking until I saw a woman in the distance. She was sitting on a park bench. She was the only living thing in sight, so I walked over to her. As I approached, she turned around. I recognised her instantly. It was me, but a younger version. She smiled at me, and I smiled back. I looked at her for a while and liked what I remembered about her. She had a glow. She was full of life.'

'But you haven't changed in that regard', says Litze.

'Thank you, sweetheart', says Blume.

'What happened?' says Litze.

'My older self asked my younger self if I could sit down, and she said yes. I was glad to sit, as I was feeling drained, even though I hadn't walked far. I remember clearing my throat before I spoke. I said: "Listen, Karla, this is a younger person's game. Sooner or later, your luck is going to run out. Give it up while you still can and don't end up like me." Then I saw my older self with a large bullet hole between my eyes. I had another entry wound in my stomach. Then maggots started crawling out of the wounds. Then out of my eyes, my ears, through my nose. They made this sucking sound as they ate my flesh. It was disgusting, but that wasn't the worst part. It was what my younger self did next.'

'What did she do?'

'She pissed herself laughing. Literally. Then she started peeing on the older me. It came out like a torrent. It was disgusting. Then dark clouds appeared. It started to thunder, and lightning appeared. Then the heavens opened, and it began to piss with rain, or it could've been piss. Then it turned red. I guessed it was blood. Then my younger self's piss turned to blood too. She just kept laughing at me and peeing until I woke up in a cold sweat. I was drenched through. For a moment, I thought I'd pissed myself. My younger self's behaviour scared me more than seeing my old self being shot to pieces. Do you believe in the significance of dreams?'

'I don't think the idea of their significance is without merit', says Litze.

'Never really gave them much thought', I say.

'Me neither', says Blume. 'Until that one. You can take all sorts of things from a dream, but I eventually worked out mine. I was telling myself that I'd taken things too lightly, and the very thing that kept me alive so long would eventually end up getting me killed. I wasn't even prepared to listen to myself, so what hope was there? But I've started listening to me. Something I used to do, but I got lost along the way.'

You and me both, I think.

'And I wasn't bought off, if that's what you were thinking, Lothar. This house, these luxuries that I have, are my treat to myself, to take things easy for a while. I'm wise enough to realise that Yumeni is someone who I don't want to be going after. I now have a cause of one', says Blume, pointing her right index finger just above her cleavage.

'OK, I'm sorry', says Litze.

'What for?' she asks.

'For questioning your courage, and for getting you involved', he says.

'No sweat', she says. Blume turns to me and asks, 'So, protégé, do you love this guy?'

I look at Litze and feel myself blush.

'Stupid question', says Blume.

I don't answer. I don't have to. My blushing answers for me. 'This is my fault. It's about me, and he's trying to help', I say.

'Hmmm. Litze is forever a gentleman, you know. A rare breed. A dying breed in my world. But I still say you should stay out of it. Be happy. Yumeni's not worth worrying your pretty little head over.'

'I don't think we could stop now if we wanted to. We're in too deep. I need to take the fight to them. The deeper I dig, the more curious I get. It's a bad habit of mine. Guess you could call it an addiction', I say.

'I can think of better things to be addicted to', Blume says, smiling.

'But what Yumeni is up to is serious. Aren't you curious? There's a lot at stake here.'

'There usually is, protégé, but you can't always save the world. Ideals are OK if you can afford them.'

'We won't impose; you've done enough already', Litze says as he rises from his chair. 'We'll deal with it.'

Blume looks at Litze; then she looks at me. 'Becker, you remind me of what I used to be like. I wish that person was still here sometimes, but that was then.'

Blume looks at me intently. I remind her of herself. I take that as a compliment.

'Fuck it, Lothar! You've saved my ass so many times; I owe you.'

'No, you don't', he says.

'Yes, I do. Let's just hope dreams don't come true.'

FIFTY-NINE

WE'RE STILL IN the kitchen as the afternoon approaches evening. As more beers are consumed, the three of us talk about everything and nothing. Setting the world to rights. It seems no subject is taboo, and I try to remember when I've had a conversation like this. Hardly ever. I don't have anybody that I can confide in. The closest was Donny Walsh until we fell out, and that now can't be fixed. Blume tells us that she has a contact near the location where Yumeni was last spotted and he'll signal when we need to move.

We're all hungry. Blume has some leftover pasta salad and French sticks to keep us going. She says she's not much of a cook (something else we have in common), so she volunteers Litze to make us a meal later. He laughs but doesn't mind and seems to know his way around her kitchen. A sign that he's been here many times before. He makes us a vegetable stew. That's more for me, because he knows I don't eat meat anymore, though I still like fish.

Blume serves us Ben & Jerry's ice cream for dessert. Later, she pours us some brandy. I'm conscious that I shouldn't overdo it, but after the day we've had, we deserve it. Then Blume offers us some dope. She says it's excellent stuff, something she indulges in occasionally, so I take a drag. And Blume was right: it's as if waves of pleasure infuse my whole body. I hand the joint to Litze, but he declines. Surprisingly, Litze doesn't seem to mind my taking smoke. And I think, *Why should I be surprised?* Maybe I got it wrong about Litze. Eight years is a long time out of someone's life. Even though it can feel like yesterday for some, it's enough time for people to change. You have to remember that there's a lot of water under the bridge. Litze was a hard bastard. But he's mellowed over the years, and I'm convinced Blume has been part of it. She'll never replace his beloved wife, but I think Silke would have approved of Karla Blume. She's not hidden the fact that she's a free spirit and that her right to be her own woman is non-negotiable. I like that about her. So does Litze.

Blume was in the German army and later worked in covert operations for the state, initially as an analyst, but she wanted to work in the field. That's where she met Litze. That was six years ago, in Belgium, and Litze agreed to mentor her as he thought that she had potential. The feeling was mutual, and they've been in contact on and off ever since. She tells me that she has German, Italian, and French heritage, which explains her exotic looks, and reveals that she speaks six languages, without boasting. Blume is stunning, and I've never been backwards in letting someone know it when I think that. I've never had an issue with my sexuality. Others have, though. I'm attracted to people, and I'm attracted to her. And I sense it's mutual but would never take that as a given, just in case I'd make a fool of myself.

I envy the fact that Blume has found someone like Litze, who accepts her for who she is. Reading between the lines, I don't get a sense that she's hung up on monogamy. I don't think there's anything wrong with it per se. But in my experience, it felt like putting toothpaste back into a tube. She seems further down the road than me. In the short time I've spent with her, I've worked out her thing: She isn't spending time trying to find the right person. It's about becoming the right person.

I leave my mentor and Blume to catch up. They don't make me feel like a gooseberry, but I want to give them some privacy. The chemistry between them is palpable, and I don't want to get in the way of that. Litze doesn't hide the fact that he likes her, but I sense he's inhibited by me. That's nice, because I believe he's respectful. But he needn't be. I'm pleased for him, and for her. They're lucky to have found each other. And it seems they have the courage and the wisdom to leave each other alone. That sounds like a proper adult relationship.

I go upstairs to the room that Blume directs me to, which is one of four large bedrooms with the same spacious feel as down below. I strip and enter the walk-in shower. I abuse the soap as the hot water pummels my skin, reanimating me. I dry myself and put on a cotton robe that I find in the wardrobe.

It's easy to forget that this place has electric blinds which are remotely operated. It's easy to forget them because out here, who would need them? There are neighbours, but no one in spying distance. There's a lot of land around the building. I estimate twenty-two acres or thereabouts. A wooded area which enhances the building's exclusive location. She's like me in that she prefers her solitude. Prefers is a tame word. For me, solitude is an essential part of my identity. Without it, I can't function. Others need people to function. I am the opposite. Being in crowds or with people too long drains my energy. Then I wonder about Blume's comments regarding her exes. Like mine, her love life's turbulent at best. But she seems not to have settled, which is good. It's hard enough to have relationships anyway, let alone in this game. But she seems to have found a happy medium, and Litze has been her constant.

This environment seems to suit Karla Blume's personality: it's vibrant, spacious, and free from clutter. Also, there's a strong independent streak that she's managed to retain. I can imagine her walking around nude. And with her body, why not? She's got it, and she certainly flaunts it. Not in an arrogant, desperate, look-at-me way, like some women do, but confidently. The fact that she doesn't have to try is the sexiest part of her. Her stillness is evident. She's comfortable, so she makes you feel comfortable too. And that's a skill I've not even begun to master, as some sense my restless energy. If you believe in that spiritualist stuff, they call it vibration. We all operate at different frequencies. I guess my vibration has got higher, but sometimes I feel like a hot air balloon with endless bags to throw overboard. That process never ends, for anyone. Blume looks like she's always been at ease in her skin, and for us women, that's a rarity. Body consciousness is one of life's challenges, for both men and women. You're constantly bombarded with someone else's ideas of what a woman or a man should look like. No wonder that we're screwed up. Training my mind as well as my body has been my path to self-acceptance. But it's a journey, not a destination. I can honestly say that I enjoy being in my own skin more than before.

As I try to sleep, I can hear Litze and Blume laugh together. It's faint but still audible. Then I realise that my door is slightly ajar as the noise carries. They talk and laugh for some time. Then it goes quiet. Which I take to mean that they're probably kissing now. Litze is probably helping her off with her jacket, and her top, and her bra. Her full breasts are revealed as they retain their firmness. She lets him suck her nipples and her back arches in response. He does this for a while, tenderly, taking his time, like the character he is. She's aroused now as she takes him by the hand and into the living area. There's loads of space and endless possibilities. They decide to do it on the rug in front of the fire. That's where I'd do it. She takes off his shirt and undoes his pants. His erection is like a diving board as she pushes him down on his back and takes him in her mouth. She works on him, and every cell in Litze's body vibrates. But he doesn't want to come inside her, not yet. I imagine he's a gentleman and he'll wait for her. He lifts her head and kisses her passionately as he puts her on her back and goes down on her. Blume's body shudders as he goes to work. He looks up at her breasts like a climber viewing the landscape. They retain their shape despite her movement as she arches her back and the groans continue like a mantra. Then Litze turns Blume on her front to get what he came for: her ass. He slaps her playfully on her left cheek, and she says it's not hard enough, and he slaps her again. That's better, she says. Then he slips inside her, holding her waist with his left hand while pulling her hair with his right. He pulls tighter, deliberately so. And she likes it. They move in unison, like really connected lovers do. They tread the fine line between fucking and making love. I never think they're the same. Blume bucks like a stallion, because she knows he likes the view. Pleasure isn't just physical. She feels him deep inside her. He responds by pulling her harder. Blume can feel Litze's droplets of sweat on her back as they reach a frenzy. Her hair and body are drenched as they wait for each other, like good lovers do. Litze is a gentleman and I imagine won't come before she does. Blume doesn't mind his coming first as she believes in equal rights. Their cells become one, and the room disappears as he explodes inside her and she erupts as they're transported into another ecstatic dimension. The room returns as they curl up together, glad they were on the same journey.

I know my imagining the way this went down might be bullshit, but this is fantasy, right? My mind is doing a little reverse engineering, which is OK. But I defy anyone to resist Karla Blume, a woman of extraordinary sexual power. She's the embodiment of pleasure, and Litze is human after all. And he's still attractive, and yes, I've thought about it. This is a welcome distraction. When you do what I do for a living, you need to take your mind somewhere else to retain any part of your sanity that you have left. They say that it's the brain's way of protecting you. I take off my robe and look at my naked body on the cool cotton sheets. Fingers aren't only for triggers. I take my mind and my body somewhere else.

SIXTY

I HEAR MUFFLED sounds of conversation from downstairs. I check my watch, and it's 7.15am. I feel slightly hung-over from the drink and the dope. But I'm mostly OK. I put on my robe and walk down the wooden stairs to the kitchen area, where Blume and Litze are sitting together, both dressed in robes. I can't help but notice Blume's breasts as her nipples make her costume look like it's embossed. Litze seems less inhibited now, and she has her arm around him. I don't think my fantasy is too far off, as they emanate sensual afterglow. She gets up from her chair and greets me with her thousand-watt smile and kisses me on the lips, which surprises and pleases me at the same time.

She asks me what I would like to eat and says that she's already made porridge and had a protein shake. I resist the temptation to say, I bet you have. Although I don't think she'd mind the joke, I don't want to embarrass Litze. He looks more relaxed than he has in years.

***

Blume wants to show us the rest of her property. She moved here three years ago after living in most of Europe's major cities and deciding she wanted a change of pace. Returning to the country was always the plan. Which makes sense, as she tells us she originally grew up on a farm. I don't ask her whether she gets lonely or scared. Blume doesn't look the type, as I can tell she can take good care of herself. Fighters know other fighters. It's a primeval thing that's passed down from thousands of years of evolution. (That's one word they should ban from the dictionary because I don't think mankind has evolved at all.) I can study the way someone moves; their balance, breathing, posture, body position; the energy they emit. A biomechanical template that only other fighters seem to know. Most great fighters won't usually pick fights until they have no choice.

One of the best fighters that I ever worked with, Master Chen, who was originally from China, trained like a demon. I met him on a visit to London and was given his number by an ex. This was an invite-only session, and I guess my ex-lover thought I was worthy enough to be given his contact details. He was small but had big energy and spoke slowly and two notches higher than a whisper. The training hall was a small, unremarkable-looking room in a converted shoe factory somewhere in East London. It was poorly lit, with little ventilation, some mats, a punch bag, and pads. The space was only big enough for a dozen people, maybe fourteen at a push. But that was the point: it was supposed to be for an elite group, and Chen came highly recommended. There were only six of us then. We trained for about three hours, steaming and stinking up the room. And I thought I was doing OK until I had to fight him. Then I realised that I wasn't doing OK. The only other person who made me feel this inadequate in a fight was my mentor.

After Master Chen had picked me up from my ass, I asked him whether he ever had to use his skills in anger. And he said no. Then I asked him how he knew if his techniques worked. He fixed me with his brown eyes. It felt like I was in a freeze frame. For a moment, I thought I'd insulted him. I was about to apologise, then he gave me a warm smile. That's when the penny dropped: Master Chen's techniques worked because he never had to use them.

Blume tells us openly of various men who drop by. And I don't detect even a hint of jealousy from Litze. That's a measure of their relationship and his security. I've never known him to be threatened by other men. Especially, for example, the special forces guys Blume cancelled because Litze asked for her help. They look her up when they're in town. She also has a few girlfriends who drop by from time to time. Some of her girlfriends don't understand how she could live out here on her own. But only someone like me, a loner, would get it. Nobody is telling you when you can or can't come in. Nobody to answer to. Nobody to be obligated to. But some would consider people like us selfish. And I would say to someone like that: And your point is . . . ?

In the middle of the building, Blume shows us her library, which is modest, as she does most of her reading on her tablet, making a physical library redundant. At the rear of the property, Blume has a gym with chrome weights, a treadmill, a punch bag, and some machines. As we walk further, I can smell the aromatic herbs coming from the spa area comprising a sauna, steam room, and hot tub with touch-sensitive switches and a remote control that can change the spot lighting to virtually any colour. She says we should take a dip later. Naked, I assume, of course. We Germans don't seem to be hung up on nudity like the people in some of the countries I've visited. I can't imagine it any other way, but Litze and I will see each other naked for the first time. And even for someone who considers herself quite liberal, given he's the closest thing I have to a parent, I honestly don't know how I will feel about that.

Blume finishes her tour of the house by showing us her collection of weapons, in what looks like a small panic room concealed behind one of the bookshelves. There are enough guns, knives, rocket-propelled grenades, and Semtex to confirm that not only can Blume take care of herself, but she's also not afraid to either. Lucky for the men in her life that she's not the jealous type. We return to the kitchen. Blume wants to collect some supplies and tells us that she's got a lead about lorries heading towards the location of Yumeni's last known whereabouts. Her contact will text her later, so we'll need to move. I tell Litze to go with her while I stay behind.

***

I must have dozed off; I look at the time. Litze and Blume have been gone for about forty-five minutes. I rest on the long grey sofa and stare at the ceiling. Then my gaze switches all around me. I wouldn't mind a house like this myself if I could stay in one place. But I feel like a shark, as if I have to keep moving, though I'll have to stop one day. We all will. I go back to the kitchen and help myself to another beer. She did say help yourself. I wouldn't mind some dope, but I don't know where she keeps it. There's some leftover stew from last night, so I reheat it in the microwave. In some ways, it tastes even better than it did last night. Litze is one damn fine cook!

I sit at the breakfast bar and wonder how much a place like this is worth. Blume has done well for herself. But she's not a show off. She enjoys nice things, but I sense that she's not attached to them in the way perhaps I am. It's nice to meet a woman who lives her life on her terms. It's much, much harder for a female to do that than a man. And before you start saying that this is some sexist bullshit I'm spewing, I'm just stating facts and observations that I've made while growing up. Blume owns her life and her pleasure. A-fucking-men to that, sister! I return to the living area and see through the huge, south-facing window that Litze and Blume are returning with supplies. I go out to help them, and we divide the bags between us and empty the contents on the breakfast bar. She asks if I'm OK and whether I've gotten some rest. I say that I have but I couldn't find the dope. Blume apologises for her oversight, saying half-jokingly that I must think she's a terrible host, and tells me that it is in a metal container in the knife drawer. I see that there are some pre-made joints, so I take one. Although Litze didn't smoke last night, I'm not naive enough to think that he hasn't partaken at some stage. As a covert operative, I'm sure he's been there, seen it, done it, done worse, and worn the T-shirt.

I light the joint, take it in my mouth, and inhale deeply. The paper erupts like a mini volcano as I melt with the surroundings and release the magic smoke into the air. And to my surprise, Litze extends his hand to me, taking the joint. He takes a puff and smiles at me. I sense he's relieved that he no longer has to stand on ceremony on my account. And this is his way of showing me that. I believe he has Blume to thank for that. Then it's her turn. Not wanting to be left out, waiting to participate in the shared experience, she takes the joint. It looks good between her lips. She kisses me again; then she kisses Litze. Then she smiles at the pair of us. Later, we'll head for the Jacuzzi. I take the joint back from Blume and take another puff. I'm feeling more relaxed about Litze seeing me naked for the first time.

***

Blume tells us that she'll join us in the Jacuzzi later as she's about to lock up and set the alarms. Litze walks ahead of me as we enter the changing area. It's made of natural wood, with lockers and towels neatly folded on the benches. Litze goes to the other side of the room, still keeping a respectful distance. I look at him and smile. He smiles back. It's as if we're both waiting to see who'll make the first move. It could be the dope, but knowing me, I doubt it, as I don't care anymore. I push to the back of my mind that he's my mentor. That somehow this isn't right. I sense Litze is trying to hide his discomfort.

I smile at him, telling him that's it's OK.

But he's feeling awkward. Uncomfortable. He's trying to be cool about it, but it's too late. The marijuana has put paid to that. I adopt the ladies-first rule and strip very slowly and place my clothes carefully in my locker. I'm now fully unclothed. Then it's his turn; we do this in silence. No words are needed as there's a sexual tension in the air. He avoids eye contact with me. He looks a bit nervous, which is reassuring. And he's turned on. How can I tell? Well, let's just say that he's spectacularly failed the erectile dysfunction test.

I decide to brazen it out and turn around to face him. I'm wet between my legs. My heart is racing a little faster than normal, so I focus on my breathing. I like my body, and I know Litze does too. Our eyes lock as we just look at each other. We've been through so many things together, worse things than this, but there's something about nudity that still freaks some people out. This is new territory for both of us. He's in good shape for his age. He looks better than a lot of men twenty or thirty years younger. I study his body for a time and show him with my eyes that I like it. Then Litze gestures with his hands for me to leave the changing room first as we take our towels. He'll be able to see my ass, and I wonder whether he'll like it as much as Blume's. I hope so, but I tell myself to get a grip.

We walk down one of the corridors that leads to the Jacuzzi area. We step into the cold blue room, and I go first into the bubbling warm water. Litze follows me in and sets the controls. We're now touching distance from each other. The Jacuzzi feels invigorating as the propelled jets of water make a gargling sound; bubbles crash and pop against our bodies. Litze seems a little more relaxed now, but not completely, not yet. Maybe that will change when Blume joins us. What did I say about monogamy? It's like trying to put toothpaste back into a tube.

I look over to Litze and can tell that this situation is strange for him. Maybe he feels that he has to be responsible. He was, after all, my mentor since I was very young. I was a child then. I'm not now, so he needn't worry. Easy to say, though. Litze's discomfort hasn't completely passed. But it must be strange for him: the mentor and mentee and a Jacuzzi. We're both stark naked, stoned, and horny. That's not the way it should be. But what way should it be? If I cared what others thought of me, I would have followed a different path. Life isn't just a colouring book or painting by numbers. Sometimes the colour goes off the lines, but I prefer to draw my lines. I want him to relax. I want him. The power dynamic has shifted in this tub, and the roles reversed, so I decide to tease him.

'So Lothar, how do you like this?'

'This is good', he says.

'What do you think of my tits?'

'What?'

'My tits. You didn't think they were real before. Remember? When we were at your flat, I got the impression that you didn't believe me.' I rise provocatively out of the Jacuzzi, stand up, glide towards him, and cup my breasts. 'Would you like to feel them?'

'What?'

'My tits.'

'Becker?' he replies. I can sense he is uncomfortable.

'It's OK. I want to prove to you that these are in fact my real breasts, Litze, not enhanced in any way. Not silicone, saline, or any of that stuff. I think they look good. Nice and firm.' I give them another squeeze. 'I'm very proud of my natural breasts. Are you sure that you don't want to feel them?' I move closer and jut my chest towards his face while I hold them in both hands.

'You've made your point, Becker; you can put them away now.'

'Are you sure? 'I say as I jiggle them while keeping a straight face at the same time. I turn my body to give him a side view of my breasts. I know I've crossed the line, but I don't care anymore.

'Enough, Becker, I was wrong, OK? I'm sorry. I can tell that your breasts are indeed real. Happy now?'

'I am. Very', I say as I return to my side of the pool and laugh at him. Litze's stern look changes and he laughs, flicking water at me with his hands.

'I had you going there, didn't I?' I say. Litze smiles at me. We've trained together, bled together, killed together; now we've been naked together. The last taboo. This Jacuzzi is even better than a karate dojo. In here, we're all the same. They say that if you want to feel less intimidated by authority, imagine your boss naked. Now I've seen my mentor, and he's seen me in all my naked glory.

I'll accept whatever happens when Blume joins us. We didn't plan this. We're just going with the flow. It will help me forget for a short time. And for that, I'm grateful. I want to jump on my mentor, but I sense there's still resistance from him. But that is fading. I won't push him. There's no need. As someone once said to me: 'Fan the flames of desire with the bellows of indifference.' When Blume arrives, we'll put Litze's legendary self-control to the test. It'll be my turn to break him for a change. Maybe we'll put on a show for him first; I sense that Blume is game. I defy any man, even him, to resist us in these circumstances.

'I'm going into the sauna room. Want to join me?'

'No, I'll stay here and wait for Blume', he says, still resisting.

'OK', I say as I step out of the Jacuzzi, I pick up my towel, dry myself down, and head back towards the corridor. The floor feels cool beneath my feet, and I leave wet footprints as I walk towards the door. The oven-like heat from the sauna envelops me, reminding me of when I opened an aeroplane door after landing in the Caribbean. I set the sand timer on the wall, which gives you fifteen minutes, but I doubt I'll last that long. I place my towel on the top of the wooden bench to protect myself from the heat and lie on it face up. You could cut the heat with a chainsaw as my pores start to open up. I'm gasping for air, but I slowly begin to acclimatise as I regulate my breathing. My skin cooks in its juices as I sit up to avoid the sweat going into my eyes. I look at the sand timer. Not even close to fifteen minutes— more like four—as I decide to bail out. I feel totally relaxed now as I take my towel and walk out of the sauna into the relatively crisp corridor air towards the steam room.

There's an immediate temperature change, and I open the smoked-glass door. It feels like I'm entering another world as I'm hit by a wave of cold air, which is a relief. It's beautiful and quiet; just how I like it. The steam room, which is a few doors down on the right towards the main pool, is decorated in blue and white marble patterns, with rocks in a circular stone cavity in the centre of the room. I sit without a towel, butt naked, on the stone-slabbed seating area. The vapour in the room smells minty, like menthol. And I can immediately feel the effect on my chest as I breathe much more easily than before. But I won't stay in here for too long. Even if I wanted to, the steam would eventually overwhelm me.

My senses are heightened now. I think I was always sensitive to things, ever since childhood. The dope has enhanced that. My body feels like a receiver, picking up good vibrations. Echoes of good and evil, flashback images, and voices from incoherent conversations, like dream sequences. I start to wonder about where Blume has got to. I'm soaking now like I've been caught in a storm. I open the door of the steam room. I walk back to go back in the Jacuzzi area where I see Litze still in the whirlpool and Blume standing at the edge of the entrance, already dressed.

'Sorry, playtime's over', she says. 'We've got to go.'

SIXTY-ONE

BLUME TELLS US that her contact has spotted activity at the AXAS site. A shipment of lorries is on the move. We change into black combat gear and arm ourselves as we take Karla Blume's black BMW people carrier with special ghost plates. Litze punches the location into the onboard satnav and Blume lets my mentor drive. It's late evening now, and it will take us at least an hour to get to our destination. We've loaded the BMW with an array of submachine guns, rocket-propelled grenades, knives, frag grenades, etc., enough to fight a small war with, and it all makes me wonder how Blume acquired such an armoury and why she needs this stuff. I also wonder how she has managed to maintain her sunny disposition despite everything. I'm sure she has her demons, but she hides them well.

The vehicle hugs the road as it cruises at a steady speed. The traffic is moderate, and Litze often ignores the satnav instructions. I joke with him and tell him that it's because he doesn't like the thought of a woman's voice telling him what to do. He gives me a playful sneer as we make progress to our destination.

***

We stop at the roadside and look at the schematic of the AXAS building on Blume's smartphone, and it's heavily guarded. There's a fifteen-foot perimeter fence, which is electrified. The building itself looks like an elongated cross, with several entry points. Blume was right about security, and I have an idea on how I can get in. Litze isn't keen, but I say it's the only way to get access to the building.

The bridge nearest to the building is a mile away; it straddles a dual carriageway, and every vehicle that goes into that place has to pass under it. If I can jump off the bridge and land on one of the lorries, I can get in undetected and disable the alarm system so that Litze and Blume can follow me. It's high risk, but they reluctantly agree it's the best option. And I'm the best person to do it. When I was training with Litze, I used to practise parkour, the free-running discipline that was invented in France. What was helpful about it was that it taught you how to land. It has also been practised by some of the best special forces units in the world. It's been a while since I did it, but I think I should be able to.

We drive to the bridge and wait. According to the intel, deliveries come in at about ten in the evening. I look at the drop. It's just over five metres. It'll be risky. There's no second try.

I check the time—it's about a quarter to ten—and I see the first vehicle pass under the bridge.

But it's not a lorry.

Ideally, it has to be big so that it will give me enough area that I'll have a chance to land on the top. An articulated lorry which is over three times the width of the bridge would be perfect. Enough room to make a decent landing. If I do this right and remember my training, then I shouldn't make too much of a noise. The key is to not tense up at the moment of impact. That's easier said than done, because that's what most people would do, especially when the fear response kicks in.

At around ten, we see a white articulated lorry travelling at about forty miles per hour.

I have to time this to perfection.

I stand on the edge of the bridge and feel the cool night air. I watch the lorry as it approaches, trundling like a metallic monster. I feel like it's in slow motion as I descend from the bridge, relaxing my muscles. I float momentarily and am awoken from my dream state with a sudden violent bump. I land on all fours, but the momentum of the lorry forces me to somersault backwards, nearly sending me off the top. My hands grab the edge of the cargo section, and I haul myself onto the top. I hope the sound of the lorry masked any noise that I made.

I lie flat on top of the vehicle and feel it shudder and vibrate as it heads towards the AXAS building. The lorry screeches to a stop, and I hear men talk. The security guard lets the driver through. I lie motionless as I wait for an opportunity. The lorry drives towards a large hangar, where it parks. I spring catlike towards the metal girders in the roof and hang until the truck passes beneath me before I jump onto some stacked-up storage boxes situated to the side. I slither to the floor, where I watch from behind the boxes. A man wearing a white coat and glasses walks through the entrance towards the lorry; he's holding what looks like a clipboard. He stands at the rear of the vehicle as the lorry driver gets out of the lorry's cabin to meet him. He unlocks the back shutters, which spring upward suddenly. I look inside and see cargo that I wasn't expecting.

SIXTY-TWO

THE LORRY IS full of people. All sizes and age ranges. Then I see a man in a blue suit enter the hangar. He shakes the truck driver's hand. It's one of those handshakes which indicates that they know each other. The gesture is more than perfunctory, but they are not close. Just enough warmth to remind each other that although they are amiable, this is strictly business.

The driver pulls out a man from the back of the trailer with a lack of regard reserved for the unimportant. Then another body; a small, delicate, and elegant woman. Then another man this time, who looks a little older. The lorry driver waits for a moment, as if he's trying to decide who's next, like it's some human lottery. Then the suited man points inside like he's trying to help the lorry driver decide, and someone else comes out. From what I can tell, it looks like a small boy. They take him out of the lorry, but I sense something different about this one: he doesn't seem as compliant as the others, as he pushes away at the truck driver. He displays a defiance I can identify with.

The lorry driver takes out three more people, seven in total. The rest remain in the lorry. The man in the lab coat with the clipboard is checking his paperwork. Most of them look docile and compliant, but the boy is still resisting. His spirit can't be contained; he shrugs

247

off the lorry driver and makes a run for it. I can feel my hands sweat on my weapon as the boy comes in this direction. He runs towards the entrance at first, but it's blocked off by two security guards. Then he comes towards the boxes.

He comes towards me.

Which means we'll both be dead. I don't want him to die, but I can't save him. I'm torn. The boy runs towards me. Then I see the suited man move into position like he's posing for cameras. The boy runs towards me until our eyes lock on each other. At that moment, we are frozen in time. I don't know how I know this, but he resists any temptation to call me. It's as if he knows that there is no point in both of us getting killed. Instead, he runs away from me towards the entrance again, even though he knows he won't make it. The suited man draws his weapon, aims, and shoots the boy in the back. The muzzle flashes as I hear the projectile impact and rupture his body. Bullet on bone and flesh. His body snaps forward. He falls to his knees, and his torso slumps face down on the floor. The blood expands around him.

I grip my gun like a vice, cursing in my head. This is a new feeling for me: remorse. But what could I do?

I'm breathing heavily, but I have to focus. I need to find and disable the alarm system so that Litze and Blume can storm the building. I was thinking of my survival. The boy instinctively knew that. A young life with an old soul who would rather have died than give in. But also, he would rather have died than get someone else killed. At this moment, I feel revulsion. I've been shamed by a child.

I have to put those thoughts out of my head for now, until, no doubt, they return.

And they most certainly will.

I have no idea how many men there are here, but we will be outnumbered, that's for sure. There are only three of us. The lorry driver locks the back of the lorry and leaves with the other two men, who escort the six people out of the hangar. The security team join them, and I wait.

I look at the lorry. There's nothing I can do for them until I have disabled the alarm system. From the schematic of the building, I remember seeing a small box which I assume is the main power supply. If I can get to it and send a signal to Litze, they'll be ready to move.

I run towards the entrance with my gun drawn and try to get my bearings. I'm facing south, which means the power supply is in front of me. Getting there will be tricky as there is no natural cover. But I'm fast, which is what I'm relying upon. I see a small truck about fifty metres away. I eat up the distance undetected. The signal box is a further one hundred and fifty metres away. Still, there's not much cover. I see two armed security guards chatting casually, without a care. I see a smaller building which is not on a direct route to the power supply, but at least it's some cover. I run as fast as my legs will allow while remaining undetected.

My breathing is heavy.

The outhouse door is slightly ajar. Even though I should be heading for the power supply, something pulls me into the building. I draw my gun and ease the door open, pushing it slowly with the outside of my left foot, maintaining a two-handed grip on my pistol. To my relief, the door doesn't creak. As I open it, I hear the flies feasting, and I can smell old urine and shit hanging in the air. The stench is burning into me. My eyes water. My throat convulses as I try not to gag. I continue despite my nausea and I step into the building.

There is enough light coming through the window to reveal a trestle table, upon which are glass bottles with faded labels and broken test tubes. The dust on the surface is old, and the lack of hygiene suggests that well-being wasn't a priority here. I scan around the room and see the windows at the rear of the building. In one of the panes of glass, I see what looks like a handprint with abnormally long fingers. It looks like someone was trying to escape but was dragged back. I put my left hand across my nose and mouth in a vain attempt to block the smell.

In the right-hand corner of the room, there is a series of open bin liners with clothes poking out of them. I get closer and see that some of the garments have been tossed on the floor. It's hard to tell the quality as they're caked in dirt, but there is a mixture of clothes. Mainly adult costumes, smaller items, and something that seems out of place here but adds to the bleakness: a teddy bear dressed in a dirty cardigan. Then my mind reverse-engineers the surroundings and I think thoughts that even I don't want to contemplate. I realised a long time ago that evil and good have at least one thing in common: they have no limits. But I've been spending too long on the dark side of the scale. I know that I'll have to deal with the crap in my head one day, but I've probably been in denial, telling myself that I'm OK. Self-delusion can only take you so far until it eventually succumbs to objective reality.

The sane part of my brain tells me finally to get the fuck out of there. I can't take any more; I burst through the door, gasping gratefully as I take in lungfuls of the fresh air. The hell is still in my head, and I want it to go quickly. My mind flashes back to times that I never buried but just parked. It's weird how sensations can take you back to places, good and bad. I head towards the main power supply. It's then I hear the click. I feel a familiar metallic coldness on the back of my neck.

If I don't get my next move right, I'm a dead woman.

SIXTY-THREE

IT'S A GUN pressed against the nape of my neck. It's happened before, but luckily not that often in a real-life situation. Mostly in training.

'Waffe fallen lassen. Hände hoch', says the voice in a strong German accent, which means 'Drop the weapon. Hands up.' I've been away for so long, I can't place his accent. It sounds like it could be Bavarian, but I'm not sure.

The man still has the gun pressed to my neck. I drop my weapon to the ground and look at it in hope rather than expectation. He sees me eyeing my weapon and knows I can't reach for my gun on the floor. That's suicide for sure. He knows it. I know it. He could pull the trigger before I can make a tenth of a blink. At least it would be quick. No suffering. One of my last memories on earth would be of me being in some shitty outhouse with some old clothes. My body would be dumped inside with a child's teddy bear to keep me company.

I slow my breathing down as he pats me with his left hand.

I have to get this next move right.

I relax even more. I want to transmit to him that I am docile. Compliant. At his mercy. Any panicked movement could cause him to react, and my head would explode over the both of us.

Litze and I trained for such an occasion. When I started, I was like an elephant in ballet shoes, but I'm nothing if not determined. My pride wouldn't let me give up. Luckily, I haven't had to do this until now.

Most people wouldn't try this move.

But I'm not most people. That's what I'm hoping for: that it will catch my opponent by surprise.

Unless, of course, he isn't most people either.

Then I definitely am a dead woman.

Relax, Becker.

Breathe.

Relax.

I make my move.

I use a Krav Maga technique involving quick footwork, swiftly rotating my body 180 degrees in an anti-clockwise motion, which means I would be facing my assailant; which means my head now isn't in the line of fire of his gun.

Half the job is done.

My momentum helps me follow through with a right elbow strike to the face. I break his cheekbone while trapping the attacker's right arm holding the gun, with my left and right hand simultaneously. I twist the weapon from his grip; disarming and pointing the attacker's gun straight at him.

I recognised him instantly: It was the man in the suit who was carrying the clipboard earlier. The man that shot the kid in the back. He was holding his right cheek and looking shocked. More bemused. And I think, a little embarrassed. At least his suit is nice. It looks Italian. Pinstriped. Maybe a Pal Zileri or an Armani. Something he'll soon be seen dead in.

The man in the suit fixes his gaze on me. He's doing his calculations. Wondering whether he can get out of this. Wondering whether he has any leverage. He can wonder all he likes.

I'm ready to send him to the next world when the ground shudders. I hear a massive explosion, which distracts me. The man in the suit exploits this, rushes me and strikes my arm with something metallic that he's pulled from the inside of his jacket, forcing me to release my gun. I didn't see it coming, but he's better than I thought. Litze always says never to pay too much respect to an opponent or too little. My right arm stings, but I try to shake off the pain. He strikes again. He misses. But not by much. The man in the suit attacks again, and the metal object swooshes. I read him and duck as the metal bar cuts the space where my head used to be. I punch him in the kidneys, and he's winded. But the man in the suit is strong. Maybe much better than I thought. He swings again at me, and I trap his right arm with an S-block at his shoulder, cutting his swing trajectory and his power, like switching off a light bulb. I land a palm strike on his left cheek. I send the man in the suit onto his back. He's covered in dirt now, and his suit doesn't look so nice, which seems to annoy him.

He gets up quickly. Neither of us is going for their gun. Under normal circumstances, they wouldn't seem that far way. But they're far enough not to risk it. The man in the suit pulls a switchblade from his belt and clicks it open like it's an extension of his hand. It glimmers in the moonlight and looks pristine, like his suit used to. We move around like boxers, circling, trying to gauge the next move. Our gazes lock onto each other, trying not to betray anything. This is the ultimate poker game. I pick up his metal bar from near my feet. The man in the suit slashes at me with the knife. It sings through the air, hissing like a snake on helium, so sharp it seems to cut through molecules. He slashes at me, wild this time. He lashes out again, but I time it perfectly as I crack the metal bar against his elbow. But not perfect enough, as he's still holding the knife. He thrusts again, more in hope now, as he seems tired. I play with him. I invite him. Give him the feeling that he's got a chance. He comes at me one last time and tries to stab me with an overarm action. I close the space between us, block his strike with my left arm, and simultaneously thrust the metal bar into his throat.

The man's face morphs into a badly bruised apple as his life drains away. He convulses and falls to his knees, clutching his throat. He looks at me one final time. Not in sorrow or disdain, but in acceptance. Then he can't look anymore. He's gone into an eternal dream, collapsing to the ground. This is a kill that I'm proud of, because this is for that little boy.

I run to see what's happened to Litze and Karla Blume. Then I look to the distance and see that the explosion was Blume's car bursting into flames.

SIXTY-FOUR

I SEE MY last chance of rescue literally go up in smoke. Then I hear footsteps and rifles being cocked and clicks as safeties are taken off. I'm surrounded by a ring of nine security men. I drop my weapon and kick it away from me. I raise my hands slowly. Then the back of my head cracks and everything goes black.

***

I wake up with the worst hangover ever. A blurred figure slowly sharpens as my eyes regain the ability to focus. I see Karl Yumeni sitting opposite me. My hands are tied, and I'm sitting on a chair. There are two security men standing either side of him. I recognise one of the other men from the hangar, the one wearing a white lab coat. I can see him better now. His receding hairline, vacant expression, and glasses make him look professorial. Yumeni looks better in real life than his photos. With his greying hair and beard, he has an exotic Middle Eastern vibe that makes him look regal. He's dressed in a crisp grey suit that looks as expensive as his surroundings. The fact he's very attractive makes his menace more unnerving. He's proof that evil doesn't care what body it inhabits.

Yumeni looks at some documents as he sits behind his huge tinted-glass office table. He doesn't engage me. It's his way of increasing the tension. He looks like a man who never rushes to do anything and is in total control. My inner voice laughs at me as I think of escaping and realise that I would be dead before I blinked. If they know anything about me, and I'm sure they do, they won't give me an inch. I scan the room for weapons. Apart from an Apple notebook computer, he has nothing much on his table except an expensive silver fountain pen, which he picks up and starts making notes with on some paper.

Yumeni looks up and whispers to the man on the left. The man then leaves and gives me a cursory glance as he does so. Yumeni looks at his mobile and swipes his fingers across the flat screen without emotion or expression. Then he finally looks at me.

'Miss Becker, I'm sorry I've kept you waiting', he says as he takes his gun from his holster and points it at me.

I give him a look that tells him that I don't believe he's sorry. And he knows it.

'And you really should have stayed out of this.'

I say nothing.

Yumeni's men cut my plastic ties.

'On your knees', says Yumeni as he points the gun at my head. I rise from the chair but stand.

'On your knees', repeats Yumeni, but I don't respond.

I look back at my life and think about the times that I've gone on my knees. Actually quite a few times. They were good times. Some excellent times in fact. Why? Because that was my choice back then. They are the only times I've willingly gone down on my knees for a man. In consensual situations. Sore knees were a small sacrifice. I will never get on my knees for Yumeni. I prefer to die on my feet than live on my knees.

At this moment, when I'm about to have my brains splattered to kingdom come, I think of all the women in history who've had to metaphorically and literally get on their knees for men: Women on their knees cleaning floors. The women who've had to apologise when it wasn't their fault. The ones who had to sublimate their looks, intelligence, and careers to make their men feel better about themselves. Women living in Saudi Arabia. The friends women had to give up. The bad jokes their men have told and they've had to laugh at. The driving: don't get me started! Statistically we rock, but try telling that to some men. The miserable marriages with contractual-obligation sex. You know exactly what I mean: that's when you're fucking him when you don't want to and thinking of someone else instead. Or the last real orgasm you can remember. That's OK if you like that sort of thing. Me personally? I prefer to keep it real. The very able women who get passed up for promotion time and time again in favour of a male colleague. The fact the we still don't get equal pay and the only time we get more money than a man is when we take part in human recreational videos. I'm not saying that porn doesn't have its place, but it's made mostly by men and all very predictable. Yumeni will have to saw off my legs at the knees.

Now I think of my mother, who was on her knees during her marriage to my fucking father. I remember girlfriends who, when their boyfriends said jump, said, 'How high?' That's the problem with men: they think they're in control, but really, we let them think that they are. That's how women survive. It's basic psychology. Little boys turning into big boys who never grow up. A great teacher of mine once said, 'The first child you will have is your husband'. He was right. I look at Yumeni and see echoes of my father: an angry child who, like lots of men—and women, to be fair—has confused masturbation with power. All the more reason I will never give in.

I welcome Yumeni's bullet because it means that I don't have to see his self-satisfied face or listen to his sanctimonious drivel. And that won't take much courage because there have been women who have blazed the trail far better than I. They're too numerous to mention. I regret that I won't be the one to take him down. But his demise is inevitable. Yumeni's already sown the seeds of his own destruction. He just doesn't know it yet.

In my final seconds, I only have my second- and third-favourite words to say to Yumeni before he pulls the trigger and puts me out of my misery. My favourite word is no, and it's not said enough in my opinion. But these will be the final things I say to Yumeni. I stand upright, proud and defiant. I look him coldly in the eyes and simply say, 'Fuck you!'

SIXTY-FIVE

THE CHEMIST CONVINCED Yumeni not to kill me. He didn't seem too pleased about that, but he agreed not to. I've been taken to this room, and my skin senses evil as it bristles with fear. It smells like an abattoir. I look around me. They say walls have ears. These walls wish they didn't. These walls wish that they were deaf at birth. Just as well that they can't see. It would be too much even for these walls to bear. I can image the horrors here: I can smell old and new blood. The walls listen like passive bystanders without the ability to act or intervene. The walls heard the blood-curdling screams that echoed and bounced around them like a ball in a squash court. The pain inflicted was so intense, the noises went beyond screams and were more high-pitched shrills, juxtaposed with the sadistic laughter of torturers.

I pass out many times after the electric shock treatment and the waterboarding. They tie my hands, hanging me from a meat hook, which is at the end of a chain suspended from the ceiling. It takes three of them to administer the punishment. My eyes are swollen. The left eye, in particular, is bad and bleeding profusely. They manage to stop the stream of blood momentarily, only to hit me again. It's like some sick game which my captors take real pleasure in. They keep asking me who I work for.

I tell them nothing.

The light above my head flicks and crackles, as if in sympathy for my plight.

The three men take it in turns to beat me. One of them is the guy Yumeni called the Chemist. They even tossed a coin. I guess that was to decide who was going first or who was going to be a bad cop, worse cop, or even worse. They strip me to my underwear, which barely covers any modesty I have left. My nipples are erect with the adrenaline and the fear I don't want to admit to. This seems to turn on my captors, helping prolong my agony. They haven't raped me. Maybe that's going to be next. It's the not knowing that is the worst. I'm trying to retain some control, some dignity in a hopeless situation. I imagine myself floating out of my body, watching myself as they do their worst. A trick I learned when I was younger. It helps me to survive.

They deliberately keep me awake. Sleep deprivation; I've trained for that too. They know this, but again, my captors want to know how far they can push me. I sense their frustration at and admiration of my resilience. A small victory which I'll take. But it's not enough to slow down the torture as they continue unabated. I'm now going inside myself. I want to find some refuge in the brain centre that helps me deal with the pain. Like I am trying to accept it, utilise it, turn it to my advantage. But even I know that's temporary.

The light flicks again.

I scan the room with my good eye and see that the door is secure. The man at the door has an AK-47. One of the others has a standard Glock pistol. The other man is holding the electrodes again. He attaches them to my back, and I let out an earth-shattering, ultimately pointless scream that nobody on the outside can hear.

The light bulb flickers.

The other man smashes his fist into my stomach. I hang like a human punch bag, which is the idea. The other man delivers a roundhouse kick to the side of my torso, expelling any wind that I still have left inside me. The pain is excruciating. I want to own my mind and not give in to the pain. I sing pop songs and lullabies to myself. One of the songs that comes into my head is 'You Won't See Me Cry' by Wilson Phillips. I am determined that whatever happens, these fuckers will not see me cry. I want to put my head in another space. But my will is fading.

The light flickers even more.

It's like it's a metaphor for my plight: my light too is about to be snuffed out.

The three leave the room. I hang there, a pathetic, weak, diminished figure. I'm mentally going through a checklist, scanning my body for injuries, but I'm too far beyond pain to know anything for sure. I wouldn't be surprised if the roundhouse kicks cracked a few ribs. I can smell burning flesh: my own. That's weird. I can barely see. Just as well that I'm not too self-conscious about my looks. My face is bloodied. My hair is soaked with sweat.

About half an hour later, the three men return to the cell. I'm half asleep. I want to sleep badly. Part of me doesn't want to wake up at all, but they have other ideas. One man throws water over me. They can't have been gone for more than a few minutes. They start on me again, this time with more ferocity. I'm a trained assassin. I know the rules of the game. I'm on my own. I can't play the gender card here; those rules don't apply in this world.

The light in the cell is getting weaker, just like me.

One of the men cups my head in his hand. He glares at me in frustration. This bitch still hasn't told them anything. He spits in my face. I just smile back. I think, I'm getting to this bastard.

The men stop momentarily. I can barely see between the sweat in my eyes and the darkly lit cell. I'm relying on my hearing now. They whisper amongst themselves, which is pointless because I can't understand their language and am no threat to them.

The light is getting weaker still. It's as if there is some symbiosis between me and it.

One of the men draws his Glock. That's a sign that they know there is no point in continuing. Things are time critical now. They've wasted enough on me.

I can't see as well as before. But I can see enough. I'm about to die.

The light in the cell is getting weaker.

The Chemist could shoot me where he is, but he wants to be in my face: up close and personal. He moves nearer and points his gun.

Then I have a light-bulb moment. Literally.

I don't know whether it goes dark because someone wants to raid the building or if there's another explanation, one of my mentor's bugbears: planned obsolescence. Litze was always moaning that we don't make things like we used to. Things aren't built to last.

That includes light bulbs.

This light bulb was only made to last a thousand hours, unlike before, when they lasted for two thousand hours. Less time means that the consumer has to buy more of them. This means more profit. Most manufacturers of pretty much everything followed suit.

Bad news for the consumer, but at this moment, a lifeline for me.

The Chemist lowers his gun, the light's flickering ember has reached its one final hour. It dies, spectacularly so—a sudden sharp pop and hot glass shards flying everywhere. This throws confusion into the cell. The men panic. The bulb's final moment has reinvigorated me. It buys me valuable seconds. But that's all I need. I trained to fight in the dark. Given the state of my vision, it's just as well.

They were probably too busy paying attention to my erect nipples to think about my hands. I've been working on breaking free from the meat hook that I'm bound to.

In the dark, I grip the Chemist with my thighs around his neck, snapping it before he has the chance to fire off a shot. I hear his gun clatter to the floor. I need to rely on my hearing big-time as I scrabble for the pistol. I keep low. The others are still confused, but I have the advantage now. My territory. I remember roughly where my other captors were situated before the light went out and shoot in their general direction.

I hear a groan to the left of me. I hit one of them. Good.

I'm not sure of the other guy. I fire again. No response. The other guy has moved. I can hear him trying to find his AK-47, but he doesn't want to spray the room indiscriminately, just in case. There is no such dilemma for me. I have an idea. I remember that there was a cup on the table ahead of me. It was full of water, which they never let me drink but teased me with. I move very slowly towards it and stroke my hand over the surface of the table. Shit. I can't find it. I'm beginning to doubt my memory as I was sure it was there.

I feel something metallic. It's the cup. Keep low. I grab it and take a swig. I swallow some. I move carefully and aim in the direction of the last man, then spit out the water with what little breath hasn't been kicked out of me. He wasn't expecting that. This gives me the element of surprise. I sense movement. The last man has decided that self-preservation is more important to him than being discriminating as he sprays his AK-47 into the cell. The bullets miss me. But crucially, the light emanating from the weapon's muzzle silhouettes his position. I fire at his location. Then there is silence. I'm not sure whether he's been hit. I keep quiet and low. Then I decide to move over to the other man on the left of the room. I can tell he's still alive, but barely.

I can feel him slumped against the wall. I drag him in front of me, using him as a shield. I fire again at the same position, giving the other man enough gun flash to wonder whether he feels fortunate enough to risk it.

My hunch is correct. The man has wised up to me, and I didn't hit him last time. The man falls for my ruse and returns fire. I can hear the thud of the bullets as they penetrate my human shield. The blood oozes from the corpse. I'm not hit. But I'm in so much pain, I probably couldn't tell if I were. The man comes closer. I can sense his position. Wait for it, I think. I could swear that I can almost feel his breath, which I hope will be his last. I wait.

I want to be sure. As does he.

He's about to fire again. But I have to go for it. I shoot again into the darkness, then I hear the last sound he makes, a groan, followed by the sound of his crumpled mass as he hits the floor. I'm tired, relieved, and grateful. But my problems are only just beginning.

SIXTY-SIX

JUST WHEN I think that I've seen the daylight, I find that I have another hurdle to overcome. I feel my way blindly towards an escape route. This place has a series of corridors like a giant maze. I don't have a plan. I just have to hope that I'll get out of here. The AK in the cell is empty. I remember where my clothes and shoes are and throw them on. I hold my gun with both hands and will fire without hesitation. There are no friendlies in here, so the law of probability suggests that anyone I'll kill does deserve to be killed.

My body is sore but not bad enough to stop me from moving or fighting if I have to. Adrenaline courses through me like an intravenous drip. I turn to my left quickly and see a man in the corridor. I shoot before he gets the chance to grab his weapon; he drops to the floor. The sound of gunfire will alert the others, so I have to move quickly. I take the pistol from his corpse, checking the mag; there aren't many rounds left. I hear footsteps in the distance.

I look ahead, and I can see a door on the left. I ease myself towards it, then twist the handle slowly, but it's locked. I move further down the corridor and take a right. It's difficult to see because of the dim light. The bulbs emit a tame flicker, and I can hear the low crackling hum of electricity above me.

The footsteps grow louder and have an increasing sense of urgency.

I'm light on ammo, so I'll have to make everything count. I can hear my assailants closing in. They're behind me now, which means I'll be in wait for them. I count the rounds I have left. I won't have enough to fend off Yumeni's men. I'll save the last bullet for me. I'd rather go on my terms.

I move further down the corridor and see another door, this time to my right. I turn the handle and enter. I see two filing cabinets to the right, and a small table with a dented grey desk lamp clamped to the edge. I close the door behind me. The room has an underused, stale smell. I look to see whether there is anything I can use as a weapon, but there's nothing visible in here. I try the desk drawers, and I see a screwdriver. At least that's something.

This will be my last stand unless I can think of something fast. The footsteps are upon me now. But I know that going into this room is just delaying the inevitable. They know that I'm probably in one of these rooms, so it's only a matter of time before they find me. But then I've given them something to think about: I've already killed four of them, and I won't give up quietly. Litze always said you might as well do something rather than do nothing.

I crouch low on the right side of the door, and I hear the soft creak of the hinge as it opens, letting a shaft of light into the room. Then it's flung open swiftly, almost hitting me. I see a gun followed by a hand poke out from the wooden panel. With all my strength, I slam the door, trapping his hand beyond the frame. I drive the screwdriver into his forearm just below his wrist with my left hand, impaling it into the wall. He screams as he releases his weapon and I shoot through the door into his centre mass. The weight of his lifeless body dislodges the screwdriver, and I retrieve it, still keeping low. The dead man's head is keeping the door open. If I step out of here now, I'm a dead woman. They'll probably decide to wait me out. I reach for the table lamp on the floor and throw it out of the room to cause a distraction and to assess the gunman's position. I also want them to waste their ammo.

I hear the rat-tat-tat of machine-gun fire as the bullets tear through the door. Even with their superior firepower, they won't risk coming in here. I hear muffled voices in the corridor now. I cautiously peer out of the door. I pull back in time as bullets shatter the door frame. More ammo wasted. Good. The dead man gives me an idea as I move his head with my right foot. A lifeless body is really heavy, but this is a chance to expend more of their rounds and reveal to me their position. Whoever is firing at me is not opposite but along the corridor, and he confirms this by shooting at the dead man.

I decide to use the dead man as a shield, just like I did before, so I roll him to his side. He's big, and I'm in agony as I do this.

I slowly slide along the dead man's body and fire in the direction of the machine gun. There's no return fire. I look left, then right, and decide to run for it, hoping he'll take the bait. My movement draws the gunman into the corridor. His impatience won't allow him to wait. He wants me as a trophy. I'm hoping he wants to impress his boss.

My mind slows everything down and I pay attention to my breathing as the gunman appears. He fires his AK-47 into the space that he thinks I'll occupy, but he's been hasty. The bullets instead pass over me and continue to the end of the corridor. He's surprised when he sees me, as I am in a backwards kneeling position, but my spine is twenty-five degrees off the floor. It's an exercise I practised when I used to be more flexible, but I can still just about do it. You see it sometimes when footballers celebrate scoring a winning goal as they slide across the grass with their backs on their heels. Or like that bullet-time sequence in *The Matrix*. The corridor floors are smooth, which allows me to do this and gives me a momentary advantage as I slide with forward momentum and shoot the gunman in the head. He drops to his knees and slumps towards me, his face still frozen in an expression of surprise.

I rise and retrieve his AK-47. I check the mag, and there aren't many rounds left, but it's more than I had before so I'll take it. I get a second wind as I hear more muffled sounds in the distance. The odds aren't good, but I put that to the back of my mind and focus on the moment. The voices and footsteps approach and I have no choice but to take the fight to them. There's no way out in the opposite direction, so I guess that the way out is in their direction. I'll charge them. They're probably not expecting me to do this, but I'm hoping the element of surprise will be to my advantage. I stop suddenly as the footsteps come towards me. I step to my left, into their path, and fire short bursts, killing two more men as their bodies explode in red mist. The arterial spray turns the corridor into a crimson scene. My mind is desensitised to the carnage, as if it's a video game, but I know that'll only be temporary.

I wait and listen for more men, but it's quiet again. A temporary respite, as I think they fear Yumeni more than they fear me. But my demonstration has given them something to think about. There's no natural cover in the corridor so I'll have to fight my way out or die trying. I run down another corridor, ignoring my pain. I estimate it's about 150 metres long. There's a fire door at the end, which means a chance to escape, or so I think.

There are doors on either side. They slowly open one by one. Yumeni's men come out like zombies, holding baseball bats, hammers, some with small hand guns. I don't understand why they aren't all armed, but I'm not complaining as it will make my job easier. They seem determined to take me on at whatever cost to themselves. I have guns, but I can't kill them all. They know that.

But they don't seem to care. They know that I will kill some of them, but they also know that if I want to escape, I'm going to have to come through them. I don't know whether their loyalty to their boss is endearing, fear based, or just plain lunacy.

SIXTY-SEVEN

THIS IS A fight to the death. I'm not going to give in, and neither are they as I fire the remaining rounds of the AKs into the rushing assailants. Two down, seven to go. They return fire and I shoot more rounds with my pistol until I hear the click-click sounds of a voiceless weapon. Three more bodies go down. This won't deter them. You can't fight an enemy like this, so this is a lose-lose situation.

There are more people coming out, so I put my other pistol to my head. The metal feels cold and reassuring against my temple as I don't care what they'll do to my body afterwards. So long as I'm not around to see it.

I feel my body relax as my mind reflects on the disturbed life that I've had. There have been some bright spots, but there's been too much pain and darkness, so it's probably better this way. I can't complain. This is the life and the code of a mercenary. No one to visit me when I'm dead and an unmarked grave at best if I'm lucky. I look at the henchmen in front of me as they come towards me. Then I pull the trigger. They still come. I pull it again and still see them moving forwards towards me. Then I realise in horror that in my excitement, I forgot to save my insurance policy: one last bullet for me. My hope of some dignity has been extinguished by my carelessness.

I drop the gun and sink in despair. But then Litze's voice won't allow me to feel sorry for myself as I draw breath and focus on the door ahead. I'm using my pain to motivate me. I used to train for this at the Facility. They called it the corridor of death, where I did my martial arts practice. Then there were two rows of people on either side. My objective was to get to the end. Theirs was to stop me. As simple as that. The difference was that the corridor had a line of students either side. Here, it's Yumeni's henchmen and two walls either side. It's like an analogy of my life. Just when I feel I can see, taste, touch, hear, or smell the goal, there is something to pull me back. I focus on my breathing and the door ahead. I recite like a mantra that I'm getting through. I reach for my screwdriver and walk purposely towards them.

This feels like a violent version of hopscotch as I skip, using fancy footwork, as I see a man pick up a hand gun from a dead colleague and aim. I'm glad he's a shit shot as he misses by miles. I take the screwdriver in my left hand as I see a gun on the floor and reach for it with my right hand, but I recoil instinctively as he shoots again. I decide to chance it again as I crouch low and reach for the gun. In a swift moment, I return fire and shoot him in the chest. I fire again but the gun is empty, so I toss it to one side and switch the screwdriver from my left to my right hand. The next man approaches me and swings wildly from the left with his baseball bat, just missing my head by inches. I trap the bat with my left hand and drive the screwdriver under his chin, simultaneously giving him a tongue and nose piercing. The blood floods my hands as I grip his weapon, thrashing it with great force to my left. I crack his skull at the temple line as his head hits the wall.

Another man swings down with his hammer; I block horizontally with the bat. The claw sticks into the wood, which is good for me as I aim a low kick to his groin to distract him. I flip the bat, so it's now vertical, and strike down two-handed on the crown of his head, making a loud sound like popcorn in a microwave. I tell myself to focus on the door as a third man swishes his blade, which I evade. Just. He swings again and slashes my right arm. He lunges; I trap the knife and, with a fast movement, break his wrist and elbow. I grab his knife and perforate him with stab wounds as he clings on to me. I push him away as he foams at the mouth.

The door is getting closer, but there are three more men. They are no less dedicated as they rush me. My footwork is crucial now and the attacker grabs air as I skip the first assault. I crash the baseball bat into the base of his skull, making a loud, hollow, percussive ringing, almost a tuneful sound.

Two to go.

The next guy looks handy. His body posture is that of a confident man with high close-quarters combat skills. But this will be quick. He telegraphs his move as he throws a right-handed punch. I block his shoulder, stopping the trajectory with my left hand, closing the space between us as I simultaneously smash my right forearm into his throat. I know just where to hit: in the right place. I don't do fancy. I prefer effective. I grab his head as he chokes. I tell myself to focus on the door ahead as I grab his head and twist clockwise 180 degrees with a sound like bubble wrap marking his death.

One left.

No time for complacency, as this man looks no less serious than the others. He's the last man standing. I move towards him, about to execute the kill. Then I hear more footsteps and my heart sinks. I've got to go through this again. I don't have the desire or the energy, and he knows it. My mentor would be disappointed in me, as he would tell me never to give up. But even he, in this situation, would understand. I'm spent. And I'm scared. I'm not even sure whether I can be bothered to kill the last man. But I remind myself that the door ahead is my escape route. The footsteps are getting closer, but I won't make it in time. I just relax. It's OK, I tell myself. I've had a good run. I've had more chances than I've had any right to. I don't believe in the Almighty so I have no fear of the other side, and anyway, it would be hypocritical now to ask for forgiveness.

Then there's a thunderous boom that sounds like God has been angered, and I'm blown back along the floor with great force. I look like I've been dipped in grey powder as I'm coated with brickwork and the ensuing cloud of dust. I gasp as my lungs are consumed by the dust and I splutter like a terminal chain-smoker. I can taste and smell the acrid cordite smoke, and I'm practically blind. My ears ring with a medium-frequency hum. My head spins like a carousel, and I just want to get out quickly. I eventually compose myself and stagger down the hall. The corridor has disintegrated, and I see a pile of rocks where the last man was standing. All that remains is a bloodied hand that pokes through the rubble. I spit on my hands and wipe the dust from my eyelids in an attempt to clear my vision. The door in front has disappeared. Instead, there's a huge cavity with an unbearable spotlight bursting through it. Then I see my maker: Litze is standing in front of me holding a machine gun. He steps into the corridor, reaches out his hand, and asks me what the hell am I waiting for.

SIXTY-EIGHT

'I THOUGHT YOU were—'

'Dead?' asks Litze as he cuts in.

'Yes', I say as I stand up and dust myself down. He hands me a spare lab coat that he finds on the floor and I cover myself.

'Did you see a body?'

'No.'

'Then never assume anything. I told you this so many times, Becker!'

'But the car, I saw it explode when I left.'

'Yes, you did, but unbeknownst to me, Blume's car had missile detection software on the satnav, which saw an incoming strike from the compound. We managed to get out in time. Fortunately, the RPG was blown from the car undamaged, so we could still use it.'

'Blume is OK?'

'Yes, but she's pissed. She loved that car.'

'Where is she?'

'Seeing her car blown to smithereens made her mad. So she took out her vengeance on some of Yumeni's boys. Don't be fooled by Blume's bright exterior. That's one lady you don't want to make mad.'

I think I'm fine, Litze, thanks for asking.

'How did you get here?' I ask.

'I got lucky. There was a truck a few hundred yards away parked on a lay-by. I was able to use my hot-wiring skills after all on it.'

'We've got to find Yumeni', I say as the pain registers in my body.

'OK, follow me', says Litze as he leads me outside. It's carnage out here. Bodies everywhere. I see Litze's handiwork. Three bodies are lying nearby. One has a big hole burst open in its back where part of his spine used to be. His insides are scattered around his corpse. Then I recognise another body that makes me smile. It's the lorry driver from the hangar.

He walks over to where I was fighting the man in the suit and sees my efforts.

'How long did it take you to kill this guy?'

I don't want to answer. I know what Litze is going to say.

'In the old days, you'd have finished him off quicker. You're slipping, Becker.'

I still say nothing. I've just fought for my life. I have no stomach to get into another fight. Not with Litze.

'I found something', he says as he walks to the left side of the warehouse. There's a cabin ahead. We walk in and see twenty people: men, women, and children. All chained together. They look scared, dirty, and hungry. Their glassy eyes betray fear. They look lost. Ghostly white. That will probably be the drugs to keep them sleepy.

'What is this?' I say.

'Something I thought I'd never see again.'

'What?' I say.

'I have my suspicions, but whatever this is about, these people aren't volunteers.'

'Have they been trafficked?'

'Looks that way.'

'But why?'

'I'm not sure yet, but we need to find Yumeni. And, Becker?'

'What?'

'You look like shit.'

'You say the nicest things.'

'Just saying.'

The place is strewn with bodies. But my thought is to go to the hangar where the lorry is.

I think two of my ribs are broken, but I can just about walk. Litze sees me in discomfort and waits for me to catch up. The hangar door is still open, and the lorry is still there. I take Litze's gun and shoot the lock, which releases the shutters. We see a group of about forty people, men, women, and children, huddled together, scared and emaciated. Then I remember that they took six away earlier and tell Litze that we need to find them.

He helps the people out of the truck. Most of them look dazed and confused. By the way that some of them are huddled together, they look like family members. All look like they haven't washed and have travelled for days.

I ask where they're from, but most don't speak English. Litze believes that they are from Syria, Afghanistan, and Iraq. Some are too weak to stand as they sit on the cold hangar floor. Some of them are covered with blankets.

'We've got to find the others', I say with more urgency.

I see another building south of the complex. I wish I could run, but I can't. It hurts just to breathe, but I want to get to the building. Then I see another body. It's the little boy. His eyes are open. I stop, kneel over his body, and despite my pain, close his eyelids with my right hand. It feels lame. It feels late, but it's the least I can do.

We continue to the building south of the compound. Litze draws his gun and shoots the locks off the entrance and opens the heavy door. We walk through a corridor and see light coming from one of the rooms ahead. Litze goes in first. Inside we see six adults strapped to leather chairs, with all sorts of instruments and electronic monitors attached to them. We check their vital signs, and they're alive but heavily sedated. Straight ahead I see a large rectangular window that's blacked out. I move closer; it looks reinforced. I press my face up against the glass but it's so dark, if feels like a black hole. It's an internal chamber, but a chamber to what? There's a white door to the right of the glass, but it's heavily secured by a keypad lock. Litze stops, then looks around for a moment. He flicks the light switch on the bottom left of the windowpane. The fluorescent beam stutters momentarily, then finally reveals the true horror inside the chamber.

I look away instinctively, but not quickly enough to avoid having the sight of the naked corpse of a young woman, sitting strapped on a chair, imprinted on my mind. It looks days old. Her face is frozen in a death stare, foaming at the mouth. Her hair is prematurely white. There are dried tears on her bloated face. Her whole body is swollen. Her visible blue veins make her skin appear like marble. She looks like she's been stung by a swarm of bees as her skin is riddled with pus-filled sores. Litze switches off the light as I nearly puke.

'Jesus Christ', says Litze. 'I thought I'd seen the last of this; I thought we'd learned our lessons from the past.' He puts his head in his hands.

'What?' I say.

'I thought these places were urban myths.'

'What are you talking about?' I say impatiently.

Then I see Karla Blume enter the room with Karl Yumeni. She thrusts him forward, pointing a gun at his back.

'I can explain', he says.

'I say we don't give him any more airtime', says Blume. 'I say we blow this motherfucker's brains out.'

SIXTY-NINE

I TAKE LITZE'S gun and point it straight under Yumeni's chin. He watches me with laser precision. I don't remove my eyes from him either as I take in what I'm about to do. I've read his file. He's a stealer of dreams. Reading about his deeds would keep many awake. In fact, he's a monster. I've seen enough people with that trait. His type can change the atmosphere in the room. Sure, these people have a degree of charisma. Otherwise, they wouldn't be successful leaders. But I don't know whether it's fear or some unwritten primal alpha code that attracts followers like the Pied Piper. I guess if you believe enough in your own bullshit, others will too.

No one should take pleasure in ending another's life. But in his case, I'm happy to make an exception as I gesture with my gun for him to kneel. He doesn't.

Well at least he'll die on his feet. At least he's facing me. Some I've killed prefer to turn away. Others want to face me, as if it's their way of imprinting their face into my consciousness. A way of haunting me from beyond the grave, and sometimes they do. I check that my safety is off. This will be one of my most satisfying kills for sure. I look at Yumeni's face one last time. I'm about to blow that smug expression off it when I hear footsteps and clicks resonating on the floor from behind me.

'Drop the weapons, now!' shouts a man with an American accent.

I look around and there is a team of twelve people, all dressed in black combat fatigues and helmets. Myself, Litze, and Blume are covered in red laser dots from their weapons. I recognise one of the men. It's Sabatini, the government guy we met a few days ago.

'I don't want to kill you, but I will if I have to', says the same voice. I assume he's the leader.

'Who's asking?' I say.

'Someone who needs this man alive.'

'If you knew who he was then you wouldn't want him alive', I reply. I press the gun into Yumeni's mouth.

'I won't ask you again, Becker', says the man.

I look at Litze and he nods at me.

'I'm not going to drop my weapon.'

'Tell your girl to stand down', says the man to Litze.

'She's not my girl', he says.

Litze and Blume step closer to me, creating a protective shield. The red dots follow them.

'Now you don't have a clean shot', says Litze.

'Then we'll kill you all', says the man.

'And risk Yumeni getting shot?' says Litze. 'Someone has gone to a lot of trouble to keep him alive, so I think he's too valuable to whoever you're working for.'

The American pauses. He knows Litze is right. Their weapons have high-velocity rounds. Flesh and bone won't protect Yumeni. I have a gun trained at Yumeni's head. If they tried to kill me with a body shot, for example, a bullet straight to my heart, I'd have enough time to shoot him. But if the assault team took a head shot, that would be different. I wouldn't have the time to kill him. Your brain stops functioning almost instantaneously. In a fraction of a second, I'd be gone.

The leader looks like he's in his late thirties, early forties. He's a white male, about five foot eleven and a half, with short blond hair and a baby face, which seems a contradiction under the circumstances.

'What do you want?' asks the American.

'Information', I say, behind my shield.

'I'm not at liberty to tell you anything', he says.

'CIA?' I ask.

'All that matters now is that I take Yumeni in.'

'Why?'

'I have my reasons, and I don't need to tell you.'

'This man is better off dead.'

'This isn't just about you, Becker. There's far more at stake here. He's part of an ongoing investigation.'

'By whom?'

'I've told you more than you have any right to know.'

'I was tasked with bringing him in, and now my team is dead. I've had a pretty shit few days, so I think I'm entitled to some answers.'

'No, you're not. Right now, I've got to get him to our exfil point. We need Yumeni alive.'

'Why?'

'That's classified.'

He's starting to irritate me.

'I know lots about you, Becker. You're a fine operative, but you don't always see the bigger picture.'

'Enlighten me then', I say.

'I don't have time for this', he says.

'I think she deserves an explanation', says Sabatini.

'I really don't have time for this', says the mystery man.

'I need a really good reason why I shouldn't shoot him.'

'You'd really sacrifice your life for Yumeni?'

'Have you seen this place? Have you seen what they do here?'

'This isn't what you think.'

'And what the hell am I supposed to think?'

'I've read your file, Becker. You're not into causes. You're a gun for hire. We need him alive.'

'Well maybe for once in my life, I'm beginning to realise that it's not about me. I want to know what the hell is going on.'

'I don't have to tell you anything.'

'If you don't tell me what I need to know by the count of three, I will kill him', I say as I put the gun against Yumeni's Adam's apple. His sweat drenches my weapon. He looks at me as he tries but fails to hide his fear. I can see his chest rise as he attempts to slow his breathing.

The assault team don't have a clear shot as they grip their rifles. We'll all be killed once I pull the trigger. Blume and Litze look at each other and hold hands like it'll be their last time.

'Please tell your men to stand down', says Sabatini to the American as the room descends into silence. The tension in the room is palpable, and time seems to slow down as I look at Yumeni and start to count.

'One . . . two . . .'

'OK, OK. Everybody stand down', says the American. Litze's hunch was correct: he needs Yumeni alive. Slowly, they do as he says. The red dots disappear. Apart from one, which is aimed at Karla Blume's heart. And I remember her dream.

'That's an order', says the American, and the final red dot disappears.

He instructs his men to escort the refugees out of the room. Only six of his men and Sabatini remain.

'May I reach into my jacket pocket to get my mobile?' asks Yumeni. He's breathing normally now.

'Why?' I ask.

'This may convince you', he says.

'Slowly', I say.

He retrieves his mobile with his right hand from his inside pocket. He scrolls down on his contacts list and calls an unknown number. It rings three times, he then presses the speakerphone icon.

'Identify yourself', says the voice.

'It's the Chameleon', says Yumeni.

'OK, putting you through.'

The line hisses and crackles for about forty seconds. Then a familiar voice comes on the line.

'Chameleon, what can I do for you?'

'Madam President', says Yumeni, 'I'm afraid we have some bad news.'

SEVENTY

YUMENI, THE CHAMELEON, or whatever he's called, tells the president of the United States that the Chemist is dead. She asks how that happened. He looks at me and says it's complicated. He explains that he will debrief her thoroughly when he returns but tells her that the undercover operation is blown. I'm trying to get my head around everything now. I've been hunting down an undercover agent working directly with President Michele Parker, and I've killed their main lead.

Litze and Blume step away from me and holster their weapons. Yumeni gulps as I remove my gun from his throat. I stand and face the American.

'So are you CIA?' I say.

The American looks at Yumeni. He nods, giving him permission to continue.

'Not exactly, Becker.'

'Then what are you exactly?'

'I used to be CIA, but I am what you would call a consultant. I report directly to the president.'

'So why doesn't the president use the CIA?'

'It's complicated, but the CIA has a long history of lying to presidents and the public, not telling the truth about its operations.

It's more concerned with its reputation than its success rate. The CIA is part of the problem. President Parker is a decent woman and has the potential to be one of the best presidents we've ever had.'

'It sounds like you really respect this woman', I say.

'I do, Becker. She's probably the first president that I've had this level of respect for. Which makes a refreshing change. She's tougher than most men I've known and inspires loyalty. One of the first things Parker said before coming into office was that she wanted to clean up the agency. You can imagine the resistance she's had. She's real brave and principled. But she has made too many enemies. Parker doesn't trust the CIA to self-regulate. It doesn't have a high standing in the world. She wants to succeed where other presidents have failed.'

'You don't say', interjects Litze. I wondered how long it would take for him to speak, as I know his view of the CIA.

'Yeah, I've heard all the jokes', continues the man as he looks towards Litze. 'Such as, "What does CIA stand for? Can't Identify Anything." But there are some good people in the organisation trying to do the right thing who get tarnished by the rest. They deserve better. It would be easier to clean it from the outside; that's where I come in.'

'So why did you leave?' I ask.

'The CIA was becoming too bureaucratic, and that made it ineffective in my opinion. There were things that I did that I never signed up to do. Things I can't or won't talk about. Things I'm deeply ashamed of. I'm a patriot and believe America deserves a more efficient secret service. I think the CIA started out with good intentions, but the lines got blurred, and the service lost its way. One of the biggest problems was its cold cash programme.'

I rack my brain because I've heard the term before, but I don't know where.

'Cold cash is a term for money used by the CIA to sponsor puppet governments', explains Litze.

'That's right', says the man. 'The CIA has been sponsoring these people for years, and they don't have a record of making good choices: Bin Laden and Hussein, for example. We get into bed with these people, don't remember to use condoms, get fucked real good, and are surprised when we get an STD. These funds got misappropriated.'

'You mean stolen?' I say.

'Correct. By our people in the CIA. They used the money for their black-bag operations within the agency. Off-the-books assignments that even the agency didn't know about.'

'So how does my ambush fit into all this?'

'I don't quite know yet. You work for the agency Coba?'

'Yes.'

'I'm sorry to say that was an accident waiting to happen.'

It seems that everybody is in on the joke, apart from me.

'So Yumeni or whatever his name is was pretending to be a terrorist to lure the real bad guy out into the open.'

'Yes. This was a sting operation to uncover false-flag attacks due to take place in Europe and America.'

'This isn't new. The CIA have been doing this for years', I say.

'That's true, Becker, but so has every other security agency in the world. Normally against enemies of the state. But that's not the real problem now. Someone else wants to discredit the CIA', says the mystery man.

'Discrediting the CIA even more that it currently is? I didn't think that this was possible', mocks Litze.

'Most people don't believe it is either', says the man. 'But what we've got coming next will make the CIA look like Sesame Street.

SEVENTY-ONE

'OVER THE YEARS', continues the mystery man, 'there have been rogue elements within the agency that feel the CIA doesn't go far enough, hence the off-books ops, secret deals, and unsanctioned assignments. We don't know how much money has gone missing, but we believe it's billions of dollars.'

'That's a lot of shoes and handbags', says Blume. Litze smiles at her.

'Have you heard of Mandrake Security?' asks the American.

'Yes', I say. 'It's one of the world's biggest security agencies.'

'Run by Jason Cross. He's five foot six but acts like he wishes the numbers of his height were the other way around. His father, Connor Cross, was originally with the OSS, which changed into the CIA and was a budget holder for these cold cash payments in the early sixties. The belief is that he used the money to, amongst other things, set up his private security company. The word was that he and many others became disgruntled with the CIA. They weren't proactive enough, in his opinion, and he wanted to create an alternative security agency. He would stage false-flag operations in Europe and America. This would embarrass the CIA so much that the US government would have to outsource the work to handle the extra capacity. Cross Junior has just followed in the family tradition', says the American.

'I don't get it', I say. 'Private military contractors have been hired by the CIA to do deniable ops for years. So why have they turned on the agency?'

'Seems as though Cross likes to bear grudges. His security company has been hung out to dry by the agency. Mandrake Security currently has twenty-one indictments pending, from botched operations in the Middle East and Africa to drugs, gun smuggling, and alleged human trafficking activities. Some of which have been orchestrated by rogue elements of the agency.'

'So this is payback?' I say.

'Exactly', says the American. 'Cross feels unloved. He feels that the agency wanted to have their cake, eat it, and fuck the baker as well. He accepted that he would have to take some of the flak. He felt that it was his patriotic duty, and the fact that he was well remunerated sweetened things for a while. But you know someone somewhere will turn on you in this game if the price is high enough, or because they don't want the blowback. Cross took his public naming and shaming personally. That rocked their agency for some time, so much so that they even rebranded it in some forlorn hope that the public would forget their association with the bad stuff and their image would improve. But people have long memories. Unfortunately, some disillusioned rogue agents within the CIA agreed with him.'

'So where do you come in?' I say, looking at Yumeni.

He looks at me in an anguished manner. But it's more than that; I see and sense grief in his expression. 'In September 2008, Cross's methods eventually came back to bite him on the ass when a team of his contractors was ambushed and killed in Afghanistan', he says.

I remember reading about it. The convoys were a man light. There were only three men per vehicle instead of the usual four. And they were travelling in soft-top vehicles which provided no protection from insurgents or IEDs. The first convoy was blown to pieces on a lonely supply road which was called the Red Route because so many died on that track. The second convoy was overpowered by sheer numbers. The mercs fought bravely but were killed one by one. What was worse was that their dismembered remains were paraded as trophies and images of them were uploaded to YouTube. The revulsion back home was instant and one guaranteed way of turning American public opinion against overseas activities.

Mercs don't have the same protection as people who work for the US military, and some of the families felt that they'd been deserted. The publicity from this hit Mandrake bad, but their handling of it was a PR disaster. Mandrake Security came across as uncaring, which they were. Cross was slow to go public, which didn't help. From what I can remember, some class-action lawsuits are pending. But Mandrake hindered the process in the hope that these families would be worn down and finally give up.

I also remember pictures and interviews of the grieving families. As much as you can put on a public front, publicity like this not only hurt Mandrake, it hurt the whole security community as they're painted with the same brush. The good thing is that there are some reputable agencies that would rather turn down work than cut costs. But that doesn't make headline news.

'But what has that got to do with you?' I ask Yumeni.

'One of those contractors was my twin brother. He was a deep undercover operative. And you've killed the best chance we had to nail that sonofabitch.'

SEVENTY-TWO

I LOOK AT Sabatini, who's been quiet during all of this.

'Why didn't you say something?' I ask.

'I couldn't. Firstly, you were working for Coba so I didn't know which side you were on, and secondly, this was a national security issue. You're a rogue operative with no clearance.'

'But Litze has clearance.'

'Yes, that's true. But he was working with you, which means he was compromised.'

'Did you send those government agents to kill us?' asks Litze.

'Yes', he says, not hiding his discomfort. 'I put in a kill order. They were rogue CIA agents. As much as I admire Herr Litze, which is why I wanted to speak to him first, I was trying to protect national interests.'

'Which are?' I say.

'We don't want a reminder of our past.'

Then it dawns on me why Litze is so upset. He's seen this before and he's not proud of Germany's darkest hour.

'You've heard of black sites?' asks the American.

'Of course I have', I say.

'Well this is a black lab.'

'As in an illegal laboratory?'

'Yes. The medical community borrowed the term black sites: secret prisons where covert activity takes place around the world. Instead of interrogations, illegal medical experiments are conducted. Some on willing volunteers but mostly on the disenfranchised, such as drug addicts, tramps, prostitutes, the mentality ill. This isn't a new idea. The CIA have been doing this for years. But it's not just the Americans. Every major power has black labs in some form. And not just governments that have these laboratories. It's also pharmaceutical companies with off-the-books operations. And sometimes, they do secret or joint ventures with their respective governments. These people don't care about regulations or documents. This is about getting their product on the market first. Drug companies are always looking for a competitive edge. And when it comes to profit, ethics go out of the window.'

'That's quite a claim.'

'All deniable of course, but they're out there.'

'Who was the Chemist?'

'His real name was Jonas Kovac. He worked for Huxcor. A brilliant scientist by all accounts, but a megalomaniac. Cross paid him a fortune to do tests on some human volunteers, but I sensed he wasn't into the money. He liked opening Pandora's box. Apparently, it was his idea to prey on people that nobody cared about or would miss.'

'You mean because they were trafficked?'

'Yes. This isn't a new phenomenon. Drug trials on the unsuspecting have been carried out by every major country since forever. It's not so difficult to work out. Major drug companies have done this for years. Testing on humans. It's better to test on subjects who will eventually use the drugs. Animal testing doesn't ultimately replicate the effect drugs have on humans. These companies will always get volunteers, especially if the price is right. But there's always a risk. Things go wrong. There could be lawsuits. It's easy for these companies to test on people nobody cares about. There's no blowback.'

'But what was the Chemist testing?'

'He was asked to do trials on subjects to find new cures for everything from the common cold to cancer. Drugs that were still in the early stages of development but where human trials were the fastest way to produce a better-quality drug.'

'But that's illegal', I say. 'With all the regulations and the paper trail needed, they would never get away with it.'

'When you have that much power, you can get away with anything', says the American.

'So what's the connection with the Chemist and Jason Cross?'

'The Chemist was testing biological weapons on unsuspecting human guinea pigs just to test the effectiveness of these weapons. Nowadays, buyers want to know that these weapons work and so they want evidence. Which means this kind of experimentation and they also want video evidence. Cross was Kovack's backer. He would pay for these bioweapons to be produced and sell them to the very people he was fighting against.'

'And I thought I was sick', I say. I turn to Yumeni. 'Which means as an undercover agent, you'd have to prove your worth to the real terrorists. Correct?'

Yumeni says nothing.

I see sadness in his eyes. And I know why. He would have gone to the same dark places I have had to, to get the job done. Now I know why he wanted to shoot me earlier. I believe he wanted to spare me the agony of being tortured by the Chemist.

'It's all in vain now', says Yumeni as he stares at his phone.

'But we have evidence', I say.

'But you killed the evidence. The Chemist was the direct link to

Jason Cross. He reports to him directly at a designated time, which would have been this evening. Without him, we have nothing.'

Litze looks at me. 'You shouldn't blame yourself, and I don't think anyone is blaming you, no matter how frustrated they are. Am I right, Mr Yumeni?'

Yumeni looks at Litze, then looks at me and nods slowly.

'Yeah, give the girl a break', Blume says and winks at me, which seems inappropriate in the circumstances but is appreciated nevertheless.

The American walks over to the window and looks outside. He seems deep in thought. He just stands there thinking for what seems a very long time. No one has anything to say. The atmosphere in the room is flat. As if there's been a great loss of something big. All that work undone by me. I'm surprised that Yumeni isn't screaming or throwing tables now. But maybe the loss of his twin brother puts things in perspective. Then the American turns around and faces us.

'Well, maybe this isn't over yet', he says.

'How so?' says Litze.

'You seem like me, old school, is that right?'

'Yes, I suppose.'

'Sometimes when the law fails, we just have to rely on good old-fashioned justice. Do you agree?'

'Yes, I do.' Litze nods.

'Cross is untouchable; at least he thinks he is. He has security everywhere. But his hubris is his blind spot. The Chemist cannot contact Cross now he's dead. He'll know something is up. Which means that sooner rather than later, Yumeni's cover will be blown. Three years of undercover work up in smoke.' He pauses for a beat, then continues. 'We, the American government, can't get involved. This would have to be a deniable op. And we'll pay handsomely for this operation. You'd have to be one crazy, arrogant, fucked-up sonofabitch to go after Cross', says the American, looking directly at me. I know exactly what he means by that. And I don't take it as an insult. I see it for what it is: he's issuing me a challenge.

SEVENTY-THREE

SABATINI TELLS LITZE that if it's any consolation, he's glad that we escaped the rogue CIA agents. Litze tells him that it isn't. Sabatini confirms Litze's suspicions about Fleischmann's knowing more than he was letting on. But Litze understands. The damage to their friendship is irreparable.

The American introduces himself as Jon O'Neill. He has a firm handshake, and I sense he's one of the good guys. His team, in cooperation with German officials and comprised of bioweapons experts, take over the site. The migrants are moved to various hospitals to be checked over and will eventually be relocated. Sabatini says he'll track down the human traffickers. Litze was right about him. He's also a good guy, even though he tried to kill us. But he sought to warn us first. That's more than I get normally, so I should be grateful for that.

Yumeni looks at me and says nothing. I don't know what else to say to him. He devoted years of his life to hunting Jason Cross, and I blew it. So it's up to me to fix it. I can't relate to his loss because he's displayed a familial love that I've never known. Yumeni would have loved to be the one to kill Cross, but he can't. He has to trust the actions of a rogue agent with no affiliation to anyone or anything. Now, that's a leap of faith! He looks at me again and nods gently. I reciprocate. I suppose it's his way of wishing me luck.

Blume walks with me to the medic tent and tells me to take good care on my mission. She says that I'd better get my ass out of there alive because we have some serious partying to do. I guess it's her way of motivating me. She slips me a business card, and I ask her what it's for. She says he's a therapist and he's the best she's worked with. I don't take offence because I know she's looking out for me. And the fact that she's not too proud to ask for help is reassuring. Blume kisses Litze on the lips and starts talking to Sabatini. I think he likes her, but for his sake, I hope he's not possessive.

The medic tends to my wounds while I sit on a wheeled stretcher in a makeshift tent on the site. She confirms that I have two fractured ribs, but apart from that, I'm OK.

Litze comes into the tent and asks the nurse to leave us for a moment.

'You don't have to do this', says Litze.

'Yes I do', I say.

'You've got nothing to prove.'

'Is that what you think? I've been trying to prove myself all my life.'

'Don't do this, Sam, this is a suicide mission.'

'I know. But for once in my life, it's a chance to do the right thing. I've messed this up. I'm the only person that can fix it.'

'But on your own?'

'Yes, Litze, too many people have died. It has to be this way.'

'It's convenient for the US government to get an outsider to do their dirty work.'

'I'm OK with that, Litze. And anyway, although I'm not a cleanskin, I'm practically a ghost.'

'And if you don't succeed?'

'Then I'm not worthy to be called one of your agents.'

'That's where you're wrong, Becker. Look at me', says Litze as his deep-blue eyes fix my gaze. 'You were always good enough. You were always ready. I wasn't the one that needed convincing.'

'Even when you were giving me hell?'

'Especially when I was giving you hell. You were different to the others. Some people are colouring books; others are blank sheets of paper. You draw your own lines. You always have. You should trust yourself more.'

'But I shot you all those years ago and never plucked up the courage to face you. I'm sorrier than you can imagine.'

'I know, Becker. I've always known.'

'Litze?'

'What?'

I fix him with my stare. 'If I was always good enough, why were you so hard on me? You treated me differently. Why did you push me away all those years ago?'

'What do you mean?'

I say nothing and wait for his reply. Litze looks uncomfortable.

'Why did you, Litze?' I ask again.

I see the sadness in his eyes. He's lost in thought. But maybe it's not that. I do believe that Litze is nervous but trying his hardest to hide it.

'Please, Litze, tell me', I plead.

He bows his head and stares at the ground. Then raises it again, slowly this time and takes a deep breath. Regaining his composure, he looks me in the eyes and says, 'I got too close.'

His words hit me like a sonic boom. My body feels lighter than it has in years.

'Now we're getting somewhere', I say as I move towards him, place my hands on his shoulders, and kiss him on the lips. 'Thank you, Litze.'

'Call me Lothar.'

He puts his hand on my right cheek and notices that a tear falls down it. He wipes it away with his right index finger with such grace that I respond by taking his palm with my left hand and rest it against my face. It feels so soothing. Something that's sadly alien to me.

'It's not much, but it's a good sign', he says. 'Baby steps, Sam. Baby steps.'

SEVENTY-FOUR

MY FIRST, AND possibly last, assignment for O'Neill is at least eight weeks away. This gives me enough time to recover. I have one thing on my list to do as I'll never get this chance again.

It's been approximately 1,408 days since Donny Walsh and I last spoke. He's been dead for half of that time. For nearly all of that time, I was clinging on to the hope of some reconciliation. And now I make the journey that I never wanted to. But I feel it's the right thing to do: to pay my respects, even though I should have done this when he was alive. It's about 9.00am when I eventually get out of bed. I'm naked as I peer out of the window and see the gloom descend outside my hotel window in Russell Square. I'm up earlier than normal, but I can't sleep. It was a restless night, which had nothing to do with my mattress or room in general. I've stayed at the Queensbury before. It's a four-star hotel and not the most expensive, with modern furniture, which looks like it could be part of a chain of some sort. My discomfort comes from my guilt. From missed opportunities. I wish I had the chance to tell him what I felt when he was alive, but the longer you leave it, the more likely it is that one of you is going to die first. In this case, it was him. The thought that we might somehow meet in the afterlife is no consolation for me. My faith is shot to pieces.

The journey to Islington & Camden Cemetery will take about forty-five minutes if I get my connections: Russell tube, overground train to East Finchley, and then walk. But it will feel like the longest forty-five minutes of my life. I'll wear a discreet black top with a black woollen overcoat, jeans, and black boots. Apart from the jeans, it doesn't seem appropriate to wear anything else. I travelled light with only a change of underwear, makeup, and toiletries as I don't plan to stay here that long. I just want to pay my respects and leave. I drink some coffee and try to eat one of the fresh croissants from the breakfast buffet in the hotel, but I feel too sick to take anything down. Later, I wait in the queue at reception to settle my bill, and it's probably the first time in my life that I want a line of people to go slowly, as my mind is full of dread. I'm in no hurry to go to the cemetery. Whether as a visitor or as one of its future customers. I've kept the undertakers busy enough for some time now.

I make my way to Russell Square tube, locked in my own universe. London can be one of the loneliest places in the world. I've lived here, and it's not easy to form close relationships. But I can't blame it on that.

The morning train is full, which is good as this is perfect camouflage for me, because I can blend in and no one will be able to register the sadness on my face. It's like grieving in plain sight. I'm standing and hold on to a railing because I fear that if I sit down, I won't want to get up again. I glance briefly at my co-passengers and wonder where they've come from, where they're going to, like a game I play to park my sorrow. Part of me wants to cry but I can't. Not yet. I don't want to embarrass myself in front of uncaring strangers who'll feel obliged to show concern when they'd rather just get on with their own problems.

I nearly forget to get off at the Holloway tube station. But do I really? Your subconscious mind has a way of protecting you and part of me just wants to stay. But I tell myself that I can't stop now and walk down the platform to the exit and take the 263 bus to the cemetery. I decide to walk part of the way to get some air. I catch my breath as I feel that my chest is tightening. I slowly compose myself as I trudge my way to the cemetery. My legs feel leaden. My hands sweat, but I will myself forward as I turn and take a shortcut through a minor road. I've never been here before, but I've memorised the route in my head. It's a simple journey really, and I visualise the long road coming off the bus stop; I take the third left and walk down a small residential side street. I already phoned the cemetery warden in advance, and he told me which lot Donny is buried in.

It occurs to me that I have no flowers as I see a florist shop on the way. They probably do good business, given that it's so near to a burial ground. I buy a single red rose, and I tell the woman to keep the change. I've never been into flowers, or romance for that matter, but today of all days, I'll make an exception. I walk up the long path of death and I see the huge church in front of me. It's a great classical design with an imposing steeple, which looks like it's keeping a paternal eye on the tombstones below. It's still early, and there is hardly anyone around. The morning mist clears and I can see the grey slabs poke out of the ivy. It looks like it's part of some decoration. I notice that some of the slabs have been discoloured over time with moss residue. I walk for a little while and briefly read some of the stones, which span decades from young to old, husband and wife, man and woman, boy and girl, children who've never had the chance to grow old, and I don't feel comfortable here as a purveyor of death.

I walk down a narrow gravel path and my footsteps kill the eerie peace. I see another lot which looks freshly created and I see headstones of different sizes, shades, colours, and designs. Some graves have dolls left on them. Others have various gifts such as keys, laminated pictures, teddy bears, porcelain trinkets, an empty whisky bottle, a small blue cardigan. I even see someone has left some foreign currency on one grave. These are touching, and even stir me out of my emotional remoteness, but these gifts serve as a reminder, if any were needed, that you can't take it with you.

I wonder what the dead think sometimes. Part of me believes they'd like to get a message to the living, telling us that it's OK and that they're in a better world. My eyes scan the graveyard and eventually settle on a space at the back: Donny Walsh's last resting place. It's in an isolated plot, which I think is typical of him. The headstone is a simple black marble rectangle, with his name; date of birth, May 12, 1980; and date of death, June 5, 2011. All neatly centred, written in gold leaf in a serif typeface.

I look at the headstone. It sets me off and my overdue tears start to cascade down my cheeks. My sorrow revisits me like the hounds of winter. It's like my grief has been gridlocked, and like a river, my tears start to flow. My legs give way as I sit against the rear of another headstone and cradle my legs with my arms. My tears soak my trousers, and I make no attempt to retain any dignity. My crying is broken up with cursing like some madwoman as frustration sets in. I wish Donny could see how sorry I am. I was too busy putting up a front and mistook emotion for weakness. I now realise that I'm not only crying because of Walsh. I'm crying because I didn't cry enough. I'm crying because of my mentor and because all the trauma of the past years is finally catching up with me. It's as if I've been trying to outrun my pain, but it's a race nobody ever wins. I almost forget my red rose. I take it out of my coat pocket and place it delicately on Donny's plot. Then I resume my position, cradling my legs like when I was a child, when I used to cry. I wait for the next flood to come, and the next.

***

I check my watch; it's 1.45pm. I've been here almost three hours, and I didn't even realise. I've sat here staring like a faithful servant trying to take everything in. I'm all cried out now, at least for the time being, and I finally get up. I feel stiff as I've stayed in this seated position all this time. I wonder how I must look—probably a red-eyed mess—as I search for my mirror and try to make myself look respectable. I use an app on my phone to reveal my image, and to be honest, I've looked better. At least my dishevelled appearance has raised my first smile today, as I look pathetic. I'm having the mother of all bad hair days. My cheeks are stained with dried tears, and I have eyes that would make Satan proud. I stand up and stretch. Then I breathe in the cool air to invigorate me. I start to walk back out the way I came, slowly retracing my steps. I turn and take one last look at Donny's gravestone. I promise that when I can, I'll visit him again. It's the very least I can do, even though this place gives me the creeps. It's a small price to pay. And maybe that's the point: there's no such thing as a free lunch in this world.

I feel better as the crying has released something. I feel lighter than when I came here. Now I refocus for my forthcoming assignment. There's much to do now as I'll have to meet O'Neill in the next few days. Cross is in my sights, and he's one loose end I'll be happy to send to a place like this. It'll take me five minutes to walk back to the exit, but I'm in no hurry. I walk a few strides away from Donny's grave onto the main path. Then something whistles through the air which sounds like a ghostly whisper. I hear a dull thud and feel a sharp sting on the side of my neck. Like a bee, but it's stronger than that. I instantly know what it is.

I manage to summon up the energy to walk some more, but my head is spinning. My stomach feels empty and sick. Then my vision blurs. I try to keep my eyes open, but everything slows down and everything is changing in front of me. I see figures in black approaching me. The gravestones, the trees, the undergrowth, and the dull grey skies are blending into each other. It's as if they are a scene that has just been painted on watercolour paper and the rain is coming down, running and blotching the hues. They begin to merge. Then everything disappears into nothing.

SEVENTY-FIVE

'WAKE UP.' I feel a hand gently slap my left cheek. I can hear voices, but my vision is blurred. I'm still out of it. My head is pounding, but I know enough to realise what that sensation is. It's familiar to me as I've felt it before: some tranquillizer or sedative. I knew as soon as the dart hit my neck. But something else strikes me; this voice sounds familiar, but my mind is too distorted with the drug to tell for certain who it is, or if I'm in a dream. It's clouded right now. I feel like I'm trying to hear underwater.

'Wake up', says the voice again, and I think that I'm listening to the voice of a ghost. The drug makes his tones echo and pulsate with different volume levels and intensities, reverberating and distorting as if he's speaking through an effects pedal on a guitar amp. It will take time for my brain to return to its default setting. My eyes start to open, but I still have no clarity as the shape in front of me has a familiarity that I can't yet place. I squint to refocus, but the signal from my brain to my eyes isn't getting through now. I think I'm talking back, but I'm not quite sure what I'm saying. I'm not sure whether I'm asleep or still in a dream state. It's probably incoherent nonsense. My veins feel bleached and my body limp. Then I hear the voice again, and it sounds like a man, but I can't be sure. In my confusion, my interpretation could be lowering the vocal register.

Therefore, I can't tell if it's a man or woman. Then I hear the same voice say a name and before I can comprehend, I drift into unconsciousness. The drug wins this round.

***

I don't know how long I've been out, but it feels like a long time. I'm on a small single bed in what looks like a holding room or cell. There are no pictures on the wall, and there's a small table to the right of the chamber. The part of me that wants to get up isn't strong enough yet as I lie down again after trying to sit. Even my instinct to escape has been diminished, so I go back to sleep, hoping the drugs will wear off soon. I hate this feeling of helplessness as it doesn't suit me. Then I hear the door open. The light bursts in like a rare visitor as I cover my eyes. They're still waiting to recalibrate. A figure pokes its head into the room like it's deciding whether or not to enter. The figure chooses to retreat. I'm at the mercy of my paralysis as I sleep and hope this will pass soon.

***

I wake once more and feel a lot better. Refreshed even. Which is an indication that I've spent a long time sleeping and probably needed it. My body is starting to feel as healthy as can be. But something is different. I'm not wearing my coat, boots, jeans, or top, just my underwear. At least I haven't been completely stripped. But I'm also in another room. A much nicer one. It looks like someone's bedroom. The bed I'm in is king size and is at the back of the room. The mattress feels more comfortable than the one before, like one of those fancy memory-foam ones, as it nurtures my body. The sheets feel like Indian white cotton; they smell brand new. The duvet cover is also white; it's thick a with an embossed design of flower petals. To the left are big bay windows with curtains falling to the floor that have a lilac paisley design and are bound back by a violet rope. Ahead is a two-drawer dressing table with curved legs and a circular mirror that looks like it can flip and is fixed on two wooden vertical rods either side. To the left, a double wardrobe made of mahogany is to the right of the door. The design is modern rather than old-fashioned. I notice how nice it smells in here compared to the other room and I wonder why I've been moved. The other place said 'prisoner'. This room says 'guest'.

I see my knee-high boots on the floor, and my coat and jeans are neatly folded on a big off-white armchair in the right-hand corner with the same flower design as the duvet. I'm feeling strong enough to get out of bed and find out what has happened to me. Then I think I was abducted despite the fact that I'm in an excellent fancy room. I can't assume anything. My survival instinct kicks in, and I'm already scanning the room for possible weapons. It would be a shame to break that mirror and get seven years' bad luck, but the shards of glass would be perfect to kill someone, unluckily for them. Then I check the drawers for any scissors that I could use. The curtain ropes would be good for strangulation. I'd prefer my Glock, but my mentor always said that anything can be used as a weapon, with a little imagination. I pull away from the duvet, which is remarkably heavy and of good quality. I would have baked under here if I were fully clothed. The bed is higher than normal, so I steady myself onto the floor.

I start to make tentative steps towards my belongings, still feeling the slight effects of the drug. But I've only gotten halfway there when the door opens, and I freeze. Now I really can't believe what my eyes are telling me. I thought I'd recovered from my stupor, but I now feel that I'm hallucinating again, though part of me wants this to be real. But my logical mind is telling me it can't be. He reveals himself slowly as he steps into the room and simply says, 'Hello, Becks.'

SEVENTY-SIX

I STAND THERE in what feels like suspended animation. I see what I see, but I still don't register it.

'Yes, Becks, it's me', he says, and breaks into a smile.

He looks different to the last time I saw him, four years ago. His hair is shorter. He hasn't aged too badly, but this ghost has designer stubble. He's still dressed casually. He's wearing a grey woollen jumper with black corduroy jeans and brown cowboy boots, but it's Donny Walsh all right.

'I'll leave you to get dressed. We've lots to talk about. I'll be waiting outside.'

'Wait', I say as he leaves the room.

'We've waited four years. A few more minutes won't hurt', he says, and closes the door slowly behind him.

I hurriedly put on my jeans, boots, and shirt because I'm scared that the ghost will disappear if I keep him waiting. Walsh is still here and is waiting in the corridor. He offers his right hand, and I take it.

'You're safe here. Sorry about putting you in that cell. That wasn't my idea; that was our leader, Fabian. He's a very cautious man. Once I convinced him that you were no threat to us, I got you moved to this bedroom. If you're wondering, I removed your clothes. I thought you'd be more comfortable. I hope you don't mind.'

I remain silent.

We walk down the corridor of what looks like a stately home. The corridor is unusually wide, but I can't place the period. My sketchy history suggests that it looks like it's from the Georgian era. The ceilings are ridiculously high and white, with cornices around the edges and wallpaper that looks like it probably cost more than the walls it covers. The carpet is plush and a rich red in colour, and it cushions my every step; it feels rude to walk on it, as it displays an intricate diamond pattern at the edges. Donny leads me to the carpeted stairs on the right, which have a brown solid wood banister on each side and flow out into the grand floor below. I imagine that it would be a great way to make an entrance amongst guests.

***

I can't calculate exactly how big the room is, but you could play an eleven-a-side football match with room to spare. Rectangular in shape, the space has six brown leather two- and three-piece sofas arranged randomly, but given the area, it somehow works. There are people sitting on them using laptops and tablets. There are also large rectangular tables with computer workstations, some occupied by groups of two or three huddled around the screen in deep discussion. Others remain empty. The room has about five doors on either side, which I assume lead to more rooms or corridors to various parts of the house. In the rear left of the room, I also see a group of children playing in what looks like an area especially for them. There is a collection of various toys and colourful beanbags for them to sit on. One woman has a small girl placed on her lap, and she looks like she's reading her a story. As we descend, I see a man at a large desk at the back of the room notice us. He rises and walks over to greet us, his form coming into view. He is a large black man who's about six foot four and built like an American footballer. He's bald, probably by choice, but has baby-faced features, though he probably is older. His smile is welcoming, and he has a serene quality about him. He's wearing a blue cotton shirt and black trousers. His movement is slow and measured, like he's never had to rush for anything in his life. But there's something else about him: an indefinable presence that I've only seen in a very few people. My mentor being one of them. The three of us meet at the bottom of the stairs, and he extends his large right hand.

'Hello, Sam, my name is Fabian', he says with his booming voice that seems to come from his shoes. 'I've heard a lot about you', he continues. His handshake is very firm and lingers, as if it's some initiation or test.

'Really?' I ask.

'Yes, Donny has talked of little else since he's been here', he says.

I look at Donny, and he almost looks embarrassed at the revelation.

'I'm very sorry about the measures we took to get you here, but we have to be careful', says Fabian.

'You were watching?' I ask.

'Yes again; that's for security. Donny will explain later.'

'Where is this place?' I ask. Though I now realise that it's a pointless question because I know what his answer will be.

'Well you're still in England if that's any consolation, but other than that, I can't say. You could call it a secret self-sustaining community. There are many like this around the world, and they're ideal for people who want to get out of the rat race, escape, or fake their deaths', he says, looking at Donny. 'We have people from all walks of life here: doctors, lawyers, civil servants, some politicians, musicians. Individuals who felt let down and disenfranchised by society and who don't identify with the rules out there. Unsurprisingly, we do also have a lot of teachers in our community.'

'So how do you keep—'

'Hidden?' interrupts Fabian. 'Despite what many say about there not being enough land in the UK, especially the anti-immigration lobby, there's plenty in this country. This isle is big enough if you want to disappear. The *Domesday Book* didn't record everything or everybody. And you don't have to go away so long as you know the right people and have the right connections. This need to get out of the system transcends race, creed, and social or financial status. Many people go missing every day. Some go abroad, some die or live on the street, some get trafficked, and some, like us, join these secret societies. People have wanted to step out of the system forever and resent the powers that be, who make these rules they don't even follow themselves. It's little wonder that they don't get respect, and somehow these people think they're entitled to it. The arrogance of it. You'd be surprised how few know of our existence, but secret societies have been around forever. That's how man has managed to survive, by keeping secrets from each other. We all have our secrets, Sam.'

I look at him and listen. It's like he speaks my words and has known my thoughts all these years. I've never felt part of society and don't know what that means. And I'm delighted by the fact that I don't do society. But sometimes I've wondered whether I've taken this alienation too far and almost rebel for the sake of it.

'Anyway, Sam, you don't want to be listening to me on my soapbox. I get carried away sometimes. You must be hungry. Donny will show you to the dining areas. I've got to get back to work. We'll talk soon.'

We shake hands and Fabian returns to his huge wooden desk at the other side of the room; that's not before he talks to a few people on the way. It's clear he's a natural leader who oozes a quiet authority.

'How did you meet?' I ask Donny.

'Fabian has a special way of recruiting people through coded messages. He sends out puzzles online, which some think are games but are in fact recruitment tests to find out whether people are suitable for the organisation', says Donny.

'So what is this place?' I ask.

'We'll have time for that. I'll take you to breakfast, and I'll answer the questions that I'm able to. Remember, I can't tell you everything, and there are even things they won't tell me. That doesn't offend me. It's for security reasons, and it's best that I don't know', Donny replies.

'This doesn't sound like you, wanting to be kept in the dark.'

'I'm sure I'll be let into the inner circle, but that takes time. I have to earn their trust. Many people would want to infiltrate this place. Many have tried, but touch wood, nobody has succeeded. I understand: if anyone found out about this location, it would be the end. We just want to be left alone to live our lives on our terms.'

'And that's why I was drugged: to protect the secret?'

'Yes, Becks. I'm sorry about that.'

'Under the circumstances, you have nothing to apologise for', I say, and put my arm on his shoulder. 'I get why you want secrecy. But there's lots of people working on laptops or PC stations. What and who are you recruiting, and for what?'

'All in good time', he says. 'I'll tell you more about our organisation later.'

Then a very tall, attractive blonde woman walks past and introduces herself to me.

'You must be Sam Becker', she says, extending her hand, which I shake. 'I'm Joss. Donny has talked about you often', she says as she kisses him on the cheek. An unjustified and surprising wave of jealousy hits me. 'We're so pleased that he joined us. He's been fantastic for us. We just love his maverick spirit', she says as she walks off.

And at that moment, she unwittingly reveals to me what this organisation is.

SEVENTY-SEVEN

I'M AT THE headquarters of a cyberterrorist group, Purple Dawn.

'You're Maverick Spirit', I say. 'You were talking to my mentor, Lothar Litze.'

'That's right, Becks. And I didn't know who he was until I did some cross-checking and realised you have connections with Litze that go back for years. To his credit, he was very discreet and held you in very high regard', says Walsh, sitting next to me.

Now I know how Litze really feels about me, this is no longer a surprise. He hid his true feelings all this time.

'Did he ever say anything else about me?'

'No, that was pretty much it. He was very focused and professional. I would have loved to have met him. I felt I knew him through our contact and we had some good conversations during our brief association', says Walsh as we continue down the stairs.

We walk to one of the many dining areas in this place. Donny tells me there are about five in total and I'm trying to work out where we are when I see the huge window. Outside it's like a sea of green that goes on forever. It could be anywhere and nowhere, and while I try to respect Purple Dawn's need for privacy, I'm naturally curious. And I wonder how you can hide whole communities within countries. I think about satellites that would be able to detect a place like this and then I remember this is Purple Dawn, who are known as cyberterrorists on the outside and freedom fighters to others. If anyone can hide from a spy satellite, then they can. In these communities they call this 'black box' knowledge: it's only available to a handful of people. I could not even begin to comprehend how they do it, but they probably hack government databases to send them false, or ghost, images so that they think they are looking at one thing but in fact, it's something else. Just the same way you would use a false tape loop on CCTV surveillance. Or maybe they create false-flag alerts in other parts of the world so that spy satellites are distracted. There is only so much that they can do. Government agencies would have to prioritise.

Agencies like the FBI, CIA, and GCHQ would have designated resources to combat cyberterrorists and take down organisations like Purple Dawn. They'd even hire ex-hackers to take out their old colleagues. Some wouldn't always have a choice as they would be threatened or tortured. But that's the way you'd do it. It would be like a game. One team is testing their expertise against another; each side is trying to outdo the other, upping their level of competence so that there's a winner. But it's really like a cyber-tennis game: when you think that you've landed a killer shot, the other side comes up with a winner. This game is never-ending; it's like finding a cure for a virus, only for it to mutate and avoid detection.

We're sat at one of the many large breakfast tables in another hall. We're relatively early, so we help ourselves to the buffet area, which has breakfast cereals with milk and fruit juices. There are also fruit and dried prunes in white china bowls. Or there's the cooked food, a traditional fried English breakfast of sausages, eggs, beans, tomatoes, and bacon with toast, or there are cold meats such as ham and salami. And there's plenty of fish, from smoked salmon to cod to mackerel. I've not eaten meat for some time, so I decide to eat some cereal to start with, and I help myself to the vegetarian English menu with Quorn sausages. Walsh decides on the meat option.

We sit down; I see more people join the breakfast area. It looks like the United Nations as I see a mixture of different nationalities.

I didn't realise how hungry I am, and I go up for my second serving. Donny is sat next to me, and I look at him, still trying to take in all that has happened. I want to know how and why he faked his death, and there's also the fact that we never talked after what I did to him, which I deeply regret. At the moment, he doesn't betray any emotion, but I want to build bridges again. I've missed him and our friendship, and I want the chance to repair it, but there's now a big hurdle to this: he seems happy here and it doesn't look like he's ready to leave Purple Dawn any time soon.

SEVENTY-EIGHT

DONNY AND I don't have any privacy during breakfast as various people say hello and join us at our table. I've never seen him so happy and at peace. He's a social animal, and I see him in a new light. Part of that pleases me, but the other part knows that he won't want to leave. After what happened, I have no right to expect anything, but I feel conflicted. I want to repair the damage I did to our friendship.

After breakfast, I feel tired and tell Donny that I want to take a nap. He says he'll come up later and we'll go for a walk. I return to my room, and the bed has been made. It looks like the sheets are clean, but my coat is untouched. I take my phone from my inside pocket and I turn it on. And I'm not surprised at what I see: there is no signal on the display. Even if I wanted to call for help, I couldn't, but I don't feel that I'm in imminent danger.

I decide to return to my bed as I feel that I need this rest. I close the heavy curtains, take my boots off, climb onto the bed, and set my alarm on my phone for about two hours.

***

I'm awoken by a knock on the door, which indicates to me that I haven't been sleeping for hours as I've not heard my alarm go off. But I feel rested. Donny Walsh pokes his head through the door, and

I gesture him in. He says to be ready in ten minutes and disappears behind the door. I get up and go to the en-suite bathroom to the left of the bed that I didn't notice earlier to freshen up. I splash my face and don't bother to dry it with a towel. I try to get my short black hair into some order as I run my wet fingers through from front to back. I check the mirror and to my relief, my eyes aren't puffed. In fact, I look well rested. I've been having more of these power naps lately, and they've helped. I've tried to listen to my body carefully and respect its need for rest where possible. I grab my coat and mobile as I head to the door. Donny Walsh is waiting in the corridor like before, and he greets me with a big smile.

We walk together down the massive staircase and at the bottom go past some of the people working on their computers. They nod to Donny as he makes eye contact with them and enters through one of the side doors on the right-hand side of the large room, through two double doors, and out to the grounds. It's not particularly sunny but nice enough to go outside for a stroll. I look around, and there isn't another building in sight. It's as if an alien spacecraft has picked up this building and transported it into the middle of nowhere. All I can see are trees and undulating hills that meet the horizon line. Donny walks me to a cluster of small saplings where there's a wooden bench, and we sit. He tells me that Purple Dawn helped him to fake his death, but with modern methods of DNA detection, the surest way to do this was to be in control of the investigation, using men and women on the inside. They also obtained a body of similar size and age to Donny, which was then destroyed beyond all recognition in the staged gas explosion in East London. Purple Dawn also hacked medical records and created a death certificate.

He looks away at first, then he looks at me and takes my hands in his.

'You should have trusted me, Becks', Donny says. It's the first time that he betrays sadness in his expression.

'I know, Donny, and I've regretted it ever since. I fucked up big time, and I'm sorry.'

'I was angry with you for a long time, Becker; that's why I didn't take your calls. I couldn't believe anyone would do this. Then I realised that I missed things about us. I didn't communicate too well. Nor did you for that matter.'

'I was scared of losing you, Donny. Anything I ever cared about seemed to turn to shit. I didn't want you to go the same way.'

'I understand all that now. I realised that you were well intentioned, but this wasn't about love. This was about control.'

I say nothing because I know he's right.

'And I concluded that you're more like your father than you care to imagine.'

That comment stings like a million wasps.

'You know, Becker, I realise you thought I was wet behind the ears.'

'What do you mean?'

'I mean that I wasn't worldly-wise and that I couldn't take care of myself.'

'But I was always intimidated by your intelligence.'

'And so you should have been. But I knew what you were before you told me. I knew you were some badass black ops assassin that most wouldn't touch with a bargepole. We make the most unlikely of friends, but we're friends for a reason. And as a friend, I have never interfered with your life choices. Have I?'

'No.'

'The fact that you have had affairs with married men and think you're some sexual Mother Teresa, saving marriages. Do you think these men respect you, Becker, really?'

I say nothing.

'They respect your discretion, but that isn't integrity. To them, you might as well be a hole in the wall with a blood supply.'

I feel like a boxer on the ropes now. The punches are coming in, but I have no response.

'I'm with you on this marriage thing, Becker. I think it's bullshit. Like some relationship advert for other people. I may not be into marriage, but I respect other peoples'. I have more respect for marriage than these losers you hook up with.'

I say nothing.

'And I don't believe you respect these men. I sometimes think you behave this way to prove that you're right about men. And that comes from your father.'

I'm lost for words. I just sit there and take it.

'The point I'm trying to make, Becker, is that you don't have to settle. There are some good guys out there, some who will treat you with respect, but you've got to do that for yourself first.'

I look at Donny for a long time. I've never heard him speak so candidly like this. 'Have you always felt this way?' I say, breaking my silence. I feel numb.

'To be honest, Becker, I didn't give it much thought. I didn't interfere because it wasn't any of my business. Maybe as a friend, I should have said something. But what you did by getting me abducted and nearly killed was the invitation I needed to say something.'

'So what you're saying is that if I'm going to dish it out, I should be able to take it?'

'That's exactly what I'm saying. You say you acted out of love, but I say that's bullshit. There are other ways. But at the end of the day, I have to make my own decisions. I want you to trust me. Not fake-trust me.'

'Fair enough.'

'Becks?'

'Yes?'

'Do you believe that we're soulmates?'

'I guess so?'

'You see, my definition of a soulmate is someone who knows the words to my song. I think in my case, you've tried to rewrite the lyrics.'

'I see.'

'Do you, Becker? Do you? I want us to know the words to each other's songs. We may not always like the lyrics, but at least we don't interfere with them. Do you get me?'

'Crystal clear.'

No one has ever spoken to me like this before. No one would ever dare, but Donny just did. Although it is hard to hear, I can't argue with any of it. Not one word. Even the father thing, which makes me sick.

'Are we still friends?' I say.

'Do you want to listen to the lyrics of my song?'

'Yes. But say them to me. Don't sing them, as you've got a shit voice.'

We laugh, then cry, then embrace. We hold each other for a long time. I don't want to let go, but I know I'll have to.

'I have another question, Donny.'

'Sure, shoot. Oops, don't take that literally.'

'Ha ha, very funny. You refused to help Litze with Karl Yumeni. Why?'

'You'd usually have to have security clearance to hear this. I suppose it doesn't matter now.'

'What do you mean?'

'Karl Yumeni isn't his real name.'

'I know that.'

'But what you don't know, Becks, is that Karl Yumeni's legend was created by me.'

I look at him and pause. 'It all makes sense', I say. 'But why?'

'That was part of the deal.'

'What deal?'

'Your suspicions about my activity online were not incorrect. I went to some dark places and hacked some very high-level organisations. These people were closing in. That was about three years ago. Then they made an offer that I couldn't refuse. They wanted me to work for the American government. I'd have to work on black ops projects. Things that you knew I would despise. But they threatened my family, so I didn't have a choice. The guy who wanted this legend came to meet me. It was Yumeni. In fact, I liked him. He told me about his twin brother and how he wanted to bring down Jason Cross. But he was honest and said that they couldn't guarantee complete immunity.'

'You mean immunity from prosecution?'

'Yes. Even though he was on their side, he was sympathetic to my plight. But he knew some evil fuckers who wanted to bury me in a hole in the ground.'

'At least he was honest with you.'

'Yes, but I think he was sending me a message.'

'In what way?'

'Yumeni had to be careful, but I sensed that he wouldn't blame me for disappearing.'

'You mean he was encouraging you?'

'Not overtly, but he was trying to distance himself from the people he was working for. I guess he blamed them in some way for his brother's death.'

'I don't understand.'

'It was working for Mandrake Security that killed his brother, but

Jason Cross is a product of the system. I sensed his anger. He was working for people who were like clones of Jason Cross. His motivation was to avenge his brother, which nullified, to a degree, any feelings he had for his employers.'

'I guess he felt it was better to work inside the system than outside.'

'Yeah, he's a better man than me in that regard. He knew that his undercover work would be life-changing. He would have to do things and justify it as being for the greater good. But as someone once said: "There's no such thing as an uninjured soldier."'

'Tell me about it.'

'OK', says Donny, looking at his watch. 'Let's walk and talk. We've a lot of catching up to do.'

SEVENTY-NINE

WE TALK ABOUT everything. My life since we stopped speaking, and his. Walsh seems happier than ever. Part of me is glad but also sad that I didn't share it.

'You know, Becker, while I was mad at you, your abduction gave birth to an idea: what if I could disappear permanently? As you know, I've never felt I've belonged. You of all people should understand that, but I thought: How hard could that be? To fake my own death. It wasn't that hard in the end. And you showed me how much you cared. I saw the grief when you visited my grave.'

'How?'

'We have a camera installed in the tombstone. So you see, I knew.'

'And you watched me sit there for three hours crying like a baby?' I say, pulling my hands away.

'Yes, Becks, I saw everything', Walsh says, taking my hands again. 'You shouldn't be embarrassed. It was good for me to see. I'm not an idiot, Becks, so don't treat me like one. I felt in my heart that you cared for me. And I had my suspicions about what you did. The sudden flights out of the country at a moment's notice, the vague way you used to talk about your "sales job." Your fatigue and the way you'd walk into my home feeling sore, saying that you'd hurt yourself training.'

'Am I that obvious?'

'To me you are, but I think I understand you better than you think. I knew you were some badass security agent or worse, and I thought one day you might confide in me. But I now know you had me abducted to protect me. I get that now. I was reckless when I was hacking all that government stuff, but I think I wasn't always in a good place then. I was drinking heavily and taking drugs, but at the heart of it, I wasn't happy. Not really. In fact, I should thank you for what you did because you gave me an out. And I didn't realise there were so many of us here. Do you know how lonely it is to be with people that you don't connect or have an affinity with? This is the first time in my life that I can truly say that I'm happy.'

As he speaks, I see the smile return to his face and I believe what he says.

'So why the camera at the gravestone?' I say.

'It's just a precaution, and vanity on my part', he says. 'Even before you set up the abduction, I felt that I was being watched. I thought that there might be people who would go after any friends that I might have had and take them in for questioning. But I needn't have worried about that. Having a covert camera on your grave is an extreme way to find out who your friends are, but as it turns out, I don't have any real friends. You're the only person who visited me in the two years since I faked my death, apart from my parents, and as far as I was concerned, that was it. So you see, I can't go back. This is where I belong.'

'I'm sorry I lied to you, Donny, and I didn't open up. It seems like we had secrets from each other.'

'We're not unusual in that, Sam. There are people in relationships all over who look back and it feels like an illusion, like they've been sleepwalking through it. Who's ever truly their real self in any relationship? I'm a great believer that everything happens for a reason and a purpose. What happened to us was meant to happen, perhaps to bring us closer together.'

'But you're happy here, Donny. I've never seen you like this. I thought I'd lost you. I've found you, and now I'm about to lose you all over again. I don't know how much I can take', I say, thinking that tears don't dry up, they just slow down.

'Becks, you never lost me and you never will. After what you've put me through, most people would have run a mile, but I always felt that I was your friend. Even though I didn't see you, I felt your presence. You know what you should have done?' he says.

'What?' I say.

'There are other ways you could've shown that you care.'

'I don't understand.'

'You should have just jumped my bones and fucked my brains out.'

Now he tells me.

EIGHTY

WE SPEND A further two hours catching up on old times. And it feels like a new relationship, an even better one, which is a relief. Apart from his activities at Purple Dawn, Donny tells me everything about what happened over the last four years after his anger subsided. He tells me again how much he's missed me. And I tell him too. Even though I will hardly see him now because of his involvement here, I'm grateful for our time together. When I thought he was dead, I felt like I'd driven over a cliff.

Donny tells me there's a meet-and-greet tonight in the big house for new recruits and we have the chance to dress up. I explain that I have nothing to wear, but he says that there are plenty of things here that will be my size and I should get one of the girls to help me out.

Fabian will be hosting the event. I'm keen to find out more about him, but he seems to be a closed book. I wonder who he knows and how he's acquired such a place. Or who he's connected with. I like the idea of an environment like this and understand it and the reason it exists. The people in here don't belong out there, and I don't either. So why don't I stay? Why don't I do a Donny and disappear? I have enough resources. I don't have any family. Maybe tonight I'll find answers and come to some conclusions.

The main hall is well prepared for this evening's events. There are over two dozen circular tables with white cloths draped over them. It looks like the kitchen staff will serve the food and it will be nice to be waited on. I've found a little black dress, and one of the girls has helped me with my hair. I was never a girly-girl. I was too busy being a tomboy and wasn't aware of fashion, so to speak, until much later on. But the woman who helps me is breathtaking. Her name is Clarissa. She is a buxom blonde with kind eyes. During our time together, she never stops smiling, and it isn't fake. It's genuine. You can't keep up that kind of smile for so long unless it's real. She's a magician with my hair, as she manages to tame it just as easily as she does her admirers. She has a gentle, soothing touch, and tells me that she's been in Purple Dawn for over four years and joining was the best decision that she ever made. And the way she speaks about Fabian—call it woman's intuition, but you can tell she has a thing for him. She tells me about what a great and inspiring leader he is and that she was in an abusive marriage. She worked as an IT consultant at Omega Industries and hated her job, but hated her relationship more. She passed the series of tests, and they allowed her to disappear. For her, it was like a witness protection program, but better. The rules of society don't apply to her, and it sounds like it would be ideal for an outsider such as me.

That's the great thing about being an outsider; they're everywhere. I've always known that I was before I knew the meaning of the word. That's why my life has taken this path so far. That's why I've met the people I've met, like Walsh and my mentor. I'm looking forward to the ball; I'm sitting at the top table with Fabian and Walsh, which makes me feel like I'm some guest of honour.

Another girl comes into my room to see if I'm OK. She is a beautiful, statuesque black woman called Simone. She looks like one of those Amazonian princesses. She must be six foot at least, has mahogany skin, and is busty without falling out of her gold-patterned dress. Again, like Clarissa, she beams like a torch. She's here to check on my makeup, and I gratefully accept as I'm not good at that either. I often put too much or too little on myself, but I've gotten better over the years. Simone leans into me. She has a gentle touch; to be honest, I'm feeling turned on by her. I try to hide it, but Simone can tell, though she's classy and discreet enough not to embarrass me and smiles. But her sensual energy is intoxicating. Different from Clarissa, but no less potent.

Simone leaves me to be on my own for a while. I look at myself in the mirror and although I wouldn't go so far as to say that I could eat myself, I think I don't look too bad. I turn and see myself in my figure-hugging black dress, and it feels good. I remind myself of what it feels like to be a woman again and I realise that in all of the chaos, that gets lost. This is a shame, and I vow to reconcile that part of me by trying to enjoy the little things. By being more girly. Asking for help. And being less proud.

I go into the room's en-suite and check my face in the mirror again. I like the job Simone has done. I'm lucky that I don't need lots of makeup and am one of those girls who doesn't live or die by it, but it has made a difference. I think I look good, and feel a surge of confidence that I haven't felt in a long time.

I smooth my dress down with my hands, put on some borrowed black stilettos, and brace myself for this evening. I don't know why I'm nervous. I shouldn't be. Everybody here seems very friendly and welcoming, always ready to put me at ease, and I realise why I'm like this: I'm not used to such an environment. An environment where I feel accepted. There's a tremendous feeling of love here. Also, there is serious work here. There are many who want to destroy Purple Dawn and don't agree with their activities. They reveal secrets. They bring down governments, and they could put many in danger, but they'll conclude that's acceptable collateral damage. Part of the greater good. I'm looking forward to meeting everyone. This is better than a holiday. But part of me is sad. And that's because of my friend Donny Walsh. He's not going anywhere; I'm happy for him and sad for me. Sad because after everything, after thinking I lost him through my stupidity and hubris, I have to come to terms with the fact that I may have to lose him all over again.

EIGHTY-ONE

AT OUR TABLE sits Fabian, who has a very attractive woman on either side of him. They look particularly close, and like the other women, they smile a lot. Part of me thinks that nobody can smile that much and have it be real. But I give them the benefit of the doubt. It doesn't look like feigned happiness. This looks genuine. Not only that, but their body language is flirtatious without being too obvious. With their sensual glow, I can guess that he has a way of keeping them happy. There are about eight of us at the table, and the seating arrangements are boy-girl. Donny is sat next to me on my right, but I'm sat with my back exposed, which is unusual for me because I prefer to sit with my back against the wall. Force of habit, I guess.

'So Sam, how are you enjoying the evening?' says Fabian in his booming voice.

'I'm having a nice time, thanks. Everyone seems happy here.'

'That's what we promote, Becker. Before people came to us, they were lost. Purple Dawn helps them find purpose. That's what we all need in life.'

'So is this some cult?'

'I don't like the word cult. For me, it has negative connotations. I prefer secret society', replies Fabian. I feel Donny's stare on my right cheek. I know that stare. It's for when I become provocative.

'So are people free to leave if they don't like it here?'

'Fortunately, Becker, that situation has never arisen. We've never had an exit interview', replies Fabian as some of the guests at the table laugh.

'It doesn't take a genius to work out that your activities will endanger peoples' lives. You're releasing top secret information to the public. Are you concerned about that?'

'Coming from an assassin, don't you think your remarks are a bit ironic? We're not that different, you and I, and I'll be honest, we never get it perfect, but we believe doing something is better than doing nothing. The reason people are here is that we understand something: we can't really rely on the powers that be to give us what we want or need. The status quo will always win. Nothing will change. We want to live our lives on our terms.'

'I take your point about my profession and accountability, but you can affect things on a much greater scale than me.'

'Hey, Sam, I'm not saying that we're perfect, but I like to consider us the good guys trying to restore balance, standing up for the little guy. The world is a nasty place out there, and unless these people are brought to account, they will continue to get away with their dubious activities. And to be honest with you, I sleep well at night. I'm no monster.'

Donny kicks me gently under the table. He wants me to stop.

'And talking of monsters', Fabian continues, 'have you seen the state of Tony Blair? He looks like shit. He tried to do a "Picture of Dorian Grey" and sell his soul to the devil for eternal life, but even the devil didn't want his soul. He's paying for sending soldiers to their deaths on that dodgy dossier. Now his picture in the attic stays young while his face grows old. And the joke is, he tells us that it was right, what he did, but the truth of his crimes is etched all over his face.'

Some of the guests around the table laugh.

'What about—'

'What about another drink?' Donny butts in. 'I could do with one.' I take the hint and change the subject.

'Why don't you join us?' asks one of the women at the table, an attractive busty blonde. She's been giving me the eye all evening.

'I'm sure that Fabian wouldn't want yet another strong woman here.'

'Nonsense, Sam. I like your spirit. I've heard so much about you from Donny. He can't stop talking about you.'

I look at Donny. Although I'm not entirely sure, I think he's blushing.

'I've noticed something else here', I say as I see Donny's expression change to one of dread. 'The ratio of men to women is at least two to one. How does that work?'

I hear a couple of the girls laugh and the buxom blonde looks at me. Then I realise.

'Oh, I see', I say, and smile, knowing I've been a complete idiot.

'People are like Quality Streets: made for sharing', says the blonde as the table starts to laugh.

'You can't accuse Fabian of not championing women here', says the blonde.

It sounds like my kind of place, I think.

***

I've had a lot to drink, which is a good thing, as I start to relax. I was in danger of becoming a party pooper. It's been a while since I've been to a party. I'm not very sociable, but it's good to see different people. The fact that they're an eclectic bunch who've opted out of society adds to the energy. And I wonder whether I could stay in such a place. This would be ideal for someone like me, and I wonder if

I'm the only assassin here. It would make sense that I'm not. I've worked with colleagues who have gone off the grid and disappeared for good. I could do that. Maybe I should do it. Especially after recent events. People like me must be crazy or supremely confident to think that this life won't catch up with you in some way or other. If someone doesn't kill you, you're left with the consequences of your choices in the privacy of your mind, which is a scary thought.

But part of me thinks that I'm not done yet. I have a strange relationship with society. Strange relationship? Well, it's no relationship. I've dipped my toe in society, and that's pretty much it. If I want to play a part, I must change, and I don't know whether I'm brave enough to do that.

I look at the assembled crowd and they look like snakes that have shed their dead skin. I don't get a sense here that people have to pretend to be something they're not. Not like on the outside. And that's always been my problem: faking it. So it makes sense that someone like me should stay in a place like this, and I wonder why I won't. I'd be with my friend, but still, something stops me.

I catch Donny's attention. He's talking to a small crowd of people, and they seem to hang on his every word. And I've never seen him like this. He was never happy on the outside, and he reminds me of that quote about caged birds. We have that in common: we don't do well in cages.

He walks over to me and smiles, and I reciprocate gratefully, as I thought I'd never see him again.

'What do you make of it, Becks?'

'It's nice here. Almost too good to be true.'

'Believe it, Becks. I've never been happier. I feel like I've got my soul back.'

'I know what you mean.'

Walsh takes me by both hands and looks at me.

'I'd love you to stay here, Becks.'

'After what I did to you?'

'You know what they say about presents coming in strange packages.'

'Yes.'

'It never came stranger than this. I owe you, Becks. I've finally escaped.'

'I've missed you like you wouldn't believe.'

'Me too. But everything happens for a reason and a purpose. Even when we weren't talking, I always felt I was with you. You'll think this is strange, but I always thought we were in communication. I never believed in all that spiritual stuff before, but time away has made me think about things a lot. Sometimes I'd talk to you when I was on my own, hoping that you'd hear, and I honestly felt that you were listening to me.'

'Well that makes a change', I say as Donny laughs.

'Whatever happens, we'll always be connected.'

'I know that, Donny, I've always known.'

He brings me closer and looks into my eyes. He brings his lips to mine and we kiss. And it doesn't feel weird.

'I've wanted to do that for a long time, Becks.'

'Why didn't you?'

'I guess out of respect. Out of fear. I'm not very good at this relationship stuff.'

'Well if you want relationship advice, Donny, you're looking at the wrong girl.'

'I suppose I was trying to preserve the integrity of our relationship, but I realise that there was this elephant in the room that we never talked about.'

'You, me, and a billion other relationships.'

'So that you know, I'm not going to sleep with you.'

'Who said I wanted to sleep with you anyway?' I lie.

'It's not because I don't fancy you. It's because I feel we've transcended that stuff. It's not that I don't want to, it's because we don't need to.'

A wave of disappointment comes over me, but I know he's right deep down. And anyway, I'm grateful that we have this.

He takes me by the hand and walks me into his room. And I momentarily think maybe he's had a change of heart.

As we enter, I can see a room not that different to the one I'm staying in. Expensive patterned carpet. High ceilings, big curtains, a king-size bed that we can disappear in, but I try not to get ahead of myself. He takes me to the double-seated, paisley-patterned couch on the left of the room, and we sit.

He looks me in the eye again. I sense hesitation.

'You're not going to stay, are you, Becks?'

'No, Donny. Tempting though it is. I'm not done with the outside world. Not just yet. And anyway, I have something to finish.'

'You mean the Jason Cross mission?'

'You know about that? Of course you do.'

Donny looks away, pauses, then looks at me. 'Please be careful.'

'I will.'

'You know I love you, Becks?'

'I do, Donny. I love you too. Even if I had a funny way of showing it at times, I've always felt it.'

'Do you trust me?'

'Yes', I say, looking at him quizzically. 'What's this about?'

He takes a cup from the side table and passes it to me. 'Drink this, please.'

Now, I normally wouldn't do this for anyone, but I know what this is about. And he knows that I know. He nods gently and passes the cup. The drink is a sedative. And it's for Purple Dawn's safety. They're going to send me back to the outside.

EIGHTY-TWO

I SEEM TO have a habit of waking up in strange bedrooms, and it's not a great lifestyle choice. But the surroundings I find myself in seem pleasant enough as my eyes, body, and brain readjust from being under. That sedative Donny gave me was very powerful, and I still feel that it's not quite out of my system. It feels like I am still hung-over, but it's not the alcohol type of hung-over feeling. I can tell the difference. It feels like my blood has bleach in it.

This looks like a hotel room. At least I think it is. I'm lying on what looks like a king-size bed and I can see a flat-screen TV in front of me on wall painted magnolia. Below it is a modern brown-oak dressing table with a chair underneath. There's a small brown leather armchair in the far left-hand corner of the room with a brown blanket. To the right of me is a large window with silver-grey curtains that caress the pale brown carpet. The curtains are drawn, so I can't even tell what time of day it is.

I'm assuming I'm still in England, but I don't know where. I'm wearing clothes, at least, which is good, and this hotel perhaps belongs to Purple Dawn, or there's some connection. How else would they get me in here? Then it occurs to me there are several ways they could smuggle a sedated woman discreetly. That's where the concierge comes in. Pay him enough, and he could hide an elephant in here undetected. I could have been sneaked in through the service entrance or even in a suitcase. Or they could have been brazen and taken me through the front door and claimed that I'd had too much and I was worse for wear. They could have said that I was a spoiled rich brat who partied too hard. Having a woman in a hotel who's out of it wouldn't be such an unusual occurrence, given what they probably have to deal with.

Part of me wanted to stay there back at the Purple Dawn headquarters. It would have been so easy, but I have scores to settle, and I made a promise to O'Neill. He seems keen for me to work with him. But I do have reservations. He's ex-CIA for a start, but he's ex for a reason, so I should think that's a good thing.

Maybe I still can't let things go. Purple Dawn was the perfect opportunity to leave. There are many in my position and with my reputation who have disappeared. Nobody would find me unless I wanted to be found. But I realise that I probably would have been happy but restless. I also understand that I get a buzz from what I do. Some people would call it thrill-seeking. But there are less dangerous ways to get your kicks. I also realise that maybe the world outside is there for me to learn. I'd have peace, sure, but I wouldn't have the same opportunities for growth. Or maybe I'm just one sick masochist who likes to bang her head against society's brick wall.

But the real reason I didn't stay is that I want to kill Jason Cross. I owe Yumeni that much. I blew the only chance to get him, and now it falls on me. I don't even have to be in the same room when he goes down. I just want to be responsible for taking him out. And I'll happily shoot him from a mile away or up close and personal.

Some would think that this mission isn't worth it and that I should walk away. But I now I know that Yumeni isn't the enemy. This isn't about me. I was in the wrong place, wrong time, and so was my team. My motivation has changed. It's now about taking out an even worse guy, Jason Cross.

O'Neill doesn't tell me much about the president's involvement but reading between the lines, he wants to distance her from this as much as possible. This operation is illegal, and if this came out, O'Neill would take the fall. She must inspire a lot of loyalty for him to risk so much. But O'Neill doesn't seem like the kind of man who can be scared or bullied. He has a natural authority that doesn't come from external things. And I feel that like me, he's been here before. Maybe we met before in a past life. I wonder about that sometimes when I meet kindred spirits. There's a familiarity about them that I can't place, but I've seen them somewhere.

This operation will take meticulous planning and will be on a need-to-know basis. I wonder how to do something like this. Any operatives I'd use on this job would be cleanskins, but there's an inherent risk because although they'd be untraceable, they'd lack experience and there'd be less chance of accurately predicting the outcome. I'd use people who could disappear. People like me. And I'd use the dark web for my communications. Something that's ideal for individuals who want to keep their identities private, but it's also a nightmare for security agencies who want to catch criminals. But this cat-and-mouse game is inevitable. One side thinks they're close. The other always ups the ante.

Cross has so many enemies that his death will be unsurprising.

Well, at least we have that in common.

EIGHTY-THREE

THE PLANNING FOR this job is much better than it was for my last one, which isn't much of an achievement. O'Neill's brief from the president is to clean this mess up. But there's an implicit understanding between them: the less she knows, the better. O'Neill is OK with that. He's a good soldier. It keeps things simpler for everybody. If this operation goes belly-up, then she'll be protected to some degree, although her enemies will say that ignorance is no defence. O'Neill is old-school and prefers to keep the president in the dark rather than to lie to her face, which is refreshing to see. Call it woman's intuition, call it mischief-making, but it's the way O'Neill speaks about the president that makes me think there's more to their relationship than a professionalism. He has a warmth about him when he talks about President Parker that even someone as experienced as he couldn't hide. Perhaps it's unrequited. But it's none of my business. In the great scheme of things, it's hardly news.

O'Neill is also a man of his word. I'd be happy to kill Jason Cross for free, but he'll have none of it. He probably feels bad too because he knows I'm on my own on this one. It is, in effect, a suicide mission. He's compensating me very well. But what's the point of that? I have nobody I want to leave my money to.

Litze probably wouldn't live long enough to enjoy it. I have no family or friends. This profession gives me some perspective. The only time I have a circle of friends is when I stand in a round room of mirrors. I'm not sure of that even then; I suppose I like myself enough to call myself a friend.

We both know that the killing of Jason Cross may not solve anything long-term. You never know whether he'll be replaced by someone worse. But under the circumstances, it's a chance the president is prepared to take. Cross isn't popular, which is good enough for O'Neill, as he won't be missed by many. The world is full of people like Jason Cross. Maybe that's the point: The world is full of arseholes. It's just a matter of degree.

I meet O'Neill at a black site in the Midwest of America. It's unremarkable looking, but again, I'm blindfolded and taken from the local private airport into a black government-issue Jeep. O'Neill apologises for the secrecy, but I tell him it isn't the first time I've been blindfolded, which makes him laugh. The journey takes about one and a half hours, and even with all my training, I can't tell where we're going. I can hear a variety of sounds merge into one another. Heavy to light traffic. Trains. Also, the aromas of gas, smoke, and manure. In the end, I fight against my natural curiosity and relax.

When we arrive, we're met at the entrance by a male and a female operative, who don't speak much. And to be honest, they aren't people I want to talk to either. They're middle-aged, perfectly dressed in their black company suits. People who'd arrest their hair if it fell out of place. Bland and smug. Company people, I figure. Probably the money. Necessary to the operation but dead from the neck up. Maybe it's my paranoia or, more likely, the chip on my shoulder, but the smell of their disdain is stronger than their cologne. I feel I've already earned O'Neill's respect, but not theirs. Or maybe they're pissed that he outsourced this job to an outsider. That's the thought I'd prefer to hold on to.

Jason Cross has a large hunting lodge outside Washington, DC, on about sixty acres of land. He goes there to get some 'me' time, but he isn't, strictly speaking, alone. He's still guarded as well as you might expect for a man like him. But if I'm going to get him, this is probably the best time and place. O'Neill is working on the premise that he'll have his guard down and that not many people know of this secret place. Only a small circle does. But his unpopularity means that Cross hasn't inspired much loyalty. Over time, people have let things slip. The walls have ears. It's as if Cross's demise is inevitable, and he is the architect of his downfall.

While I wait for the operation to get the go-ahead, I lie low. Mainly back in London. I haven't heard much from Litze. A few messages but nothing substantial. I haven't heard from Walsh, but he said he would be in touch. And I wonder where he is. I couldn't even begin to figure it out. But I'm glad he's happy, and in a perverse way, I contributed to his new life.

After three months, I get the signal to move and the temperature has hit the high thirties. I want to go in at night, which would be much better. I have a sniper rifle for the task at hand and carry small arms for close-quarters personal protection. I set out on foot for the last two miles and set off on a brisk walk. Crossing the land is beautiful. The earth is dry and firm. The trees seem to touch the clouds, they're so high. The clouds look like candy floss on a stick. The air is good and makes me realise even more that I need to get out of the city. I can already feel the difference in my breath. I understand why Cross would come here for relative solitude. This setting seems paradoxical with his character and is everything he isn't: pure and uncorrupted.

From the aerial reconnaissance photographs that O'Neill showed me, the target will be staying at a purpose-built log cabin, which is on a flat piece of land. The immediate area surrounding the building is bare, an ideal killing zone for attackers or would-be assassins approaching on foot and caught out in the open, but as you move outward, the land is covered with more trees. Which is perfect for me as it'll provide some natural cover. I only have a forty-five-minute window to get back to the exfil point. If I don't, I'll have to make it out on my own. O'Neill explained this in great detail and looked at me intensely, as if he was saying with his eyes, *Are you sure about this?* He hoped for the best but feared the worst. And in the short time we've gotten to know each other, we've developed a mutual respect. I hope that this won't be the last time I work with him, and I often wonder whether he feels the same. He's probably sent even better operatives than me to their deaths, so I think he probably wouldn't want to risk tempting fate.

The intel suggests that the guard duty is light, so they shouldn't be a problem, but in this game, you assume nothing.

I decide to wait awhile, until it gets dark, which will be late because of the time of year. I switch on my night-vision goggles, which I tested prior to the start of the mission, and take a quick look through them. They give everything an ethereal shade of green and make the scenery look like something from *The Matrix*, but without the vertical numbers. It reminds me of old computer screens before they changed to colour.

I check my location using the satnav facility on my phone. I'm making good progress. I'm also in radio contact with O'Neill on the ghost network, but we maintain radio silence as per standard operating procedure. I can't radio for backup. In this situation, I'm General Custer. Some would say that I'm a crazy bitch with a death wish who can't help trying to prove herself all the time.

The air is cooler now. I can hear the songs of wildlife, which sound beautiful and untamed. I feel strangely at peace here and it reminds me of the times when I've appreciated nature. But now I'm hunting. I want to stick Cross's head on a mantelpiece, but I'd settle for blowing it off instead.

I check my watch. It's 11.30pm.

Showtime.

EIGHTY-FOUR

I CAN SEE the lodge with all its green distortions through my night-vision goggles as I approach. The scene looks creepy, like something from a sci-fi movie. It's very freeing to be able to see like this in the dark. The outside light bounces around the immediate area, which creates a glare. That's the problem with night vision. You can have too much light, so there's no visual contrast. The scene is oversaturated making it difficult to pick out a target. I understand why some people prefer thermal imaging cameras, because they see heat and contrast much easier. But this is better than nothing.

I can feel my heart race and my breath quicken, so I remember what Litze taught me about controlling my nerves. Live in the moment. Detach from the outcome.

Head of ice. Heart of fire.

Unlearn everything that I've been taught or programmed to do when it comes to fear.

I move closer to the target and raise my rifle, quickly scoping the area to the front of me, taking in the general layout of windows and doors, but more importantly looking for signs of life, even though it will soon be extinguished with extreme prejudice if all goes to plan. But something is wrong. It's too easy. I can't see any guards. I can't hear any sounds. Nothing. It's too quiet; I expected to see someone outside the perimeter on guard duty, or at least someone at the lodge carrying out watch duties.

I didn't expect to get this close.

I shouldn't have gotten this close.

I should have faced some resistance by now. If it's too good to be true, it usually is. I stop for a moment and wait. I move closer to the building, but I can't hear anything. I can't see any movement. No shadows; no sound apart from the faint echoes of nature in the distance.

Then my paranoia kicks in.

Am I being set up again? Did O'Neill double-cross me? For a moment, I feel a tidal wave of fear. I curse myself for taking this job. I let my ego get in the way. Again. Litze would be having a field day. I can see his face in my head telling me off for being so reckless. He wouldn't have taken this job. But there's no telling me. I should learn from my mistakes. I just hope I live long enough to do so.

Then I grab my paranoia by the throat and tell myself to get a grip. My darkness gets the better of me at times. I need a drink. Litze would give me hell for that too. I'm good at this. I can do this! I can do this!

I move closer to the building. There's an old pickup truck just a few yards from the main entrance. I cover the ground quickly, using what I can to conceal my position. I smell gas as I near the pickup; I feel the bonnet and it's warm to the touch. It could mean many things, but I'm not sure which. I move closer to the old building, but there is still no resistance.

Nothing.

I still have a bad feeling about this, but I proceed anyway. I'm crazy like that. I'm the one who would dare to touch the fire. Litze would be pulling his hair out. My ego and common sense are out of balance. Now I'm sure that there's no one about, I make my way stealthily along the side of the building, heading for the door that I saw on my initial 'eyes on' using the Schmidt & Bender scope. Upon reaching the door, I take a breath and try the handle. I'm in luck; the door is open. It doesn't look forced. I lead with my Glock 17 as it's better for close-quarters battle than trying to swing a 'long' around inside, and I gently ease open the door with my left hand, then quickly hold the Glock with both hands and push the door the rest of the way open with my foot.

The corridor is clear, so I check the ground-floor rooms. No signs of life. No signs of any activity. There is a smell of stale coffee in the air. I head to the central area of the house, the kitchen. My goggles reveal a large, rectangular table and chairs and large windows. I can also see the shiny metallic-green appliances in the cooking area. My mind momentarily tries to imagine what the room would look like normally. The room is an open-plan lounge diner.

I still can't see any signs of life. I decide to go upstairs to the bedrooms. It's still dark. The curtains are partly drawn on some of the rooms. But nothing here to indicate signs of activity. I start to question the intel, but no intelligence is ever 100 percent reliable. I count four bedrooms, confirming the floor plans from O'Neill's briefing. The beds are untouched, and so are the rooms. Through my night-vision goggles, I can see the bedroom furniture shimmer from the green-tinted light bouncing off the shiny handles and glass and the shards of rays creeping in through the edges of the curtains.

I go back downstairs to the kitchen area. I walk to the rear of the room and see some stairs leading to a basement. I ease down, but the stairs creak. I think, shoot anything that moves. I reach the basement floor and stop. I can smell something wrong in the air. Something familiar, but I'm not sure what it is.

I reach for a light switch on the side wall and remove my goggles. Then I realise instantly why I haven't seen any of the guards. And why I haven't seen Jason Cross. He is one amongst the six dead bodies that lie on the basement floor.

Someone has beaten me to it.

EIGHTY-FIVE

JASON CROSS HAS a large entry wound between his eyes. The back of his skull has exploded. Brains and blood ooze out around his head like a psychedelic think bubble. The others were cut to shreds by a semiautomatic. I can see the arterial blood sprays snaking up the walls and across the floor of the basement. I start to wonder how you get everybody to assemble in one room like this. This was way too easy. It looks like they were caught off guard. Perhaps by someone they knew.

But there's no doubting this was a professional hit, and I momentarily admire the clean efficiency of the kill before my survival instinct kicks in and I decide it's not a good idea to hang around for too long.

O'Neill was right about Cross having enemies. But where would you begin with a man like him? That's as pointless as wondering how big the universe is. Cross would have many people wanting to kill him. And although I'm glad he's dead, I'm sorry that it wasn't me who took him down. As far as I'm concerned, the job isn't complete and I feel a tinge of dissatisfaction. Us killers—well, at least some of us—have professional pride. And we're only as good as the last job we did.

This is a job I didn't do.

I switch the light off, put my goggles back on, and walk back upstairs. My pride won't let me take credit for this, even though it'll cost me a massive payday. I wouldn't get away with it as someone, sooner or later, would take credit for it. I look at my watch, and I figure that I have twenty minutes to get to the exfil point where O'Neill and his team are waiting. But then my paranoia starts again. Am I being set up? Maybe O'Neill wants no evidence. After all, this is 'black bag', this is a deniable op, and it makes sense to get rid of all the evidence. Or perhaps O'Neill wanted to make doubly sure and had a team sent in ahead of me just in case. It would've been expensive, but with a man like Jason Cross, the expense was not the issue. He was the architect of so much misery; it seemed that no expense would be spared to take him out.

I must get out of here fast.

I focus on my breathing as I can feel my heart rate quickening. I admire that ability in others. Though calmness is relative. Compared to my teenage years, I'm a lake without ripples. Compared to some of the martial artists that I've trained with, I'm more like a tidal wave of emotion.

My senses are heightened now as I feel another presence. How could I have been so reckless? That's a dumb question as reckless is my middle name, the only one I'll admit to.

I look at my watch again and see that I have only eighteen minutes to the exfil point. That's assuming that O'Neill is true to his word and hasn't already left or indeed set me up. I look for one final time at the carnage behind me, half pleased at least because Jason Cross is dead, though I feel cheated out of this kill. I reholster my Glock and leave the cabin to see the eerie green night sky through my night-vision goggles. It seems the only thing I can hear is my panting and my weight hitting the ground as I race to my exfil point, trying to retrace my steps. As I get into my rhythm, I'm enjoying the clean woodland air, which seems to invigorate me despite my fear, which I'm trying to control. At least I'm still alive, for now. And for the first time in a while, I think about my team who were killed, and the fact that I didn't get the chance to avenge them, but to be honest, I didn't know them that well, and my professional head is telling me that they knew the risks. Will I now become the hunted? Litze taught me that's also part of the game, which is why you must never assume anything in life.

I visualize myself reaching the exfil point, where O'Neill is waiting. My mind is hoping for the best, preparing for the worst. *This'll be OK, Sam*, I keep reciting to myself like a mantra. The words I wish I heard when I was younger from parents who should have known better.

***

My trancelike state seems to accelerate time as I look at my watch: fifteen minutes to the exfil point and I'm still alive. You have to savour these moments, Litze used to tell me. He was a great man, and I was too immature, too arrogant, too everything to appreciate him.

I stop for a moment.

I thought I heard something, but maybe it's my mind playing tricks. My hands sweat on my semiautomatic as I feel that I'm having a déjà vu moment: that moment when the world stays silent and then there's the impending smell and feel of death coming out to claim what's his, and to collect his dues.

My night-vision goggles suddenly fill with a bright green light, blinding me, as I feel my own weapon being smashed to pieces. Pain sears through my hands, causing me to drop the shattered remains of my weapon as my brain finally computes that a bullet was the cause of this devastation. I feel another round smash to the left of me as I begin to move. I could be dead, I should be dead, but that's not the point: I'm not supposed to be. I'm being teased. Played with as a cat plays with a mouse just before delivering the coup de grace. I have a sinking feeling in the pit of my stomach as I realise something: my past has finally caught up with me.

EIGHTY-SIX

NOW I'M IRRITATED. Not because I'm about to die, though that doesn't help. I have accepted that now. But the fact that this fucker has decided to prolong this. If he's expecting me to beg for my life, then he'll have to wait awhile. I lie still on the ground as I see a figure approach me. He emerges like an alien from the green-enhanced night light in my goggles. Slowly. Confidently. I can tell just by his gait that this person is a professional. He's about six foot one but moves gracefully and unselfconsciously, like someone who's always been comfortable in his skin; like my mentor. He aims his gun at me, which has a tac light attached to it, which emits a green beam in my goggles. He closes the space between us and gestures with his gun, indicating for me to get up. I rise slowly. Both hands raised. He moves behind me, preventing me from standing. I'm on my knees, something I hate. He takes my Glock from its holster and presses his gun to the nape of my neck. He pulls me up onto my feet. I don't want to provoke anything. I don't even take off my night-vision goggles. I'm still alive but still pissed.

I always wondered how this would end. But this is hardly a surprise. It's karma doing its work like a faithful servant of the universe. Litze always said that there's no such thing as a free lunch, and finally, the owner of the restaurant called Destiny has caught up with me so I can pay the bill.

I'm not about to ask God for forgiveness or to save my soul. That would be hypocritical, not that having double standards bothered me before. That's part of the job. But I think my soul is probably in the possession of the man downstairs. Even in this desperate situation, I'm not sorry. I never much was before, so why should it make a difference now?

The man walks behind me, and I can feel his weapon pointed at my back, even though it's not touching me. He turns his tac light off. We amble along the path in the opposite direction to where I was going. My survival instinct is bereft of ideas. I try to think of ways of getting out of this, but I know it's pointless. That's not me being a defeatist. I'm a realist. I'm only delaying the inevitable. That's not unique to the life of the assassin. But who am I trying to kid? Assassins accelerate the inevitable.

We walk for what seems like an age as I briefly consider talking to him, but I don't think he's the talking kind. More the strong, silent type. I could always offer myself to him like I've done before. That's usually a good way to buy time, but to be honest, I'm not that desperate, and he strikes me as someone who'd laugh at me anyway and shoot me for insulting his intelligence. He wouldn't respect me. No real man would, and I wouldn't respect him. This is based on experience.

I'm thinking that he's taking me to a grave. Or maybe that'll be my last act: to dig my own. I've only done that, metaphorically speaking, all my life, so this situation is apt. The man points me to a clearing in a thicket. I'm now going back to nature, and I console myself with the knowledge that at least my end will be somewhere decent. I relax and feel the cool air caress the trees and soothe my skin. I think of the place where I finally met Litze for the first time in all these years. That was nearly his resting place. This will be mine now. Not of my choosing, but beggars can't be choosers.

I walk further on this path, and I cannot seem to tell the wood from the trees. Literally. I've lost track of time and space now, and I think it's my brain's way of bowing to the inevitable. The only thing I can take comfort in now is that I'm not begging. And that's not necessarily down to watching my victims' pleas and being disgusted by them. That's down to my fucking father and the defiance I showed him for all those years as a child. He trained me well, even though he wasn't aware of it. He prepared me for this moment. What irony! I suppose I should thank him, but my magnanimity won't stretch that far.

We walk for about half a kilometre more in silence, hearing only our almost syncopated steps crush the dry leaves and twigs. The ground starts to level off, and the land feels harder on my feet, which seems to suggest that the composition of the earth isn't merely soil, but a mixture of granite and limestone. That would explain why some of the pine trees have fallen over time. This isn't the most fertile, sustainable ground for vegetation, where things last for hundreds of years. And that makes me think that he probably won't bother with a grave for me. He'll shoot me and let nature take its course. Who'd care anyway? I have no family, no friends to speak of apart from Walsh and Litze. But maybe calling them friends is a little grandiose and desperate.

I see a tree trunk lying on its side, and I stop instinctively, as I know he's going to do it here. The man comes closer, so that he's in my peripheral vision alongside me, which is slightly restricted by the casing of my night-vision goggles. He points to the tree trunk with his gun, which I understand to mean that he wants me to sit. I walk calmly and sit, but I face him. I'm not going to close my eyes. I want him to know that the last thing he'll remember is my stare. A stare of defiance. One that's completely detached from the outcome.

Something that I've tried to cultivate all through my life, especially when I've been under pressure. It seems strange that my detachment is easier now when I'm staring down the barrel of a gun.

EIGHTY-SEVEN

I WONDER WHAT he's waiting for as he points his gun. This isn't the first time someone's pointed a weapon at me, so you'd think I'd be accustomed to it. But you hope it isn't the last thing you'll see.

'They said you were one cold bitch, and to be honest, you haven't disappointed', says the man, who's still standing over me by the way. This is his opening line. An insult or a compliment, depending on how you look at it. It's an American accent, but not distinct enough for my inexperienced ears to determine where he's from. He speaks with a quiet authority. His delivery is that of someone who talks without rushing. Like someone who'd be great at narrating an audiobook. Like someone who respects his energy. So he's going to call me names, then he's going to kill me.

'Who's "they"?' I ask.

'The word gets around, Becker', he says. So he knows me. Or at least, he knows of me.

'Can we get this over with?' I say, partly as a bluff and partly because I'm too weary to be bothered to engage in small talk.

'In time, Becker, but there are a few things you should know first.'

'Like what?'

'Like the fact that your mission to capture Karl Yumeni was a setup.'

'Tell me something I don't know.'

'There's lots you don't know, Becker.'

'OK, so tell me, then get this over with.'

'The famous Becker impatience. I suspect that's what's got you into this mess in the first place.'

He's going to lecture me, then he's going to kill me. Great! 'I assume that you killed my team? You were the shooter behind my ambush?' I say, looking straight at him as I slowly calm down my breathing.

'Correct.'

'But I'm a loose end now. I got away, and now you want to clean house?'

The man says nothing.

'Who hired you?'

'Jason Cross.'

'And you killed him and his team?'

'Yes, that's right. You could say he was double-crossed', he laughs.

I get the lame joke, but I won't indulge him. My nonreaction seems to get him back on track.

'Do you think that the US government is the only party who wanted to kill Jason Cross? He's pissed off so many people. If you got a bigger offer to kill Cross from another party, you'd be a fool to turn it down. They made me an offer I couldn't refuse.'

'Who are "they"?'

'Doesn't matter who. All you need to know is that they're too big, bad, and dangerous to go into a detailed explanation. The thing is, Jason Cross practically signed his death warrant as soon as he sucked on his mamma's titties. It was inevitable. There are two things he didn't know: the word no and the number zero. His folks probably indulged poor little Jason and never said no to him, which explains a lot; added to the fact that their child-rearing skills didn't involve zero tolerance, it means that he was a man who felt a sense of entitlement all his life. Everybody's actions lead them down a path. He was just too arrogant to know it. Or it could be that his parents weren't the problem and that his DNA was encoded so that he would turn out to be a total prick.'

'So why did you take the job? Sounds like you didn't like him.'

'If liking a client was a prerequisite for taking a job, there'd be no work. But you already know that, right?'

He has a point. I'm racking my brain to think of the last client I liked. It seems like a long, long time ago.

He continues, 'The people that hired your agency, Coba, were the CIA, set up as a shell company', which only confirms my suspicions. 'They were on to Cross about his desire to control the security market and wanted to stop him. Yumeni was his man on the ground. He was his rent-a-terrorist, or so he thought. What Cross didn't know was that Yumeni was a double agent working for a large corporation interested in taking Cross down.'

'You mean another security agency? I thought he was working directly for the president.'

'Is that what you were told?'

'Yes.'

'Becker, have you checked your birth certificate lately? Because I sure as hell didn't think you were born yesterday. Yumeni answered to the president, but she wasn't at the top of the tree. No president is. They're just the public face. And to be honest, the president is on a need-to-know basis. The people behind her are so powerful and scary, this stuff is way above her pay grade. This corporation makes the president look like she's on minimum wage.'

'So the story about Cross trying to discredit the CIA and President Parker wanting to clean it up is just bullshit?'

'No, it isn't, but there's more to it. What we also have is a turf war between competing agencies. Cross wasn't the only show in town who wanted to dominate the market. The government wants a company that'll play nice. Cross didn't play nice. Like I said, he was too arrogant to realise where he was at.'

I let it sink in for a moment as what the man is saying to me starts to make sense.

'And how the hell do you think they're going to clean up the CIA anyhow?' asks the man.

Eventually, my mind starts to join the dots. 'The other security agency is the one they'll use as a stick to beat the CIA with if they step out of line.'

'Well done, Becker, you're learning.'

'So why kill my team?' I ask.

'Your team? Are you serious, Becker? Really?' he says mockingly.

'What are you talking about?'

'That so-called team wasn't there to capture Yumeni. That was a hit squad. They were there to kill you. I saved your sorry ass.'

EIGHTY-EIGHT

I STAY SILENT for a while. Then I feel a cold sensation like a ghost walking through my body.

'If that's true, why did you shoot me?'

'That wasn't me. It's easy to think it was in all that confusion. But I assure you, if I wanted you dead, you'd be dead already. I'm a great shot if I don't mind saying so myself. Why, I could've shot off your nipple ring if you were wearing one from over a mile away and left you intact if I wanted to.'

I start to feel a tingling sensation.

'That was Matt Doyle, another shooter who I took care of, but not quick enough to prevent him from taking a shot at you. It was the team's backup plan. He was far enough away and had the opportunity to do it. He was their fail-safe. But clearly, he was a shit shot.'

Then I think back. I know why Blake had that confused look on his face when he saw me running to the SUV. I mistook that look, but when I rerun the image in my head, it wasn't so much a look of confusion. It was one of surprise. Surprise because he thought he'd seen a ghost. He wasn't expecting me.

'Avery, Gains, Madison, Blake, and Doyle were all dirty. Rogue CIA agents that were working for Jason Cross all along. There are factions in the CIA who think that they are not hard enough. Can you believe that? The CIA, responsible for some of the most reprehensible acts known to man, not hard enough? These hardliners became disillusioned with the agency and wanted Cross to take over. All the fuck-ups and missed opportunities of past years had made the organisation seem weak. They felt that the CIA had let their country down. The US had become a laughingstock in the world, especially after 9/11. They wanted America to become great again, and they thought the CIA was the past. The best way to achieve that aim was for Cross to further discredit them. That's where Yumeni comes in.'

My instinct says that he's telling the truth. And in my world, this doesn't seem as crazy as it sounds, which is even more worrying.

'Do you mind if I take my goggles off?' I ask. Sweat drips into my eyes, and I feel it's getting light enough to see as the moonlight bathes the landscape.

'Slowly', he says. Even though he's pointing the gun and at a great enough distance that I can't do anything, he still exercises caution. A real pro. I'm relieved as I can feel the cold night air on my face. But I cannot clearly make out his features.

'So why did they want to kill me?'

'Your mission was to take in Yumeni. Theirs was to give him a free run. It was a conflict of interest. This wasn't personal, Becker. Just business. You'd have been in the way. Sure, they could have killed you at any time before the mission, but it made sense that you'd be killed in theatre. It would be easier to explain away. I know that your agency, Coba, are idiots, but they didn't know who hired them. They were too busy looking at the cheque to care.'

And that was my problem too.

'The fact that Coba fucked up would have suited Jason Cross too. Yumeni was a prized asset and Coba's so-called reputation would have suffered. They would be another agency out of the way', says the man. He starts to check his left wrist, like he's looking at his watch.

'So what now?' I say to the man, who's still pointing the gun at me.

'An excellent question, but I have a dilemma', says the man.

When people use that word, dilemma, it normally doesn't end well.

'Let me guess: I have a price on my head, and you're supposed to kill me?'

'Something like that', he says.

'What do you mean "something like that"? It either is or it isn't.'

'OK, it's like that.'

'Who?'

The man shrugs in a 'how the fuck should I know?' manner. I feel that I'm now back to zero. This conversation has been pleasant. Enjoyable even. It's been a long time since I've shot the breeze with someone in this way. But he's a professional. A gun for hire. Just like me. It's not personal, it's business. The mere thought of that makes me feel even calmer. In a perverse way, I'm glad he's the one who's going to kill me. Glad seems an odd choice of word, but if you were in my shoes, I'm sure you'd understand.

'Don't you get tired of working for idiots, Becker?' asks the man. This seems a strange question under the circumstances.

'I don't recall a time when I didn't. You could say I'm desensitised to them.'

'When you do this long enough, you start to question things; at least you should, like an assassin's midlife crisis. I've always known I'm a killer, even before my first kill. I think my mom knew when I kicked her so hard in her womb. I think our kind do. We scare people. I'm sure even my first pet knew. Animals always know. But does killing get any easier? For some maybe. But we are who we are.

I've accepted my nature. It's not the same as liking it, but acceptance helps. We're all here for some purpose. Don't you think that sometimes?'

'I've never given it much thought, to be honest.' Maybe I should've. Guess I won't get the chance now.

'I've gotten to thinking, Becker: this life, yeah, I chose it, or maybe it chose me, who knows? But everybody's good at something. You gotta admit we're real good at killing. There was a time I enjoyed it. Maybe too much. But the sane part of my brain tells me off for enjoying it too much. And I'm glad that part is still there. It's like checks and balances. But we still clean up other people's shit just the same. Just like garbage men. Hell, we're like substitute teachers with guns, only the pay is better. I started thinking: is this it?'

'We're not paid to think. Well, not by most clients.'

'Yeah, wouldn't it be good if we were? I never gave this much thought before. I'd go out and do my job, like a true pro.'

'So what's made you reflect?' I ask, cutting him off and surprising him.

The man pauses for a moment, then resumes. 'I met a guy ten years ago on a mission in Russia. When I say "met", that wasn't exactly how it went down. He was the target. At the time, he was one of the most wanted. You could say he was the assassin's equivalent of the golden ticket. I wanted to prove myself because of the reputation of this man. We were on opposite sides, but in another life, we would have been best buddies. There was something about him. He became an obsession for me. I studied his files, learned about his habits, the guns he liked to use, his fighting techniques, what he liked to eat and drink, his background. I wanted to get inside his head. The more I got to learn about him, the more I liked this guy, even though I knew I'd have to take him down. To be honest, that made me a bit sad. Maybe that was a mistake, to get emotionally attached. Anyway, the intel I got on the target was bad. He was supposed to be in a hotel in Moscow and somehow, he must have gotten wind of this, because the target wasn't there. He was watching me all along. He'd turned the tables. The hunter became the hunted. I returned to my car, and he was inside with a gun pointed at my back. He made me drive a few miles out of the city to a quiet suburb. He walked me out of the car, and I stupidly tried to take him, but he was way too good and knocked me unconscious.

'Next thing I knew, he was standing over me with a gun pointed at my head. I thought that was it. Game over. My life flashed before me like a pop video: every kill in vivid Technicolor. I could smell the blood, hear the screams. Much like what's going on with you right now. We spoke for a while; it was strange, but I had studied this man for months and meeting him face-to-face, it confirmed my instinct: he was someone I liked, even though he was about to kill me. But I sensed he was struggling. He looked weary. Haunted maybe. After putting two and two together, we worked out we were set up by a third party who wanted us both out of the way. I'll never forget what he said as he pointed his gun at me.'

'What did he say?'

'He said, "When you can't tell the difference between the client and the target, it's time to reconsider your choices." That's the only reason why you are still alive.' The man slowly lowers his gun.

I breathe slowly in realisation. My mind commands my hands not to shake. I can feel my muscles relax from my head right down to my toes, as if I were conducting an auto-scan on my body.

'He didn't have blue eyes and grey hair by any chance?' I ask.

'Yes, as a matter of fact, I remember he did.'

'Litze!'

'You know Litze?'

'Yeah, I know Lothar Litze, he's my mentor.'

'No shit?'

'The one and only', I say. I begin to stand up very slowly and rub my numb legs. He's saved my ass yet again. It seems I'll always be indebted to him.

'Wow!' says the man as he steps back. 'Talk about everything being connected and all. Do you believe in coincidence, Becker?'

'No, I don't.'

'Me neither. If you see him, please send him my best. Because of Litze, I became choosier about what contracts to take. I've turned lots of work down. Some clients hate that, but I like the thought that they think they can buy you only for you to give them the finger. I find that empowering. I can even afford to do pro bono work.'

'No offence, but you don't strike me as the helping-a-little-old-lady-across-the-road type.'

'None taken. Guess I don't but working for assholes becomes soul destroying after a while. Pro bono may not be all rock 'n' roll, but there are people out there who could use guys like us.'

'So is not killing me your way of paying it forward?'

'If you wanna put it that way. You could do the same. It's up to you, Becker. That's if anything I've said resonated with you.'

'To be honest, it did.' The man walks slowly towards me, pulls out my gun, and gives it to me handle first. After a brief hesitation, which he senses, I take the Glock. Even though we have a mutual connection in my mentor, it takes a brave person to do that, especially with me, but he's taking a leap of faith, which uncommon to someone like me. He's trusting me not to kill him. But even if I did, he doesn't strike me as someone who regrets showing faith. Maybe he's reached the stage where he's detached himself from the outcome. I guess that some would call that enlightenment. Something that Litze has reached, or at least trying to. And he's clearly made an impression on this mystery man. He's the kind of person you could meet for five minutes, and you'd never forget him.

'What do I call you?' I ask him.

'Death has many names. I'm known as many things, depending on who you talk to or what country you're in. I'm the Angel of Death, the Change Agent, the Waste Manager, the Fixer, the Reaper, Diablo, Mephistopheles. My personal favourite is the Wallpaper Man. You can call me that.'

I'm trying to work out why in the dimly lit night. He is blandly handsome. Unremarkable features; long, thin face. Designed to be invisible. But that isn't it, as some wallpaper is exciting. I think his code name is to do with the fact that he can cover things up.

He looks at his watch again, which prompts me to look at mine.

'I realise I missed my exfil pickup. I suppose you could give me a lift?' I ask.

'No, you suppose wrong.'

'But my contact point is miles away.'

'Really, Becker? Listen, don't go trying to pull that damsel-in-distress crap, because you ain't no lady. No offence.'

'None taken', I say.

'Thing is, I didn't kill you; I've just given you back your gun, and I wouldn't even do that for my own mother; you can take credit for the Jason Cross hit and still get paid shitloads, enhancing your reputation as one of the world's most feared and sought-after assassins; and you want a lift as well? Do you want to destroy your reputation as a cold-hearted bitch?'

'I suppose not.'

'I'd say you got an excellent deal tonight.'

'I guess when you put it like that', I say, breaking into a half smile. I need to work on that gratitude thing. 'Thanks', I say.

'Don't sweat it, Becker, and besides, it suits my client that their fingerprints aren't on this. And anyway, I'm late for a date', says the man, looking at his watch.

'A date with a woman? I see.'

'No, Becker, you don't see. There will be no romance involved. It's with my mentor. She's a lot older than me and one mean sonofabitch. We're supposed to spar later, and she hates it when I'm not on time, so she's going to beat the shit out of me.'

Yeah, I know that feeling.

EIGHTY-NINE

I KNOW THE rules of the game, even though I don't always abide by them. So there's no point in me going to the exfil point. O'Neill won't be there if he has any sense. It would be too risky. I wouldn't have waited. I decide to make my own way out, but I don't know where I am.

I walk down some nameless freeway. Apart from the occasional pockets of vegetation, the land is mostly flat, but at least it's warm out here. I've been walking on the side of the road for about fifteen minutes when I see a car approach. This causes me to be on guard. As it slows down, the shape looks familiar. It's a black SUV, the same model that brought me here.

As it pulls alongside me, O'Neill sticks his head out and tells me to get in. I'm about forty minutes late. He explains that he disobeyed a direct order from the president to get the hell out, but told her he wouldn't leave me behind. He says said that if he'd obeyed every rule, nothing would get done. He didn't have to wait, of course, but I think it's a nice touch. It's the second leap of faith I've been shown by complete strangers in the space of two hours. If I think about it too much, I could get quite emotional, so I try not to. The other members of his team have gone, and I suspect he sent them away, even though they would have stayed out of loyalty to him, not to me. After all, I'm the outsider.

As I enter the vehicle, I confirm to O'Neill that the job is done by a simple nod. He smiles back in a way which suggests that it's all he wanted to know. He puts the car into drive, and we set off. The sun starts to discreetly show itself in golden bursts through discordant cloud formations that Donny Walsh could name as easily as reading the menu of a fast-food chain. Pretty much all of the journey to the private jet waiting to take me where I want to go is in silence. No twenty questions, no debrief, nothing. O'Neill is a respectful guy and leaves me to my thoughts. I also figure the less he knows, the better for him and the president he's trying to protect. This was supposed to be a deniable op after all. He isn't really here. I don't exist, and I'm on my own if the shit hits the fan. Which makes the fact that he waited for me even more remarkable. I don't like lying to him, and I don't like taking credit for a job that I didn't do, but in the scheme of things, this all makes sense. I'm not that proud. This is a great payday, and I'm being strategic for once in my life. Maybe all those lessons with Litze have finally paid off, and I'm growing up after all.

But there's a price for this too: it'll be known that I've taken down Jason Cross and I'll be one of the most feared and hunted assassins in the world. My ego likes the kudos, especially with those who wrote me off so readily, but I now have to be even more careful. There's going to be some young Turk after my crown. Maybe the Wallpaper Man wasn't so altruistic when he let me take credit for the Jason Cross kill. Maybe it was his way of dumping the shit on me instead. But it's shit I can just about handle.

Many hours later, I watch CNN on the TV monitor of the government private jet with O'Neill and some of his crew. News of Cross's death breaks, which results in Mandrake Security shares plummeting, while Landcare International and other security companies' shares skyrocket. And there's no news of Huxcor's involvement in all this, surprise, surprise. I think back to the conversation with the Wallpaper Man and the fact that he didn't disclose the client who ordered the hit on Cross. There's no such thing as coincidence.

I haven't spoken to Litze for months, but given that we hadn't spoken in years, this is no real hardship. But I plan to keep in touch with him. He's made me realise that I need him more than my pride was willing to let me admit. Blume drops me a note to say that she's pleased I made it. As for Donny, I should be happy for him that he's found his nirvana, but part of me isn't. I know I'm being selfish, but I miss him. He said he'll be watching over me, which gives me some comfort. I haven't contacted Coba, nor have they contacted me, which says everything.

And what about the voices in my head? My fucking father. I'm learning to let that go. It's about time, I think. I'm even seeing the counsellor that Karla Blume recommended. Something I should have done years ago, and it's helping. I don't tell him everything, of course, and he senses that, but he's a good guy and very discreet. He's helping me learn how to listen to the voices in my head and not judge them, just be an observer. Something Litze tried to help me with, but I wasn't ready. I read somewhere that critical people are trying to help you but are doing it in an unusually harsh way. I prefer to believe that my father was a bully who couldn't deal with his pain, so he took it out on me. When I once told Donny Walsh that my dad had ruined my life, he turned around and said that my life wasn't over and it was up to me what I did from then on. Donny was right of course. It was up to me. I was giving my father too much power. The power he never really had or deserved.

I've also decided that I'm going to be choosier about my assignments, just like the Wallpaper Man. The last one was too close a call. I'll try not to be so shallow and just look at the cheque. Maybe it's my turn to help little old ladies across the road.

I have more money than I know what to do with. But what good is money if it's just there to collect dust as well as interest? I think that I'll take a long-overdue holiday. The Caribbean sounds good. It always looks good. I seem to come alive in the sun. Every cell of my body feels reenergised. A complete change of scene where I can disappear sounds great. Well, that's the theory anyway. But I know an assassin's life is never simple, and I'm a born trouble magnet. Litze said I could start a fight in a Buddhist retreat.

I think about the times that I didn't help people when I had the power to. Then I try not to think about it because I'll start regretting. Maybe the same thing happened to the Wallpaper Man, hence his decision to do pro bono assignments. Helping the less well-off may not cleanse my soul, but at least it's a start. I guess that was the point of the Facility, which I turned my back on all those years ago and has disavowed me. The only reason I'm still breathing is because Litze stayed at the Facility longer than he wanted to in order to protect me.

My mind is racing now about my new mission and how I can get this thing started. But I need a break as my head is fried. And before I disappear, there's one last thing I need to do. I need to get back to Germany for one of the hardest things I'll ever have to face. I tell myself that this is the start of my turning over a new leaf. But my dark side is never far away and says to me: Good luck with that!

NINETY

I DON'T NEED too much information to find her, and we do eventually. I gave Walsh the location when I was at Purple Dawn, and he did the rest. He checked all the recent land registry records and hacked into various databases and found that the family were extremely wealthy landowners who had been in that particular region for six generations, through the changes in the country's history. From what Walsh could see, the Kohlbergers were politically in the middle, though some of their bloodline had links to Germany's dark history. Something that, according to the records and newspaper cuttings, they were ashamed of.

I walk towards a beautiful residential area in a place called Keyshoffen near Mainz. It's where the girl is studying at a private fee-paying school. It's a mixed environment with a hundred students and a good pupil–teacher ratio of eight to one. It's about 11.00am, which is break time, and I look at my phone. There's a picture of her so that I can recognise her. I didn't get a good enough look at her the last time. Although I think I have a good memory for faces, I don't want to take any chances.

I approach the school gates and see the students in the playground. I've taken precautions by disguising myself with a wig and contact lenses. This is a loose end I need to tie up. I see the sign on the front which reads Lomberg Privatschule, lettered in green against a white background on the entrance. The success rate is very high here. Given the fees, I'd expect it to be.

I see the girl and notice that apart from the occasional greeting, she's on her own, holding her red leather satchel and what looks like a mobile device. She's still dressed in her grey school uniform: the same jacket with purple trim on the lapels; a crisp white shirt; a purple tie, which still isn't done up at the top; and a pleated knee-length skirt. She walks towards a bench under the big oak tree on the left of the courtyard, and I discreetly catch her attention.

'Brigitte?' I say in a loud whisper. She initially looks startled. Then I see that I look familiar to her as she smiles and walks over to me.

'Not the greatest disguise in the world', she says to me. She hasn't lost any of her precociousness.

'How did you—?'

'Know that it was you?' she interrupts. 'Well, I think that the wig looks like a wig, for a start, and your contact lenses don't seem natural to me. I almost didn't recognise you without your gun. What's wrong, have you had a change of heart?' she says, half joking.

'No, Brigitte, I'm not here to kill you.'

'Then why are you here?'

I pause for a moment. Then I compose myself. My throat feels dry. I'm nervous. Christ, this is harder than I thought. I notice that there's a wooden bench a few feet away from us.

'Can we sit?' I say.

Brigitte nods as we walk and sit down next to each other. She rests her left arm on the back of the bench. I rest my right arm on the back too. We're almost touching.

'This is hard for me', I say. 'I'm not a great talker at the best of times, especially when it comes to confessional, emotional stuff. But this feels like verbal constipation. I shuffle to my right on the bench and look her in the eyes. I want to make her believe I mean what I say now.

'What I said in the barn, about life not getting better? It's not true. I suppose I was talking about myself. I've learned some things.' I pause for a moment. I've rehearsed this in my head many times, but it doesn't come out the way I planned.

'And?' Brigitte asks, looking at me with those penetrating deep-blue eyes. She senses my discomfort.

'Well, um . . . well, what I'm trying to say is that life is what you make it. I always blamed circumstances and didn't realise that I'd always have a choice. It's complicated, but when I said those things before in the barn, that was my stuff. I wasn't fair to you. At that moment, when I had a gun pointed at your head, your courage taught me that you always have a choice, even when your life is about to end. You can choose how you react. What I'm trying to say—and you may want to record this rare event—is sorry. There, I've said it.' I breathe a slow sigh. I feel a sense of relief, shame, and embarrassment.

'Oh. Thanks, I guess', replies Brigitte. We pause as we watch the other kids, but they seem too busy to notice us. She rummages through her satchel and takes out an apple.

As she reaches out her hand, I notice marks on her forearm which peek out from her shirt cuff where she's self-harmed. My heart sinks. This is the girl I considered killing a few months ago.

'Would you like this?' she says.

'No thank you.'

'I have another.'

'I'm not hungry.'

'What about this?' she says with glee in her voice as she hands me what looks like a joint.

I don't believe I'm about to say this.

'Brigitte, be careful with that stuff. Too much isn't a good thing', I say as I feel like a total hypocrite. I discreetly look around, take the joint, and put it back in her satchel.

'OK, if you say so. It's excellent stuff. Are you sure?'

'I'm sure', I say.

Brigitte closes her satchel.

'Do you have a name?' she asks.

'My name is Sam', I say.

'Any middle names?'

'No', I lie. I don't like lying to Brigitte. In such a short time, she has gained my respect, but my contrition doesn't stretch this far. Not just yet.

'Nor do I', she says, winking at me. There's no fooling this kid.

I smile back at her. 'I'm also sorry about stealing the vehicle.'

'Another sorry? I'm honoured', she says. 'Don't overdo it. You didn't technically steal it as I said you could use it. Anyway, Papa was insured and was glad for the upgrade.'

Brigitte sits on the wooden bench and shuffles her feet. I recall the number of times I've sat on wooden benches or had to sleep on them. It seems a cliché, especially in spy movies, but I've met many contacts on park benches. This is a first for me: an apology on a wooden bench.

'Can I see your gun?' she asks.

'What?'

'Can I see your gun?' she asks again.

'No, you can't see my gun.'

'Why not?'

'Why not? What do you mean, why not? What kind of a question is that?'

'I want to see your gun.'

'You're crazy!' I say.

'You said that to me before in the barn. As we know, a mental state is relative. And anyway, you owe me.'

'How do you figure that?'

'You were going to kill me in the barn, or at the very least, you considered it, right?'

'Yes', I say hesitantly.

'I figure the very least you could do is to show me the weapon you were going to use.'

It's messed-up logic, but after she stares me out, I find myself checking to see who's around, then I pull my jacket away to reveal the weapon in my side holster.

'Wow. Looks like a Glock', she says.

'How do you—'

'How do I know?' she interrupts. 'You're not the only one with toys. My father is a collector, but I've always been fascinated.'

'If you knew the destructive power of these things, you wouldn't refer to them as toys. It's a mistake I've made too often', I say. I feel the same discomfort I felt when I first met her in the barn. 'Guns kill people', I say.

'People kill people', says Brigitte. She's right again. There's a pause, then she continues. 'How many people—'

'Never ask me that question again, Brigitte', I say before she can finish her sentence.

'Why?'

'There are some places you should never go.'

She looks at me determinedly. Like a dog with a bone.

'Please, Brigitte?' I say in a soft, tired voice. I can see her expression change, as if she senses my awkwardness.

'OK', she says.

She's one of the few people in the world who makes me feel awe and shame at the same time.

'How's your love life?' Brigitte asks, throwing me completely. My cheeks redden. The girl isn't backwards in her forwardness. At least she's not asking me about guns.

'You don't want to know', I laugh. 'It's complicated.'

'Try me.'

'Maybe another time.'

'OK.'

'How's yours?' I ask, trying to deflect the attention.

'Busy', she giggles.

'Oh really? Interesting', I say, my voice rising. 'I hope you're careful?' I say to her, again feeling hypocritical.

'Always', she says. And I believe her.

'These boys: they're not called Heinz or Fritz by any chance?'

'No.'

'Good.'

Brigitte shifts on the seat to look at me. 'When we met, I was in a bad way. I guess I was an angst-ridden teenager who wanted to fight the world. But you knew that, didn't you? I sensed that you got it. That you got me. I knew you understood the loneliness. I could see it in your eyes. Even though the circumstances of our meeting were weird, I felt then that we had much in common. I've never felt that connection with anybody before. I'd finally met someone who spoke the same language. You know what that feeling is like? You feel that at last, you're no longer alone in the world or crazy. You did me a big favour, Sam. So it is I who should thank you.'

'How so?' I say, confused.

'It's not every day that you have a gun pointed at your head. And I thought I didn't have much of a life to flash before me. But then I realised that I didn't appreciate what I had before. I'm spoiled, you see, which makes you think you're entitled. That's not OK. But when you can get things so easy, life seems meaningless. It's only in the moment of truth that you find out what you're made of. That day in the barn showed me that I had more courage than I ever believed, and I had a lot to be thankful for.'

'Oh!' I say as I look away from Brigitte and sit back on the bench to reflect. Most people I've pointed a gun at aren't around to thank me, so this moment is weird.

'Anyway, I've already learned today that life does get better', she says, smiling.

'How so?' I ask, looking directly at her.

'You came back.'

THE END

Enjoy this book?
Then I'd love to know your views.

I appreciate the time you've already taken to read my book. If you could spare a moment to leave a review, it would be gratefully appreciated. It can be as short as you like on the book's page.

Thank you very much.

ABOUT THE AUTHOR

Walter Clearfoster was born in Ipswich, UK. But for most of his life, he was known as Trevor Ford. When searching for a pen name, he resurrected his much-loathed middle names.

Digging in the Dirt is Walter's debut novel. You can contact him online at:

Website
www.walterclearfoster.com

Twitter
@walterclearfos1

Facebook
https://www.facebook.com/walterclearfosterauthor

Email
walter@walterclearfoster.com, to join the mailing list

Printed in Poland
by Amazon Fulfillment
Poland Sp. z o.o., Wrocław

53271319R00228